"I demand to know what is to happen to me."

"I tried to explain before, but you would not allow it," Arturo replied.

"I might believe your story if there was something for you, some reward in this endeavor. But you say you do not want a ransom. You do not intend to sell me. You do not want me for your mistress. What *do* you want?"

"I would be willing to reconsider that last idea, if it will make you happy."

"That is not what I said!" she protested indignantly.

"What am I to think, *cher?* You keep bringing it up."

"You are an insufferably conceited scoundrel."

"*Oui.* And you are too timid and well-bred to ask me to share your bed. But I will help you over your shyness." He crossed the room toward her.

"Believe me, *capitaine,* I have no intention of being mistress to you or any other man," she assured him proudly, retreating two steps for every one he took.

"I *could* change your mind, *cher.*"

Dear Reader,

Welcome to the world of Harlequin Historicals, where April promises to be another exciting month.

In *Sun Woman,* by Lindsay McKenna, a young Apache woman becomes an army scout in a desperate attempt to save the last of her band of Geronimo's followers. On a lighter note, Kate Kingsley has written *Ransom of the Heart,* a fanciful tale of a penniless Louisiana belle and her swashbuckling rescuer.

Mari, by Donna Anders, is the first of two books set in exotic Hawaii, so be sure to look for the sequel, *Ketti,* in June. And with *Mission of Mercy,* Kathryn Belmont brings to life the whaling industry as we travel with Mercy Randall on a voyage of discovery and danger in the South Seas.

You'll have to wait until next month to read our May books, but I can at least tell you that you have stories from Lynda Trent, Patricia Potter, Marjorie Burrows and Peggy Bechko to look forward to. Don't miss them!

Yours,

Tracy Farrell
Senior Editor

Ransom of the Heart

Kate Kingsley

Harlequin Books

TORONTO • NEW YORK • LONDON
AMSTERDAM • PARIS • SYDNEY • HAMBURG
STOCKHOLM • ATHENS • TOKYO • MILAN

Harlequin Historicals first edition April 1991

ISBN 0-373-28672-4

RANSOM OF THE HEART

KATE KINGSLEY

loves to write historical romance. A native of New Orleans, the author certainly has the background to bring that history to life. Kate, who now lives in the San Francisco Bay area and does volunteer work at a local hospital, enjoys reading, biking, knitting and especially traveling—whenever she can find some extra time. Now that her daughter's in college, Kate has a bit more time to spend with her husband, an actor and television announcer whose sexy voice can be heard on numerous network and cable programs.

For my husband, family and friends,
who have loved me, supported me and believed in me.

Chapter One

New Orleans 1824

Danielle Valmont rolled back the isinglass covering of the coach window and thrust her face into the narrow opening, blinking against a gust of wintry wind that bore the scent of the Mississippi River a few squares away. As the carriage rolled along Rue Royal, she lifted her eyes to view the familiar iron galleries overhanging the narrow street, shadowy in the moonlight. Here and there, lanterns were set on posts, their flickering light illuminating the wooden banquettes, which glistened with a coating of heavy mist.

"Oh, look, Yves," she breathed with delight before her disapproving elder brother could reprimand her for leaning out of the coach, "doesn't the ballroom look beautiful?"

A frown flitted across Yves's handsome face, so like his sister's, before he smiled indulgently and peered out over her shoulder. "*Oui*, beautiful," he echoed.

Tonight the Orleans Ballroom, which sometimes housed the infamous Quadroon Balls, was the site of a gathering of Creole aristocracy. In honor of the Winter Masque, the dignified building wore a dazzling costume of candles, which shone from every window. Outside, festive paper lanterns swayed on the cross-posts of the lamps along the banquette, casting a rosy glow upon the street.

Music could be heard from the ballroom as liveried footmen sprang forward to assist new arrivals. Entire Creole families stepped down from carriages, some of which had carried their passengers nearly a full day's journey from their plantations. In a rainbow of silk, taffeta and lace, younger women emerged with delighted shivers of anticipation, while their black-clad mothers did not so much sober the scene as provide a contrast to the swirls of brilliant color. Smoothing voluminous skirts, ladies of all ages chattered gaily and accepted the arms their escorts gallantly offered. Then they disappeared through the doors to be washed in the warm crystal glow of chandeliers.

Outside the ballroom, a score of people had gathered on the narrow street. Slaves, tradesmen and free people of color waited to glimpse the elite of New Orleans, *les bonnes familles*.

Into this mad crush, the Valmont coach discharged its passengers. Debonair in his evening clothes, Yves alit first.

"Look, Mama," murmured a lovely octoroon woman who stood nearby, "it's M'sieur Yves, and he looks even more handsome than he did when we danced at the Quadroon Ball last week."

"*Oui,* handsome with his yellow hair," her dusky mother confirmed quietly, "but as wild a roué as ever lived. And they say his sister is his match."

Fortunately, Yves did not overhear the women's comments as he motioned the footmen away and turned to assist his sister. Onlookers drew awed breaths in unison as the tall golden-haired girl, her black cloak drawn tightly around her, seemed to materialize from the dark interior of the carriage.

Danielle descended slowly into the dim light, after pausing gracefully on the step of the coach. Her cloak ruffled in the breeze to reveal the promise of rich ivory and black. Her bearing offered no hint of her nervousness. Behind her black satin half mask, her face was as composed as a finely chiseled sculpture. Only the sparkle in her brown eyes and the high color in her cheeks were evidence of her excitement.

Her proud brother led her inside, privately looking forward to the drink that awaited him in the card room. The ride from Félicité, the Valmont plantation, had been long and cold.

"*Bonsoir,* Madame Barrios," Yves said with a nod to a stout matron, who frowned in disapproval as they entered the cavernous marble entryway filled with massive statuary. She nodded coolly, then averted her eyes to stare over their shoulders at the revelers who were just coming through the door.

Seemingly unfazed by Madame Barrios's cool greeting, the girl halted to shed her cloak with a shrug of her shapely white shoulders. She was equally unaffected by the woman's gasp of shock when she saw Danielle's velvet dress, its bodice cut dangerously low. The gown was fashionably high-waisted and hung in heavy ivory swags over a black lace pettiskirt edged with gold. The girl's honey-blond hair was drawn back in a simple style, her glossy curls cascading down her back. A plain gold chain shimmered around her slender white neck and tiny golden pendants adorned her ears.

"*Mon Dieu,*" Yves exploded in a hoarse whisper at the sight of his sister. Immediately he dragged her out of sight behind a statue and loomed over her, so close she could smell the brandy he had sipped to warm himself during the ride into town.

"Danielle Marie-Christiane Valmont!" he hissed. "So this is why you were wearing your cloak when you came downstairs. I thought it was because we were late, but it was because you knew I wouldn't let you out of the house wearing that dress."

"What is wrong with this dress? It is the latest fashion from Paris and I think it is beautiful." She smoothed the cream-colored velvet lovingly.

"Beautiful," he conceded, "and inappropriate. Even though you've attended few balls, you knew better. I told you unmarried girls wear white to this masque."

"This gown is nearly white," she insisted stubbornly.

"I also told you unmarried girls do not wear velvet. The dress is too mature for you. And your pettiskirt..." he faltered, his fair aristocratic face aflame. "It is black. What will people think?"

"Why should we care what people think?" The frown the girl turned on him was genuinely perplexed. "Haven't you always told me, 'We are Valmonts and we...'"

"And we shall live our lives as we please," Yves finished for her ruefully. "*Dieu,* I wish I had known how my words would come back to haunt me." He cast around for the proper argument and tried a reasonable tone. "Look, Dani, I know I have not always been the best example for you, but you don't want those old cats in there to gossip about you, do you?"

"They are already gossiping," she countered calmly.

"*Oui,* and you brought it on yourself."

The girl's chin tilted upward, a sure sign of defiance.

"There is no use to argue." Her brother sighed. "Come, we are going home."

"No," Danielle declared mutinously, "I'll decide when I shall go home, Yves. I do not intend to miss this ball because you are old-fashioned. Isn't the reason we are here tonight that you want to find me a husband? Well, here I am, well displayed for potential buyers."

"It is not like that," he growled in protest.

"How is it then? First you want me to marry, then you treat me like a child. Well, I am not a child and I am not leaving."

"Very well, we shall stay," Yves relented unexpectedly and offered his arm. "But do not say I didn't warn you."

Danielle looked about the elaborate entryway, ignoring the whispers around her, eager for the experience to come.

Despite his anger with his sister, Yves regarded her proudly. At eighteen years of age, she was tall and slender, and she carried herself like a queen, her blond head held high on a graceful white neck. Her large brown eyes, too direct for a Creole maiden, were set wide in a delicate oval face and fringed with long dark lashes. Although they could blaze with temper, in their depths lurked the glint of humor. The lips of her generous, expressive mouth seemed always willing to curve in a smile, which revealed even, white teeth. Other women might powder their faces or heighten their allure with Spanish paper, but Danielle needed no such artifice. She was that most devastating of females, a beauty who was unaware of her effect on men. Her charm was natural and graceful . . . and innocent.

The young Creole was acutely aware that every eye in the hall was on his sister. There might be a challenge to a duel before this night was out, he thought darkly, noting that more practiced observers admired Danielle's creamy bosom, swelling against her décolletage.

Just inside the ballroom, the Court of the Winter Masque, a group of aging "princesses" and matronly ladies-in-waiting, was ranged in a receiving line headed by its "queen," the regal and imposing Martine Arceneaux. A chain reaction of nudges and murmurs alerted them to the pair framed in the doorway.

"Look at that dress!" One of the middle-aged "princesses" made herself heard over the music by speaking directly in Madame Arceneaux's ear. "It is absolutely indecent."

"It is rather daring, but since her *maman* died, she has no one to guide her," Martine maintained sympathetically. "The poor child probably didn't know any better, Sylvie."

"Of course, you are right . . . even though she is old enough to be married by now. She certainly could not rely on the counsel of that brother of hers." Sylvie sniffed. "Yves Valmont is such a roué. When I think how gentle and proper his mother was . . . She would be disappointed indeed to see what has become of her family."

"Are you talking about the Solange Valmont who was my best friend? She was high-spirited and proud, and there seems to be a great deal of her in her daughter." She nodded toward the girl.

"And we live our lives as we please," Yves muttered as the music ended and he led his sister into the ballroom. Her head high, Danielle spread her black lace fan and surveyed her surroundings haughtily. The brilliants in her hair threw flashes of light against the ballroom's rotunda ceiling. For a moment, the circle of Creoles and the girl regarded each other silently. The eyes of several in the crowd slid toward the Queen of the Masque to see how Martine Arceneaux, undisputed arbiter of New Orleans society, would deal with the pair.

"Yves, Danielle . . . I am so glad you are here." Purposefully, the woman stepped forward and greeted them graciously. She would not allow Solange's children to suffer embarrassment.

"Our pleasure." Yves bowed respectfully, his relief mirrored on his face. He kissed the hand the woman offered as Danielle dipped in a polite curtsy.

"*Bonsoir,* Madame Arceneaux," Danielle answered self-consciously, feeling the curious stares upon her. "I am happy to see you again."

"You look lovely tonight, *cher*." An inscrutable flicker crossed the Creole woman's face as her eyes swept Danielle's Paris creation.

"*Merci*. Is Angelique here?"

"*Oui*...and Augustine, my second son. You remember him, of course. He is just younger than Yves." Madame Arceneaux summoned her children across the room, then frowned toward the bandstand. "Music, *s'il vous plaît*," she instructed the dumbfounded orchestra, which obediently launched into a lively reel.

Angelique, plump and appealing, was two years younger than Danielle, but already quite the lady. She had been trained in the proper mien and aptitudes for a Creole girl and was ready for the marriage her parents would soon arrange for her. Pleased to be the center of attention at the moment, she glided across the dance floor on her brother's arm to greet Danielle, her white satin skirt rustling. Behind her pink half mask, Angelique's dark eyes were wide as she beheld the other girl's dress.

"Oh, Danielle, what a beautiful gown! You look lovely. Doesn't she, Augustine?" she demanded.

"*Très jolie*, Mademoiselle Valmont," the slight young man lisped enthusiastically.

"I have always envied you, Dani," Angelique announced ingenuously. "You are always pretty and always daring."

"And always my favorite among all your friends," Augustine interjected eagerly. "May I have the pleasure of the first dance, *mademoiselle*? If your brother does not object."

"Give her time, Tin-Tin," his sister chided before Yves could answer. To Danielle, she said importantly, "You must watch him. He will try to fill up your dance card. Don't let anyone sign for more than one dance at first." She flashed a warning glance at her indignant brother.

"What about me?" a male voice cried. "I want all the waltzes."

"Vincent Gauthier, you can't do that!" Angelique greeted Danielle's most determined suitor with shock. "No one else would have a chance to dance with her."

"My intentions exactly," the elegant young man retorted good-naturedly. "You do not mind if I steal the brother's prerogative, do you, Yves, by claiming Danielle's first dance of the evening?'' At Yves's nod, he led the girl onto the floor before Augustine could protest or any other rival reach them.

"Wait, Dani!" Angelique called. "Leave your card with me. Tin-Tin must have the next dance or he will sulk all evening.''

With a smile, Danielle slipped the ribbon of her dance card over her wrist and tossed it to her friend. Vincent shot a quick look of annoyance at Angelique, then, unmindful of anything but the girl in his arms, he guided Danielle into the ever-circling pattern of dancers.

On the upper gallery, which edged the interior of the huge ballroom, Arturo De Leon lounged on a balustrade. His back against a carved post and one booted foot slung over the polished rail, he swung his leg idly, swaying the garland of flowers that draped the decorated banister. A study in boredom, he did not even bother to stifle a yawn. The warmth generated by thousands of candles and the dancers below made him sleepy.

Arturo stirred and nodded amiably as Yves Valmont passed on his way to the card room. He noticed the fashionable young Creole pause on the shadowy gallery to sip from a silver flask. Restless, Arturo stretched, flexing his broad shoulders. He would have considered going downstairs, but for a certain young matron with hot eyes and an equally hot Creole husband who was sure to seek him out. He thought about going outside for a breath of fresh air, but he could not bring himself to move. Lethargically, he loosened the green scarf he wore knotted about his neck and mopped his brow with the end of it. He shook his head drowsily and pushed his yellow satin mask up on his forehead, mussing his curly shoulder-length black hair and adding to his rakish appearance.

Pulling an elaborate watch from his striped vest, he glanced at it. *Mon Dieu,* was it only midnight? The ball had barely started. He replaced the watch in his vest pocket and began to fish in the pockets of his well-tailored blue jacket.

Sometimes Arturo wondered why he attended these interminable affairs. Even without the bribe an invitation cost him, the price of admission was exorbitant. And once he was here, he found the gaming rooms dead, the music practically a funeral march, and Creole girls nothing more than babied, overprotected virgins. There was nothing to make attendance worthwhile, yet he came. It was a childish weakness, he mused, that made a grown man ache to shock the respectable people of New Orleans from their smug stupor. But he had been shocking them for most of his twenty-six years.

For a moment he toyed with the idea of seeking out the caterer's giggling assistant with her springy curls and tempting curves. A self-satisfied smirk flitted across his darkly handsome face as he recalled his latest conquest. He shifted his position slightly for a better view of the dance floor. At the same time, his fingers located the object of his distracted search.

"Havana?" he asked his companion, offering a leather packet of thick black cigars.

"Merci," Denis LeBlanc, a young Creole whom Arturo knew from the gaming tables, accepted apathetically.

Side by side, high above the dance floor and disapproving stares, the two men performed identical rituals with more animation than either had shown throughout the evening. After first sniffing his cigar appreciatively, each cut the tip with a small silver knife, then lighting it, took a long, luxurious draw. They smoked companionably, lost in thought.

Suddenly a movement below, a rich swirl of ivory and black, caught Arturo's eye. He leaned over the banister, scanning the ballroom with interest.

"LeBlanc—" he nudged Denis from his reverie "—who is that? And why have I not met her before?"

Denis's eyes followed the other man's line of vision. "Oh, that's Valmont's sister," he drawled. "This is her first season."

"So *that* is Danielle Valmont," Arturo breathed, full of wonder. "I have heard of her often since I returned last week, but she is not at all what I expected."

"What exactly did you expect?" Denis regarded the other man with amusement.

"I don't know." Arturo shrugged. "Valmont kept her hidden away for so long in the country, I thought she would be gauche...rustic, you know?"

"She is...a little."

"You know her?"

"I used to see her once in a while when I went to Félicité to play cards, but in the past few years Yves has become very protective of her. Now he looks at all unmarried men as prospective suitors for his sister."

"Were you a suitor?"

"Not me," Denis said with a laugh. "She was scarcely more than a child when I knew her, but intelligent and entirely too well educated for a girl."

"A minor flaw," Arturo answered distractedly.

"You think so? I remember one night in particular when she debated with Monsieur Soulé, the attorney, on the subject of slavery. It seems Danielle freed her maid, the only slave she ever owned, when she was ten years old. Good thing she did not have more than one. Freeing slaves is hardly a way to attract a husband in Louisiana."

"No," Arturo agreed with an absent shake of his head, though he had hardly heard a word the other man said. "How could I have missed her entrance to the ballroom?"

"You were otherwise engaged . . . with the redhead in the pantry," Denis baited him.

"Oh, yes, Rita. You would enjoy her." Arturo was engrossed in watching the girl below. "This one you must leave to the men, LeBlanc." He flashed a brilliant smile and needled the other man in return. "She is *magnifique, oui?*"

"She does have a certain style," Denis granted. "But with enough money, anyone can. If nothing is done about that damned import tariff, pirates—pardon, De Leon—privateers like you will have all the style that money can buy," he joked lazily.

Arturo ignored the reference to his recent daring smuggling triumph as his blue eyes took in every detail of the scene below. "This Danielle Valmont, she has more than style," he countered. "She has beauty and golden hair and creamy skin. What she does *not* have is a dance card."

Abruptly he stood and straightened his silk tie. "I am wasting time with all this talk. I know a prize when I see one, *mon ami,* and this girl is a prize worth having. I will go and make her acquaintance." Pulling his mask into place, Arturo smoothed his long hair and brushed at his mustache with a bent finger. "I hope, as a woman of learning, she knows what to do with a man of the world. I hear girls learn of passion early in the country. Perhaps she would make a match even for me," he added with a wicked grin.

"Perhaps Yves Valmont would have something to say about that," Denis muttered as he watched the privateer's progress across the crowded ballroom below.

Purposefully, Arturo stepped behind Danielle and her partner as the orchestra began the next tune. He tapped Vincent smartly on the shoulder. One arm possessively encircling her waist, the compact young Creole glared up at the intruder.

"Pardon, *m'sieur*." Arturo looked over his disgruntled rival's shoulder and bowed politely to Danielle. "This dance is mine, Mademoiselle Valmont," he declared.

"A moment, *monsieur*. Is your name on her dance card?" Vincent objected hotly.

"Of course." The tall man smiled down at him patronizingly. "Go and see for yourself," he suggested with a careless shrug. Then, taking Danielle's arm gently, he extricated her from her beau's grip and swept her onto the dance floor before anything more could be said.

"Who are you? How did you know my name?" Danielle asked, tilting her masked face toward his.

Her voice was low and pleasing, her accent refined, just as Arturo had known it would be. She placed one hand on his muscular shoulder and stared curiously at him.

"I am one of your many admirers," he responded smoothly, "and we all know your name."

"Have we met before, *monsieur?*" she asked stiffly, discomfited by the practiced flattery of her mysterious partner.

"*Non,* but we should have."

"Are you a friend of my brother?"

"I have met him," the stranger answered noncommittally. "Now, no more questions," he silenced her. "Just dance." Despite his powerful build, Arturo cut a graceful figure as he led the girl skillfully through an intricate series of steps.

But Danielle could not resist one more inquiry. "Is your name really on my dance card?" she challenged.

"What do you think?" Arturo grinned down at her.

"I think it probably is not." She looked away to hide the pleased smile that inexplicably lit her face.

"If you are right, *mademoiselle,* I will be found out for the cad I am." The man sighed tragically, drawing her amused gaze back to him. "I would have signed your dance card. But those ridiculous formalities are a waste of time . . . time better spent dancing with the most beautiful woman at the ball."

Although his tone was light, his azure eyes seemed to burn through the slits of the golden mask, caressing her face, her hair, her shoulders. His muscular arms tightened around her, drawing her nearer to his hard chest.

Danielle's body stiffened in his grip as she raised her face, straining to see the features behind the disguise. To her dismay, she found his full, sensuous lips dangerously close to hers.

"Please, *monsieur* . . ." She ducked her head self-consciously.

"*Capitaine.* Capitaine De Leon." His breath stirred her hair.

"Please, Capitaine De Leon, do not hold me so tightly."

Contrarily, Arturo clasped her even tighter, reasoning, "But, *cher,* I do not want lose you now that I have found you. And you do not want to lose me, either, do you, when we dance so well together?"

This time Danielle did not hide her smile. The couple spun around the dance floor without speaking until the dance was over. With a calculating glance at Vincent, who was shoving his way through the crowd toward them, Arturo steered the girl in the opposite direction.

"Sit here—" he nodded toward an empty chair "—while I get you a drink . . . a cordial, perhaps, or some punch."

Who was this bold stranger? Danielle wondered as she perched on the edge of the chair. He was handsome, even elegant, in his flamboyant velvets and brocades, but she did not recognize him. She could not, hindered by the mask. Had they met before?

Her puzzling was interrupted by a loud voice. Looking over her shoulder, Danielle discovered Madame Dufren, one of her neighbors, indignantly addressing a small attentive knot of women.

"What a pair," she announced with shrill disgust. "A blackguard pirate and a willful orphan. Yves Valmont may have thought he was protecting that girl, keeping her at Félicité while he sowed his wild oats, but I tell you she ran free all over the parish without a chaperon! I heard she even visited that old man who just died—what was his name?—Monsieur Doucet. Her tutor," the woman said with a snort. "I never heard of such foolishness." Her voice dropped confidentially. "She attended his funeral, too. Appalling behavior for the daughter of one of *les bonnes familles!* Ladies simply do not attend funerals in New Orleans. Who does she think she is?

"And did I mention the time she raced that huge black horse of hers with a peddler?" Madame Dufren continued without even pausing for breath. "It was shocking, yet just a few days later, I saw her with my own eyes—scandalous it was—riding that beast again. Bareback."

Danielle cared little what the woman said about her, but she was considering whether to defend Péril, her beloved gelding, when Capitaine De Leon returned, bearing two small crystal cups of punch.

"Are you a blackguard?" the girl asked ingenuously as she accepted one from him.

Arturo's cup halted halfway to his lips, which curved with amusement. "Some seem to think that I am."

"Are you a pirate, as well?"

"The word for what I am, *mademoiselle,* is privateer," he corrected gravely. "Perhaps I must even admit to being a smuggler, but never a pirate. Why do you ask?"

"It was just something I heard," she replied vaguely.

"I see." Arturo glanced knowingly at Madame Dufren's broad back. "I may have heard the same conversation."

"Such is my lot, always to be the topic of gossip." He sighed, bending near to ask, "If you are to share my fate, do you not think you could call me Arturo?"

"All right . . . Arturo." Danielle smiled.

"Come, *ma belle,*" the privateer teased gently, "let me claim you for another dance and we will give them more to talk about."

In the chandelier's glow, Arturo and Danielle spun around the ballroom with a fierce abandon. They were a well-matched

couple, the virile man and the tall, graceful girl. They whirled
past a line of disapproving old spinsters and a beautiful young
matron who tried in vain to catch the privateer's eye. Arturo's dark head was bent close to Danielle's blond one, and he
smiled exultantly at his prize, holding her tightly.

As they swept past another couple, Danielle caught a
glimpse of her brother's angry face. Yves watched them intently, nearly treading on the feet of his partner. Danielle
wished the dance could go on and on, but it ended and Yves
loomed at her elbow.

"I believe my name is next on my sister's dance card," he
informed Arturo brusquely.

"Beaten at my own game," Arturo groaned, but he acquiesced. "As you wish, Monsieur Valmont. My pleasure,
mademoiselle." He kissed her hand, then turned and disappeared in the throng.

As Danielle watched him go, Yves, his face dark with displeasure, gripped her in rigid arms. She was nearly staggered
by the brandy on his breath. "What are you doing, wasting
your time on a pirate?" he demanded.

"Capitaine De Leon is a privateer."

"He is a pirate, a cutthroat and a seducer of decent
women," he growled. "If he were a gentleman, I would call
him out."

"I was not seduced and I will not have you dueling over
me," Danielle informed her brother heatedly. "I know what
you do. First you drink, then you look for a fight. I heard
about your last duel, and I do not wish to be your excuse this
time."

"It does not matter what you wish. Arturo De Leon is a
scoundrel. Although I would rather not, I will defend your
honor against such a man if I must," he said pompously.

"Yves Valmont, my honor is not so fragile that dancing with
the *capitaine* will ruin it," she protested in a loud whisper.

He looked around apprehensively to see who might have
overheard. "Be reasonable, Dani," he coaxed. "You are
making Vincent angry. Don't say it," he commanded when she
would protest. "I know you do not love him, but Vincent
Gauthier would be a good match for you. He is only one of
many eligible young men here tonight. If you would just re-

trieve your dance card from Angelique, you'd find every dance is spoken for.''

As Yves had said, every line of her card was indeed filled, and Danielle was drawn onto the dance floor by admirer after admirer. Vincent watched sullenly, making no effort to approach her until the music for their next dance had begun. At the first chords, he presented himself, bowing stiffly. ''My dance, I believe, *mademoiselle.*''

Vincent's arms were stiff around the girl and he held her at a distance. Every silent step seemed an accusation. At last, Danielle could stand it no longer. ''Are you not going to talk to me, Vincent?''

''I am pleased you honor me with this dance, *mademoiselle,*'' he replied stiltedly, ''particularly when you have so few to spare me.''

A flare of anger shone momentarily in the girl's brown eyes, but she controlled it and merely sighed, ''It is my pleasure, as well, Monsieur Gauthier.''

All at once, Vincent's reserve crumbled, and his arm tightened around her. ''Oh, Danielle,'' he muttered miserably. ''I wanted this evening to be perfect for us.''

''I think it is wonderful,'' she assured him.

''But we have only one more dance together all evening,'' he complained petulantly.

''Then we must enjoy it.''

''You are right, I suppose,'' Vincent finally muttered, ''but how am I to enjoy it when you are surrounded by so many admirers?'' Holding her even closer, he swung her recklessly around the floor.

When their dance was finished, Danielle's suitor unwillingly relinquished her to her waiting partner and trudged away. He and Yves stood at the sidelines and sipped punch liberally sweetened from Yves's pocket flask. Danielle's brother watched proudly as she danced with first one partner, than another.

The evening passed in a pleasurable blur for Danielle as she danced and laughed and talked. Exertion brought a becoming pink to the girl's cheeks. Vincent's jealous green eyes never left her until Yves finally persuaded him to withdraw to the gaming room until his last dance of the evening with Danielle. She did not even notice when they made their unsteady ascent.

At last, Danielle found herself stumbling through a reel with an awkward American boy who stepped on her toes nearly a dozen times and apologized twice that, before suggesting they sit down. Gratefully, she waited while he went to fetch the obligatory cup of punch.

Suddenly, Arturo appeared in front of her. Bowing deeply, he took her hand and drew her onto the floor. "Surely your brother cannot claim this dance."

"*Non,* but someone else can," Danielle protested weakly, peering over her shoulder for her partner.

"I believe the American has danced as much as he can," the captain chuckled. "It is up to us now."

Danielle looked up at the privateer, ready to argue, but she did not. In a heartbeat, his smile disappeared and his blue eyes met hers and held them. The music seemed to fade and she nearly missed a step. She longed to escape the intensity of his gaze, but it was impossible.

With effort, she shifted her eyes. Through the dark veil of her eyelashes, she concentrated instead on the golden earring in his left ear, the sun-bronzed skin of his cheek and the minute smile lines around his mouth below his raven mustache. She blushed suddenly, disconcerted at the unbidden thoughts of those lips on hers. As if he knew what she was thinking, Arturo's grin broadened and his arms tightened around her even more.

From the gallery, Yves Valmont caught sight of his sister with the privateer. He gripped the balustrade with white-knuckled hands, and his aristocratic face, already flushed with alcohol, deepened in hue. Would Danielle never learn to obey? No matter what he told her, she always did just the opposite. He had warned her that De Leon was a dangerous man, and now she was dancing with him again.

Wrathfully, Yves made his way downstairs, pausing on the bottom step to glare at the couple over the heads of the crowd. He considered crossing the floor to break them apart, but his legs felt too unsteady to negotiate a path between the circling dancers. Instead he watched them venomously until he lost sight of them in the crowd.

When the music ended, Danielle placed both hands flat against Arturo's chest and pushed away lightly. She was relieved when he allowed her to retreat, but ill at ease under his bemused stare.

"I must go now," she blurted breathlessly, distressed that she could not read his expression behind his golden mask. "I—I really must go. The next dance belongs to Vincent."

"He will not mind if you dance with me again." Arturo stood very near; his voice was low and intimate.

"He minded when you took his last dance," Danielle reminded him coolly, but she took another step backward, hoping he could not guess how her pulse was pounding.

"But now he is nowhere to be seen." The big man made a show of looking around. "I believe he is upstairs, drunk. It is such a shame what jealousy does to a man!"

The music resumed, and Arturo swept Danielle onto the dance floor once more.

"Please, you must let me go," she demurred.

"Why?" The disturbing blue eyes were fixed on her again.

"Because my brother will be angry," she answered reluctantly.

"Ah...your brother. And you do everything he wants? *Bien,* I see you do not." Arturo laughed as Danielle's chin rose rebelliously in response to his goading. "I knew you were a woman who does as she pleases."

"Indeed, and what I please, *capitaine,* is for you to release me. I warn you, Yves has been drinking and he has a very hot temper."

"And you fear he will demand satisfaction. Don't worry, I don't believe he will challenge me."

"He said he would if..." the girl began hotly, annoyed by his smug smile, but she faltered.

"He would if...what?" Arturo crooned ominously.

"He would if you were a gentleman." She met his gaze uneasily and was startled when he laughed aloud.

"If I were a gentleman, *cher,* it would not be necessary for him to call me out," he informed her. "There would be no danger—at least, no more than you wish yourself. In fact, *I* am the one who is in danger here. Creoles and their damned affairs of honor. Dueling is such a waste of time and energy."

Arturo shook his head in mock exasperation. "Still, if I must, I must. Whom do you suppose I will have to fight first—Yves or young Gauthier?"

"Do not make jokes about it," she snapped.

"I wouldn't think of it," Arturo replied, suddenly serious. "But I tell you, Danielle, I would not fight for honor, though I might fight for you."

A thrill of unfamiliar emotion surged through the girl at his words. She suddenly felt very young and at a loss for words.

"Come with me, Danielle." Yves's infuriated voice cut across their conversation. Standing unsteadily at her side, he gripped her elbow tightly and spun her from Arturo's grip.

The captain grimaced with irritation, but he surrendered the girl without protest. "*Bonsoir* once again, *mademoiselle.*" He bowed politely. "I hope we may finish our dance the next time we meet."

"There will be no next time, De Leon. Keep away from my sister," Yves snarled, placing his hand deliberately on the hilt of the colchemarde he wore at his side.

Arturo's eyes narrowed, but he made no move for his sword. He glanced at Danielle's tense, pale face. The girl was obviously frightened of what the next few moments might hold. Bystanders shifted nervously, their eyes fastened on the two men.

"There is no reason for bloodshed, Valmont. Surely your sister is old enough to choose her friends," the privateer suggested quietly.

"My sister is—" Yves began in a clipped voice.

"Your sister is quite capable of making her own decisions," Danielle interjected furiously. She knew her brother well; knew his rashness when he had been drinking.

Intent on their confrontation, both men turned to regard the girl with blank looks of surprise. Yves opened his mouth, as if to speak.

"When there are choices that concern me, Yves, I will make them," she told her brother, "and *now* I choose to go home."

Without another word or even a backward glance, Danielle marched from the ballroom, leaving him to follow angrily in her wake.

Chapter Two

A breeze from the river ruffled Danielle's hair as she stood on the small balcony outside her bedroom. The sun was warm on her shoulders despite the morning chill. She usually enjoyed this view of Félicité's rose gardens and she should have been in a good mood. But this morning the girl stared at the neat flower beds with a distracted frown, drawing her shawl closer around her. Below her, pale green shoots showed through the rich soil at the bases of dormant bushes as the first daffodils of spring struggled to life. She scarcely noticed them.

Her thoughts were on Yves. Downstairs in the dining room, her brother was eating his breakfast, waiting for her to appear, but Danielle procrastinated.

For weeks, something had been troubling her reckless, carefree brother. Yves had his faults; his reputation for gambling, drinking and carousing was well deserved, becoming more exaggerated each year, but the girl did not care. She idolized him and Yves doted on her in return.

Recently he had shut her out. He had not gone out in the evenings, but disappeared after dinner into his study with a bottle of bourbon. When Danielle listened at the door, she heard him pacing within. She went away sadly without knocking; he made it clear he did not wish to be disturbed. Long after she had gone to bed, she heard his unsteady tread on the stairs as he retired to his room. Yves appeared in the morning with dark circles under his eyes and an invisible wall around him. She longed to talk to him, to discover what bothered him, but when she tried, he became falsely jovial and told her not to worry.

Perhaps it was her fault. Things had not been right between them since the masked ball more than a month ago. Yves's pride would not allow him to forgive Danielle's dramatic exit that night. And she resented his accusation that she had interfered in his affair of honor, embarrassing him. Since their clash at the ball, they quarreled almost daily, usually about her impending spinsterhood.

When the muted rattle of dishes from the dining room finally roused Danielle from her brooding, she realized she was cold. Opening the glass-paned French door, she stepped inside.

She could delay no longer. As she gave her appearance a quick inspection, her glance strayed to the black satin mask hanging on the corner of the mirror where it had hung since the morning after the ball. She picked it up, fingering it dreamily, and a smile fluttered across her lips. Humming an airy tune, Danielle danced lightly around the room, imagining the warmth of Arturo De Leon's arms around her. But when she caught sight of her reflection, her smile faded and she gave up the fancy, returning the mask, almost guiltily, to its place.

Hurriedly, she arranged her hair into a sleek chignon at her nape, then, setting her shoulders, went downstairs for another skirmish with her brother.

"*Bonjour,* Danielle," Yves greeted her. His dapper appearance belied the ache in his head. The young Creole was immaculately groomed as always, but his eyes were bloodshot and the hand that held his coffee cup shook ever so slightly.

"*Bonjour,* Yves." Danielle bent to kiss his clean-shaven cheek. The skirt of her merino dress with its satin piping swayed gracefully as she took her place at the table. Unobtrusively, a dusky maid appeared from the butler's pantry to pour a cup of fragrant black coffee and set it in front of her mistress. "*Merci beaucoup,* Lydie."

The master of the house nodded toward his cup and instantly the maid supplied more of the steaming liquid. He sat back and looked at his sister, his dark eyes taking in her blue dress quizzically. "You look lovely today, *ma petite.* Are you going somewhere?"

"Just shopping with Angelique."

"That should be nice, I am sure," Yves responded properly, sipping his coffee. He was pleased with his sister's planned outing, for he approved of her friendship with the Arceneaux girl, through he refrained from saying so. Lately it seemed he and Danielle were not able to talk without shouting.

He cleared his throat anxiously and said, "If you are going with Mademoiselle Arceneaux, I suppose there is no reason to tell you to behave like a lady."

"No reason at all," Danielle answered with a tight smile.

"Bien," he replied heartily. Yves longed to ask her about Vincent's visit last night, but he could see no invitation to conversation in her eyes. Awkwardly, he refolded his linen napkin and laid it on the table. "I must go now," he excused himself. "I will be riding the fields with the overseer today. Perhaps we can talk this evening."

The girl was finishing her solitary breakfast when a carriage rolled up the *allée*. Before the servants could reach the door, a rapid knock sounded and Angelique entered, audible well before she was visible.

"Bonjour, Zeme," the vivacious Creole girl greeted the Valmonts' ancient Negro mammy. "Is Danielle in the dining room? Oh, something smells good. Is there any *café* left?"

The short, round brunette burst into the room, bringing with her a storm of chatter. "Ah, there you are, Dani. Are you ready? We must hurry. *Oui, café,* please, Lydie.

"What is wrong, *cher?"* Angelique asked, plopping unceremoniously into a chair across from her hostess. "You look exhausted."

"I did not sleep well."

"Oh, dear, are you and Yves still arguing?" the other girl asked knowingly as she drew off her gloves.

Danielle nodded and watched her friend measure three heaping spoons of sugar into the coffee Lydie set before her.

"I vow I've never seen such a stubborn family as you Valmonts, not even my own," the Creole girl commented nonchalantly. Even the gossipy Angelique would not be so brash as to mention the latest rumors making the rounds about Yves.

"I don't know, Angelique," Danielle sighed. "Yves seems bothered by something. Sometimes he is gone for days and I worry about him. And then when he comes home, I wish he would leave again for he always picks up the argument right where he left off."

"The argument? The one about Vincent Gauthier?" the other girl asked, her voice still casual.

"Oui," Danielle nodded bleakly. "I'm surprised he said nothing this morning. Vincent was here last night."

"Oh," Angelique squealed, setting her cup down with a clatter. "Vincent was here? Tell me all about it! Did he propose again?"

"He didn't have time," Danielle replied dryly. "He was too busy interrogating me about my other suitors."

"Oh, *non,* what did you tell him?"

"Nothing. I don't want to be responsible for a duel."

"I suppose. But still . . . a duel under the Oaks . . . wouldn't it be romantic?" The little Creole sighed. She picked up a cold *beignet* and munched it dreamily. "Ummm . . . it must be wonderful to have a man so much in love with you."

Danielle winced at her friend's naïveté. "It is not wonderful when he questions me about my every move. Vincent's jealousy ruins everything."

"He's only jealous because he loves you," Angelique insisted unsympathetically. Her eyes widened when the clock in the foyer chimed, and she gulped her *beignet,* wiping a dusting of powdered sugar from her lips. "Ten o'clock! Can it be so late? Come, we must hurry. You won't need a maid to accompany you. I have Chantal with me," she called over her shoulder as she rushed from the room in a flurry of skirt.

Danielle donned her dark blue pelisse with its matching bonnet and joined Angelique in the open barouche, where Chantal was arranging a woolen carriage robe over the girl's legs.

"You'll never guess, Dani," the little Creole whispered excitedly as her friend settled in the seat beside her. "We are going to the Pirates' Market . . . in Barataria."

"The Pirates' Market?" Danielle repeated incredulously, allowing the maid to tuck the lap robe around her knees as well. "Your mother does not object?"

"*Maman* does not know." The plump girl giggled. "And Chantal and Bruno will not tell her." She nodded toward the slaves who sat beside each other on the driver's bench. "This shopping trip is an excuse for them to be together. They are in love and it's so..."

"Romantic?" Danielle could not resist teasing.

"Yes, romantic. And thrilling and daring. You're not the only one who can be reckless, *ma cher,*" Angelique retorted. "And admit it... you have heard about the infamous Pirates' Market all your life. Haven't you always wanted to see it for yourself?"

"*Oui,*" Danielle agreed against her better judgment.

"*Très bien,*" Angelique cried exuberantly. "Then that's just what we'll do. Have a care that your bonnet shades your face, though. We do not want to look like red Indians when we get there.

"I knew you would go with me, Danielle," she confided as the carriage clattered onto the River Road. "In fact, you are part of the reason I wanted to go. Do you think *he* will be there?"

"Who?" Danielle frowned blankly.

"The pirate... Capitaine De Leon, of course."

"*Non,* I will probably never see him again. Yves says his ship sailed the morning after the ball."

"Oh, and he was so interesting." Angelique looked crestfallen, then she brightened. "Are you secretly in love with the *capitaine?* Is that why you won't marry Vincent?"

"I only met the man once," Danielle protested.

"Once is enough," the other girl assured her hopefully. "I think he is terribly rash and exciting. Do you think he is as wicked as everyone says?"

"No," Danielle answered curtly.

"Then I just don't understand it, Dani," Angelique declared in exasperation. "Why don't you love Vincent? He loves you. And he's the handsomest man in New Orleans. You mustn't mind that he's shorter than you. He's kind and polite and rich and..."

"He is all of those things," the object of his affection agreed with a gusty sigh. Then gently, firmly, she changed the subject and, for the next few miles, appeared unusually inter-ested in every word of Angelique's chatter.

Their carriage stopped briefly on the levee to wait with sev-eral other vehicles for the rickety ferry. Once they were safely across the river, the rigs ranged in an uneven procession along narrow, rutted roads lined with moss-laden trees. Despite the sunshine, the late March weather was chilly. Danielle pulled the short cape of her pelisse tightly around her and wished they would reach their destination.

At Barataria, they found merry pandemonium. The fa-mous Pirates' Market was no more than a clearing in the swamp, surrounded by a scraggly stand of cypress trees. A bevy of carriages ringed the soggy field where the goods were displayed. From many of them, ladies, shaded from the wintry sun by bonnets and parasols, dispatched slaves to fetch mer-chandise they wished to examine more closely: some of it, booty; some, imported items that could not be bought for love or money in American shops.

Hardier ladies, their hems trailing in the mire, were es-corted by gentlemen through the confusion. Cautiously, the shoppers skirted wooden sawhorses bearing ornate Spanish leather saddles and picked paths through stacks of bags con-taining rare spices piled next to rattan baskets overflowing with lemons, limes, coconuts and pineapples.

Everywhere, luxurious velvets, satins and silks were draped in bright disorder over crates and casks. Along a rough ap-proximation of an aisle, blankets, their corners hastily tied to poles, formed makeshift stalls for the sellers. On the damp ground, weather-beaten seamen spread exquisite Turkey car-pets where they displayed silver candelabra, golden snuff-boxes, all manner of gems and jewelry, ivory combs, ostrich feather fans and frothy feminine undergarments.

Across the aisle, wooden chests with brass hinges proffered an astonishing array of laces, ribbons and trims. Here was a barrel of Delft china; there a painting of a sober old gentle-man leaned against an overstuffed chair. All around were goods, detoured from their journey by privateers who were protected by letters of marque signed by governors of various Caribbean islands.

From the edge of the clearing came a loud cheer from the spectators assembled around a shallow pit to watch a cockfight. Pickpockets and cutpurses worked their stumbling way through the crowd and, along the fringes, wrinkled old crones hawked charms and potions to promote health, wealth, love and revenge.

The smells of the fish vendor's stall and of crab boiling in a big pot nearby mingled and threatened to overpower the potent aromas of fresh fruit and pungent spices.

Angelique wrinkled her nose delicately, but she alit from the carriage with a purposeful air. "Come on, Danielle," she urged gaily, unfurling her lacy parasol, "this will be fun. You might get muddy, but just think of what else you'll get!"

"Pneumonia? Ague?" Danielle stepped out of the carriage, almost losing her half boot immediately in the muck.

"No... all kinds of bargains." Laughing, the other girl hitched up her skirt as much as she dared and made her way laboriously toward a vendor of exotic feathers and plumes.

Amused by her enthusiasm, Danielle slogged behind her toward firmer ground. When she arrived, Angelique was already haggling with a squint-eyed sailor over the price of a bonnet.

"Lessee naow, mistress," he growled, "if ye wears hit like this, ye fairly makes a picture, see?" Removing his knitted cap, he shoved the hat onto his own untidy head and posed prettily for Angelique. Smiling sheepishly when she dissolved into peals of laughter, he thrust it toward her. "'Ere, you try hit."

Merrily, the girl obliged him. "How do I look?" she preened.

"Fact is, *mam'selle*," the man replied unctuously, "the 'at looks so much better on you than me, I'll give hit to ye for less than I first allowed."

Danielle left the delighted Angelique to her negotiations and wandered on to the next booth. She was engrossed in an inspection of elaborate silverware when she was interrupted by a deep flirtatious voice behind her.

"Mademoiselle Valmont, is it not? How good of you to grace our humble market today with your presence."

Although she had heard it only one time before, the voice was gloriously familiar. Danielle whirled and saw the speaker standing in the sunny aisle between the stalls.

Arturo De Leon was even more handsome than she had remembered, tall and lean, yet muscular. Dressed in the fashion of the buccaneers, he wore fawn-colored breeches that were tight on lithe legs and tucked into the cuffs of high kid boots. A green silk scarf was knotted carelessly at his throat and a yellow silk sash encircled his trim waist and held a brace of pistols in place. A long, deadly-looking knife was sheathed in the hollow at the small of his back. His billowing shirt, made of fine white lawn, was open under his leather jacket to reveal a browned, lightly furred chest. His glossy raven hair hung to his broad shoulders and, in his left earlobe, a golden hoop glittered in the sun. His blue eyes regarded her warmly, unrestricted by the mask he had worn at the ball. Below his thick black mustache, even white teeth flashed against tan skin as he smiled in welcome.

"Capitaine De Leon!" There was no guile in Danielle's greeting. The surprise on her face gave way to a radiant smile. The privateer was taken aback by the feelings it stirred in him.

"Come, *cher,* let me look at you," he said, taking her hand and drawing her into the sunlight where he regarded her with wonder. "I was sorry when you did not stay for the unmasking at the ball, but I see the wait was worth it. You are even more beautiful than I imagined."

Danielle blushed becomingly and extricated her hand, embarrassed by his ardent words.

"Bonjour, capitaine." She curtsied self-consciously. "I did not realize you would be here."

"How can that be?" He sighed dramatically. "I was certain you came to Barataria especially to see me." His dancing blue eyes sought hers beneath the broad brim of her bonnet and held them. "After you ran away from me at the ball," he accused softly, moving closer.

The girl retreated a step, searching for a response, fighting the attraction she felt. "I thought it was best that . . ."

"That I would not see you again?"

"That there be no bloodshed," Danielle corrected.

"Would you have wept if my blood was shed?" Arturo moved closer yet; his voice was quiet, yet somehow demanding.

"I would weep more if it were my brother's." She held her ground and frowned up at him, vexed that he made her feel defenseless.

"But you would weep," he murmured insistently.

"I do not weep for just anyone," the girl said firmly, stepping back.

"But I am not just anyone, *cher.*" Arturo smiled confidently.

"Oh, Danielle, just look what I bought!" Angelique's gleeful trill interrupted the couple. A scowl on his rugged face, the man swung to glare at the new arrival.

The Creole girl bustled toward them, juggling parasol, reticule and a huge hat box, but her step faltered when she saw Arturo. *"Bonjour."* She smiled in tentative greeting. No matter what Danielle had said, Angelique was still frightened of the notorious privateer and the murderous expression on his face convinced her to be cautious.

"Angelique, may I introduce Capitaine Arturo De Leon? *Capitaine,* my friend, Mademoiselle Angelique Arceneaux," Danielle blurted, the words rushing from her in relief for the interruption.

"Angelique . . . a charming name for one so fair." Arturo forced his brow to unfurrow and bowed chivalrously. "My pleasure, Mademoiselle Arceneaux. Welcome to Barataria."

"How do you do, *capitaine,*" she said, giggling nervously.

"Call me Arturo, please." The big man was flirting, winning over the plump girl immediately.

Forgetting her fears, Angelique chattered excitedly about the Pirates' Market. When she paused to take a breath, she looked around the marshy clearing and asked dubiously, "You do not live here, do you, Arturo?"

"I do, at least part of the time when we are in port." The privateer positioned himself between the girls and offered each an arm. "Will you ladies allow me the honor of showing you around? Outside of the market, there is very little to show. Barataria has seen better days, but we call it home."

He led them through the cluttered stalls, past a makeshift alehouse where a sultry, sloe-eyed girl danced for coins, to the outer edge of the clearing where the bayou flowed. Away from the crowds, dragonflies darted in the crisp, clean air and the cry of a wild goose could be heard in the distance.

"You see, just a small village in the midst of the swamp." Arturo pointed toward the compound of huts, built on stilts, nearly obscured by a thick screen of vegetation. "As I told you, it is not much to look at, but this was my chance to be alone with the two loveliest ladies in New Orleans," he teased.

"*Merci,* Arturo," Angelique replied daringly as Danielle, seemingly oblivious to the man's lavish compliments, stepped closer to the water.

Angelique shaded her eyes against the sun and surveyed the tiny village on the other side of the bayou sadly. "It is so...plain. I always thought there would be mansions, built from booty."

"There was a mansion once that belonged to Jean Lafitte, but it burned long ago. I was young, but I remember it well." Arturo's tone was nostalgic a moment before he continued briskly, "Those days are gone forever. Lafitte is gone, his men are gone. Hellish banditti. That is what Andrew Jackson called them—before the Battle of New Orleans.

"Ah, well, some say Lafitte does well in Texas. Who knows? Now my men live here...quietly. They are simple family men. Most of them have pirogues so, when we are not at sea, they can trap and hunt and fish."

"Not a very exciting life for pirates," Angelique muttered. "I thought you murdered and pillaged and..." Her voice trailed off in distress when she realized what she was about to say.

"Murdered and pillaged and what?" Arturo prompted roguishly.

"Oh, nothing." She turned deep red in hue and refused to meet his mischievous blue eyes. "Did you ever kill anyone?"

"No one who did not deserve it," the man responded. Then he added with a wicked smile, "Do not worry. I would never harm a lady as lovely as you. I only kill the very ugly ones."

"I see," the Creole girl murmured with a dubious sidewise glance. Suddenly, she gasped and pointed at what looked like a log sliding by in the muddy water, "Oh, what's that?"

Arturo's gaze followed hers as the log disappeared under a tangled growth of water hyacinths. "An alligator...a big, sleepy fellow." He smiled tolerantly. "He wants no more to do with you than you do with him."

A little apart from the conversation, Danielle leaned against a tree and watched a pair of pelicans effortlessly skim the surface of the water to light on a nearby cypress knee. Contentedly, she took off her hat and let the breeze ruffle her hair, ingenuously unaware of Arturo's distracted, admiring glances.

"What is the name of your ship, Capitaine De Leon?" she asked, turning unexpectedly. Arturo also leaned against the tree trunk, his face close to hers. Hastily, Danielle looked away.

"She is called the *Magdalena,* after one of the women in my life."

"How romantic," Angelique twittered.

"Oui." Arturo nodded with an amused grin. "You should see my ship, *cheri."* He leaned forward to murmur in Danielle's ear. "She is beautiful, almost as beautiful as you."

"Merci," the girl muttered, shifting uncomfortably. "Where is the *Magdalena* today?"

"Being fitted out for our next voyage," the man answered lazily, his gaze roaming her face.

"Where will you sail this time?" Angelique piped from behind them, anxious to be included in the conversation.

Arturo looked back at her in surprise. "I cannot divulge our destination, *mademoiselle,* but rest assured, we always sail to where treasure awaits. Come, now," he invited, gesturing grandly, "you do not want to miss another moment of the famous Pirates' Market." Gallantly, he offered an arm to each girl to escort them back to the busy stalls.

As the man drew Danielle's hand through the crook of his arm, he leaned close to whisper, "Perhaps you will come to Barataria again soon, *mademoiselle*...to see the *Magdalena."*

"I do not know. Perhaps," she agreed cautiously, dodging slightly in an effort to retreat from his overly warm invitation.

"Alas, you will come to see the market, you will come to see my ship. Why will you not come just to see me?" he jested.

"I have not said for certain, *capitaine,* that I will come even to see your ship," the girl retorted, but a smile hovered about her lips.

"You will break my heart, Danielle. I know it," the privateer pronounced with a hearty laugh. But as they walked back to the hubbub of the market, Arturo's sapphire eyes were thoughtful.

When they approached the stalls, Angelique stopped suddenly to announce, "If you two will excuse me, I must see if the bolt of pink watered silk is still for sale. The more I think about it, the more certain I am that I must have it for the next ball. It was good to meet you, Capitaine De Leon." She offered her hand to the man, who obligingly kissed it.

"I am honored by your visit today, Mademoiselle Arceneaux," he flattered smoothly. "I hope you and Mademoiselle Valmont will visit us again soon."

"We'd love to," Angelique gushed with a dimpled smile. Then she bustled off to find the silk seller.

"Ribbons! Me, I got ribbons . . . fine satin ribbons for your hair, *mam'selle,* penny a length," a wizened Cajun seaman croaked as Danielle and Arturo wandered past his stall.

"If you find one you like, perhaps you will permit me to buy it for you?" the captain suggested hopefully, drawing the girl toward the display.

"Non, merci." She sidled away from her attentive escort, disturbingly aware of his nearness. "I couldn't let you do that."

"But I want to," he insisted. Picking up a length of blue ribbon, he held it against her hair.

"Perfect," he announced. "Perhaps I could buy you two or three . . . for your birthday." He selected a pink ribbon and a yellow one.

Danielle retreated again. "My birthday was the second of November, Capitaine De Leon . . . long past. I will buy my own ribbon, *merci."*

"Oh, very well," the privateer agreed grudgingly.

Intent on her selection, Danielle did not notice Arturo's meaningful nod toward the old sailor nor see the quick look of understanding between the two men.

"I will take these." The girl showed the vendor her choices.

"That'll be two cents, *mam'selle*."

"Two cents?" Danielle looked down at the three lengths of ribbon in her hand. "I thought you said a penny a length."

"Oui," he answered gravely, "but, me, I was forgetting about my three-for-the-price-of-two sale, today only. Two cents, if you please, *mam'selle*." He extended a grubby palm.

Obligingly, Danielle rummaged in her bag for the two coins, missing the smile and the wink exchanged by the men.

But Vincent Gauthier saw it from across the field. At first, he had been so engrossed in watching the cockfight, he was unaware of Danielle's presence. But when the battle was over and the victorious bird strutted over the body of his opponent, the young Creole peered around and rubbed his neck like a man awakening from a deep sleep.

Through a gap in the wall of people ringing the pit, he spied Danielle and he could not believe what he saw. She was strolling brazenly through the Pirates' Market with Arturo De Leon. The privateer possessively covered the hand she placed on his arm as he escorted her from stall to stall, smiling down intimately at her, ducking his head to hear what she had to say. But what Vincent could not bear was the fascination in Danielle's eyes when she looked up at the privateer.

Rage distorting his aristocratic face, the young Creole charged across the marshy field toward the girl, calling her name.

"Vincent!" Danielle greeted him, her brown eyes round with surprise. *"Bonjour.* I did not expect to see you here."

"That is obvious," he spit, glaring at Arturo.

The bigger man met his scowl coolly, not even bothering to release Danielle's hand.

"What are you doing here?" the Creole demanded of Danielle, pointedly turning his back on the privateer. "This is no place for a young lady . . . and certainly no place for my wife-to-be." He wheeled on Arturo belligerently. "I will thank you to take your hands off of her, De Leon."

"I have never said I will marry you, Vincent Gauthier," Danielle protested hotly before Arturo could respond.

"No, but it is...it is understood," Vincent stammered, taken aback by the girl's vehemence.

"Only by you and my brother," she snapped.

"It would seem Mademoiselle Danielle prefers my company today, *mon ami*," Arturo suggested with a smirk.

"She does not know what a scoundrel you are, De Leon. She is too young and genteel. If you do not withdraw immediately and allow me to take her home, I will be forced to defend her name on the field of honor," Vincent insisted arrogantly, taking his sword cane in both hands as if to unsheathe it. "At dawn tomorrow."

"Why wait, Gauthier?" Arturo drawled dangerously. "I could fight you as well now as later."

"Enough, both of you!" Danielle exploded, glaring back and forth between them. Uncomfortably conscious of the attention their scene was attracting, she drew herself up proudly and directed the young Creole, "Vincent, you may escort me to Angelique's carriage."

Her head high, she turned to the privateer. "Capitaine De Leon, *merci* for showing me the amusements of the Pirates' Market. Today, however, you may not count a duel among them."

Chapter Three

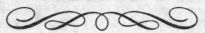

A black expression on his handsome face, Arturo De Leon drove along the River Road toward the home of his silent partner, Jaime Montera. The spring day was unseasonably hot. The morning breeze had died and now the sun, high in the sky, beat down, magnifying Arturo's temper and inspiring his recall of oaths in five languages.

Damn the boy at Hébert's Livery Stable for this jangling rig and bony nag, he fumed. A curse on Montera for insisting he drive all the way out to his country home. But most of all, devil take the luck when he agreed to have a partner and carry legal cargo aboard the *Magdalena*. Arturo De Leon was a free-booter, not a merchant!

The swaybacked mare that drew the rented cabriolet had been lackadaisical in the heat, but now she shied skittishly for no reason and kicked up dust, which drifted into Arturo's face. The man sneezed and swore, his bad humor communicating itself to the horse. She halted in the middle of the road and would go no farther.

"Peste," Arturo muttered, at the end of his limited patience. *"Allons!* Giddap, Circe, or whatever your name is, you miserable excuse for an animal," he shouted, sawing at the reins. But when the mare deigned to move, she ambled slowly off the road, veering toward the levee where she stopped under a shade tree to graze.

In exasperation, the captain pushed back his Panama hat and mopped his forehead with the end of his scarf. Turning to place one booted foot on the wooden seat, he lit a cheroot and scanned the sunbaked road, glad no one passed to witness this indignity. He would have a word with Hébert when he returned to the Vieux Carré...if the independent Circe could be persuaded to take him.

Beyond the levee to his right, Arturo could hear the gentle lapping of the Mississippi against the bank. The sound of birdsong came from the forest of huge trees across the road. Lulled by the heat and the stillness, he began to relax. Montera would wait. It was not unpleasant here in the shade. Perhaps the horse had more sense than he had given her credit for.

Idly surveying his surroundings, Arturo realized he was stopped near the gates to Félicité, the Valmont plantation. Although not the biggest, it was reputed to be one of the most gracious homes along the Mississippi. Curious, he tried to peer through the screen of trees hung with gray wisps of Spanish moss, but the house was invisible, set far back at the end of the *allée*.

So this was where Danielle Valmont lived her sheltered life. The privateer settled back on the seat with a lopsided smile and allowed his thoughts to turn to the girl.

He had not seen her since she came to the Market nearly three weeks ago, but she was never far from his thoughts. When modesty demanded, Arturo counted his conquests only in the hundreds. Why, then, did this girl stay in his mind? She was beautiful, but he had known many beautiful women. She was also proud, haughty and hot-tempered, and she held herself to be above him, he knew that. These Creoles...they considered themselves pieces from the thigh of Jupiter. Danielle Valmont was a spoiled child, like every other Creole girl he had ever met.

No—Arturo's smile broadened at the memory of her—Danielle was different. She was spoiled, it was true, but she was not a child. Naive was the word he would choose to describe her, and how she would hate that description. No doubt her inexperience could be remedied. It would require only a short time alone with her to teach her what she needed to know. Leaning back more comfortably, he blew smoke rings toward the cloudless sky and wondered what kind of student she would be.

He was jolted from his musings when Circe suddenly lurched forward in search of better grazing. Determined to take advantage of any forward motion, the man jammed his cigar between his teeth, grasped the reins firmly and shouted, *"Allons!"* The surprised mare trotted a few steps, then stopped and started all the way to the bayou that marked the boundary of Félicité. Finally, she pulled the rig over a narrow wooden bridge toward a belated meeting with Jaime Montera.

In her room at Félicité, Danielle was trying to read a book of poetry Vincent had given her as a token of his devotion. She closed the slim volume with a sigh for, try as she might, she could not concentrate while she listened for Yves's return. After the trip to the Pirates' Market, she had avoided her brother, but now he was avoiding her. He had been absent for three days with no word. They had argued often before. What had she said this time to drive him away so completely?

Bleakly, she remembered the return to Félicité that day nearly three weeks ago. It had been a long, silent ride from Barataria. Vincent rode sullenly beside the open carriage, throwing occasional hurt looks toward Danielle. Angelique sat across from her, quiet for once, her eyes wide with fear at having been discovered at the Market. On the driver's seat, Bruno edged away slightly from Chantal and glanced nervously in the direction of the young Creole man. Danielle herself stared straight ahead, seething with anger at Vincent's possessiveness, and said nothing at all. A pall had fallen over her day's adventure.

When they arrived at Félicité, Vincent tied his horse to the back of the barouche before opening the door for Danielle.

"Come, Mademoiselle Valmont, I will walk with you," he pronounced formally. In a kinder tone, he suggested to the other girl, "If you will wait here for a moment, Mademoiselle Angelique, I will escort you home personally."

Danielle's injured suitor accompanied her to the door. "I will be back soon," he said sadly. "We have much to talk about, you and I." Then he marched back to the carriage.

Numb with dread, the girl walked into the house, past the questioning looks of Zeme and Lydie, who waited in the foyer, and directly to her brother's study. She settled there apprehensively, mentally rehearsing what she would say to Yves when the inevitable confrontation occurred.

She did not have long to wait. Apparently Vincent had met Yves on the River Road and must have immediately reported her offense.

The study door flew open and Yves stormed into the room, his face mottled with rage. Still clad in his riding clothes, he tracked mud from his boots across the Oriental carpet and positioned himself arrogantly in front of his sister. She could smell his familiar masculine scent: cigars and horses and whiskey...a great deal of whiskey.

"Danielle Marie-Christiane Valmont! What were you thinking—or were you thinking at all?" he roared in greeting. "To take Angelique Arceneaux to the Pirates' Market?"

"As it happens," she answered calmly, standing her ground, "Angelique took me."

"I don't believe that any more than anyone else will. How am I going to explain to her mother?"

"Explain what? I did nothing wrong," the girl insisted.

"You never do," Yves retorted sarcastically, "yet I constantly hear of your escapades. Don't you know what everyone is saying?" he asked hotly. "That you're wild and headstrong. You are certainly making a fine reputation for yourself, Sister."

"It must run in the family, Brother," she snapped, the acid in her tone matching his.

Yves's lips curled in a furious snarl and his fist clenched and opened spasmodically. Controlling himself with effort, he sank into a leather chair and closed his eyes wearily. The weight of responsibility had always been great, for he had become the guardian of his sister when she was eleven years old and he only eighteen. Even after all these years, Yves was uncomfortable disciplining the girl. And it was becoming more and more difficult.

"If you'd only listen to me, Yves," she coaxed.

"Listen to what?" he asked hoarsely, opening his eyes to glare at her balefully. "More arguments? I swear I should never have let you talk me into hiring a tutor for you at all. I should have sent you to the good sisters at the Ursuline Convent. At least they would have taught you to cook or to sew . . . or something useful.''

"What does that have to do with it?'' she protested.

"Everything,'' he stated flatly. "Too much education ruins a girl. You are far too argumentative. But I warn you, there will be no more arguments now, Danielle, no clever debating. I have denied you little and given in far too often. I tell you now, it must stop. *Dieu,* when are you going to grow up?''

The girl's chin rose defiantly. Let Yves think what he wanted, she decided furiously. He had already decided her guilt. She should have known better than to think they could talk calmly.

In the silence, Yves leaned back in his chair and glowered at his sister. He had often thought Danielle's honey-colored hair and creamy complexion deceptive, but never more than today. Still wearing the blue dress, she looked soft, even fragile, standing in front of him. But bright spots of angry color burned on her high cheekbones and her brown eyes met his without flinching, the challenge in them plain.

"Sit down.'' He gestured to the chair across from his. "There are still matters to be discussed.''

When she complied, he continued, carefully choosing his words. "Vincent is extremely hurt. He has asked for your hand three times in the past six months. Each time you refused and I put him off. He is your last suitor. You have chased the others away with your willfulness. Today you may have ruined everything, I do not know.

"And I cannot even call out De Leon in good conscience,'' he fumed. "Vincent said you were flirting with the scoundrel in a most unseemly fashion.''

"I was not flirting!''

"It does not really matter. Vincent thinks you were. He has loved you since you were children, Dani, but I do not know how much longer he will wait. I shouldn't think it would be very long, given your current behavior.''

"We were talking about the Pirates' Market, not marriage,'' the girl asserted icily. "If you have finished . . .'' She rose and swept out of the room without waiting for an answer.

"I have not finished," Yves bellowed, following her into the foyer. "Mark me, Danielle, I forbid you even to set foot out of Félicité. You will stay at home until you can behave as a lady."

She paused, staring at him coldly before she whirled and marched up the stairs. In the foyer below, Yves and Zeme winced at the slam of her bedroom door, which set the crystal chandelier over their heads ajangle.

"Do not worry too much, M'sieur Yves," Zeme said, her lilting Jamaican voice soothing. *"La petite maîtresse,* she gets mad, but she gets ovah it." To the stout Negress who had cared for Danielle from childhood, the girl was still the little mistress. "Sometimes she's as stubborn as a mule an' she jus' mus' have her own way."

"She comes from a long line of mules, Zeme," Yves replied grimly. "Champion, thoroughbred mules."

The young Creole picked up his hat from a table near the front door and called over his shoulder as he left, "I know Dani's tricks. Tell her she can come down for dinner. I won't be here."

True to his prediction, the girl stubbornly took her meals in her room, pleading illness. After several days, Yves's daily jaunts into town turned into overnight stays and soon he was gone from home more than he was present. As usual, accounts of his dubious escapades reached Félicité, much to Danielle's dismay.

Now, as she gazed out at Félicité's manicured grounds, a perfumed breeze reached her through the tall windows that opened onto her balcony. This sunny afternoon was too good to waste, she decided suddenly. Resolutely, she rose and tossed her book on the high tester bed. Crossing to the carved armoire, she selected a rust-colored riding habit with a split skirt. She had had enough waiting and isolation. No matter what Yves had said, she was going riding...now!

Excited by the prospect, the girl hastily changed her clothes, not even bothering to summon Lydie to help her. She searched for the hat with russet plumes, which went with her habit, but when she did not immediately find it, she gave up and hurried downstairs, nearly running to the stables with Zeme on her heels.

"Where you think you're goin', *mam'selle?*" The rotund old woman was panting, her bare feet raising small puffs of dust as she ran.

"For a ride." Danielle did not even bother to slow down.

"You cannot. M'sieur Yves don' want you goin' out." With surprising speed, the old slave maneuvered around Danielle and planted her ample body in the girl's path.

"My brother hasn't been here to know if I'm at home or not," Danielle replied dryly.

"No," Zeme conceded, "but he said, 'You cannot leave the house.'"

"He said I could not leave Félicité. And I won't," she reassured her. She dodged around her old mammy and beckoned the groom. "Hippolyte, saddle Péril for me, *s'il vous plaît.*"

"But, *mam'selle*..." the stubby adolescent croaked in dismay.

"Saddle Péril," she repeated in measured tones. "I will answer to my brother."

"Ain' right her ridin' like a man," Hippolyte muttered disapprovingly to himself while he hastened to do her bidding. But by the time his mistress swung into her saddle, he mustered the courage to remind her of another of Yves's orders. "Jus' a minute, *mam'selle,* I mus' saddle Bébé and go with you, like M'sieur Yves said."

"That will not be necessary," Danielle answered. "I won't be leaving the plantation."

"*Oui, petite maîtresse,* it is necessary," Zeme interjected firmly. "M'sieur Yves has said many times you should not go ridin' out alone...evah."

"I do not need a chaperon on Félicité, Zeme," the girl insisted through gritted teeth.

"Likely you do not," the old servant reasoned, "but 'Polyte here will be in trouble if he don' follow along behin' you."

Danielle grinned mischievously. "All right then, he can follow—if he can catch me." She set off at a gallop, leaving the young groom to trail behind.

The girl galloped past the double row of slave cabins and burst into the open fields. She glanced back to see that Hippolyte had given up the chase and was reluctantly leading Bébé toward the stables.

As she drew near the bayou that marked one of Félicité's property lines, Danielle walked Péril toward a thicket of trees beside the River Road. She would have liked to cross the road to the levee, but if Yves found out . . . Instead she dismounted in the shady stand of trees and led the gelding to the water's edge.

"Magnifique, mon ami," she murmured, patting him admiringly while he drank. "After that run, you are barely breathing hard."

She laughed aloud when he returned the tribute with a nudge of his wet nose. "What? Now that you've had a drink, you are looking for something to eat?" The girl searched her pockets, but came up empty-handed. With an aggrieved snort, Péril turned his back on her and began to graze on the tender young blades of grass at his feet.

Danielle felt giddy, lighthearted, liberated. She stretched, arching her back lazily, then swooped forward, bending at the waist, allowing her arms to hang loosely. Catching sight of her reflection in the water, she smiled at what she saw. She was flushed and disheveled, but the face that looked back at her was happy for the first time in days.

"What is this, Péril?" she asked, straightening to look around. She spied a tangle of blackberry vines within the glade of trees nearby. Tying the horse to a tree, she went to pick one and popped it in her mouth. The berry was ripe and luscious, so she picked another.

Péril whinnied insistently. "I know. They are my favorites, too," she answered, laughing, harvesting a handful of juicy berries. She returned to the shade tree where the horse waited, and sat down.

To the big gelding's delight, he received two berries for every one Danielle ate. But, after three trips, his mistress refused to respond even when he butted her gently with his head. "No more, you big baby," she chuckled, rubbing his velvety nose affectionately, "even though you look at me with big sad eyes."

She had gone to the bayou's edge to wash her hands when she heard a masculine voice. Crooning and melodious, it seemed to come from the road. Some of what the man said she could not understand, for it was a foreign language. But part of what he spoke was French. And the words made her ears burn. Thinking she was hidden by the trees, Danielle peeped out curiously.

"*Allons,* let us fly, *ma belle* Circe. You are *muy hermosa, cara mia,* giddap," Arturo De Leon encouraged the nag pulling his open carriage. Although his attention seemed to be focused on the reluctant mare, his brilliant blue eyes caught a glimpse of the girl through the trees.

"You are beautiful, *cher* Circe, but not as beautiful as Danielle Valmont," he called loudly. With a sharp tug on the reins, Arturo brought the mare to a lurching halt and gazed expectantly toward the thicket.

With a rueful smile, Danielle stepped out, the thorny vines behind her grabbing at her clothes. The privateer had the most disconcerting habit of making her blush, she fumed as she scrubbed at her sticky hands with a lace handkerchief, chagrined at having been caught gorging on berries.

"*Bonjour, mademoiselle.*" Arturo's mustache framed a grin that was equally sheepish. "It is an embarrassment indeed to be discovered talking to a horse."

"*Bonjour,* Capitaine De Leon. Do you always speak to your mare that way?"

"She is not mine. In fact, we never met before today, but I found she responds better to words of love than to curses. It is usually so with women. And what are you doing this fine afternoon?" His easy behavior made it seem as if Danielle's scornful departure from the Pirates' Market had never occurred.

"I was just, er, riding." She thrust her stained hands behind her and looked at him innocently.

"Riding . . . I see." One eyebrow rose as Arturo took in her unconventional riding habit, tumbled hair and disturbingly vivid berry-stained lips. She looked positively guilty, lurking beside the tangle of berry bushes. He squinted, trying to see if anyone awaited her within the shady stand of trees.

"You ride alone?"

"*Oui.*"

"Yves Valmont does not insist on a chaperon for his sister?" he demanded in mock horror.

"Oh, he does, but none of the grooms can keep up with me."

The big man roared with laughter. "Your brother should not worry about you. From what I have seen, no one can keep up with you, not even your suitors."

She seemed nonplussed by his teasing, so he asked lightly, "Where is your horse, *mam'selle?*"

"Hitched to a tree beside the bayou."

"Would it be all right to leave him for a while and take a ride with me?"

"I am sorry, I cannot." She averted her eyes.

Arturo's brows knit in a perplexed frown. What was wrong with the girl that she hung back and would come no closer? "Will you come and sit in my carriage then, so we can talk?" he suggested.

"I . . . I can't."

"Why not?" he asked challengingly.

Danielle met his blue eyes, tempted to take the dare she saw in them, but she thought better of it. "Because I promised Yves I would not leave Félicité," she admitted grudgingly.

"Of course, I should have known! He was angry to learn you had been to the Pirates' Market and he warned you not to go where I might be. Am I correct?"

"He asked me not to leave Félicité," the girl maintained stubbornly, feeling a flash of annoyance at the man's conceit.

"If you cannot come to me, then I will come to you . . . if I can find a place to hitch this nag. Eh, Circe, *mon amour?*"

He alit from the carriage and led the mare to a weeping willow on the bayou's edge near the bridge.

Uncertainly, Danielle followed, debating with herself. Yves had not said she could not see Arturo. He had not said she couldn't see anyone she wanted. He had simply ordered her to stay at Félicité. And she had obeyed; she was on Valmont property.

Still, he had also warned her that Arturo de Leon was a dangerous man, and now she was alone with him. Instinctively, she sidled away and eyed him warily. Except for the golden earring gleaming in his ear, he did not look like a pirate or even a privateer. He scarcely looked dangerous as he bent to the task of tying Circe's lead rope to the tree, grinning at her over his shoulder. Through the broadcloth of his tailored jacket, she could see well-defined muscles rippling in his back as he skillfully tied a formidable-looking sailor's knot.

Arturo De Leon was the most interesting man she had ever met, and Danielle decided she would stay and talk to him.

"*Et voilà!* All secure." He turned and offered his arm, sighing, "I tell you, *mam'selle,* there are better modes of transportation to be had than a horse."

"Such as a ship?" She smiled, her qualms forgotten.

"*Oui,* most certainly a ship," he agreed. "Come, shall we enjoy the breeze on the bridge?"

"Er...*non, merci.*" She balked beside the road.

"Oh, yes." He chuckled. "You must not leave Félicité. *Très bien,* we will follow the letter of the law, if not the spirit."

The couple found a pleasant shady spot out of sight of the road and sat down. Danielle was careful to keep a distance from him, sitting with her back against a massive oak tree, but Arturo smiled inwardly. He had wanted to be alone with her since the first time he laid eyes on her. How lucky he was to have met her today. He could almost taste the berries on her lips.

"It must be wonderful to sail on a great ship," she said, resuming their conversation primly.

"It is." He stretched out on his back, one arm cushioning his head.

"I must go on an ocean voyage someday," she said nervously, trying not to notice that his blue eyes roamed over her admiringly.

"I sail to Morocco soon. Perhaps I could take you along as a cabin boy," he drawled. "You will soon be able to pass for a little blackamoor if you do not wear a hat. Didn't anyone ever tell you brown skin is not feminine?"

"I'll wager what you know of femininity, you did not learn from a lady," Danielle retorted, feeling very sophisticated.

"Many ladies," he corrected lazily. "You might be surprised by my teachers, *ma petite,* and even more surprised at what I taught them."

Recently, the girl had learned of many of Arturo's more notorious conquests, thanks mostly to Lydie, an inexhaustible source of accurate information. The maid had told her how the beautiful young Madame Camille Marquette tried to kill herself after the Winter Masque, for love of the privateer. When her wronged husband challenged him, the *capitaine* had drolly chosen Turkish scimitars as weapons, knowing full well no gentleman would duel with such an uncivilized weapon. And the *capitaine* probably knew how to use them, Danielle thought. Wondering suddenly if she were perhaps in danger, after all, she sat erect and started to rise.

"Don't go." Arturo rolled onto his side, facing her, and propped himself on one elbow. "We will talk of something besides my conquests. Tell me, do you often go out riding alone?"

"When I can get away and when Yves is not around to stop me." Danielle sat back against the tree, but her brown eyes watched him guardedly.

"A brother can be a great problem to a girl," Arturo sympathized. "I take it, you and Yves quarrel about your solitary rides."

"Yves and I quarrel about almost everything lately," Danielle said glumly.

"Let me see if I can guess the problem. He treats you as a child."

"*Oui.*" Danielle regarded the man suspiciously, unsure if he was making fun of her.

"And he never lets you do as you wish."

"Not anymore. And for the past year, he had thought of nothing but finding me a husband."

"He sounds no different than any other father or brother." The man shrugged.

"But Yves has always been different from other fathers and brothers," she declared. "'We are Valmonts,' he said. 'We shall live our lives as we please.' But marriage is not what I please."

"Never?" Arturo was surprised. He had not expected this, even of Danielle.

"Oh, certainly someday. When I am ready...and I will wed whom I please," she added emphatically. "I am old enough to make my own decisions, but Yves refuses to understand. At one time, I could have made him see, but now—"

"You are not going to cry, are you?" The privateer sat up in alarm. He always hated it when women wept.

"Of course not," the girl quavered, her delicate jaw jutting forward stubbornly.

Reassured, Arturo lay back and asked conversationally, "Why can you not bring him around to your point of view this time?"

"Because we cannot even talk without arguing." Suddenly the words spilled out. "I think sometimes he would like to talk to me, to tell me his problems, but we have grown so far apart. I wish things were as they were in the old days. Then I wouldn't worry when he goes away for days . . . and I hear things."

"What kind of things?"

"Oh, that he gambles and spends a lot of money and that he likes the ladies," she answered lightly. "The usual things for a bachelor in New Orleans."

"Ah, yes, the usual," Arturo agreed solemnly, then waited for her to continue.

"But I think he drinks more than he should sometimes." She glanced tentatively at him, but the man was occupied, chewing the end of a tender blade of grass and he did not comment. Danielle continued hesitantly. "I suppose I worry most about his drinking because when Yves drinks, he fights. You saw him at the ball. And I heard yesterday he killed his fifth man under the Dueling Oaks."

"Actually it was only his fourth," Arturo corrected gravely, gesturing with his bedraggled blade of grass. "And it was at St. Anthony's Garden three days ago."

"What difference does it make?" she asked vehemently. "He will either kill someone or be killed himself. This duelist is a stranger to me. The Yves who fights men over imagined slights to his honor is not the brother I know."

Arturo frowned in annoyance. The afternoon was not going as he had hoped. He had planned to while away some time with a willing girl, and now he felt awkward in the face of her intensity. At the moment, the man wanted nothing more than to calm her and perhaps turn their tête-à-tête down a more flirtatious path.

He sat up abruptly and faced her, cajoling, "Do not worry, *ma petite,* Yves will be fine. If you fret too much, your brow will become furrowed. And you are much too young for that. Not to say you are not nearly a grown woman," he amended hastily when he saw the flicker of irritation in her brown eyes.

"I *am* a grown woman, *capitaine.* Even you should be able to see that," Danielle snapped, drawing herself up proudly.

"*Oui,* especially I can see that," he murmured huskily. He leaned toward her as if drawn. "You are indeed a woman, *cher,* a very beautiful woman."

Her eyes round, the girl shrank away, suddenly very aware of their isolation as his gaze swept over her almost caressingly.

He reached out to trace her berry-stained lips with one finger. "I wonder, how would it be to be your suitor, Danielle? It might be difficult to keep up with you, but what fun the chase would be. And I might be the man who finally catches you."

"That would hardly be possible," she sputtered, scrambling to her feet.

"That I should chase you or that I should catch you?" he asked insolently, rising to stand beside her.

"That you should be my suitor at all," she said, retreating until her back was against the oak. "My brother would never let me marry a pirate."

Arturo's eyes darkened to the color of the stormy sea. He stepped nearer and placed his hands on the broad tree trunk on either side of her head, trapping her. "What about you, Danielle?" he crooned. "You nearly weep that you would marry whom you please, when you please. Would you marry a pirate, or perhaps a privateer? If a privateer is not good enough, would you prefer a fine Creole mama's boy? Tell me, *cher,* did you have a rendezvous with a beau in this berry patch or were you waiting for me?"

"I had no rendezvous—" she exploded, anger overcoming fear.

"Then never let it be said you waited in vain," he muttered, bending to kiss her. His lean hard body pressed against hers, pinning her against the tree.

When Danielle realized his intent, her fear returned in a rush and she fought wildly, stiffening her body and twisting her head to elude his relentless lips. But Arturo's mouth found hers, demandingly at first, then more gently as he drank in the sweetness of her lips.

The kiss lasted only a moment, but it might have lasted forever, the two were so lost in time. The girl shuddered deeply as a fire of passion kindled within her, a small flicker that burst into flame and melted her resistance, leaving only sweet, pleasurable sensation. With a moan, her lips parted and she returned his kiss hungrily.

As his tongue gently explored her mouth, Arturo savored the taste and the unexpected heat of her. Mindlessly, instinctively, she molded her body to his, her breasts straining against him, igniting an urgent blaze of yearning that took him by surprise.

He tore his lips from hers with effort and drew away, his arms still forming a supple cage to hold her against the tree trunk. He regarded Danielle wonderingly, and one big hand moved to stroke her cheek. Her bosom was heaving with emotion and, for a moment, the girl looked as shaken as he felt. Collecting herself, she jerked from his touch as if burned, her stunned expression rapidly replaced by one of fury.

"I did not give you leave to kiss me," she said coldly, ducking under his restraining arms.

"I saw no reason to ask it," Arturo countered lightly. He followed her, cursing himself, trying to ignore the ache in his loins.

"Then you are no gentleman, *monsieur*," Danielle snapped, wrathfully untying Péril. Once astride the huge gelding, she glared down at Arturo. Her lips curved downward in displeasure; full and sensuous, they bore the signs of their recent kiss.

"Non," Arturo agreed with deceptive mildness, "but I warned you of that on the night of the ball. And I warn you now, Danielle, if ever I have another opportunity, I will probably kiss you again. There are two lessons I never learned— how to be a gentleman and how to resist a beautiful woman."

"O-o-oh," she said, seething in outrage, her brown eyes flashing. "You are a cad!" With that pronouncement, she wheeled her horse and galloped through the lengthening shadows toward Félicité.

"A cad?" The man chuckled humorlessly. "Undoubtedly." But his face was severe as he stood at the edge of the field and watched the girl ride away, her fair hair streaming on the wind. Three times he had met Danielle Valmont and three times she had run away from him. When there were so many willing women in the world, why did he waste his time with her girlish games? And why did the memory of her lips disturb him so?

Still red-faced and flustered, Danielle stormed around the corner of the house and paused for a moment on the long shell-covered *allée* to collect herself. How dared that pirate kiss her as if she were one of his common waterfront strumpets!

She forced herself to slow her step when she felt the curious stare of Hercule, one of the groundsmen, on her. The burly slave nodded courteously, but continued to trim the grass under the great trees, the rise and fall of his scythe never faltering.

Determined to put Arturo's smirking face from her mind, the girl looked for something to which she could turn her full attention. Not far from the house, the small rose garden that had been her mother's was badly in need of weeding. Filled with angry resolve, she bent to the task with more determination than finesse.

Awkwardly stooped over a weed-choked bush, Danielle was waving mosquitoes away from her face when she heard the sound of a horse's hooves on the drive behind her. She straightened slowly and turned with as much dignity as she could muster. A skinny pockmarked man mounted on a bay mare stood behind her, watching her expressionlessly.

"Howdy." The man's nasal voice was flat. He did not dismount or even remove his hat. Carelessly, he allowed his horse to amble across the lawn and graze on the manicured grass near the girl's feet.

"Bonsoir," she answered, her brown eyes raking the visitor disapprovingly. What a rude man, she thought, and obviously an American.

"This Yves Valmont's place?" His mud-colored eyes took in the big two-story home, set among the river oaks. The house was built high with a sloping roof along West Indian lines, its green hurricane doors, their color softened by the sun, and the pair of graceful curving staircases, "welcoming arms," leading up to the formal entrance in the middle of the long upper gallery.

"Oui." She nodded proudly. "This is Félicité, *monsieur...?"*

The man ignored the unspoken question to ask, "Yves around?"

"Monsieur Valmont is not in at present." Suddenly Danielle felt strangely ill at ease. With a slight gesture, she beckoned the watchful Hercule, who immediately moved nearer, his scythe still in hand. "I shall tell him that Monsieur..." She paused and looked up questioningly at the man on horseback.

"Lynch, Jack Lynch." The answer came grudgingly. "You can tell Yves that Mr. Lynch was here."

"You certainly chose a hot day to ride all this way, Monsieur Lynch," Danielle ventured, when the man made no move to leave. Having never spoken with a Kaintock, she was curious, for she had heard they were full of tall tales. "Was Yves expecting you?"

She was disappointed when the man stared off into the distance and mumbled a single syllable, "Nope."

Unaccustomed to such terseness, she decided to rid herself of this uncouth man. "I do not know when Yves will return, sir. Of course, I will be certain to give him your message," she stated dismissively.

There was a creak of leather as the man shifted in his saddle and looked at her. "You Valmont's wife?"

"His sister," she answered, nervous under his scrutiny.

"Waal, yer a purty little thang," he observed with a thin smile.

"Merci," Danielle muttered, wishing Yves had been home to deal himself with Monsieur Lynch.

"You Creole gals don't cotton much to compliments, do ye?" Lynch emitted a sudden humorless laugh. "Unless they come from one of yer own. Don't matter, 'cause I ain't here to stay. I left the makin's of a fine poker game at the Arcade an' I'd like to get back to it.''

He looked her over appraisingly before continuing, "Jest be sure to tell yer brother this: Jack Lynch expects him to make good on his pledge by this time tomorrow.''

"His pledge?'' She looked startled.

"Don't go pokin' yer nose in where it don't belong, gal,'' he advised impatiently. "Jest tell him what I said.''

He gathered his reins and was about to turn his horse to go when Yves appeared, charging his horse down the River Road toward the house. Bellowing Lynch's name, the young Creole galloped toward the Kaintock. His fair-skinned, aristocratic face was flushed with anger, as he swiftly dismounted.

"Seems you don't hafta deliver my message, after all,'' the scrawny American told Danielle. He dismounted and led his horse onto the drive where he stopped to speak with Yves. Danielle could not hear their conversation, but she saw her brother's angry gestures and the other man's indifferent shrug in response. After a moment, Lynch remounted and trotted down the drive. He rode past Danielle without even a glance while Yves stood at the head of the *allée,* his fists clenched into balls of anger.

Danielle went to stand beside her brother. "Who is this Monsieur Lynch?'' she finally asked, unable to stand the curiosity.

"A Kaintock,'' was Yves's curt reply.

"I could tell that.'' She frowned. "But how do you know him?''

"I run into him from time to time,'' he answered evasively.

"At the gambling houses?'' Danielle knew she should not press, but she had to ask. Fearfully, she watched the fleeting changes in expression on her brother's face.

"What do you know...? Never mind. Always I get questions from you, little sister,'' Yves teased, his manner suddenly jocular as he tried to hide his tension. "Don't worry about it.''

"'Don't poke my nose in where it doesn't belong'? That is what *l'Américain* told me.''

"That is not such bad advice,'' the Creole said dryly. "You would do well to follow it.''

He squeezed her nape playfully. "Aren't you going to dress for dinner, Dani? Here you are in that awful habit when I just bought you another new gown. Don't I get to see you in it?" Hand in hand, they walked toward the house as the first candles of the long summer evening were being placed in the windows.

Chapter Four

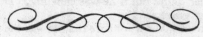

"There you are, De Leon! I should have known I would find you wasting your time on women."

On the balcony of Madame LaRue's bordello, Arturo took his feet from the railing and set his chair down onto all four legs. Rising, he peered through the dusk, seeking the source of the voice that hailed him.

"Wasting time, eh?" He chuckled when he saw young Denis LeBlanc astride his gelding on the street below. "What better pastime is there than a warm, willing woman?"

"Gambling," the dapper Creole answered positively, "and there is a card game tonight at Félicité."

"Valmont's home?" Arturo looked interested.

"*Oui*. I thought you might like to come along." Denis controlled his prancing horse gracefully and frowned as two men emerged from the brothel to linger on the banquette nearby. His scowl disappeared when he saw they were Arturo's men.

"It hardly seems polite to beard the lion in his den," Arturo drawled, grinning at the other man's air of impatience. "Valmont was rather angry the last time we met, you know."

"Yves is not one to bear grudges, except when it comes to his sister."

"I have not seen her for weeks." Arturo's brows knit in annoyance at the mere mention of Danielle Valmont.

"Then why not come along?" Denis urged. "Paul Brignac and Emile Letreau will be there. Besides, I have gambled three times with Yves this week and won every time. I could use a challenge."

"Do you think the *'méricain coquin* will be there?" the big captain asked casually.

"Lynch? It is possible," Denis said, a dark expression on his aristocratic face. "That Kaintock . . . he is a snake, *oui?*"

"*Oui.*" Arturo's mind turned to a night a few months earlier, a friendly card game to which Yves had brought a newcomer, the American, Jack Lynch.

"We never found out if he was cheating," Denis reminded the privateer gravely.

"And I do not know for sure that he was the one who shot at me and relieved me of my winnings, but I have my suspicions."

"It is true Lynch left first that night," the Creole mused.

"That is not proof. I would know if I could see whether he carried a pocket pistol."

"You would not cause trouble tonight?" Denis had begun to regret his invitation.

"*Non,* I only want to watch him."

"*Très bien,* De Leon," he called over his shoulder as he wheeled his horse in the narrow dirt street. "See my groom when you are ready. He will have a mount for you."

"*Merci.*" Arturo watched the elegant young Creole ride toward the River Road. Then he called to a big man who was lounging against a lamppost nearby, "Jacques!"

"*Oui,* Turo." Jacques Foucher, Arturo's first mate, lumbered over to stand below the balcony.

"Go and find Hector, *mon ami.* Take him back to the ship before he can pick another fight."

"I might have to hit him, me," the brawny sailor suggested mildly.

"Probably," the *capitaine* agreed, "but try not to hurt him too badly. He is a good hand with the sails. And, Jacques," he added, as the Baratarian prepared to depart, "take Narcisse with you. He will be safer facing Hector than he will be with those two." He nodded laughingly toward a slender, handsome young man who was flirting with two painted women on the corner.

"*Oui, capitaine.*" Jacques beckoned Narcisse Duval, the helmsman of the *Magdalena.* With a regretful smile for the strumpets, Narcisse joined Jacques to carry out Arturo's orders.

Less than a hour later, the privateer lounged moodily against the wall of Denis LeBlanc's stable, watching the groom saddle a sleepy-looking mare.

"Here you go, Cap'n," the servant announced, patting the horse's flank with an air of finality. "Be real good to ol' Hurricane here and she'll be good to you."

"Hurricane, eh?" Arturo muttered. *"Merci."* Gloomily, he mounted the beast and turned her toward Félicité.

"But, *mam'selle,*" Lydie protested, following her mistress out onto the balcony, "your brother said you were to stay upstairs while his gentlemen friends are in the house."

"I know, but I must find out what is going on," Danielle insisted, all the more determined because she had just seen Jack Lynch ride up the drive. "I will listen at the window and be back before anyone misses me."

"If Zeme misses you, she will have both our hides," the maid predicted, her lovely face bleak.

"She won't find out. She thinks I have a headache. She even brought me a tisane for it. Are you going to help me or not?" Leaning far over the railing, Danielle grasped a bough of the huge tree nearest the house and strained to pull the limb toward her. "Here, hold this."

Lydie obeyed, but she continued to argue, "This is not right, Dani. Terrible things can happen to a girl out alone at night."

"You think a zombie will carry me off?" Danielle teased as she climbed over the railing and lowered herself onto the branch.

"I do not believe in spirits," the servant said with an air of wounded dignity. "But something could happen. If anyone sees you dressed like that—"

"You cannot expect me to shinny down the trees in silk and petticoats," the other girl responded tartly, looking down at the boyish attire she had donned. Cinched around her narrow waist with a piece of frayed rope, the pants were too short and bared much of her calves and the borrowed gingham shirt strained over her breasts. "Don't worry, no one will see me. And I'll get these back to Hippolyte before he even knows they're missing. Now, let go," she ordered, holding on with both hands.

The maid relinquished her grasp, wincing when the limb swayed, her beloved *petite maîtresse* on it.

"I'll be right back," Danielle whispered as she eased backwards and then down the huge trunk. "Wait for me here."

On the ground, the girl darted from tree to tree on the shadowed lawn, treading lightly, grimacing as the shells that paved the *allée* jabbed her bare feet. Stealthily, she made her way toward the open windows of the library through which the indistinct rumble of voices could be heard. With single-minded determination, she crouched low and raced across the dew-wet lawn toward the camellia bush that grew below the windows.

Suddenly Danielle heard a noise and glanced over her shoulder as she ran, fearful of discovery. She did not lessen her speed, however, and when she turned forward again and saw a figure before her, she could not stop on the dewy grass. Colliding headlong into a solid masculine chest, she heard the mighty rush of air the man expelled at impact. Caught in a pair of strong arms, she immediately lashed out at her unseen captor.

Arturo swore and maintained his grasp on the squirming figure with difficulty. "Be still, you little ruffian," he growled when he recovered his breath. Thinking he had hold of a slave boy, he gripped the girl's shoulders tightly and frowned down at her in moonlight. To his surprise, his fierce scowl was met with equal intensity. Danielle's face was a pale blur in the darkness, but he could see her brown eyes flashing in fury.

"Unhand me at once, *capitaine,*" she demanded in a wrathful whisper, trying to ignore a disconcerting flutter in her stomach as Arturo pulled her into the shadows, out of sight of the library. "How—how dare you creep up on me?"

"I am not the one who was creeping, *mademoiselle,*" he informed her, keeping his voice low. He continued to hold tight to one of her arms. "What are you doing out here alone in the dark?"

The girl's eyes widened at his words and she swallowed deeply. "Not that it is your business," she replied in a tone that she hoped betrayed none of her nervousness, "but since I live here, I go where I please."

"Always in such a becoming outfit?" He took a step back, his blue eyes sweeping the girl appraisingly, taking in the ill-fitting pants, the expanse of naked leg, the gap in the tight cotton shirt.

"Just what are *you* doing here, Capitaine De Leon?" Abruptly Danielle wrenched free of his grasp and glared at him. Now that there was some distance between them, she could think again.

"I came to play cards with your brother, but before I could even make it to the house, I was met by an apparition of feminine grace and charm," he teased with a comical wag of his eyebrows. "You still have not told me why you are creeping around like this."

"It is still none of your business," the girl retorted, stung by his amusement at her expense.

"Perhaps I should ask your brother?"

"*Non!*" she protested at once.

"I am surprised at you, Danielle Valmont. Such manners." He sighed reprovingly. "Spying on your own brother? I suppose you must be forgiven since you are young," he concluded beneficently.

"Arturo De Leon, you—" she began hotly.

"Do not say anything you will regret, *cher*," the man cautioned, recapturing her arm to guide her across the lawn. "Come, we must get you inside before someone else sees you."

"I am perfectly capable of seeing myself back inside."

"And how do you intend to do it?" he asked politely. "By marching through the front door, past your brother and all his friends?"

"I will manage just fine without you," she answered stiffly, unwilling for him to see her climbing a tree.

"No man likes to be told he is unnecessary," Arturo said, wincing for effect. "You must let me escort you."

"*Non, merci.*"

"I am not going into the house and leaving you out here." Arturo's tone would brook no argument. Unwillingly, the girl allowed him to accompany her. They stole around the house, past the *pigeonnier*, the smokehouse and the cistern toward the servants' staircase at the back of the house. But when they reached the thicket of banana trees that served as a screen between the squat, detached kitchen and the main house, they found their way blocked by several slaves who lounged on the bottom steps enjoying the cool of the evening. Silently, the couple returned the way they had come. Arturo's eyes inspected every window and door they crept past, looking for a clear entrance, but none was to be seen.

In the rose garden below Danielle's balcony, she halted and dismissed the man with a formal nod of her head. "*Bonsoir, capitaine, et merci.* I have troubled you enough."

"No trouble, *mam'selle,*" he replied. His amused eyes sought hers in the dimness as he bent to kiss the hand she offered. It would be better if he left at that moment; he knew it. But suddenly he wanted to prolong their curious interlude. His hand tightened on hers and he murmured, "*Mon Dieu,* you are beautiful in the moonlight, *cheri,* here among the roses."

"How like you to say something of that sort." Disdainfully, the girl reclaimed her hand, but she made no move to leave.

"What do you mean?" Arturo frowned, baffled by her response.

"Only that you cannot seem to resist the urge to flirt even for a moment," she answered curtly. "Your remarkable reputation, it seems, is well deserved. Well, I am not the kind of woman you are apparently accustomed to."

"What kind of woman is that?" His tone was ominous.

"*Une fille . . .*" The girl faltered over the words. "*Fille de joie.*"

"I am shocked that you would even know about daughters of joy." Arturo rolled his eyes dramatically.

Danielle glared at the man. "I know that men visit such women," she snapped. "You, probably even Yves, though it would break our mother's heart if she were alive."

"Not everyone is as eager as you to condemn a man because he enjoys waking up next to a beautiful woman," Arturo said with a shrug. "You will understand someday, little one."

"Do not call me that. I am not a child!" She turned in a huff and started toward the house.

"So you keep telling me," Arturo drawled, his blue eyes drawn to her shapely hips, their outline visible even through her loose trousers. With one long step, he caught her wrist and spun her to face him. "You talk about *that* kind of woman. Tell me, my fine Creole lady, what kind of woman steals around in the night wearing a boy's clothes? And what kind of woman grants hasty kisses in the berry patch?"

Danielle could feel a flaming blush spreading all the way to her hairline and was thankful for the darkness. "You cad," she seethed. "*You* kissed *me*."

"*Oui.* And even now you are remembering what I said, aren't you?" With his free arm, he pulled her close, capturing her hands against his chest. His face was dangerously close to hers. "Remember, Danielle? I said that if ever I had the opportunity—"

"*Non,*" she choked, shaking her head. She tried to wriggle free, but he held her with an iron grip around her waist.

"If ever I had the opportunity, I would kiss you again," he continued relentlessly. "You *do* remember and you are waiting for it. Do not tell me you would not like it."

"You—you wouldn't dare," she argued unconvincingly. But her struggling ceased as her dark eyes met his glittering blue ones. She lifted her chin defiantly, but her traitorous heart was racing and she longed to feel his lips on hers.

"A man might dare many things for the want of you, *cher,*" Arturo murmured, his warm, demanding mouth descending on hers. Danielle felt as if her entire body was afire. His hand that ensnared hers slid around her shoulder and he embraced her, molding her body to his.

She could not move, could not breathe, could not think; she only felt and responded. Compared to this caress, their kiss in the berry patch seemed chaste and passionless. Her breasts ached and swelled against his chest and the strength in her legs melted as she swayed against him.

The girl's body stiffened when she felt his hand on her breast. She wore only Hippolyte's cotton shirt, and Arturo's thumb traced lazy circles where no man had dared to touch her before. Her hand, still caught against his chest, shoved against him with all her might. Their lips had no sooner parted than she slapped his face. The crack of her hand against his cheek seemed to reverberate through the dark garden.

"You are terribly mistaken if you think—" she fumed.

"I am not mistaken," Arturo broke in harshly, nursing his stinging jaw. "You *are* a little tease, a spoiled child in a woman's body. I do not know why I keep forgetting that. *Bonsoir,* Danielle." Without a word, he disappeared into the darkness.

Danielle walked slowly toward the house, trembling with rage and pent-up emotion. She did not realize it when Arturo stopped under a huge moss-bearded river oak to watch as she scampered up the sloping tree branch beside the balcony and over the railing, her bare legs pale in the moonlight.

Ruefully rubbing his cheek, the privateer pondered the nature of women. He loved them, whatever their age, shape, size or marital status. He reveled in their varied beauties and talents, enjoyed their company and conversation, but he would never understand them.

Hell, he could not even understand himself. Even in her inexperience, Danielle had excited him more in the moonlit garden tonight than any of the whores he had seen at Madame LaRue's this afternoon.

Suddenly in no mood for card games, Arturo rode back to town, cursing as Hurricane, his borrowed mare, wished to live up to her name and gallop all the way home, bouncing the privateer wildly the whole way. Perhaps he should go back to Barataria for a while, he thought, and avoid females altogether.

When Arturo awoke the next morning aboard the *Magdalena,* his cabin was stifling. Yawning hugely, he rose and went to look through the open porthole at the city. He blinked sleepily as a gentle river-scented breeze lifted his tangled hair from his shoulders. The sun was already high, beating down on the tarred dock where sweating crews of Negroes worked. Gulls wheeled above them, squawking harshly, then swooping to perch on pylons at the water's edge.

Lulled by the sway of the ship, he lounged, listening to the Mississippi lapping against the hull, soft and soothing under the strident voices of the roustabouts. From the wharf, little could be seen of the French Market on Levee Street, but he heard its indistinct mélange of sounds, complemented by the cries of vendors and the peal of bells from St. Louis Cathedral.

The man luxuriated, enjoying the breeze, savoring the sounds, until a rap at his door jarred him from his musings.

Felix Fontaineau, the *Magdalena*'s aged cook, thrust his grizzled head into the cabin and asked querulously, "Will you be wanting breakfast before lunch, Your Daintiness, or is it your pleasure to wait till after?"

"No breakfast. I will get a cup of *café* at the market."

"Me, I can bring you a whole pot," Felix countered stubbornly.

"A whole pot of that tar and gunpowder mixture you call *café? Non, merci,* I value my stomach."

The peg-legged old man was unfazed. "I only use gunpowder to cure hangovers, me, when all the leaves of *palm de Cristi* in the world will not help. You do not have a hangover, do you, Turo?"

"Still trying to be my nursemaid, old man?" the privateer growled affectionately.

"*Mais non!* I never saw a wharf rat who could get into so much trouble," Felix retorted, digging an envelope from the pocket of his baggy trousers. "Here, a boy brought this for you."

Arturo opened it curiously and found a small page filled with graceful feminine handwriting.

Dear Capitaine,

    I am sending this note in utmost secrecy to thank you for your recent attempt to come to my aid.

    You have shown yourself to have a tender heart, so please permit me to ask one more service of you. I beg you to forget that last night ever occurred.

    As you travel the world, I pray you to remember me only with kindness.

Adieu,
D.

The little vixen. She thanks me politely and considers our dealings done. Well, Arturo De Leon will not be dismissed so easily, he thought darkly.

"A note from one of your admirers?" Felix asked eagerly.

"You might say that." Arturo snorted. "When did it arrive?"

"Not more than an hour ago. A boy brought it, one of the ones you can hire for a picayune at the square."

"I see." The captain went immediately to the basin to wash, so preoccupied that he did not notice when the cook slipped out of the cabin.

Arturo dressed and went topside, nearly bowling Felix over as the old man hobbled toward his cabin with a steaming cup of black coffee. Unable to avoid it, the privateer accepted the cup and sipped the bitter brew while standing on the deck of his nearly deserted ship. The *Magdalena* was to sail in less than a week and the men who were not in Barataria were ashore, enjoying their last days of leisure before the voyage.

He looked toward the breaks between the stalls of the market where people could be seen milling around, but the distance was too great to recognize anyone. He would go ashore to the Vieux Carré. The girl must still be nearby, and he would have the meaning of that note from her own lips.

In the lovely, parklike Place D'Armes, faint calls could be heard from the open market, though they were nearly drowned out by the shouts of a black woman who hawked sugary pralines from a basket she balanced on her head. While the captain strolled, he scanned the crowd in vain for Danielle's face. At last he spied some of his men gathered under a tree and joined them, but he paid scant attention to their conversation as he watched for the girl.

When he was about to give up, Arturo saw her. Trailed by her maid, Danielle came out of the cathedral and paused on the steps, blinking in the sunlight. How could the girl affect him so? he wondered, watching her appreciatively. Clad in a simple lavender-sprigged day dress and a straw bonnet, she looked fresh and lovely despite the heat.

Danielle's dark eyes widened in alarm when the privateer caught her attention. She had just come from church where she had made a silent vow to be good. At the sight of Arturo, she gulped deeply, feeling her conviction slip away. She was not prepared to face him after last night, and certainly not in public. In truth, she had hoped he would sail before they met again.

But there he stood, head and shoulders above his rowdy crew. The captain had removed his jacket in the heat and his shirtsleeves were rolled, revealing tanned, muscular arms. Under his Panama hat, his black hair was clubbed back in a style that cared little for fashion. The green scarf was tied jauntily at his neck, and he looked every inch the adventurer Yves had warned her about.

She could faintly hear his companions' raucous laughter as one of them told a bawdy story. The buccaneers' frowzy women emitted insincere squawks of protest as they were hugged enthusiastically against sweating chests. A youthful, inexperienced constable looked on helplessly as the Baratarians passed cold bottles of beer among themselves in merry disregard for the early hour.

Arturo pulled his jacket on as he crossed the square, noisy clouds of pigeons rising in front of him. As he made his way unerringly toward her, Danielle was rooted to the spot. Fervently, she wished to be somewhere else. Panic-stricken, she willed her legs to work and bolted toward the shops on Rue Chartres, unmindful of grace or dignity as she dragged Lydie with her.

Arturo hesitated at the edge of the square for an instant, irritation plain on his face. The girl and her games were maddening. But if she wished to play chase, they would play chase.

Purposefully, he crossed the street and followed Danielle's fleeing figure along the banquette. He chuckled aloud as she flew ahead of him, glancing occasionally over her shoulder in dismay. With a sardonic smile, he tipped his hat and advanced. Just ahead of him, she stationed her maid in the shade outside a dry goods store and hurried inside.

"*Bonjour,* Mademoiselle Valmont." Mopping his balding pate with a wilted handkerchief, Victor Balliet greeted Danielle courteously. "What can I show you today? Silks from Cathay, lace from Belgium or perhaps tortoise combs from Portugal?"

"Nothing so exotic, Monsieur Balliet," she replied, darting a distracted glance out the window. "Just some ribbon to trim a gown."

If the shopkeeper was disappointed by her mundane request, he did not show it. "This way, *mademoiselle*," he said gesturing expansively. "I have ribbons of every color.

"Take care of the customers, Mathieu," he instructed his assistant as he led Danielle through narrow aisles toward a corner in the back of the shop, hidden by tall bolts of fabric.

"That bell has been ringing all morning," Balliet muttered when the door opened again. When they reached the ribbon counter, he stepped aside so his customer could admire his inventory. True to his word, there were spools of ribbon of silk, satin, and velvet in every hue.

"The gown you are trimming, it is for the Fourth of July Ball, *oui?*" he guessed rightly. "Then you must have satin. Blue, perhaps?" Choosing a roll of lustrous ice-blue ribbon, he unfurled it with an extravagant gesture on the cutting table. "Or yellow...or pink...or green?" Three other bright loops of ribbon cascaded over the first.

"There is the door again," Balliet said testily when he heard the bell again. "Perhaps you would like time to think," he suggested with a deferential bow.

"*Oui, merci,*" Danielle agreed, engrossed in making her choice.

"If you will excuse me then..." He bustled away, red-faced from heat and irritation, shouting for Mathieu as he went.

Danielle lingered over her selection, wielding her fan energetically in the sweltering heat.

"How delightful to find you looking at ribbons again," a voice growled playfully in her ear. The girl spun to find Arturo De Leon behind her. Although he smiled, his blue eyes were grave as he looked down at her.

"*Bonjour,* Capitaine De Leon," she greeted him breathlessly.

"Did you think you could escape me so easily?" he asked. His voice was soft, yet urgent. "Listen to me, Danielle. I will not be dismissed like a hired man nor snubbed on the street. If you are angry with me about last night, let me make it up to you."

"Please, *capitaine*..." The girl looked miserable and Arturo knew it was because of the truth in his accusation.

"It seems a shame that buying ribbon is all rich women find to do with their time," he teased, suddenly playful, taking pity on her.

"We find few other things of such importance," she retorted, obviously relieved by his change in tack.

"Did I hear you say you were trimming another ball gown? Shopping and dancing . . . what a waste." He shook his head. "I know a better way for a beautiful woman to spend time," he murmured suggestively, moving closer to touch a straying tendril of hair peeking out from beneath her bonnet.

Involuntarily, Danielle retreated again. She had not wanted to meet the privateer in public, but his intimations in private were worse. She glared at him, furious at the satisfaction on his handsome face. He seemed to enjoy her distress as much as he did his precious reputation as rogue.

Jerking her head away, she challenged him. "*Monsieur,* you presume too much."

Arturo's hand dropped, but he grinned remorselessly. "I do presume, and always too much." He leaned against the cutting table and remarked casually, "You are out early this morning."

"I went to church," Danielle admitted after an uneasy pause.

"To confession, I imagine." His grin grew even broader. "I hope you did not tell all, *cher.* Priests hear many things, but Père Antoine is getting old. Shock cannot be good for him."

"Did you get my letter?" she demanded in a low voice, ignoring his joking remark.

"*Oui.*"

"Well, did you read it?"

"*Oui,* but I thought you might like to explain."

"What is there to explain? I want you to forget last night— as if it never happened." She fidgeted with the ribbon on the table, refusing to meet his eyes.

"That might be difficult," the man answered quietly, but Danielle did not have time to respond to his serious remark before he added lightly, "As you say in your letter, *cher,* I have shown myself to have a tender heart. But you do not know how it grieves me that I cannot make you fall in love with me."

"You must know plenty of other women who will soothe the pain," she retorted, irritated by his playful mockery.

"Many." Arturo shrugged carelessly. "But not one among the entire hundred can hold a candle to you, *mon amour*."

Monsieur Balliet reappeared from behind the bolts of cloth in time to hear Arturo's last remark. With a scant nod to the privateer, from whom he bought most of his goods, the merchant broke in disapprovingly. "*Mademoiselle,* pardon the interruption, but have you found what you were seeking?"

"I would like to think so," Arturo interjected, smiling lazily at the girl.

"*Oui,* Monsieur Balliet," Danielle blurted, her face burning. "Twenty-five yards of the pale blue ribbon, *s'il vous plâit*."

She followed the storekeeper to the front of the shop with Arturo on her heels. Absorbed in signing her bill, she would not look at him as he lolled at the counter beside her, watching her.

When she turned to leave, the privateer took three long steps and arrived at the door ahead of her. With a courtly bow, he opened it and followed her when she swept past him.

Monsieur Balliet looked after them, a troubled expression on his shiny face. The Valmont account was long past due and rumors flew regarding Yves Valmont's finances. It was said that five of Félicité's best hands were about to be sold to bring in cash, a dangerous solution to the problem. Many of Valmont's fields already lay fallow without enough slaves to work them. But the shopkeeper had said nothing to the girl. How could he? He did not wish to embarrass her, especially in front of that rascal, De Leon. Let no one say Victor Balliet was a hard-hearted man.

Out on the banquette, Arturo reached deftly around Danielle and plucked the small bundle from her hand. "I will carry your package," he offered gallantly.

"Lydie will carry it," Danielle contradicted and retrieved it.

"I thought she came along to protect you," Arturo baited her.

"Protect me from whom?" The girl handed the parcel to her maid.

Silently, Lydie placed it into her wicker shopping basket and watched the couple through wary black eyes. This fascination *la petite maîtresse* had for the pirate was dangerous. Had she not seen them herself last night in the garden? No difference that it might be love. If M'sieur Yves ever found out... The maid shuddered at the thought.

"We should be going, *mam'selle*," she advised, trying to steer her mistress toward the carriage.

"Without enjoying some of the finer points of the city?" the privateer asked slyly.

"Such as?" Danielle regarded him skeptically.

"Such as a promenade or a cool breeze from the river or..."

"Or?"

"Or the company of a charming man." He smiled, his blue eyes wickedly confident.

"Let me think," the girl riposted, "are we speaking of anyone I know?"

"Arturo De Leon, of course," he said, striving to look wounded. "Join me for *café, cher,* so I may convince you of his charm."

"Non, merci." She moved past him on the banquette.

"I understand," he said gravely, capturing her arm to detain her. "It is because you fear you will fall in love with me, *oui?*"

Danielle glared up at him, prepared to protest, but seeing the mirth in his blue eyes, she suddenly smiled. Yves was not at Félicité, and the idea of returning to the hot, silent house was repugnant. She had wanted to spend the day in town, and now she knew how she wanted to spend it... with Arturo. Surely a promenade with him would be a wonderful, harmless adventure.

"Très bien, I will have *café* with you, *capitaine,*" she said, "but I cannot stay long."

"Then we must make the best of our short time together. Come." Attentively, he offered his arm and led her toward the river as Lydie trailed them watchfully.

They picked their way among stacks of barrels and bales of cotton left uncovered on the levee and stopped to gaze at the forest of masts lining the riverbank behind the market. The bows of the great sailing ships towered over them, for the level of the Mississippi was higher than the city.

Positioning Danielle in front of him, Arturo bent so their cheeks were nearly touching and pointed. "See that brigantine there? The ship with two masts?"

"The one with the Spanish lady for a figurehead?"

"*Oui*, that's the *Magdalena*," the captain proudly announced.

"Oh, she *is* beautiful," the girl breathed delightedly.

"Since you would not go to Barataria to see her, I brought her to you," he declared outrageously. "I wanted you to see her before we sail."

"To Morocco?"

"First a short voyage to the Caribbean, then a long one to Morocco."

"Very long?"

"Long enough that you will probably be an old married lady by the time I return," he answered airily. "So come, *ma cher*, let us enjoy life while we can."

Although Danielle felt an unexpected pang at Arturo's jest, she said nothing as he led her to the *banquette café*.

"How did the *Magdalena* get her name?" she asked nervously when they were seated, sipping coffee from sturdy white mugs.

"I told you, she is named for one of the women in my life— my mother," the privateer answered, grinning.

Danielle tried to hide her surprise. "Magdalena De Leon. What a lovely and gentle-sounding name."

"My mother is lovely to me," Arturo said, laughing heartily, "but she is far from gentle. She has a Spanish temper—one I fear I inherited. When she is angry, everyone runs for cover."

"Even your father?"

"I never knew my father," he answered soberly.

"That must have been hard for you when you were a boy."

"Not really. My mother has four brothers. They tried to keep me in line. Mostly by pounding sense into me. When I was fifteen, I fought back. I started with Alejandro, the youngest. Then Mateo—the peacemaker—butted in, so I fought him, too. Emilio is hotheaded, always looking for a fight, so he jumped in. When it looked like all three of them together could not take me, Juan, the eldest, settled it. Tío Mostacho, I call him. He just seized me by the scruff of the neck and threw me to the ground. No punches, no shouting, just a growl—'Back to work, Turo.' ''

"Did you get back to work?"

"Oh, yes, but the next day I ran away to sea. I signed on with the first ship I could find, a trader going to the Orient. We did not return to New Orleans for more than three years. Then I signed on with one ship and another. I even served on a whaler out of Boston for a time, but I did not like it, pursuing whales and killing them." He made a sour face.

"So instead you pursue ships and their passengers," the girl baited him.

"Oui," he agreed mildly, "but I do not kill anyone. Well, perhaps in battle I kill a few, but I do not murder them. I rob them. And if their ship is damaged in the fight, think how I help by lightening their loads!"

The girl laughed in spite of herself. "How did you become a pirate?"

"A privateer," he corrected exasperatedly. "First I found myself a rich backer—by finding his wife. Felicia was young and beautiful and married to Don Reynaldo, the governor of a Caribbean island. She fancied me and her old husband found out. He doted on her, but he was also a businessman. So instead of throwing me in the brig to rot, he proposed a partnership.

"If I would leave the island, he would turn over to me an impounded ship. I had my doubts, but the *Magdalena* changed my mind. She is fleet and well armed. When Don Reynaldo offered me a letter of marque in exchange for half my booty for two years, I accepted. He made it clear that if I did not keep my bargain, he would hunt me down and hang me from the yardarm. It seemed fair.

"The wily old fox!" He roared with laughter. "He rid himself of his wife's lover and made money, as well. Everyone was happy."

"Even Felicia?"

"Even Felicia. In truth, we were beginning to tire of each other. The governor showered her with jewels to recapture her affection, and I was soon forgotten. But it does not matter. I would trade her for the *Magdalena* any day. No woman is worth my ship."

Yves Valmont was in a foul mood when he rounded the corner and plunged into the traffic of the congested market-place. The blazing sun reflected on the uneven cobblestones of Levee Street did little to improve his temper as he surveyed the press of humanity. The Creole's eyes were drawn to the famil-iar slender form of Lydie, sitting in the shade outside one of the cafés. She saw her master the same moment he spied her. Her eyes widened guiltily, and she ducked too late to escape detection.

"Lydie!" he hailed her. "Where is Danielle?"

She faced him as if she had just noticed him and smiled brightly. "*Bonjour,* M'sieur Yves."

"Where is Danielle?" he repeated.

"Nearby. I am to wait for her here," she answered uneas-ily.

"Then I will wait with you," Yves announced, peering shrewdly down at her.

"Do not trouble yourself, M'sieur," Lydie said quickly.

"Not at all," he drawled, his dark eyes searching for his sister. An ominous scowl came to his face when he spotted her in an open café with Arturo De Leon.

"Go and fetch the carriage," Yves instructed grimly.

"I promised I would wait."

"Do as I tell you, Lydie." The man's tone left no room for argument. Reluctantly, the maid hefted her basket and set out.

Her back to the street, Danielle did not notice their ex-change, but Arturo saw. Rising cordially, he greeted the other man. "Valmont, what an unexpected pleasure."

"So I see," Yves snarled.

Danielle turned innocently in her seat to welcome her brother, but her smile faded under his hostile stare.

"We were just having some *café*." Arturo gestured toward their cups. "Would you care to join us?"

"I have come to fetch my sister home."

"Home?" Danielle repeated incredulously. "But I have been here only a few minutes."

"Long enough for every tongue in New Orleans to wag," Yves retorted, leaning to pull her roughly from her seat.

Arturo stepped forward to block him. "No need for a scene, Valmont," he counseled reasonably. "She has done nothing wrong."

"Perhaps not today." Yves's shrug was eloquent. "But everyone in the Vieux Carré knows your reputation, De Leon, and I will thank you not to practice your womanizing on my sister."

"No danger, *mon ami,*" Arturo crooned menacingly. "Apparently I have more respect for her than you do."

"That is hardly possible." Yves's face flushed with anger. "Come, Danielle."

Aware that every eye in the crowded café was upon them, the girl was deceptively submissive, fighting to maintain self-control, as she prepared to leave.

Arturo was also conscious of their audience. Reveling in his unaccustomed role of gentleman, he kissed her hand and murmured, "Until next time, little one."

"There will be no next time," Yves assured him contemptuously, steering his sister toward the street.

"Oh, but there will, *mon ami,*" the privateer murmured, watching their departure through narrowed eyes. "And soon."

"Yves Valmont, I have never—" Wresting her arm from his grip, Yves's sister rounded on him when they reached the banquette.

"I will not tolerate a scene on the street, Danielle," he warned.

They stood on the corner, awaiting the carriage. Danielle was rigid with anger. "How dare you humiliate me?" she asked angrily under her breath while nodding to a matron who approached on the banquette.

"How dare you throw yourself at that pirate?" her brother shot back, tipping his hat politely to the woman.

"I will have you know," the girl whispered venomously, "my behavior with Capitaine De Leon was above reproach."

"But not above gossip," Yves answered sanctimoniously. "You are supposed to be a respectable, marriageable young lady. Remember?"

"I remember," she jeered. "As *Maman* would say, 'Let us wash our dirty clothes in our own family,' Yves. I have listened to enough gossip about you and your escapades. What is wrong with my joining Capitaine De Leon for *café* in public in broad daylight?"

"Keep your voice down," he growled as their open coach rolled toward them. "Now, listen to me. Gauthier is coming to Félicité tonight and he may ask for your hand again. Do you not understand how lucky you are? Your marriage to Vincent will be a great match."

"For you perhaps," Danielle muttered mutinously.

"We will discuss the answer you are to give your intended later," he snapped, handing his sister into the carriage none too gently. "Otherwise, an extended retreat to a convent might help you make up your mind. Many long and fruitful marriages have been decided upon in the solitude of the cloister."

Danielle's brown eyes rested furiously on her brother as he turned to walk away. "Mark me well, Yves," she grated, just loudly enough for him to hear, "I will have something to say about my future." She could not see his face, but she saw his shoulders stiffen just before the carriage rolled away.

Chapter Five

Wearing only a light nightgown, Danielle stood in the middle of her bedroom and brushed her hair. It shone in the candlelight as she applied herself energetically to the last few strokes.

The night was sultry, the moon was full, and from the slave quarters came the sounds of a *charivari,* a cacophonous wedding serenade. Even the dignified Lydie participated as house servants and field hands gathered to clatter pots, ring bells, shout and whistle.

Danielle had attended the ceremony, staying long enough to watch the couple jump the broom, a bayou country tradition. Then she returned to the big house, leaving the slaves to celebrate.

Now she was ready for bed, but there was no hope for sleep. She paced, made restless by the heat, the noise and the mood of the night. It was late when she mounted the steps to her tester bed and closed the baire, or mosquito netting, around it, settling back to brood on her problems.

As Yves had predicted, Vincent had indeed proposed again. Dismayed, she had evaded his question, never saying yes, but never really saying no.

"You have had a lifetime to think about marrying me, Dani," the young Creole pressed when she asked for more time to think. "I told you how I felt about you when I was twelve."

"I know, but . . ." she began miserably.

"But you do not love me?" A corner of Vincent's mouth twitched as he tried to control his emotions.

"I do love you," the girl assured him hastily, "but as a friend." Her brown eyes filled with tears; she could not bear to hurt him, even with the truth. Why did he insist on becoming her husband?

"Friendship is enough for now," he persisted. "Many good unions start that way. You will learn to love me as I love you."

"Oh, Vincent," Danielle sighed, "it is not that simple."

"You are in love with someone else," he accused. "It is that scoundrel, De Leon, isn't it?"

"Of course not," she protested, shocked by both the suggestion and his vehemence.

The young man's narrow shoulders sagged with relief. "I am sorry," he apologized. "I was afraid you ... Never mind.

"All right then, you may have more time to think, but I would like your answer by my birthday ... July 6th. If you say yes, I will buy you an alliance ring the very next day. We could be married by New Year's. Would you like that?"

"It sounds lovely," she answered distractedly, her mind racing so she hardly noticed when he took the liberty of planting a timid kiss on her cheek. Two weeks, she thought, two weeks until the inevitable. Only that day she and Yves had quarreled again and he had made her choices clear: marriage to Vincent or life in a convent until he allowed her to come home to live as a spinster. Her mind churned, rebelling against either possibility.

Danielle examined her reflection critically in the full-length mirror. Dressed for the Fourth of July Ball, she knew she looked lovely even though the gown she wore was an old one. She had been angry at first, not understanding why Yves refused to furnish her with a new gown. But thanks to the ice-blue ribbon she had bought at Balliet's and Lydie's skill with a needle, she was pleased with her refurbished gown.

The simple white dress, made of diaphanous gauze over satin, was nipped in at her slender waist. Its split skirt belled becomingly over a blue pettiskirt the same pale shade as the ribbons that trimmed the outer dress. The fitted bodice with its short sleeves bared her shoulders tantalizingly. The cold fire of aquamarines flickered at her ears, but no necklace marred the expanse of creamy skin revealed by her plunging décolletage. Her glossy blond curls, intertwined with more of the lustrous blue ribbon, were gathered loosely atop her head and cascaded down her back.

But the girl's face looked tired and strained, its pallor marked with two bright spots of color burning on each cheek. She bit her bloodless lips to bring color to them and smiled at herself in the mirror. Her mouth curved upward, covering signs of her dissatisfaction, but none of her customary merriment showed in her dark, shadowed eyes.

What was wrong with her? Danielle asked herself. This ball would be the biggest event of the summer. Held at the home of Lester Parker, an influential American, it would be a great celebration and one of the first times that Creole and Kaintock mixed socially. But all she could think was that her time was nearly gone. In two days, she must give Vincent his answer.

She sighed gustily, feeling odd and discontented and very much alone. She thought of summoning her maid to keep her company until it was time to go downstairs, but she did not want to discuss Hercule, Lydie's current infatuation. Restlessly, Danielle went to her vanity and opened the small wooden casket that served as her jewelry box, rummaging through it until she found what she sought: an ornate, old-fashioned opal ring that had belonged to her mother. Its gentle iridescent fire did not match her ensemble, but when she put it on, the girl felt as if she were not alone.

The clock was striking ten when she picked up her white lace fan and went downstairs. Yves awaited her in the foyer, smiling appreciatively when she appeared. Dressed in virginal white, she was lovely, looking every inch the marriageable, biddable Creole maiden.

But she felt far from biddable. Her cheeks burned with an unaccustomed fever as the carriage rolled along the rough dirt roads to the Parker home, carrying her to the American section for the first time. It hardly seemed fair. She was being forced into an engagement when she wanted still to laugh and dance and play coquette with many admirers. This ball was her last chance. Tonight neither Yves nor Vincent could mar her good time. She thought of the evening to come and felt a sudden rush of reckless excitement.

Danielle entered the ballroom, animated, engaging, borne on a cloud of desperate gaiety. She danced first with her host, then with Yves, who turned her over to Vincent the instant the music faded. The ardent young Creole beamed, holding his beloved close while they waltzed.

He was sullen when he was forced to surrender the girl to Augustine Arceneaux for a lively reel. As he had at the Winter Masque, Vincent stood at the sidelines and glowered at every rival until he could reclaim Danielle. She did little to relieve his jealousy, flirting equally with each partner, young or old.

At last, she found herself dancing with Martin Hannibel, a visitor from Tennessee who was no more than sixteen years old. Although she was nearly as tall as he, the boy held her as if he feared she would break until he realized a closer embrace was acceptable to the Creoles. Then he gripped Danielle so tightly he nearly cut off her wind and whirled her around the floor with brash, adolescent enjoyment. She laughed aloud as her surroundings became a blur in the glow of the candles. Then, unexpectedly, one figure leaped out in sharp detail.

Arturo De Leon leaned insolently against a carved doorpost. Clad in resplendent velvets and satins, he stood out among the gentlemen in ordinary formal evening attire. His arms folded across his muscular chest, he observed the dancers disinterestedly. But feeling Danielle's surprised gaze on him, he looked directly at her and winked one blue eye outlandishly.

Drawing a quick breath, the girl nodded to the privateer, grateful that neither her brother nor Vincent had witnessed the exchange. Her pulse quickening, she wondered if Arturo would even want to talk to her after Yves had embarrassed them at the café. Her face burned when she recalled the scene. She would like to have an opportunity to speak to him, to apologize for her brother's behavior. Yves and his temper... She sighed.

"Is something amiss, Miss Valmont?" Martin Hannibel inquired solicitously.

"No, no," Danielle assured him. "I just saw someone I know."

"Someone you do not wish to see? Only say so, and I will stay by your side all night to shield you, if need be," he said, his gallant declaration ending in a soprano squawk when his voice broke. The teenage boy blushed furiously, then, lowering his head, said huskily, "We Americans know something of chivalry, too."

"Thank you, Monsieur Hannibel—" Danielle smiled sweetly at him "—but I am sure that will not be necessary."

The lad was utterly smitten, charmed by her smile, her voice, even the way she said his name. "As you wish, whatever you wish," he pledged with youthful sincerity.

When their dance was finished, he released her and bowed stiffly. "Thank you for the dance, Miss Valmont. Would you like to sit down? Or should I get you some punch? Or anything at all?"

"*Non, merci,* but you are very kind." Danielle rewarded the young American with another dazzling smile from behind her fan, reveling in the effect she was having on him.

"Then may I have the honor of another dance?" Martin proposed shyly when the music began again.

"Do not be so greedy, my friend," a deep voice reproved. "You have already danced with the most beautiful woman at the ball. You must allow others the same pleasure."

"Good evening. Captain De Leon, is it not?" the young American squeaked reluctantly.

"Oh, yes, M'sieur Hannibel, we met earlier. *Bonsoir.* And you, *mademoiselle,* are lovely, as always." Arturo bowed suavely.

"*Bonsoir, capitaine.*" Danielle nodded graciously, offering her hand to be kissed.

The man was quick to oblige, but after his lips brushed her hand, he did not release it. "You will give me the pleasure of this dance, *mademoiselle?*"

"*Oui, merci.*" She was anxious for the chance to speak to him alone. "Please excuse me, Monsieur Hannibel."

Martin bowed amiably, but he looked crestfallen when the privateer took the girl into his arms. Their eyes on each other, the couple did not notice Vincent's angry face over Martin's shoulder as they joined the dancers on the floor.

"*Capitaine,* I wanted to talk to you," Danielle began at once.

"And I, to you," he murmured warmly.

"I want to apologize—"

"Do not say it, *ma belle,*" he interrupted smoothly. "Let us speak instead of how beautiful you are." His admiring eyes dipped to her décolletage. "Who would have thought that a bit of plain blue ribbon could look so lovely?"

Blushing wildly, but resisting the urge to cover her exposed cleavage, the girl acknowledged his compliment. *"Merci, capitaine."*

"Arturo, *cher.* Why must I always remind you? You promised to call me Arturo the first time we met. In fact, this reminds me of that night," he whispered, his arms tightening around her.

"Only because you still hold me too close," she protested wryly, straining to pull away.

He loosened his hold slightly, but complained, "I hold you close because I do not wish you to escape me again. You are always running away from me."

"I thought it was you who was leaving. Were you not due to sail last week?"

"Our departure was postponed." The privateer did not wish to admit that he had searched for her at the theater and the French Opera. When the Valmonts had not appeared at either, he had changed the *Magdalena*'s schedule in order to attend this ball.

A determined gleam coming suddenly to his blue eyes, Arturo twirled the girl toward the doors that stood open to let in the cooling night air.

"Non, s'il vous plaît—" Danielle demurred.

"Please, *cher,* you said you wished to talk to me. Let us have a few moments in private. I will behave myself, I swear it."

Danielle allowed herself to be danced outside, and the couple emerged onto a shadowy patio with a fountain in its center. The delicate fragrance of flowers perfumed the air, and muted music floated to them from the ballroom as they waltzed in the moonlight. When the last strains of the music died, Arturo released her reluctantly, took off his jacket and spread it on a bench so they could sit down.

"What a lovely ring you are wearing tonight," he complimented her, taking her hand in his. "An opal, is it not?"

"Yes, it belonged to my mother."

"I thought opals brought bad luck, especially in affairs of the heart." He leaned nearer and breathed in the scent of her hair. "You have not found that to be true, have you?"

"Do not tell me you are superstitious, *capitaine*," the girl said, edging away a bit.

"Only about a few things," he admitted honestly, but his expression soon turned playful. "Did I tell you an old voodoo woman once taught me to tell fortunes by reading palms?" He turned Danielle's hand over and stared at it in the moonlight.

"What does it tell you?"

"That you are unhappy."

"You cannot know that by looking at my hand," she countered, attempting to withdraw it, but Arturo did not release it.

"I know by looking into your eyes. What is wrong, *ma petite?*" Arturo asked. "Does Yves still insist on your marriage?"

She did not answer; she did not think she could bear to discuss the subject with him.

"Ah, Danielle, it pains me to see you look so sad," he whispered. Her pale face was luminous in the moonlight, and Arturo was tempted to kiss her, to chase the sorrowful expression from her brown eyes, but he remembered his promise. Instead he contented himself with bringing her hand to his lips and gently kissing the fingers.

An angry voice ripped through the quiet. "What a cozy picture this is!"

"Vincent!" Yanking her hand away, Danielle jumped guiltily to her feet.

"Get out of the way, Danielle," the compact young Creole ordered, glaring at Arturo murderously as he rose from his seat.

"It is not what you think, Gauthier," the big captain informed him mildly.

"What is it then?" Vincent snarled.

"Danielle and I were only talking."

"Talking—alone in the dark?"

"Talking to a girl alone in the dark can be a pleasant way to pass the time," Arturo said lightly. "You should try it sometime."

"I ought to kill you, De Leon!" the enraged man shouted, advancing on him.

"Relax, *mon ami,* it was only a joke," Arturo protested, astonished by Vincent's vehement reaction. "Not a very good one, but a joke all the same."

"I do not find it amusing. Nor do I see any humor in finding Danielle 'passing time'... again... with a scoundrel."

"Vincent!" Danielle gasped indignantly.

Ignoring her protest, he faced Arturo proudly. "I will deal with my intended later, but you and I have a matter to resolve at the Dueling Oaks."

"Oh, no," the girl moaned, her face blanching.

Arturo cast a glance toward her and forced himself to state reasonably, "Nothing has happened here that requires you to settle a debt of honor, Gauthier."

"What do you know of honor?" Vincent's tone was insulting.

"Hmmm, honor..." Arturo pondered. Tugging thoughtfully on the golden earring he wore, the privateer paced, coming closer to the irate Creole. "I do find it difficult to understand, *m'sieur.* I suppose because honor is for gentlemen, as are duels." Without warning, his doubled fist lashed out and caught Vincent squarely on the chin.

"Sorry," he apologized insincerely as the other man skidded across the terrace, leaving a furrow along the moss-covered flagstones, and came to rest near the fountain. "But you are right, I do not know much of honor. And as we discussed once before, why wait until dawn to fight?"

The brawny privateer turned to Danielle, who stood transfixed with shock. "You see, *cher,*" he announced magnanimously, "if you must marry, at least you know this jealous fool loves you. He is willing to duel for you."

"I do not want him to duel for me, or his honor!" Danielle's hot words ended in a screech as Vincent lurched to his feet, shaking his head groggily, and charged at his opponent's back. The force of his lunge carried both men to the ground where they rolled, knocking the girl off balance.

Hair atumble and her skirt in a tangle, Danielle leaped to her feet. Circling the fighters as they rolled on the ground, she pounded furiously on the back of whoever was on top, first one and then the other. "Stop it!" she shouted. "Have you both lost your senses?"

The sounds of combat attracted an audience of avid Kaintocks, equipped with lanterns. They thronged eagerly from the house at the first signal of a fight; fisticuffs always made better sport than dancing.

"Not much you can do, Miss Valmont, 'cept get out of the way." Lester Parker appeared from nowhere to pull the girl from the fray. "You're liable to get hurt while those boys knock some of the meanness out of each other. And Lord knows they could use it," he added, watching the clash appreciatively.

Flanked by her host and Martin Hannibel, Danielle stood by helplessly as the crowd swelled and bets were placed. Men and women ringed the fighters, cheering excitedly. At the windows of the ballroom, disapproving Creole faces appeared, but none came out of the house.

On their feet again, the combatants exchanged jarring blows. Grunts of exertion punctuated the sound of fists pounding against solid bodies.

"Can you not stop it?" Danielle begged her host. "Someone will be killed."

"Don't reckon so," he argued, unwilling to break up the fight. "De Leon'll stop before he hurts the little fellow."

"Please, *monsieur*," she turned imploringly to Martin Hannibel.

The infatuated young man acceded immediately. "Come on, Mr. Parker," he urged, "they've had their fun."

The other American gave in sorrowfully. "Oh, all right. Come on, boys," he hollered, wading into action amid boos from the spectators, "enough is enough." Ducking blind blows, he seized the bruised and bleeding Vincent and dragged him off of the other man.

Martin had no trouble controlling Arturo. Within moments, the privateer stood to one side and mopped blood from his battered nose with his ever-present green scarf. The fighters eyed each other angrily across the courtyard. With no brawl to interest them, the guests drifted into the house.

"Let us finish what we have started here, Monsieur Parker," Vincent demanded hoarsely.

"Much as I hate to see a good sluggin' match bust up, you boys have to stop. This is s'posed to be a party. Besides, you're upsettin' the little lady here."

Both opponents turned resentful stares on the disheveled girl. As if they sensed the impending explosion, the Americans retreated.

Arturo regarded Danielle with disappointment. "You should not have interfered, *cher.*"

"What was I to do?" she snapped. "Stand by and watch you kill each other?"

"You should have more faith—at least in one of us," he rebuked her sadly. "What I did was for you, to teach Gauthier a lesson on the evils of jealousy."

"By pounding him?"

"He pounded, too." Arturo's peevish retort was all but drowned out as Yves joined them.

"Enough, Danielle!" the Creole roared at his sister.

"It is not enough." She turned her back on Yves and divided her anger between the two fighters. "The two of you, fighting like a pair of tomcats."

"*Mon Dieu,* Valmont, what a sharp tongue your sister has," Arturo noted sympathetically as he pulled on his jacket.

"And you!" Danielle spun on him. "How could you fight a boy?"

"Who are you calling a boy?" Vincent yelled.

"*Oui,* who are you calling a boy?" Arturo echoed, dabbing at his battered nose.

"You struck without warning! Vincent did not even have time to defend himself," she ranted. "And he is smaller than you. You might have hurt him."

"This is the gratitude you show for all I have done for you?" Arturo stormed, becoming angry for the first time that night. He stalked away, muttering direly in several languages.

"Men!" Danielle screeched in frustration and limped back toward the house with as much dignity as her tousled appearance would allow. The heel of her slipper had broken when she fell, her gauze overskirt hung in tatters, and ice-blue ribbons trailed from her ruined finery.

Before she reached the French doors to the ballroom, Vincent intercepted her. Yves was on his heels.

"You have made a fool of me for the last time, Danielle," Vincent accused through puffy lips. "I do not need your answer day after tomorrow. I do not want you for a wife any more than you want me for a husband." Stiffly, he pivoted and marched away.

Yves stared witheringly at Danielle, who watched Vincent's departure in stunned silence. "Get our things and meet us at the carriage," he commanded. "I will see if I can straighten this out." Then he followed her injured suitor into the darkness.

In the house, the guests were being served a midnight supper. Rumpled and upset, Danielle sought out her hostess to apologize.

"Your handsome captain is just a high-spirited young man, dear," Mrs. Parker comforted, patting her hand. "He will mellow with age. By the time you are married as long as Lester and me, you will see."

The puzzled girl did not explain she would probably never see "her captain" again and was not sure she wanted to. Choking back tears, she fled to the carriage to wait for her brother.

Arturo slumped over a rough-hewn table in El Reposo de los Marinos, his mother's tavern, and reached for the bottle of rum. He held it up and squinted at it, focusing with difficulty.

"Empty," he muttered. "Coulda sworn s'more."

"So there was, *mon capitaine,*" Jacques slurred, his Cajun accent even thicker than usual, "but tha' was some time ago, yes."

"Ver' long?" Arturo hiccuped and swatted ineffectually at a mosquito buzzing around his head.

"Long enough tha' your *maman*'s ve-ree angry," Jacques answered solemnly. "Don' think she likes it tha' you come home to get drunk. I don' speak Spanish, me, but I know she was cursing." He wagged a drunken, disapproving finger at the other man.

"She n-never stays mad a' me," Arturo responded with a tipsy smirk. Listing slightly, he sat back, braced his hands on his knees and regarded his companion gravely. "S'only one thing to do now, amigo, an' I'll do it im-im—now."

He lurched to his feet. At this hour, only a few sailors lingered and they scrambled from the big man's path as he weaved across the worn plank floor. "More, rum, *tío, por favor,*" he requested, presenting himself at the bar with a lopsided smile.

Juan De Leon glanced at his nephew sourly and did not stop wiping the glass he held. "You have already had too much, Turo."

"Y'think so?" Arturo seemed to ponder the question.

"*Sí,* I think you should go and sleep it off, but your mother said when you were on your feet again to send you to the kitchen."

"O-o-oh." Arturo looked pained, but he swaggered unsteadily toward the kitchen. "If I'm not back inna hour, sen' th' coroner, *mon ami,*" he called over his shoulder, receiving a sloppy salute from Jacques.

Guardedly, Arturo looked at his mother over the swinging doors. Up to her elbows in soapy water, Magdalena did not realize he was there. To her watching son her stocky figure and strong face seemed formidable. Self-reliant and independent, she had reared him alone while running her thriving tavern, sometimes assisted by, sometimes hindered by her four brothers, who wandered in and out of her life as easily as they ate in her kitchen or drank at her bar.

Although Magdalena's beauty was now faded and toil-worn, it was not hard to see where Arturo had gotten his sensual good looks and startling blue eyes. Her eyes were greener than her son's, almost turquoise in color, and when she spotted him over the half doors, they narrowed disapprovingly.

"*Mi madre,*" he mumbled, slipping naturally into Spanish. Swinging the door open with a flourish, he attempted to stroll casually into the room. Instead he stumbled over his own feet and staggered against the heavy table, sloshing her dishwater.

"Sit before you fall down, Turo," Magdalena commanded sharply, drying her work-roughened hands on her apron.

She wiped up the spill and set a plate bearing a large rubbery piece of steak on the table in front of her son. "Here, I've been keeping this warm for you. Eat, then go back to your ship. Don't you sail in the morning?"

"Sí." He looked down at the meat queasily and swallowed hard.

"You are drunk," his mother accused. "What kind of fool does this the night before a voyage?"

"A fool who is also a sailor?" Arturo hazarded a guess, vastly amused by his cleverness.

"And what if he is a *capitán?*" Magdalena snorted in disgust. "What is wrong with you, *mi hijo?* Is it a woman as Jacques says?"

"Jacques talks too much."

"Well, is it a woman?" she persisted. "You have always had a heart like an artichoke, as the old ones say, a leaf for every girl. Can it be you have fallen in love, Turo?"

"No. *No!*" His denial became emphatic as he pounded his fist on the table, setting the dishes aclatter and bringing the dishpan dangerously close to the edge. "I'm not in love. Plagued, pestered, driven mad by th' women in my life, but *not* in love."

"A big problem, all those women. But it only takes one to make a man *loco,*" Magdalena suggested slyly.

"Sí, one woman." Arturo's slurred voice took on a melancholy tone. "Wasn' *loco* 'fore she came 'long. F'rever arguments from 'er. *Dios,* what a temper she has! An' I ask you, did I getta kiss 'fore sailin'?" He threw a disgruntled frown toward his mother before answering his own question, "No, insult's what I got, an' she can' do tha' to Turo De Leon." Unsteadily, he got to his feet and reeled toward the door.

"Where are you going, son?" Magdalena called after him, expecting the answer that floated back on the summer night.

"Goin' to getta kiss from 'er 'fore I sail!"

The moon peeped out from behind the rolling clouds when Arturo stumbled across Félicité's lawn, uncertain how he came to be there. Because all the livery stables were closed for the night, he had prowled the streets until he came across a truck farmer on his way to market to secure a stall. Resisting the Italian's valiant attempts to haggle, Arturo rented one of his draft horses for an exorbitant price. Then he mounted the nag, with her heavy plodding hooves and tattered straw hat, and was jostled all the way to the Valmont plantation.

Pausing now in the rose garden below Danielle's window, the captain was uncertain what to do next. Even in his addled state, he knew he could not make noise that would rouse the house. And he would hardly be welcome here. Besides, he reflected as he swigged from a nearly empty flask, he wished to see the lady privately.

For the moment, the moon was hidden and the night was dark. Arturo silently cursed himself for coming. But now that he was here, he *would* see Danielle. He looked up to the balcony where he could see the glass-paned door to her room opened slightly to admit the breeze. There was nothing to do, he decided, but to climb up. If he could scramble up the ratlines of a pitching ship, he could manage a stationary tree.

Moving with the comical exaggerated care of an inebriate, Arturo removed the elegant jacket and waistcoat he wore and folded them meticulously. Placing them quite illogically on the dew-wet grass, he laid his hat carefully atop them, then tiptoed to the enormous oak and hoisted himself up heavily. Straddling the curving branch, he began laboriously to scoot up it.

By the time the man reached the top, he had come close to falling only ten times or so, but there he met with a real obstacle: the distance between the branch and the balcony. Peering down woozily, he discovered the ground was about a mile away.

Taking a deep breath, Arturo gripped the limb tightly with his knees and leaned in an attempt to reach the rail. He became overbalanced and found himself clawing thin air as he slid to the side. Muffling a curse, he hauled himself upright with effort, then he braced himself and tried again. This time his fingers curved around the rail. Gingerly, he pulled the branch toward the balcony and eased himself over.

The moon broke through the clouds as Arturo entered Danielle's bedroom. He hesitated, pulling the door partly closed behind him, and stepped into the shadows. The acrid scent of burned juniper berries filled the air in an attempt to keep mosquitoes away.

He could see the girl faintly on the bed in front of him. She lay, asleep, on her back, her blond hair spread on snowy pillows. Above a light quilt, her thin nightgown was open at the throat, revealing a tantalizing glimpse of rounded white breast. She looked ethereal and beautiful through the gauzy baire and it took his breath away. The besotted man felt he must touch her to know whether she was made of flesh and blood. He started forward and bumped into a small slipper chair he had not seen in the dark.

Startled, Danielle sat bolt upright and turned wide eyes toward the shadows. "Who's there?" she whispered apprehensively.

"Don' be 'fraid, li'l one. S'Arturo," he slurred softly.

"Arturo! What are you doing in my room?" She yanked the cover up under her chin and frowned in the direction of his voice although she could not see him in the darkness.

"I—I mus' talk to you." He stepped nearer, a vague silhouette against lace curtains that covered the French door.

"Do not come any closer," she whispered urgently. "You must go at once. Yves would kill you if he found you here."

"Then 'e mustn' find me, eh, *cher?*" Arturo staggered toward the bed, bent on sitting beside her. But his toe caught the edge of a straw floor mat and he landed heavily across the foot of the bed, taking part of the baire with him.

"You—you are drunk," she whispered in outrage, yanking one of her legs out from under him.

"P'raps a li'l," he agreed with an amiable, crooked grin. Propping himself on one elbow, he clawed the mosquito netting from his face and declared amorously, "But not so drunk tha' I cannot see how beau-beautiful y'are, even in the dark."

"Have you forgotten I am angry at you?" she started bravely, but she faltered when he scowled blearily at her. "What . . . what do you want?"

"Wanna talk to you 'fore I sail. Couldn' bear 'f our las' words were angry." Suddenly very weary, Arturo stretched out on his side. The bed was soft and smelled of vetiver. Contentedly, he closed his eyes and cushioned his head with one arm; the other was looped loosely around Danielle's quilt-covered feet.

"Get up," the girl commanded. Forcing herself to keep her voice low, she punctuated her order by nudging his broad chest with her toe.

Arturo mumbled unintelligibly and hugged the bunched coverlet close as the girl yanked her feet away and climbed out of bed behind him. Without taking time to don slippers or robe, she ran around to the other side and tugged at him.

"Come on, get up," she pleaded when he opened one eye to regard her hazily. "You are mad even to be here."

"*Oui*, mad," he grunted in agreement, but he did not move.

Desperately, she went to the door and threw it open. "Look," she begged, "the sky is getting light. It will be dawn soon. You *must* go."

With a quick intake of breath, the man sat up. The waning moonlight clearly silhouetted Danielle's slender body through her flimsy nightgown. She stood, naturally graceful, unaware that Arturo's stare was fixed on her as he rose, swaying slightly on his feet.

Afraid he would fall with a crash that would wake the entire household, she hurried to him and thrust a shoulder under his arm to brace him. Wrapping one arm round his waist, she guided him determinedly toward the door.

"Come," she said, sighing with relief as he took a few wobbly steps. "Let me help you."

Suddenly, the arm that draped over Danielle's shoulder, tightened, drawing her closer to his side, nearly lifting her bare feet from the floor. Raising her gaze to his, the girl shuddered at the desire glittering in his blue eyes.

"*Cher,*" he murmured, his lips very near hers, "I mus' have a kiss 'fore I go."

"You *are* mad." She attempted to draw away, but suddenly found herself caught by two muscular arms.

"*Oui*, mad," he agreed for the second time, lowering his mouth to claim hers.

The lingering taste of rum on his lips warmed her, and she returned his kiss tentatively at first, then willingly, urgently. Feeling the now familiar fire of passion rising within her, she wrapped both arms around his waist and pressed against him as her hands explored his back, delighting in the hard muscles that rippled beneath his shirt.

Arturo's lips moved from her mouth, trailing feathery kisses down the slender column of her neck, and nestled in the warm, pulsing spot at the hollow of her throat.

"Can you not see how I want you, Danielle? And you want me, too," he whispered. Although his voice was thick with desire, his words were distinct and he sounded sober for the first time since he stole into her room.

"No, I cannot, not here, not like this," she nearly sobbed, struggling to resist the passion that threatened to possess her.

"Come away with me then," he murmured insistently. Lacing his fingers through her hair, he cupped her head and gazed down at her intensely.

"What...what are you saying?" His eyes held hers and she was helpless, mesmerized by his closeness, by the feel of his lithe, hard body against hers. Through the thin cotton of her nightgown, she felt the scalding, solid evidence of his need.

"You do not wish to marry Gauthier."

"After tonight, there is not much chance of it." Her whisper came like a sigh.

"Then sail away with me. I will give you money, jewels. I have a fine home in Tortuga. It will be yours. I give you everything a woman could want."

"Everything?" she asked explicitly, stepping back to search his face.

"Oh, ho," he laughed quietly, quick to comprehend the meaning of her question despite his drink-muddled condition. His hand slid from her thick tresses and dropped heavily to his side. The slur returned to his speech. "You mus' mean marriage?"

"*Oui,* marriage...and love," she replied simply, but hope was dying in her eyes.

"I vow 'm fond of you, *cher,* but I think we could do 'thout either. No man in his righ' min' wants to be tied down. 'Sides, I thought you wouldn' con-consider marryin' a pirate." He hiccuped.

"I would not run away with one, either," she snapped, drawing herself up proudly. "I am not the sort for *la scandale.*"

"You could be," Arturo suggested with a drunken leer, "ver' eas'ly. I think you'd make a fine mistress," he added generously.

"Out! Get out!" Danielle exploded hoarsely, shoving the man onto the balcony. Realizing he was too tipsy to start his descent alone, she yanked the tree branch closer so he could climb onto it. "Hurry up," she urged.

Unfazed, he clambered onto the limb and straddled it, grinning lasciviously. "How'm I to leave you, *cher,* 'thout one more kiss?"

"I am sure I do not know," she answered grimly, "unless you go the same way you came." She released the branch so it swung wildly in midair, nearly unseating Arturo. Ignoring the man's muffled curse as he slid backward for several feet down the rough bark, Danielle went inside and closed her door.

Chapter Six

As the *Magdalena* sailed upriver, the sun, now a fiery ball in the western sky, played tag with the brigantine. First to the left, then behind, then suddenly, blindingly, ahead, it seemed to shift as the ship followed the meanderings of the Mississippi.

From the quarterdeck, Arturo watched the shoreline of the delta slip by, its vegetation tropical and verdant. No matter how many times he sailed away, he always enjoyed the feeling of homecoming that rose in him at English Turn just downriver from New Orleans. His crew seemed infected with the same pleasure. The return from the Caribbean had been uneventful and they were in high spirits, singing raucous Cajun ditties while they worked.

When the *Magdalena* rounded a bend in the river and the Vieux Carré came into sight, a cheer rose from the foredeck. Nearing the docks, the sailors could see that word of their arrival had spread quickly. Plump wives and barefoot families waited on the wharf. The sweltering heat of the August day was over, their men were home and the mood was festive.

Arturo wished he could share in the gaiety, but as the *Magdalena* was hauled by straining sailors toward the pier and the ropes were secured, the captain spotted a familiar face in the crowd. Trouble, not pleasure, awaited him.

Jaime Montera, his partner in the upcoming voyage to Morocco, stood apart, sallow and dour, rigid and judgmental. A wealthy merchant, Jaime was a descendant of a soldier who was garrisoned in New Orleans during Spain's possession of the Louisiana Territory. Despite their intermarriage with some of the oldest French families in Louisiana, the Monteras remained solidly Spanish, always separate.

"There is Jaime," Arturo told his first mate. "You will have to check in with the harbormaster while I deal with this one."

The plank had scarcely touched the wharf when Montera charged aboard. Jacques stepped back quickly to avoid being bowled over by the purposeful little Creole.

"*Madre de Dios,* it is about time you were back, De Leon," Jaime greeted the privateer flatly.

"*Bonjour,* Jaime," Arturo replied, stubbornly refusing to speak Spanish for the other man's benefit. "My business in Tortuga took a little longer than expected, but I would have hurried if I had known you missed my company so much, *mon ami.*"

Although he was annoyed by Jaime's rudeness, he tried to ignore their natural antipathy. Both men felt the sooner the business between them was completed, the better. Their only tie before this unwelcome partnership had been Diego Montera, Arturo's friend and Jaime's cousin.

Diego, an old shipmate of Arturo's, had tired of pirating and turned his ships to commerce in northern Africa. Prudently, he had converted to Islam, adopted a Muslim name, married and retired to Morocco to enjoy a fat, prosperous middle age as a merchant.

But now Diego worried his ships would be prey to the very pirates with whom he had sailed. Casting about for a way to prevent it, he developed an ingenious plan. He would strike a deal with one of his old experienced shipmates, offering huge profits for spices from the East. The man he chose was Arturo De Leon, and he had instructed Jaime to recruit him.

That he had accepted the Monteras' proposal was a fact Arturo had come to regret—almost immediately.

"I am sorry, Jaime," he offered in a conciliatory tone. "Come, I have an excellent bottle of brandy we can share."

As soon as they were in his cabin, the Spaniard rounded on him. "Do we or do we not have an agreement, *capitán?*"

"We do," Arturo conceded mildly. "I will carry a cargo which you will assemble—"

"Which I have already assembled," Jaime interjected hotly. "Perique tobacco and molasses."

"So soon? Sit down, Jaime, you must have been hard at work while I was away."

"*Sí.*" The Spaniard dropped into the nearest chair, only slightly placated by the compliment.

"Then the next step is for me to take the cargo to Diego in Morocco," Arturo said, setting a flat-bottomed decanter and two glasses on the table. "I return with a load of spices, you sell them to your buyers and we all split the profits. What is the problem in that?"

"The problem," Jaime snapped, accepting the drink the captain offered, "is that I have not seen one cent from you."

"Is that all?" Arturo saluted him with his glass. "Do not worry, amigo. Let us drink to the success of our venture."

"To success," Jaime echoed automatically. He sipped his brandy, then demanded, "What about the money you owe me?"

"You will have it." The privateer shrugged. "How much?"

"Two thousand dollars." Jaime watched the other man intently.

"Two thousand?" Arturo's face was impassive, but he knew without looking that the money chest locked in his trunk was nearly empty. During the past month, almost every cent he had had gone into Désir du Coeur, his struggling plantation near Tortuga. "I do not have that much aboard, Jaime. To come up with it, I must go ashore."

"To gamble, I suppose," the Spaniard muttered with a disapproving frown.

"What difference, as long as I come up with the money?"

"No difference." Jaime suddenly smiled, the benevolent expression out of place on his thin face. "Very well, amigo, today is Tuesday. If you do not pay me by Friday, our bargain is no longer valid. I will hire Capitán McNamara." Deliberately, he placed his empty glass on the table.

"Angus McNamara?" Arturo snorted derisively. "His *Bonnie Mary* is a slow, ungainly old tub."

"But she is dependable, as is her *capitán*." The insinuation lingered in the air as Montera rose to depart. "I would prefer to do business with you, De Leon. Diego likes you and, though only *Dios* knows why, he trusts you.

"By the way, you might be interested to know that one of your gambling cronies was killed in a duel while you were away. You knew my neighbor, Yves Valmont, did you not?"

"Valmont is dead? What of his sister?" Arturo started and rose from his chair.

The Spaniard's eyes narrowed speculatively as he gazed up at the man who towered over him. "The girl is penniless. Everything, even the plantation, down to its stock and its last slave, had to be sold to pay Valmont's creditors. I myself bought a magnificent black gelding, the one she rode with such spirit."

"What about Danielle?" Arturo repeated his question urgently.

So something had finally gotten under the privateer's skin, Jaime thought with satisfaction. It was good to know another man's weakness. He regarded his unwilling partner with interest. It was true Danielle Valmont had a reputation for wildness, but surely she did not consort with pirates. Self-righteously, he decided he would not tell Arturo where she was . . . even if he knew.

"I heard young Gauthier plans to marry her as soon as it can be decently done," Jaime said with a careless shrug. "Well, until Friday, De Leon." He hurried for the door before the other man could question him more.

Arturo prowled the deck, waiting for Jacques. Why should it matter to him if Danielle married Vincent Gauthier? he asked himself savagely. Hadn't he always known she would in the end? He should be thinking about business now. *Peste!* He had just passed up the perfect opportunity to withdraw from this insufferable, unwanted partnership. Carrying cargo went against his very grain. There was no excitement, no danger. Only the remote possibility that the *Magdalena* might run into one of a dwindling number of pirates on the high seas.

The privateer had to admit to himself that his decision was based on profit; there was almost as much money to be had in spices as in contraband. Two thousand dollars was a sizable investment, but he could easily triple, even quadruple it on this one voyage—if he could raise it. His credit was good with many of New Orleans's solid citizens, but time was short.

"How was our friendly harbormaster?" Arturo greeted his first mate the moment he trudged up the gangplank.

"As charming as ever, him," Jacques answered, uncharacteristically wry. "He says we can berth here only until Saturday when the *Delta Maid* is due from Pensacola."

"That is enough time, if we take on cargo Friday and sail Friday night."

"That will take some arranging," the Baratarian fretted.

"*Oui,* but it is not impossible. Right now, tell Felix to heat some bathwater, will you? Whether we sail to Morocco at all depends on the work I do ashore tonight."

Still damp from his bath and clad in only a pair of trousers, Arturo lit the lantern above the table and counted the money in his small chest: three hundred dollars. To turn into two thousand, with luck. Fortunately, vingt-et-un had always been his lucky game.

Jacques rapped softly at the door and opened it. Sniffing the moist air, he grinned. "That is you, Turo? You smell like a two-dollar whore, yes."

"You have never had two dollars for a woman in your life," the captain growled good-naturedly.

"If I did, I would spend it for a couple of one-dollar ones," Jacques retorted mildly. The big Baratarian reached around the door to pluck a shirt from the pegged rack and held it toward Arturo. "There is, er, someone waiting to see you, *capitaine.*"

Frowning, Arturo accepted the shirt and pulled it on as Jacques disappeared from view for an instant to beckon the visitor.

"*Merci,* you are kind to see me, *capitaine,*" said the graceful young black woman, having waited to speak until the door had closed behind her. Her voice was low and modulated, and it reminded Arturo of someone else.

"My pleasure, *mam'selle,*" he answered slowly, staring at the woman in open curiosity. She was familiar, but for a moment he could not place her. Suddenly it came to him. "You—you are Danielle Valmont's maid—the one she freed."

"*Oui,* my name is Lydie, *m'sieur,*" she explained. She took the seat Arturo offered and continued, "Mam'selle Dani would be angry if she knew I was here, but I had to talk to you. I do not know what to do. You must help her.''

''Help her?'' The man nearly hooted with laughter. ''The last time I helped your mistress, she slapped my face. The last time I saw her, she nearly unmanned me. Why doesn't her fiancé help her?'' he sneered as an afterthought.

''Her fiancé?'' The girl seemed puzzled, but Arturo refused to be taken in.

''Do not bother to deny it,'' he ordered harshly as he paced the tiny cabin. ''I heard Gauthier plans to marry her, and soon.''

''Just because he plans to marry *la petite maîtresse* does not mean she plans to marry him,'' Lydie protested indignantly. ''Dani has no fiancé, *capitaine*. She has no one.''

The pacing stopped and Arturo came to sit in the chair across from Lydie.

''I have offered to take care of her for a while,'' the girl went on. ''I am good with a needle and have taken a position at Madame Lambert's dress shop. But, even after all she has done for me, Mam'selle Danielle will not allow me to help her. I think it is because she knows I wish to buy the freedom of my . . . of Hercule, the man I love,'' she whispered shyly.

''I have a little money,'' Arturo offered, his voice quiet now.

''Do you think she would take it? *Non, m'sieur.* She is proud and will not accept charity from anyone. It was all I could do to make her take the mourning gown I made for her.''

''What are her plans then?''

''She says she will find a position. But she is pale and tired, *m'sieur,* and the spirit seems to have left her. I fear she will be ill. She cannot even weep.''

''I do not know what you expect me to do,'' Arturo said sighing. ''She made it clear the last time I saw her that she wanted nothing more to do with me.''

''A woman can change her mind,'' she urged. ''I thought that since she has no protector, perhaps you . . .''

''And who will protect me from her?'' the man asked sourly, remembering the force of her rejection that moonlit night several weeks ago.

''I am sorry,'' Lydie muttered, tears in her eyes, as she collected herself to leave. ''I was wrong to come here. I thought you cared for her. I thought you would keep her from danger.''

"What danger?" His tone stayed her.

"Not really danger, *capitaine,* but please understand. My mistress is open and generous and she follows her heart. Some think she is wild. Now just because she went to her brother's funeral . . ."

"Not another funeral!" he groaned, recalling the gossip he'd previously heard about Danielle.

"Oui." Lydie nodded uncomfortably. "I went, too, but she did not know I was there. When I stood outside the cemetery, I heard the men talking among themselves. One *coquin* wants Mam'selle Danielle as his mistress and swears he will have her."

"What a surprise he's in for if he tries to lay a hand on her," Arturo muttered, amused at the thought in spite of himself.

"What did you say, *m'sieur?*"

"Never mind. Where is Danielle now?"

"After the auction at Félicité, M'sieur Soulé, the attorney, took her to his town house. He and his family are summering in the country. I worried for her there alone, so I have taken the maid's room for now. But soon we must both find new places to live. I will rent a room above the shop, but Danielle . . ." Her voice trailed off helplessly.

"Zut!" the captain muttered to himself as he considered the situation.

Zut, indeed, Lydie thought, but wisely she remained silent. Let the footloose privateer feel responsible for Dani, for in a way he was. He had made her fall in love with him. Lydie knew it even if Danielle did not.

"I do not know what I can do," Arturo said hoarsely after a long silence. "She will not accept my money. I do not even know if she will agree to see me before I must sail. But I swear this to you, whatever protection Danielle will allow me to give her, I will give."

"That is all I ask, *m'sieur.*" Lydie smiled wanly and rose. "You will work it out between you, I know."

"Work it out or fight it out," he muttered bleakly as the door swung closed behind his departing guest.

In the gaming rooms of the Orleans Ballroom that evening, Arturo played cards distractedly, made several lucky wagers and raked in his winnings. His mind was not on the game, but fortune was with him.

At last he returned wearily to the ship and deposited his winnings in his small chest. Despite his fatigue, he was restless. The sultry night did not help and music came faintly from the taverns along the waterfront. At last he removed the fine jacket he had worn earlier, donned a rough vest and a brace of pistols and set out toward El Reposo.

The night sky overhead flared with the sudden jagged bolts of heat lightning common in the height of summer. Thunder rumbled distantly. It was odd, the captain reflected as he strode along the levee: he had grown up among the taverns and brothels and had fought to leave them, but now the waterfront beckoned him. Outside of his ship, it was the only home he had ever known until he bought Désir du Coeur. To stay in that gracious plantation house someday was indeed his heart's desire, but he could not afford to live there yet.

As Arturo turned down the narrow street toward the tavern, he noticed a knot of people gathered outside one of the saloons. Jacques detached himself from the group and met his captain with a worried frown. "Turo, we have some trouble, us."

"What now?" he asked wearily.

"Hector" was the gloomy answer.

"What? Another fight?"

"His last one." Jacques nodded to where the body of Arturo's crewman was being borne away by an undertaker's wagon.

"Damn, I knew this would happen one day. He was a good sailor, but he loved a brawl too much. Since he had no family, I will see that he is buried." Arturo sighed. "You must find a replacement for him."

"That will not be easy on such short notice, *capitaine.*"

"Do what you can. We need a quick hand on the halyard."

"We may find one with the help of *le bon Dieu,*" Jacques intoned dubiously, "but, me, I will help by spreading the word." The big Baratarian lumbered away to search the bars for recruits.

Arturo paused on the rough banquette outside his mother's tavern. Indoors, it would be stifling, the heat of the summer night intensified by lamps on every table and a crude chandelier that hung from bare rafters. Magdalena did not skimp on candles or oil, for she liked to see what her unpredictable clientele was going to do before they did it.

When the captain entered the crowded barroom, the stale smells of smoke and beer and unwashed bodies hit him in a wave. Juan, Magdalena's eldest brother, was working behind the bar, the ends of his waxed mustache drooping in the heat. On the stage at the far end of the room, Arturo's other uncles were playing music with varying levels of enthusiasm. Emilio and Alejandro listlessly strummed guitars while Mateo pumped a squeeze box energetically, sweat pouring down his round face. The product of their endeavor, an inharmonious melody that they might or might not finish together, was nearly drowned out by hoarse voices of El Reposo's customers and the shrill laughter of their women.

Arturo ordered a drink, visiting with Juan for a moment, then found a seat beside a window away from the worst of the press and the noise. His problem had not disappeared with company, and he needed to think. What was he to do about Danielle Valmont?

Jack Lynch appeared, a glass of rye clutched in his hand and an unctuous smile on his ravaged face. "A word with you, Cap'n?"

"If it is brief," the privateer agreed inhospitably. He still had no proof Lynch had robbed him, but he didn't like the scrawny man with his murky eyes.

"Brief enough. A business proposition." The man slouched uninvited, on the bench across from Arturo and hunched over his drink. "Don't know if you heard about Yves Valmont."

"I heard," Arturo answered curtly.

"Well, he left more debts than money. Creditors got his bank account an' there ain't nothin' left fer those of us holdin' his IOUs from the gamin' tables."

"What does that have to do with me?" The captain watched him through hooded eyes.

"Don't tell me Valmont didn't owe you. He owed ever'one he ever played cards with." Lynch smiled scornfully. "Anyhow, I come up with a way for us to git some of our money back. We jest got to work together. Your part is easy. Lemme tell you what you do.''

The privateer did not know whether to be amused or annoyed by the man's audacity. He was about to refuse the proposal brusquely when Lynch was jostled by a drunken sailor.

Whirling, the American drew a pearl-handled pocket pistol from inside his jacket and thrust it roughly under the sailor's chin. "Why don't you watch what you're doin'?" he snarled.

"S-sorry. S'accident," the other man mumbled apologetically. Holding his head stiffly erect, he crossed his eyes and blinked stupidly down at the small man who held the gun.

"Don't let it happen again," Lynch barked. "I've killed men fer less."

While Lynch bullied the bigger man, he did not notice Arturo's eyes narrow, their characteristic twinkle gone. That pistol. It was the one the bandit had used the night he was robbed. He had been right all along; Jack Lynch had robbed him.

For an instant, he thought with relish of breaking the scrawny bastard in half. But Magdalena did not tolerate fights in her tavern, and there was a better way to strike back at the greedy little American. Lynch spoke of recovering his losses? Well, Arturo De Leon would recoup his, as well, and have a fine revenge.

"What exactly is your plan?" the privateer prompted nonchalantly when Lynch sat down again.

"Waal, Valmont's sister—"

"The girl had nothing to do with Yves's gambling debts," Arturo protested.

"Don't make no never mind. She kin still help us git our money back . . . 'less yer squeamish 'bout a bit of kidnappin'."

"Who would pay a ransom? She is alone in the world."

"All the more reason no one'd miss 'er if she up an' disappeared," Lynch argued craftily. "We don't need no ransom. The way I figger it is, I grab 'er an' bring 'er to yer ship. I ain't greedy, so you pay me two hundred dollars on delivery an' our dealin's are over. Then you take the gal an' sell 'er as a whore

r a bondwoman at yer next port. She's purty an' she'll bring
a good price.''

"I see," Arturo drawled dangerously.

"So I git my money," Lynch concluded, "you make a
profit, an' you an' me an' the Valmonts'll be square. What d'ye
think?"

His brow knit with thought, Arturo seemed to study the
proposal. If he refused, Lynch might try his scheme with
someone else. If he left the girl behind, someone else might
decide to kidnap her. Lynch was not the only unsavory character to whom Yves had owed money. Besides, there was the
roué who planned to make her his mistress....

Somehow Arturo would have his revenge on Jack Lynch,
but first he must remove Danielle from danger. The captain
did not permit himself to analyze his fragmentary plan. What
would happen after the *Magdalena* sailed, he did not consider, did not want to consider. He knew only that he must
move quickly.

"We can do business, M'sieur Lynch," the privateer agreed,
"if you bring the girl to my ship tomorrow night."

"Tomorrow? Wednesday?" The other man sputtered. "I
heard Foucher say you weren't sailin' till Friday."

"Jacques is not *capitaine* of the *Magdalena*. I have decided
we will sail sooner," Arturo answered coolly.

"Don't gimme much time, but you got yerself a deal,"
Lynch acquiesced, lifting his glass to seal the bargain.

Arturo returned the toast, but before he brought his glass to
his lips, he added casually, "One thing, Lynch. I do not accept damaged merchandise. That girl is from a fine Creole
family and is surely a virgin. I expect her to remain one in your
hands."

A flush crept up the American's skinny neck, but he drank
to their agreement. Damn that pirate! He had been of a mind
to sample the wares, but now he couldn't—not if he wanted
two hundred dollars from Arturo De Leon.

The next day, a sweating crew toiled on the pier, which
seemed to shimmer in the heat as the men loaded heavy barrels of molasses and bundled bales of tobacco leaves into the
Magdalena's hold. The harbormaster had not been happy
about the inconvenience of finding extra roustabouts, but his

protests lessened when a twenty-dollar gold piece was pressed into his hand.

By noon Montera had also been paid. Despite his reservations about doing business with Arturo, the Spaniard seemed relieved to accept his money. Worry lurked in his deep-set eyes when Jaime revealed that the *Clara Corey* out of Mobile was to sail for Africa next week, and like the *Magdalena* she was to bring back spices. Who knew what might happen on the open sea? Arturo's partner offered an extra percentage of the profits if the *Magdalena* returned before the *Clara Corey*. The South, indeed the entire country, was hungry for spices, and Jaime Montera planned to be there first.

At the dock, Arturo concluded some personal business and interviewed the only candidate Jacques had found to replace Hector. The skinny Cockney, named Harry Hinson, seemed competent, if not likable. Arturo planned to sail that very night, so Harry was signed to a seaman's berth.

Late in the afternoon when the cargo was loaded, the captain stood on the quarterdeck, his mind on the night to come. Going to his cabin, he hastily scribbled a note describing his plan and stuffed it in his pocket. Then he walked through the familiar, shadowed streets to El Reposo.

There was no one in the bar when he passed through on his way to the deserted kitchen. Juan dozed in the waning sun outside the back door, his white mustache flapping gently as he snored. Nearby, Alejandro, the youngest of Magdalena's brothers, practiced his knife throw. With a monotonous thump, his weapon found its mark again and again on a battered board propped against the levee.

"Turo, what are you doing here?" Alejandro greeted him. "I thought you sailors were always whoring when you came ashore."

"I tried," his nephew retorted, "but all the *putas* are in love with you."

The older man roared with laughter. Still slender with a thick mane of black hair and a devilish smile, Alejandro De Leon considered himself a ladies' man. "You flatter me," he said with a chuckle. "You must want something."

"You are too modest, *tío*," Arturo joked quietly, one eye on Juan, who muttered in his sleep and scratched at a mosquito bite.

"What is it you want?" Alejandro also lowered his voice to keep from waking his brother.

The privateer drew the envelope from his pocket. "Would you deliver this for me? I cannot trust any of the street urchins with it."

"*Sí.*" His uncle accepted it, staring at it with interest. "It is a good thing to read and write. I should learn someday. This message is *muy importante, sí*? Who is it for?"

"A Negro wench named Lydie."

"Aie-e-e, what a beauty! She was here this morning looking for you, *diablo*." Alejandro threw back his head and laughed aloud again. Juan started and opened one eye, glaring at him balefully. Then, without ever realizing his nephew was there, he settled himself more comfortably to continue his nap.

"What did she want?" Arturo asked urgently, drawing Alejandro to one side.

"She left the strangest message. She said she believes they are being watched." His tone made the statement a question. "This Lydie, she is one of yours?"

"No."

"Is she a whore at all?"

"She is a seamstress at Madame Lambert's."

"No matter. I like all kinds of women," the older man declared with a crooked smile so like his nephew's. "Do you think I could make her fall in love with me?"

"I think you would die trying," Arturo warned teasingly. "She loves someone already."

"A man can only try." Alejandro shrugged. "And what a way to die, eh, Turo?"

Catching sight of his mother in the kitchen, Arturo went inside to say goodbye, still laughing and shaking his head.

He returned to the *Magdalena* long after the sunset gun. Laden with cargo and riding low in the water, the ship rocked in her mooring, buffeted by the rising wind. The crew was aboard, quietly making ready to sail.

Worried mutters floated up to the captain on the quarterdeck as the sailors watched the sky uneasily. Dark clouds swirled overhead and no stars could be seen. The sky was rent occasionally by searing blue flashes of lightning, and thunder rumbled close at hand, the harbinger of an advancing storm. But Arturo lingered, awaiting a delivery from Jack Lynch.

A fine mist formed in the air, dampening his spirits as he wondered whether the American would appear before they had to sail. Finally, just after midnight, a wagon rolled along the dock and stopped. Lynch got down and hailed the ship.

"Evenin', Cap'n, think I could get some help with this here bundle?"

Immediately, the first mate and the man closest to the gangway descended and hoisted a bulky package from the back of the wagon. As he watched, the captain was grateful that its contents were not easily discernible.

"Put it in my cabin, Jacques," he ordered as the men came aboard. Ignoring the first mate's questioning look, he turned to the American and instructed so only he could hear, "Wait here, Lynch. I will settle with you after I see that she is all right."

When Arturo opened the door to allow Jacques to back into the cabin with the unwieldy burden, he was uneasy to discover the man supporting the other end was Harry Hinson, his newest crew member. Arturo did not understand the reason for his apprehension nor have time to analyze it before Harry panted, "Thankee, Cap'n. 'Ere's yer precious bundle, safe and sound."

They laid Danielle on the bunk and Arturo tugged at the rope that held a coarse cover around her unconscious body. The wrap fell back loosely to reveal her face. Her lips were bloodless and with her dark lashes etched against high, colorless cheekbones, the girl looked as if she were sculpted from alabaster.

"*Mon Dieu,* what has that *'méricain* rascal done to her?" the privateer noted anxiously. "She is not breathing."

Harry leaned close to her and sniffed. "The lady hain't dead, Cap'n. Smells like she's 'ad a bit of the poppy elixir. Nuffin' 'armful in hit. Just makes 'er breathin' shallowlike for a time. Hit'll get deeper when she's closer to wakin' up."

"*Très bien.*" Arturo recovered his composure. "Carry on."

Jacques waited until the little Englishman had gone before urning to his captain. "Why have you brought this girl here, uro?" he asked.

"To save her life, *mon ami*," the captain answered grimly.

"From the Kaintock? He is a bad one, him."

"*Oui.* Make ready to sail as soon as I give the word."

"We are taking them with us?" The Baratarian seemed uzzled.

"Only the girl."

A look of understanding crossed Jacques's unshaved face. Ah, *non*," he said, laughing, "you know what they say, uro, that if you wash your face in the Mississippi, you will me back again, yes. What will happen if this 'méricain takes whole bath?"

"I do not know," the captain answered with a wry smile, but we will not stay to find out, eh?"

Arturo emerged from below deck to find Jack Lynch pac- g just outside the passageway. The crew was assembled near e bow, out of earshot, awaiting their orders.

"'Bout time," the American greeted him. He did not no- e when Jacques went forward to carry out Arturo's com- ands.

"My apologies for taking so long," the captain said mock- gly.

"She to yer likin'?" Lynch asked with a leer. "Heerd y'er ht fond of the gals. Thought mebbe you were figgerin' on ether to keep 'er fer yerself."

"You never know." Arturo's answer was quiet, but it rang h steel. "Now it is time to settle with you."

"That's what I've been waitin' fer."

'It is what I have been waiting for, as well, M'sieur nch . . . for some months now," the other man said danger- sly.

or the first time, Lynch seemed to recognize the menace in privateer's manner. Involuntarily, he retreated a step. 'hat're you talkin' about, De Leon?" His murky eyes, wide h foreboding, were locked on the big man. He did not no- the sailors bringing the gangplank aboard.

"Do you not remember the night we met?" The buccaneer's eyes were two chips of cold blue flint.

"Can't say that I do." Lynch emitted a ragged laugh, desperate to appear cool. Guardedly, slowly, his hand moved toward the inside of his jacket, his action illuminated by a jagged flash of lightning.

"Surely you have not forgotten." The privateer's voice was low and threatening, nearly obliterated by a clap of thunder as a torrential storm broke over the city. "It was at a card game. You left early. I was robbed later that night by a masked man."

Arturo's hand shot out and gripped the other man's wrist in a viselike hold, causing him to drop the small pistol he had pulled from his pocket. Huge drops of rain spattered the deck where the little gun lay.

"A masked man shot at me with a gun quite like that one," he continued relentlessly as the ship rocked and the wind howled in the rigging. "In fact," he concluded grimly, "it was that one."

"Y'er crazy. Jes' settle with me an' lemme be on my way," Lynch blustered. He attempted to wrench his arm from Arturo's hold, blinking rapidly to clear rain from his eyes.

The captain was also dripping, but unaffected. "Indeed, we must settle," he said, almost pleasantly. "Let me see, you took from me five hundred dollars, *oui?* And I owe you two hundred dollars. Tell me if that is not right. I was never good with numbers. So I propose to take Danielle Valmont and call us even."

"I don't call that even," the American sputtered.

"No? Then this is my last offer. I take the girl, you keep your life. Cast off," Arturo shouted suddenly over his shoulder.

As the *Magdalena* drifted on the current, the privateer dragged Lynch to the rail where the increasing distance between the ship and the pier could be fully appreciated. "I will give you more of a chance than you gave me, *m'sieur,*" he said coldly, bending the other man forcefully to look at the muddy water churning below. "If you jump for the dock now, you might make it. If not, beware the undertow. The Mississippi is a treacherous river and takes many lives...."

* * *

A short distance down the levee, Lydie clutched Arturo's note tightly in her hand and drew her cloak tighter against the wind-whipped rain. She watched the *Magdalena* disappear into the night and hoped with all her heart that she had done the right thing.

Chapter Seven

The rain-washed wind was with the *Magdalena* as she glided out of the pass at the mouth of the Mississippi toward the sunrise. The trim brigantine's figurehead, a Spanish lady, peered through the spray, a smile on her red lips, as the bow beneath her sliced through the blue water of the Gulf of Mexico. A painted white mantilla draped over her blue-black hair and yellow hoops in her ears, the elegant carving gazed out at the world through turquoise eyes, inviting new adventure.

The fury of last night's storm was a memory as the sails filled and billowed in the wind. Against the rose and gold of the dawn, gulls circled overhead. Soon, even the birds dropped back, leaving the ship to dodge small coastal islands.

Arturo stood on the main deck, relishing the salt tang of the breeze and the aroma of freshly brewed coffee, which reached him from the galley. He was glad to be under way. Being at sea could almost make a man forget his worries.

The captain watched his crew on the deck below as they braced the yards on the foremast. Skillful sailors, they had sailed together for so long that they worked as a single graceful unit.

Jacques joined him and, for a moment, they were silent. Then the big Baratarian, his eyes fixed on Harry Hinson, muttered darkly, "I do not like him, Turo."

"Nor I, *mon ami*," the captain said, sighing as his newest crewman clambered up the rigging in front of them, "but we were lucky to find him. If only Hector had not run into someone better with a knife than he was."

"*Oui,* poor Hector, *Dieu* give him rest," Jacques murmured. He made the sign of the cross upon his tattooed chest, then returned to the original subject. "But this Harry, *capitaine,* he seemed pleased when we brought the girl aboard. He said you must agree with him, yes, that females are better cargo than tobacco or molasses."

"He told the crew this?"

"*Non,* but they know there is a woman aboard, Turo."

"What else did he have to say?"

"That the girl is pretty so she will bring a good price from a bordello. Me, I told him to keep his thoughts to himself, for this woman is under your protection."

"*Très bien,*" Arturo muttered, his blue eyes darkening. "What sort of scoundrel is this Harry that he thinks we would sell her? You will observe him for me. I do not trust him."

"*Oui, capitaine,* I will. I placed him in my watch crew." With that reassurance, the faithful first mate departed.

Unscrupulous crew members were the least of his worries, Arturo reflected, although he was glad for Jacques's warning. The regular hands of the *Magdalena* were loyal to him. They were likely to settle with the troublesome little Cockney themselves.

The greater problem was the girl. Not only was the *Magdalena* ill equipped to carry a female passenger, but the men were superstitious, opposed to having a woman aboard at all. Arturo could not help but agree with them. Danielle Valmont had been nothing but trouble to him. He would never have brought her aboard if it had not been necessary. And now that she was here, he was not sure what to do with her. There would be time enough to figure it out, he thought bleakly, for he might be forced to take her with him all the way to Tangier. If, as Montera said, the trade run was to be a race with the *Clara Corey,* he would have no time for unnecessary stops.

Staring moodily at the disappearing coastline, Arturo's thoughts returned to his cabin where Danielle slept,. She was lovely, and he had always had a weakness for beautiful women. But he could not forget—nor forgive—her treatment of him when they last met. At the Parkers' ball, he had fought for her

and she had taken sides against him. Later when he had crept
to her room like a love-struck idiot, she had ejected him in a
most unfeeling manner. He did not know whether he was an-
grier at her or at himself. He still smarted at the memory,
though it had happened weeks ago. What had possessed him
to come up with this ill-conceived plan?

As the ship skimmed over the open sea, the captain strode
toward the hatch that opened under the quarterdeck. Accord-
ing to Harry's calculations, Danielle would awaken soon and
he wanted to be the first person she saw.

He told himself ruefully that she was going to be as angry as
a hive of hornets and all of her wrath was going to be directed
at him. They might as well have it out immediately. It would
be better that she knew straightaway who had taken her and
that she understood who was master of this ship. Once she was
over her ire, she could not help but be grateful when she realized he had saved her life. Although, as he paused outside the
door to his cabin, Arturo was forced to admit her gratitude was
not what he wanted.

Inside, Danielle slept a drugged, peaceful slumber. In contrast to her stiff mourning gown of unrelieved black, her face
looked pale and childlike in repose and her golden hair was in
disarray on the pillow. Gazing down on her, Arturo experienced a rush of irrational anger at the tenderness he felt; he
was supposed to be her protector, not her suitor!

Summoning his old resentments with effort, he tried to recall the edge of rancor in the girl's voice after he had kissed her
in the garden, tried to visualize her brown eyes snapping when
she had left him hanging on to a tree branch. But in his reverie, the man heard the sound of her laughter, was warmed by
her smile, tasted her lips. He wanted to stay angry at her, but
he could not, no matter how he tried.

Stroking her velvety cheek thoughtfully with the back of his
hand, Arturo knew what he would do about Danielle. When
the *Magdalena* finished her trading run, he would take her to
Tortuga. There he would install her on his plantation and there
she would stay, at least until they tired of each other.

She would be free from the dangers in New Orleans. She
would not face a life of penury or servitude; she would not
suffer the indignity of becoming a Creole scoundrel's mis-

tress. Through his intervention she had escaped the fate Jack Lynch had planned for her: indenture, prostitution, exile in a harem or worse. He would keep the girl beside him, protect her with his able sword arm, shower her with riches. He would see she had only the best—and the best was Arturo De Leon. How could she hate him for that?

The privateer prowled the tiny cabin, engrossed in his plans. It would not be easy. It might take a long time to win her, but at least he would have her with him at Désir du Coeur. He had never wanted a woman as he did Danielle. And it was proving to be a novel experience.

Arturo's fantasies fled when the girl's eyelids fluttered. When she groaned and rolled heavily onto her side, he moved to the foot of the bed and watched her silently, giving her time to rouse slowly, steeling himself for her wrath.

Suddenly, Danielle drew a sharp breath and her eyes flew open. Blinking several times rapidly, she surveyed the small, unfamiliar room, sluggishly taking in the details from the swaying bunk.

A rich Persian carpet covered the wooden floor. Closed cabinets lined the wall opposite the bunk where she lay. They stretched from floor to ceiling, except for a small space in the center where a tiny window was placed. Below the short blue velvet drapes, a trunk with pillows carelessly tossed on its leather lid, served as a window seat. A massive square table, hewn of honey-colored oak, and two sturdy chairs were positioned in the center of the room under a gimballed brass lantern, suspended overhead.

The entire room seemed to be moving, she thought dully. It creaked and rocked and would lull her back to sleep. Suddenly, her eyes narrowed suspiciously and she shifted on the narrow bunk. Where was she? she wondered with heightened interest as her head began to clear.

She lifted herself on one elbow and immediately clutched at her pounding head. Licking her dry lips, she gazed around. The room did, indeed, seem to be in motion, and her stomach somersaulted three times without a pause. Giving a pitiful moan, the girl lay down once more.

"Bonjour." Arturo stepped into view. "I thought you would sleep all day."

The girl's eyes rolled balefully toward him, but she did not attempt to lift her head from the pillow again. "You," she groaned accusingly. "Where am I?"

"Aboard the *Magdalena,* bound for Morocco."

"Morocco? That is impossible!" she shrieked. Unmindful of her discomfort, she sat bolt upright. The last pin holding her ruined chignon dropped to the floor with a soft tinkle, and her hair poured like molten gold to her shoulders.

"I am afraid it is entirely possible." Sympathetically, Arturo held a tin cup toward her. "Here, drink this. I would give you something stronger, but I am told water will make you feel better."

She took it and drank deeply, grimacing when the cold liquid hit her queasy stomach. *"Mon Dieu,"* she groaned again, "you have poisoned me."

"Tsk tsk, such language from a young lady," Arturo chided. "You were not poisoned, only given a little too much essence of poppy. I am told it will wear off soon and you will be as good as new. You are not going to be sick, are you?"

"No," she insisted, her white lips set tightly. When her nausea passed, she slumped against the pillow at her back and glared at him. "We are not really on our way to Morocco, are we?"

"Oui, since last night."

"You kidnapped me?" she uttered incredulously.

"I did not *kidnap* you," he contradicted. "I simply—"

"You simply had one of your men do it," she cut in so certainly he did not bother to argue. "You must take me back."

"Alas, I cannot." Feigning a compassionate sigh, Arturo sat on the edge of the bed and waited expectantly for her next move.

"Then put me ashore at the next port."

"I cannot do that, either."

"I will not go with you." She shook her head, wincing at the throb in it. "I will escape at the first opportunity."

"In northern Africa? I think not," he contended mildly, taking her hand in his. "And while we are at sea, where would you go?"

"What is it you want? Money?" the girl demanded, furiously snatching her hand away. "Send word to Monsieur

Soulé and he will pay, I know it. He was my family's lawyer and he is a good man.''

"I do not want money, *cher*."

"What then?" But before he could answer, Danielle's brown eyes, smoldering with rage, met his. She drew herself up stiffly and, without moving, seemed to increase the distance between them a hundredfold. "How dare you?" she gritted. "Just because I would not run away with you when you burst into my room in the middle of the night, just because I did not swoon or allow you to take the uncouth liberties you wished."

"May I remind you, when I made these uncouth gestures, you flirted and teased and matched me kiss for kiss?" He had thought he was ready to face her, but he was unprepared for the sting he felt at her words. Leaning toward her, he crooned sarcastically, "Why not just admit it, *ma petite?* You are just as fascinated by me as I am by you."

"Oh-h-h, your conceit is intolerable!" she cried, shoving him away. "I cannot imagine what makes you think you can kidnap me. Even though I no longer have the protection of a family, do you think the abduction of a Valmont will go unnoticed? My reputation has suffered some indignities at your hand, *capitaine,* but I would not have believed this—even of you."

"Indignities? I might tell you of indignities." Arturo sprang to his feet and towered over her, angered by the venom in her voice and the condemnation in her eyes. "You have caused me nothing but trouble, Danielle. Yet, when I heard Yves was dead, I came for you, to help you."

"You help by abducting me?" she scoffed. "What an agreeable excuse for the crime you have committed against me."

"I have committed no crime against you yet, although murder is not out of the question," Arturo suggested grimly, his temper growing short. He yanked the girl from the bunk so she stood in front of him and gripped her shoulders tightly. "Listen to me, damn it," he snapped, "there is nothing for you in New Orleans anymore. I am offering you a new life."

"I do not want a new life." She glared up at him, her chin lifted defiantly, her chest heaving in anger.

"*Mon Dieu,*, I never met such an unreasonable female. You have no money—"

"You know the saying, *monsieur,* poverty is not a sin, but a mighty inconvenience," she retorted coolly.

Arturo would not be deterred. "No money, no family, no husband, no prospect of one."

"That is not true," the girl protested hotly, attempting to wrench from his grip. "Vincent—"

"*Oui.* I keep forgetting him. And so do you, from what I've seen," Arturo taunted, refusing to release her. "I suppose eventually you could marry Gauthier or someone like him, or be kept by him."

"I would not!" she gasped.

"Than what does it leave? Governess to someone else's brats? Is that what you want?"

"It would be preferable to abduction," she declared evenly. Abruptly, the tension left her and the girl sagged wearily. "I have been through a great deal recently. Why don't you tell me what your plans are for me and leave me alone?" She lifted her face to him heroically, obviously prepared for the worst.

Pitilessly, Arturo decided to oblige her. "There are several possibilities. But I seek the one which would suit you best. I can easily see you giving pleasure to a man. Do you think you would enjoy life in a brothel, *ma cher?* Or perhaps you would prefer the harem of some Oriental sultan? If neither of those appeal to you, you could become a bondwoman. You might even have a chance for marriage, to some boorish planter in the Indies. I can arrange it, if you do not wish to go with me."

"I am sure you can, but you cannot frighten me. I will not be your mistress," she maintained staunchly.

"Ever the haughty Creole belle, eh, Danielle? I do not remember asking you to be my mistress," he said flatly, his blue eyes glittering with displeasure, "but since you bring it up, it is not a bad idea." Entwining his fingers in her hair, he drew her head back and brought his mouth down on hers forcefully. This time there was no warmth or tenderness in his kiss, only savage passion.

Danielle struggled in his grasp but his arms tightened around her, locking her against his lean hard body. Determined the privateer would not have the acquiescence he sought, she stiffened and tried to pull away. Stubbornly, she clenched her teeth and refused to respond to his impassioned assault on her senses. She drew a shuddering breath and concentrated on resisting the languor that threatened to steal through her body if she let down her guard for the merest instant.

Suddenly Arturo released her, an odd expression in his eyes. "I will not force you, *cher,* but I feel sure you will come around to my point of view."

"I would die first," she snapped, reeling slightly without the support of his arms against the gentle roll of the ship.

"What a shame to choose death over the glorious adventure we would have together, you and I." He flashed her a shameless grin.

"Get out!" she screeched, her temper stretched to breaking. "Get out of my sight at once!"

Only when the big man ducked through the door, slamming it behind him, did he realize he had been chased from his own cabin.

"I will come back later for my things," he called through the panel as he locked the door. He did not actually think Danielle was foolish enough to throw herself overboard, but she might be stubborn enough to attempt it, just to prove her point. "I may unlock this door later, if you promise never to come topside unless I accompany you. Think about it while I am away." He winced when Danielle's cup hit the door in response.

She had behaved exactly as he had known she would, the man told himself with a conceited smile. She was furious and she resisted. But she would soon come to accept her fate, perhaps even to welcome it.

Until she did, he was willing to be patient. Unfortunately, it meant sleeping in the first mate's tiny cabin. As a result, Jacques would displace Falgout, the second mate, who would swing a hammock in the forecastle and grumble about the crew's snoring. But so went life aboard a ship. And after all, it was only for a few nights, Arturo reflected confidently, setting out to find Jacques and tell him of the new sleeping arrangements.

Locked in the cabin, the girl hunched, dry-eyed and miserable, on the bunk. The privateer's summary of her plight was correct. In the past month, she had lost her last living relative, her home and her freedom. Everything had been taken away...everything but dignity and honor. Although she did not know what would become of her, she knew two things certainly. She would never allow Arturo to make her cry. And she would never, never become his mistress.

Her resolution made, she realized her stomach was rumbling, not from seasickness but from hunger. She was always hungry in the morning, and she had missed dinner last night. Surely he did not intend to starve her into submission. It would take more than hunger to make her docile, she thought rebelliously.

She emptied the pocket of her skirt onto the table, hoping some forgotten scrap of food might be there. No sticky praline wrapped in crumpled paper, no broken crust of bread were to be found. But there was an olive wood comb, a carved ivory fan, even a small collection of coins. The money did not amount to much, but every cent could be useful as bribes.

Suddenly she remembered her mother's ring, one of the few possessions left to her. She had carried it in her pocket because it was not proper mourning attire. Arturo might be a kidnapper, she thought tartly, but he was not a thief. Surely he would not have stolen it. Digging deep into the pocket, she was relieved to find it. She slid it onto her finger and felt a little better.

Danielle smoothed the rumpled skirt of her dress and washed her face in a basin of tepid water. She searched for hairpins among the bedclothes, then looked around curiously. After she had freshened up, she would take her mind off her hunger by exploring her new quarters.

Behind the short drapery, she discovered a porthole. A narrow section of deserted deck was visible through the round glass, its foot-worn planking edged by a carved railing. Beyond the railing, all that could be seen was the shimmering blue water stretching to the horizon where it met the cloudless sky. No sandy coastline, no island broke the measureless expanse Danielle surveyed.

Carefully, she adjusted the brass fittings on the rim of the porthole, feeling the vibration of the ship in motion as she swung it open to admit a slight breeze. On tiptoe, she thrust her face near the opening and listened to muffled voices, floating from the forward section of the ship where the crew labored at the sails. Craning her neck, she discovered that her cabin was located on the starboard side of the ship about halfway back the main deck. But she could discern little of the activity taking place near the bow because the cabin section seemed to be sunk into the deck and the foredeck was even lower.

Stepping back, Danielle gauged the width of the porthole appraisingly, then looked down at her willowy body. It would be tight, but the opening was large enough that she might be able to squeeze through if she took off all her petticoats. For whatever good that might do, she reflected despairingly.

A lilting youthful voice echoed her thoughts. "Wouldn't be tryin' to go out that porthole if I were ye, miss. 'Twould avail ye nothin'. We're already well out to sea."

The girl whirled to find an untidy adolescent watching her merrily from the doorway. His wrists and ankles protruded from faded outgrown clothing. A mop of unruly red hair framed his broad, likable face, and his blue eyes sparkled as a brigade of freckles marched unevenly across his turned-up nose.

"Yer breakfast, miss," the lad announced officiously, flourishing a tray covered with a towel. "Patrick Ahern O'Reilly, at yer service."

"*Merci,* Monsieur O'Reilly." Danielle watched as he set the tray down. A ring of keys, hanging from his bony wrist, jangled with every move.

"Pat, if ye please, ma'am. I'm but a lowly cabin boy."

"Sit down, Pat," she invited, attacking her breakfast with zeal. "My name is Danielle Valmont."

"I know." The boy's mind was not on the conversation. He sank into a chair and incredulously observed as the girl began to devour a large plate of ham, grits and fluffy scrambled eggs. "Beggin' yer pardon, Miss Valmont," he interrupted delicately. "Lord knows, I admire a woman with an appetite. Me own mother, bless 'er, is a fine eater. But 'twould be to yer advantage to slow down a bit and enjoy those eggs. They're the last y'er likely to see till we anchor in foreign waters—unless the cap'n is inclined to give ye his. The *Magdalena* carries a hen or two, but if they're not good layers, they find their way to Felix's cooking pot about halfway out, much to their obvious distress.''

"You are right," she agreed ruefully, offering the boy one of her biscuits. "I was just so hungry. I missed dinner last night."

"But 'twas so late when ye were brought aboard, the cap'n said ye weren't hungry."

She watched the boy eagerly split the biscuit, dribble a spoonful of honey over it and pop the entire thing into his mouth.

"What else did the *capitaine* tell you?" she asked casually, eyeing the keys.

"Well, Cap'n De Leon is not one to kiss and tell, mind ye, but rumors have a way of gettin' around," Pat said through the remainder of his biscuit.

"What rumors?"

"Just that ye've prevailed 'pon the cap'n to spirit ye away from that horrid drunken beast yer family wishes ye to wed. An' that ye find our cap'n a great deal to yer likin'." He looked to her confidently for confirmation.

"That despicable liar! If I wished to be here, why am I locked in this stuffy cabin?" Danielle asked logically.

"Why, for yer own protection. 'Twould never do for a lady of quality to be roamin' around a ship of rough sailin' men. They're liable to forget themselves. Cap'n De Leon trusts only me to help care for ye. I'm just about his most trusted man, ye know—next to Jacques."

"And who is Jacques?" she asked nonchalantly, pressing another biscuit on the boy, hoping for more information from him.

"Jacques Foucher, the first mate, a great huge Baratarian," he told her, slathering the biscuit with honey. "He's been with the cap'n nigh on seven years. They've seen some adventurin', those two."

"How did you come to be with Capitaine De Leon? Do you also seek adventure?" Danielle settled back to listen to his story while secretly pocketing the fruit knife from her tray.

"No, ma'am, 'twas nothing so excitin'." Pat wished he had a more glamorous story to tell. "Me brother and me went to

New Orleans to work on the canals. After three months, Kevin died from dysentery. I knew that diggin' ditches was not what I wanted in life, so I struck out on me own. But Gus, the foreman, found me in a café at the waterfront and told me I couldn't be quittin' till I settled with the company store and paid for Kevin's buryin'. Ye never fully pay off a company store, ye know. Y'er better off indentured," he advised solemnly. "At least, ye can buy yer way free one day.

"Anyhow, I allowed I would pay...in cash made from honest wages soon as I got a job. Then Gus allowed 'twas not possible. With all that allowin', one thing led to another and he decided to take the payments out of me hide. He decided right in Cap'n De Leon's ear. The cap'n was tryin' to have a quiet dinner and all the bellowin' upset him considerable. So he suggested real civillike that Gus fight him, instead of me, and the winner get me services.

"Gus took to the idea of moppin' the floor with a Frenchie right away. He was even happier when the cap'n stood up. Gus loved to brawl and he was glad to fight another strappin' fellow.

"Anyway, when he went to take off his coat, the cap'n give him a boot in the family jewels and we both ran like hell, beggin' yer pardon, ma'am. And that's all 'twas to it."

"Ah, yes, I have seen Arturo De Leon fight before."

"Have ye now?" Pat looked interested, but he was distracted by duty. "Mayhap ye can tell me about it sometime, but I've tarried too long now as 'tis," he informed her importantly as he scooped up the tray. "The cap'n may be needin' me and I'm not of a mind to let him down."

"*Merci* for the food and the company, Pat," she said politely.

"'Twas nothin', miss," the boy mumbled, blushing. "Thank ye for the biscuits. I'm to tell ye to make yerself comfortable. 'Tis a fine feather bed ye'll enjoy in the cap'n's cabin, not like the forecastle where all we have are donkeys' breakfasts."

"Donkeys' breakfasts?" The girl looked mystified.

"Aye, straw mattresses." Pat grinned, pleased to teach her some of his knowledge of the ship. "The cap'n also said to tell ye there are books in that locker yonder if ye'd like to read."

When the cabin boy had gone, Danielle ransacked the room for a place to hide her stolen knife. A poor excuse for a weapon, it was tiny, with a flimsy blade, but it was the best she could do under the circumstances. Just having it made her feel better. If Arturo or anyone else tried to force himself on her, he would meet steel.

Danielle concealed the fruit knife in the space between the head of the bunk and hull and plumped the pillows over it. Then, going to the locker, she browsed through Arturo's library. The choice was limited: Bowditch's, *The American Practical Navigator,* two astronomy books and four novels. Finally, she selected a novel and settled down to read.

She was disappointed to find the book was a juvenile adventure story about a pirate of unlikely honor and derring-do. Leave it to Arturo to read such trash, she thought uncharitably. But she read it, if only to fill the hours, until her head nodded and the book slipped from her hands to the mattress beside her.

Danielle awakened when Arturo returned to the cabin for his belongings. She sat up and glared at him, but she did not speak.

"Ah, you are awake," he greeted her. Dragging a chair near the bunk, he sat down and looked at the book she had been reading. "One of my favorites, but is it suitable for a lady of gentle breeding?" he teased with a charming smile. "Besides, I thought refined ladies found it a detriment to be too well studied."

"The book is hardly educational, although I can see how it would appeal to you," she snapped.

Arturo's eyes were cold as he sat back rigidly. "Perhaps it appeals because I was eighteen before I learned to read it at all. I think it is wonderful to read—anything. I am the only one in my family who can."

He rose, knocking the chair aside with an angry swipe of his big hand. Danielle watched with cold satisfaction while the man gathered the ship's logbook and charts, navigation instruments and his shaving box, juggling them with an armload of clothing. Then he stomped toward the door, stringing shirts behind him as he went.

"Just when I think you are something other than a spoiled child, Danielle, you always prove me wrong," he pronounced with an air of wounded dignity before he slammed through the door and locked it behind him.

Furious, the girl jumped to her feet and began to pace. How dared he act as if he were the injured party, she fumed, after he had kidnapped her? She kicked the chair that blocked her path and sent it skidding heavily toward the table, nearly breaking her toe. In the next instant, she retrieved the chair and positioned it with a thud, so it faced the door. Then she sat down to wait.

Several hours passed before a key was heard in the lock, but the girl leaped to her feet, primed for another skirmish with Arturo. Pat entered alone, juggling a tray.

"Brought yer lunch, miss," he announced cheerfully. "Cook caught a fine flounder for ye."

"Where is the *capitaine,* Pat?"

"Topside. And his face is black as thunder. Did you two have a lovers' spat?" the boy asked shyly.

"No, we did not have a lovers' spat!" she yelled, regretting it immediately when the cabin boy backed hastily toward the door. "Wait, Pat, I am sorry, I should not have shouted at you. Would you tell Capitaine De Leon that I would like to see him?"

"I doubt he'll come, miss. He's in a foul mood, to be sure."

"Then tell him this for me...."

"Er, Cap'n De Leon, sir."

Glowering ominously, Arturo sought the source of the hesitant voice.

Pat grimaced ruefully at the fearsome figure glaring down from the quarterdeck, but he swallowed bravely and plunged into his message. "Cap'n, Miss Valmont requests yer presence in her cabin."

"*Her* cabin?" the man roared at the unfortunate courier. Pat retreated even though he was not within reach of the irate man.

"I'm just tellin' ye what she said, sir," he stammered.

"I know." Arturo controlled his voice with effort; his knuckles showed white as he gripped the railing in anger. "Tell Mam'selle Danielle that I do not wish to see her." He dismissed the boy and was surprised when he made no move to leave. "Is there something else?"

"Aye, Cap'n," Pat said reluctantly. With an uneasy glance toward Narcisse, the helmsman, who was listening with interest, he stepped out and lowered his voice so only Arturo could hear. "The lady said to tell ye if ye do not come, she will commence screamin' and she'll scream until she has the attention of yer crew. Then she will tell them, in great detail, how you had her kidnapped and brought aboard against her wishes."

"She will, will she?" Arturo's words hung on the wind as he leapt down the ladder to the main deck. He stomped toward the cabins with the anxious boy dogging his steps.

"Ye'll be wantin' the keys, sir," Pat panted, shoving the burdensome key ring toward the man. Then, with the sagacity of youth, the cabin boy darted astern, out of harm's way.

Danielle waited for Arturo, her wrathful speech ready. She heard his pounding footsteps as he approached and his muffled curse as he fumbled with the key. But the force with which he threw open the door startled her; she jumped back as it bounced off the wall and swung wildly on its hinges. The privateer hovered in the passageway, his icy-blue eyes locked on the girl's angry brown ones as they exchanged glare for glare.

"There is something you need?" he prompted impatiently.

"Oui," she snapped. "When are you going to let me out? Since you will not be persuaded to put me ashore, you cannot keep me locked in this stuffy cabin."

"The *Magdalena* is my ship," he replied tersely, "and I can do anything I wish aboard her. You would do well to remember that."

"*Très bien,* you are the master of the ship," she conceded, "but earlier you said that I could go out on deck if you accompanied me."

"That was before you insulted me—again."

With effort, Danielle maintained a moderate tone. "I must go out, *capitaine.* Surely you understand. I grew up outdoors, free, with the wind in my hair."

"I grew up in a barroom, *mam'selle*. Poor, with a mop in my hand," Arturo countered coldly. "A person can become accustomed to anything. I suggest you get used to this cabin." With those words, he turned on his heel and left his furious captive to ponder her fate.

Chapter Eight

Danielle clung to her pitching bunk, her face buried in a pillow, and prayed fervently for the day when her feet would touch solid ground again.

The *Magdalena*'s first three days at sea had been uneventful, almost pleasant, until a squall was sighted in the distance. Three blasts on the first mate's whistle brought all hands on deck. Hastily, the sails were reefed and the course was altered. The *Magdalena* scudded bravely before the approaching storm in an attempt to outrun it.

Chasing the little brigantine across the water, the gale overtook her, engulfing her, blotting out the sun. Blinding bolts of blue-white lightning scored the sky and explosive claps of thunder rolled across turbulent water. All day and well into the night, the *Magdalena* was awash, mercilessly tossed on white-capped waves as sheets of rain pelted the decks and washed out the scuppers.

In the captain's quarters, Danielle could faintly hear the shouts of the crew over the creak of the timbers and the howl of the wind, as they fought to keep the ship afloat and on course. She watched with growing consternation as foam-flecked water crept under her locked door.

Looking for something constructive to occupy her mind, the girl hurriedly removed her shoes and stockings and waded through the now ankle-deep flood to rescue Arturo's small library. Hauling the books from the bottom shelf of his locker, she placed them on the bed, out of harm's way.

Although she dreaded the utter darkness it would bring, Danielle extinguished the lantern for safety's sake. Lying on the bunk, the books gouging her, she was protected from the heavy furniture, which careened past her and halted with a thump against the bulkhead. The tinkling of glass told her Arturo's shaving mirror had fallen and been dashed against the washstand. Although she was not superstitious, Danielle shut her eyes tightly, willing away the bad luck. Certain their fates were in the hands of God, she prayed for either safety or sudden death.

"Are you all right, miss?" Pat's concerned voice came from nearby. She had not heard the boy let himself into the cabin. Lurching with every roll of the ship, he staggered to where she lay. When she lifted her head to look at him, she was blinded at first by the feeble light of the lantern he carried. But she was comforted to see his kindly face as he knelt beside her bunk. His oilskin was wet and dripping, adding more water to the flood.

"I am . . . as well as can be expected. *Merci.*" She raised herself on one elbow and summoned a brave smile. But her eyes widened as a crash came from below and the ship seemed to shudder. "We are not going to sink, are we?"

"Not in this puny squall," Pat assured her with a cocky grin. "We're not even bailin' water. Cargo's shiftin' a bit in the hold and that's not good, but we'll redistribute the load when we're through this weather. Never fear, the cap'n's brought us through worse. Even hurricanes."

"Ah, your *capitaine,*" she gritted, "he locks me in his cabin, sails me into a storm and leaves me to die."

"He tried to avoid the storm," the cabin boy defended his hero, steadying himself as the ship yawed and was corrected. "And y'er not really goin' to die. 'Tis just what ye wish when the seasickness has got ye. 'Sides," he argued tactlessly, "no matter what ye say now, ye wouldn't really like for him to see ye all green-faced and sickly, would ye?"

The girl tried to frame a retort, but could not. Instead she sank onto the mattress and sniffed disdainfully. Pat appeared not to notice as he went back out into the tempest.

After the worst of the storm was over, Danielle rose, relit the lamp and surveyed the waterlogged cabin. With a sigh, she tucked her skirt into her waistband and set to work, replacing the damaged mirror on its peg as she scoffed at her earlier fears. Then she managed to roll up the sodden rug and mop water from the floor with a towel, wringing it into a light wooden bucket that floated away each time she released it. Mentally, she rehearsed the tongue-lashing she would give the captain when he came to see about her.

As the night advanced, the girl dried the bulkheads and set the cabin aright. When the pale dawn broke, she finally went to bed. But for a long time, she did not sleep, sulking instead with no way to vent her anger.

She had not seen Arturo since he stormed from the cabin her first day aboard the *Magdalena,* although she knew he slept just across the passageway. Each night she heard his footsteps when he retired and watched the latch as he made sure the door was locked.

The next morning Danielle did not even catch a glimpse of the man through the open door when Pat and Jacques carried the soggy rug out to dry in the sun. Relieved to find there was little damage, due largely to the girl's efforts, Jacques flashed a respectful glance in her direction and left the cabin silently.

That afternoon, at Danielle's request, Pat furnished a cake of beeswax and she removed the water marks from the furniture. She persuaded him to bring water to wash the bed linens and set him to polishing the brass lantern over the table. By evening, the cabin shone and the pleasing odor of beeswax replaced the former mustiness. Unaccustomed even to simple household chores, the exhausted girl fell into her bunk and slept deeply after her labors.

If Arturo was aware of the changes wrought in his quarters, she did not know because Pat did not say. Since she awoke aboard ship, the cabin boy had been almost her only visitor. She was always glad to see him and invited him to share her meals. While they ate, he talked, relaying news of the outside world, limited though it was aboard a ship at sea. When accounts of deck work and cabin duties wore thin, he brought tears of laughter to Danielle's eyes with his reports on an endless domino game between the second mate and the ship's carpenter. Pat seemed to enjoy her company, too, even when she put him to work, and was dejected when their project was finished and he could come again only when duty dictated.

When Danielle was not reading or playing solitaire with a dog-eared deck of cards she found in the locker, she paced the airless cabin, stopping frequently in front of the porthole in hopes of a breath of fresh air.

Sometimes when the girl perched on the window seat, she saw a scrawny old man near the gunwale at the stern. Even if he had not worn a stained, threadbare apron, she would have recognized him as the *Magdalena*'s cook from Pat's vivid description. Felix was no idler, the cabin boy insisted; he was sometimes pressed into service as sail maker or ship's doctor.

The cook was a grizzled scarecrow with a wooden leg, whose faded, oversize clothing dwarfed him as he hobbled along. His Adam's apple was the most prominent feature of his bony body; it jutted magnificently from a wrinkled neck, which was none too clean. Felix's skin was weathered and creased from years at sea and his pate shone brightly through his thinning hair. A bushy gray mustache almost obscured his tremulous mouth, the lips collapsing over toothless gums.

Although the galley was located after the cabins on the port side of the ship, he often came to the starboard railing to throw refuse into the sea and cast curious nearsighted glances toward Danielle's cabin. But he never came near the porthole and, although she could see him clearly, the girl could tell Felix was unable to distinguish her face in the shadowy opening.

She was sometimes seen by brawny crewmen passing along the main deck, but they shifted their eyes uncomfortably to avoid looking at the porthole. When Danielle asked the cabin boy about the crew's unwillingness to acknowledge her presence, he hedged before he answered her question.

"Truth is, ma'am, the men try not to see ye because they don't wish to. No offense to ye, but sailors are a superstitious lot. A woman aboard is bad luck. Though they're not sayin' it to the cap'n, they're not happy he brought ye aboard. I reckon they think that if they don't see ye, then ye ain't really here and cannot harm 'em."

"I would not harm them, even if I could," Danielle protested.

"I know that and ye know that, but they're a might unenlightened, ye understand."

She was forced to be satisfied with that answer, but the isolation wore on her. Confinement allowed too much time to think and to wonder what her fate would be. At times she wondered if anger at her abductor was the only thing that kept her from giving in to despair.

One morning, Danielle noticed Pat's elbow poking through the sleeve of his blue shirt. As a child, she had dodged Zeme's sewing lessons, so she had never been a skilled seamstress, but she was anxious for any activity. She suggested the cabin boy bring her a needle and thread and she would mend the tear for him.

When he returned at midday, wearing a red-checked shirt, which clashed drastically with his fiery hair, Pat brought a little embroidered sewing kit.

"This is lovely," the girl said, admiring the dainty satin case. "Where on earth did you find it?"

"Ye'd be amazed what ye'll find on the *Magdalena*. This gear belongs to Felix," Pat answered. "Cap'n brought it for him years ago from China. 'Twas a grand adventure he had and even grander to hear him tell about it. One day I'll have such stories to tell."

Taking advantage of his first chance for a visit since they had worked together, the boy trimmed and filled Danielle's lamp as an excuse to stay longer. When no one summoned him, he sat down to chat while she sewed. She pricked her fingers as often as the fabric while she drew the boy out. She was pleased for his company, but even more gratified by the information he imparted.

Although they were scarcely into the voyage, the cap'n was like a lion with a thorn in his paw, Pat gossiped. No one, not even Felix, who had known him all his life, had ever seen him this way. So far, everyone had the good sense to steer clear of him. Whether Arturo's condition was due to the strain of legitimate shipping or to having a woman aboard, even Jacques would not hazard a guess. The first mate grumbled that the passage to Morocco could not be fast enough for him, for it would be that much sooner they reached home.

When Danielle finished her awkward mending job, she examined it dubiously, but Pat was delighted. "Thank ye, Miss Danielle. Is there anything I can do for ye?"

"Indeed there is, Pat." She seized gratefully upon his offer. "I would like some water for bathing."

The boy looked incredulous. "Ye want to take a bath?"

"*Oui,* I haven't had a bath for nearly a week."

"Seems recent enough to me," he mumbled. "Well, I'll see what I can arrange. Maybe a sponge bath for ye, though. With the cap'n bein' so angry, I don't think he'll be willin' to lend ye his tub."

"His tub?"

"Aye. Cap'n De Leon has a fascination for bathing, too. I think it just come over him suddenlike in the Japans one time. Perhaps when he's over his fit of temper, I can talk him into lendin' it to ye. I've the gift of gab, ye know," he assured her, gathering up his shirt and Felix's sewing kit. "But this afternoon, ye'll have to make do with a bucket of hot water."

"Gladly, Pat. After a week of cold water in a basin, a whole bucket of hot water sounds wonderful," the girl agreed eagerly.

Pat returned later with heated saltwater for Danielle's bath. The adolescent boy seemed embarrassed because he knew its intended purpose. Mumbling to himself, he rolled back the carpet, positioned the broad-bottomed wooden bucket in the center of the waxed floor and hurriedly departed.

Still chuckling at his discomfiture, the girl placed towels around the bucket, covered the porthole and braced the door with a chair so no one could blunder into her cabin. She stripped off her clothing eagerly and tested the water with her toe, then she stepped into the bucket, wincing as the steaming water lapped around her ankles and splashed out onto the floor. Her pained expression turned into a smile of contentment when she wet her cloth and squeezed the warm water onto her head, allowing it to sluice in streams down her body.

Happily, she repeated the process again and again until the water had cooled. She did not even mind that she could only rinse her hair; washing would have to wait because Pat had come up with only a sliver of disreputable-looking soap and one bucket of water.

Her bathwater was cold when Danielle stepped out and wrapped herself in a skimpy towel of indeterminate color. She plunged her chemise into the bucket and scrubbed it, following it with her dress and black petticoats. She spread her clothing over the chairs to dry and took one of Arturo's shirts from a peg in the corner. He had dropped it when he stormed out of the cabin. Now she would make good use of it, she decided. The crisp shirt, which billowed becomingly on the captain's muscular frame, hung nearly to her knees, leaving her long, lean calves bare.

She mopped the spills from the floor and replaced the carpet to its original spot. Then, relaxed and refreshed, the girl sat down on the bunk to comb the tangles from her wet hair.

Suddenly hearing the key in the lock, Danielle jumped up and grabbed her dripping petticoat from the nearby chair. Clutching it in front of her, she ran to the door. "Not yet, Pat. I am still half-naked."

"What?" Arturo's enraged bellow reached her and he began to pound. "What has that young pup been up to? I knew he was spending too much time in there. I will strangle him with my bare hands."

The door rattled on its hinges from the force of his blows. Certain the man would kick it in, Danielle attempted to open it before he could break it down. Shoving the heavy chair clear, she danced out of the way as the door flew open. She lost her petticoat in her retreat and Arturo caught sight of her flashing, naked legs as he charged into the cabin with a murderous glint in his eye. His booted toe caught the heavy bucket, which had been waiting beside the door for Pat, and sent it skidding into the corner, sloshing its contents on the floor.

"What the hell is going on?" he yelled, even more infuriated by the pain in his foot.

"I am taking a bath," Danielle spit from across the room, "not that it concerns you."

"A bath? So that is why it is so hot in here," the man muttered, tenderly rubbing the top of his bruised foot against the heel of his other boot.

"How dare you burst in this way?" the girl stormed, forgetting her state of undress. "For days you did not even come

"*Oui*. And my mother's ring." She drew the opal from her finger and placed it on the table. "It is very valuable."

The man picked up the ring and examined it critically. "A pretty trinket, but not nearly enough. I value you too highly to risk you for that. I think you have something worth more to me."

"My earrings?" She touched the dangling jet pendants questioningly.

"More trinkets," he scoffed.

"What then?"

"Your freedom against a night in your bed."

His proposal had the effect of a blow on the girl. She drew a sudden breath and her face colored, but her brown eyes met his and did not shirk. She was unaware that a gamut of emotion stole across her face, causing her to look young and vulnerable for one unguarded moment.

"One night?" she asked, her voice tight.

"One night with you as a willing partner," Arturo amended hastily.

"I see." After a long moment's consideration, Danielle's face set with resolve and her chin lifted. "I accept." It was a gamble, she decided, but she had won steadily. She had learned the strengths and weaknesses of Arturo's game. She could beat him.

"*Très bien*. Would you like to deal?" the privateer offered, extravagantly polite.

"Let us cut for it." She would not have him accuse her later of taking advantage of him. "Low card will deal."

After he had mixed the cards and set them before her, she drew the queen of hearts. Then Arturo drew the ten of clubs and, with it, the job of dealer.

Without a word, he retrieved the deck and began to shuffle the cards, rapidly and efficiently. He dealt expertly with one hand and a certain grace. The girl blinked in perplexity. This was not what she expected.

Nor did she expect Arturo to cheat, but he did…shamelessly and with such great skill that she never realized it.

Danielle looked at her cards, a four and a five, and elected to take another. She was uneasy at first when Arturo decided to stand, declining any more cards, but the ace he dealt her brought her score to an even twenty. She could not get much closer to the ideal score. She leaned back in her seat and relaxed slightly, then she turned up her cards.

"*Vingt!*" she cried triumphantly.

But her smile faded when Arturo revealed his cards, a king and an ace.

"*Vingt-et-un*—twenty-one. You win," she whispered in horror.

"*Oui,* I win," Arturo responded with a mocking smile. But his tone was devoid of emotion. He watched the girl intently.

Danielle's pale face looked stricken when she lifted her stare from his cards. She had lost, she thought dully. She had been so certain she would win that she had wagered her honor against her freedom. All that was left now was pride, her very downfall. And that same pride would see that Arturo was paid, though she would be ruined by it. Very well, let it be...but for tonight only. That was the wager. She would not think of tomorrow.

She got to her feet unsteadily, the scrape of her chair loud in the silent cabin. Her knees felt as if they would buckle and she leaned against the table for support. She would not meet his eyes as she fumbled with the tiny buttons of her bodice.

"Wait, *ma cher,* let me." Arturo rose and went to stand in front of her. Gently, he brushed her nerveless fingers away from their task and began to strip the buttons from their holes himself, murmuring soft endearments all the while.

Easily, he slipped the open bodice down so it formed a soft snare for her arms and leaned to kiss the smooth skin of her shoulders.

"Do not be afraid of me, *ma petite,*" he whispered, his dark brows meeting in a frown as she shivered beneath the tender advance of his lips.

"I—I am not afraid," she demurred, determined to perform her part of the bargain with dignity.

"Of course not," he agreed huskily. Carefully, he loosened her hair, causing the pins to spill onto the floor as he combed the luxuriant locks with his fingers, exulting in their fragrance and silken texture. Then, with one smooth upward movement, he divested the girl of her dress.

When she stood before him in her chemise and petticoat, her glossy hair cascading over her shoulders, he encircled her waist with his hands and held her at a distance so he could admire her. Above the lace edging of her chemise, her bare neck and shoulders took on a pearly sheen in the lantern light, and the dark circles that crowned her firm breasts were clearly visible, straining against the sheer fabric.

"You are beautiful, Danielle," he breathed in wonder, "so very beautiful."

Almost unwillingly, she lifted her eyes to Arturo's face. His blue eyes were tender. For the first time since the card game, her fear was forgotten. She watched, fascinated, while the man removed his shirt. The white bandage on his arm stood out in sharp contrast to his skin, bronzed from working under the tropical sun without a shirt. A souvenir of a battle past, a long, even scar that ran from below his heart along his rib cage showed silvery-white in the lamplight. His broad chest was muscled and lightly furred, the triangular mat of black hair narrowing to a line that swept down his lean, hard torso and disappeared below his belt. Below that belt, she could see, through his snug breeches, the bulge that bespoke his desire for her.

He took the girl in his arms again, and she swayed against him as if she had no will of her own. He kissed her tenderly, his lips exploring the corners of her mouth, brushing over her eyes, lingering at her temple as he breathed in her sweet scent. Her own lips curved in an involuntary smile as his mustache prickled her cheek lightly. He trailed kisses along her jawline, resting a moment on her throat where her pulse throbbed under creamy-white skin, before returning to claim her mouth with fiery expectation.

Arturo loosened the tabs of her petticoat and Danielle felt the warm night air on her legs as it fell to the floor with the slightest rustle of sound. His arms tightened around her, lifting her from the puddle of fabric at her feet. In that instant, the length of her slender body was molded to his, naked thigh against sinewy leg, firm breasts flattened against his solid chest. And the heat of his body seemed to burn through her thin chemise.

When he released her to untie the ribbons at her shoulders, the girl resisted an almost uncontrollable urge to lean against him, to follow the motions of his body, to seek out and revel in the new feelings he aroused. Instead, she was still, as her chemise slid downward and she stood naked to Arturo's inspection.

"Danielle, *mon coeur,* let me love you," he whispered, his breath stirring the tendrils beside her ear. "How I have wanted you...waited for this moment." Tenderly, he cupped her breast and his mouth sought hers again. Her eyes closed and she moaned under his touch, his large warm hand against her bare skin thrilling her, exciting sensations she had never felt before. Their kiss deepened and her lips parted under his, inviting his intimate exploration.

The man drew away with a shuddering breath. Without a word, he swept her up into his arms and carried her to the bunk.

Steadying himself with one knee on the mattress, he laid the girl down with elaborate gentleness. When he made no move to join her on the bed, she lifted her eyelids, heavy with passion, to look at him. Some of her fear had returned and was visible in her eyes, mingled with yearning, but she made no protest. Instead she seemed to hold her breath and watch him expectantly.

Arturo poised beside her, his hands on his belt buckle as if he would undress. The light from the lantern behind him glinted on his golden earring, burnished the ridged muscles of his shoulders and hid his face in shadow. Danielle could not know what he thought, but his desire was obvious.

Suddenly, his hands dropped and his arms hung limp at his sides. When he spoke, his voice was raw with emotion, "*Mon Dieu,* what am I doing? I am sorry, *cher.*"

The mattress bounced abruptly as he withdrew, the movement matching the girl's jolt of intense emotion. In her confusion, she could not discern whether what she felt was relief or disappointment.

"You are sorry," she repeated dumbly, "that you won?"

"I won nothing," he muttered. Retrieving his shirt, he turned and slammed the door behind him, leaving her numbed.

Nothing? she thought dully. Arturo thought that he had won nothing? Did he find her so unattractive despite his honeyed words? Was he disgusted by the lengths to which she would go to secure her freedom? Did he not understand that she came to him willingly because she had given her word? As always, he spoke of desire and never of love. How he must hate her.

Danielle crept under the blanket and lay awake for a long time. Her mind roiled with unanswered questions and her body ached with a shameful longing for his touch. She could not bear even to think of tomorrow, but one thing she knew with certainty—she was alone again in the world. And she had never felt so forlorn.

Chapter Ten

Narcisse Duval sighed contentedly, his hand caressing the smooth wooden king's peg at the top of the ship's wheel. How he loved the helm on moonlit nights when the warm salt-kissed wind ruffled his hair and snapped the sails overhead.

The hour was late and his shipmates dozed on pallets and coils of rope, seeking a breeze. To Narcisse, even the faint glow of the binnacle light seemed bright, blinding him to the still forms on the unlit foredeck. He could easily imagine that there was nothing in the world but the brigantine he steered, the dark measureless sea and the bright stars above to guide him.

He was a fortunate man, glad to be a part of Arturo's crew and content that the life of a sailor was free and simple.

His sense of well-being ebbed, however, when Arturo, bare-chested, stormed from the cabins onto the main deck. The captain mumbled curses in a multitude of languages as he yanked his shirt on and glared through the darkness toward the quarterdeck where he knew the helmsman stood. Even from a distance, Narcisse recognized the dire warning in his manner and wisely held his tongue.

Still muttering, Arturo went to the port rail and glowered out at the night. His back rigid, he lit a cheroot with choppy motions and smoked silently, jamming the cigar between clenched teeth, savagely chewing its end. Finally he threw the butt over the gunwale with a gesture of disgust and stomped off to bed.

The simple life becomes complex when a woman comes into it, Narcisse mused, watching him go. His own life had been complicated many times by women, sometimes happily, sometimes not so happily. No doubt the girl was the cause of the *capitaine*'s ill temper. Turo had not been the same since she was brought on board. He tried to shield her, even to hide her, but the entire crew knew the *Magdalena* carried a woman. Narcisse had caught several indistinct glimpses of her during her evening walks and longed for a better look. But only Jacques and Pat and Harry Hinson had seen her so far. The little Cockney said she was a beauty.

This could be bad for his old friend, who had a weakness for women, the sailor reflected sadly. He, too, missed the company of the gentler sex, and surely *les femmes* missed him, as well, since he pleased them so. Perhaps he could help Arturo and himself if he made the girl fall in love with him, he thought logically. How nice a discreet affair of the heart would be to while away the hours at sea.

Singing softly in concert with the low hum of the rigging, the helmsman soon gave up his speculation and turned his attention to navigation.

As Arturo strode the quarterdeck the next morning, shouting at Felix, at Pat, at anyone who did not move fast enough to suit him, he mercilessly reexamined his actions of the night before. He had cheated at cards and come close to deflowering a virgin, but what was worse...he no longer knew his own mind.

He had not taken her. For once in his life, he had done the right thing and he knew it. Why then did he feel so guilty? Danielle was old enough to know the results of what she had proposed. The man was furious that she had set him on such a course in the first place.

As the day wore on, the wind rose and waves buffeted the *Magdalena*. Accustomed to the mild pitching, Arturo hardly noticed it. So embroiled was he in his inner conflict, he might not have noticed a hurricane. His anger ricocheted at each memory. He was infuriated with the girl and with himself. He did not trust himself to be with her and, after last night, he could not trust her, either. He had to get Danielle to Nassau, give her her liberty and be rid of her.

He must stay away from her, he told himself. Anyone could accompany her on her evening walk...Jacques, Felix, Pat, even that womanizer, Narcisse. Unaccountably vexed at the thought, Arturo slapped the rail in frustration. He'd be damned if he would be jealous. He would avoid the girl altogether. Yet, when evening came, he went to her.

"But I thought—" Danielle greeted him in surprise.

"What did you think?" Arturo cut in dangerously.

"That you wanted nothing to do with me." She met his eyes dauntlessly, but her face reddened at the memory of his rejection.

"I am here, am I not?" he growled.

"*Oui,* you are here," the girl said with a sigh and lowered her gaze. Silently she followed him up the companionway, gasping when the wind hit her. It whipped her heavy skirt around her ankles and nearly knocked her off balance.

Because the sea was rough, the captain decided they would stay on the beam where their footing would be more stable. The couple was silent, painfully aware of each other and almost absurd in their efforts not to touch on the rocking deck. When a wave buffeted the tiny brigantine, Danielle was thrown against Arturo. He steadied her, but did not immediately release her. Sliding one arm around her waist to pull her close, he turned slightly to shield her from the wind.

She could feel the warmth of his body under his linen shirt, and she fancied she heard the pounding of his heart. As if his eyes were magnets that drew her own, she lifted her head and looked at him. One of his hands rose to smooth her hair gently, capturing a loose tendril that floated on the wind. His fingers cupped her head as he bent to kiss her.

He felt the girl's sigh under the gentle pressure of his mouth. Then her lips parted and she returned his kiss. Her skirt billowing behind her, Danielle molded her body to his. His arm tightened around her and lifted her from the deck to meet his ardor. Her hands, which had rested lightly on his chest, now crept upward until her arms forged a tender chain around his neck.

Arturo had not intended for it to happen, but choice and rationality were lost to him. He was plunged into a desire as natural and relentless as the windswept sea around them. And he felt as if he would drown in the sweetness of her kiss.

He drew away, gulping for air, for reason, for sanity. He set her back on her feet abruptly and scowled down at her. "This is madness," he muttered. "I should have known better."

"Indeed, you should have," Danielle snapped. Her breathing ragged, she retreated. The wind lashed at her, but she held her head high, grateful the man could not know her haughty demeanor masked the pain she felt. She had wanted to believe an unexpected nobility in his character had caused him to leave her last night, but now she understood. He could not bear to touch her. "It is too late to claim last night's winnings now, *capitaine*," she informed him acidly.

"I claim nothing because I won nothing," Arturo growled.

Danielle expelled her breath as if she had been struck. "At least you are honest about your feelings," she said, her voice shaking with emotion. "Then allow me to be just as honest. I will never forgive you. I have lost everything to you. My freedom, my pride, my honor—"

"You lost nothing to me, you little fool. That is what I am trying to tell you. I cheated."

"You . . . cheated?" Danielle braced herself with one hand on the gunwale. Her face was a white blur in the darkness, but Arturo did not have to see it clearly to know that her eyes were accusing. "You cheated," she repeated scathingly, "and let me give myself to you, so you could refuse me. How amusing you must have found it!"

"It was not like that." He gripped her tightly by the arms, drawing her toward him. "Listen to me."

"*Non*," she cried in a strangled voice. "I will not listen to you, ever again. I hate you." She wrenched free and raced through the hatch to the cabins. Arturo heard the slam of her door over the wailing of the wind.

The captain remained on the deck all night as the *Magdalena* sailed past small islands, dark and uninhabited, following the channel toward the Bahamas. He did not find the peace he usually found at sea, for a bothersome question lurked in the back of his mind. What had Danielle done to him? She was a fever in his blood. He only hoped he could be cured.

The next evening, Arturo sent Jacques to accompany Danielle on her walk. From the quarterdeck, he watched as they emerged from below. At first she did not see him and Arturo was free to observe her. Even from a distance, he could see that her face was pale and there were dark smudges under her eyes, evidence she had not slept.

As if she felt his scrutiny, Danielle lifted her gaze, and in the dimness her hostile eyes met his. She glared at the man, who stared back at her from the height. Not a word passed between them. Suddenly, she spoke quietly to her companion, then turned on her heel and strode back to her cabin, leaving the first mate looking after her, puzzled and concerned.

At once, Arturo vaulted purposefully to the deck below and hurled himself into the passageway, just as the girl was about to let herself into her cabin.

"Wait," he commanded, catching her arm before she could close the door, "I want to talk to you."

"We have nothing to discuss."

"Pat said you did not eat all day."

"What business is that of yours?"

"As captain, I am responsible for the well-being of my passengers. I cannot have some spoiled *bébé* weeping in her cabin and refusing to eat until she starves herself."

"I won't starve. And believe me, *capitaine,* I will *not* cry," she announced coldly, freeing her arm. Then she closed the door.

"Land ho!"

Danielle leaped from her bunk when she heard the cry just after dawn. She could scarcely believe her ears. Hurrying to the porthole, she looked out at a lush green island jutting from the turquoise sea. As the brigantine sailed nearer, she saw many ships anchored in a large crescent cove around which a small settlement was built. In the harbor, men from the other vessels called to the crew of the *Magdalena,* and Arturo's men answered with ribald good humor.

Along the windswept shore, a strip of sparkling white sand separated the rolling surf from the little town. A bustling waterfront street was lined with low, pastel-colored buildings between which could be seen the dense green foliage of swaying palms and the vivid color of tropical flowers.

When the anchor was dropped, Danielle could barely restrain her excitement. She watched as the small boats kept on the *Magdalena*'s deck were lowered into the glistening water. After what seemed hours to the impatient girl, Pat appeared at last with her breakfast.

She pounced upon the cabin boy before he had even set the tray down. "Where are we? Why have we stopped?"

"That's Nassau, the island of New Providence, miss. We're in the Bahamas to take on water and supplies and to repair the damage done by the storm—"

"You mean we were in danger of sinking all this time?"

"No, ma'am, the damages are minor. We're not so much as listin'. But us men—" he paused to savor the word "—us men are also to have a bit of liberty before we sail on."

"How nice. Will everyone be going ashore?" the girl asked, deliberately casual.

"Not right away. There's much work to be done. Jacques and Felix are goin' to see to provisionin' now. The cap'n already went ashore, for he had business to tend to."

"Who is in charge then? You?"

The boy's chest expanded proudly that she would think so, but he admitted he was not. "Cap'n De Leon left Narcisse Duval, the helmsman, in command."

"I see. And when will all 'you men' go ashore?"

"Tonight everyone'll go," Pat responded. "Everyone but the cap'n and the watch, that is."

"I see..." the girl repeated thoughtfully, already plotting her flight. Since her door was no longer locked, she might be able to steal out and over the side. She would have to swim, but she felt certain she could make it. If she foundered, she would call for help, and surely some kindhearted sailor from a neighboring ship would fish her out of the water and see her on her way.

Absorbed, Danielle paid no heed as Pat moved around the cabin, using Arturo's key to unlock the trunk and withdrawing a small heavy wooden chest. She scarcely noticed him at all until he left.

"Beggin' yer pardon, miss, but the cap'n asks that ye stay inside as usual. He said the trade winds will commence blowin' directly, and he hoped ye won't suffer too much from the heat in the meantime."

"She should not have to suffer at all, *non, mon ami,*" a man said with a teasing tone from behind them.

"No, but 'tis the cap'n's orders that she is to stay out of the way of the crew," Pat said reluctantly when he turned to find Narcisse lounging in the doorway.

"Then I will see to it. But first, Pat, are you not going to introduce me?"

"Aye," the cabin boy agreed, even more reluctantly. "Miss Valmont, may I present Narcisse Duval."

"At your service, *mam'selle.*" The handsome young Cajun came forward to kiss her hand, admiration unmistakable in his dark eyes.

"And this is Miss Danielle Valmont, who the cap'n is lookin' out for personally," Pat mumbled rapidly.

"*Oui,* I have seen you with Turo sometimes in the evening, *mam'selle.* May I say that you are indeed a rare woman, one who is lovelier by the light of day than by moonlight."

"*Merci,* Monsieur Duval." Taken aback by the pretty compliment and the winning smile that accompanied it, Danielle nevertheless regarded her benefactor hopefully.

Narcisse was not as tall or muscular as Arturo, but she sensed power and strength in his lithe form. Short, curly black hair framed a pleasing, clean-shaven face, bronzed by the sun. But the man's most appealing feature was his dark, luminous eyes. It seemed to the girl that sensitivity and compassion shone from them. Here was a man to whom she could appeal for help.

"You must call me Narcisse and I will call you Danielle, *oui?*" At her nod, he gestured toward the door. "Now that proper introductions have been made, let us repair to the deck where it is cooler. Lead on, Patrick."

Danielle accepted Narcisse's arm, and they followed the boy out on deck. Enjoying what little breeze there was, she tried to ignore the odor of the hot pitch being used to caulk the ship's damaged seams. Looking around curiously, she quickly realized she was being regarded with undisguised interest by the sailors who worked nearby. She was relieved when Narcisse led her toward the gunwale in hopes of escaping the stench of tar.

The couple stood facing the island, the helmsman frowning over his shoulder at his shipmates, indicating they were to continue their work. The sun beat down, nearly smothering the girl in her black clothing, but she did not care. She was glad just to be out of the stuffy cabin. "The island is beautiful, is it not?" she said, sighing contentedly and shading her eyes with her hand.

"Not nearly so beautiful as you," Narcisse insisted fervently.

Danielle was suddenly aware that the handsome young Cajun stood very near. Uneasily, she edged away and continued to survey the scene in front of her. One of the *Magdalena*'s boats, laden with fruit and foodstuffs, bobbed on the surf, weaving among fishing boats with brightly colored sails, toward the ship. Felix was perched among the crates and baskets, his peg leg on a huge turtle, which was lying on its back in the bottom of the boat, legs waving futilely in the air. When Felix saw their figures at the *Magdalena*'s railing, he squinted and waved. Danielle doubted that the nearsighted old man could identify them.

"Narcisse," she asked impulsively, "can you take me ashore?"

"Not unless Turo says it is all right."

"He will not."

"Then I cannot." The sailor seemed amused, though he refused her firmly.

"But he has kidnapped me. He is keeping me prisoner."

Narcisse shrugged charmingly. "He must have a good reason."

"A good reason?" Danielle's disbelief was apparent.

"Let us not argue, *non*. It will ruin the time we have together. Besides, I already risk *mon capitaine*'s wrath by bringing you out on deck at all."

"You are right, of course. I am sorry," she whispered, chagrined. "I do not want you to get into trouble because of me." Her eyes, bright with tears, avoided his. Her gaze was fixed on a boat that approached, but she did not really see it.

"Have no fear, *mam'selle*," he murmured soothingly. "The pleasure of your company would be worth it."

"He is a terrible man," the girl muttered more to herself than to her companion. So absorbed was she in her thoughts that she hardly noticed when Narcisse led her to the other side of the ship to escape the fumes that threatened to overcome them as the wind began to rise.

"Turo is not bad, just bad-tempered." Narcisse chuckled. "I do not like to speak so well of a rival, no, but we have been friends for many years."

"Rival?" Danielle exploded. "I would not have Arturo De Leon if he were offered to me on a silver salver."

"It is good, then, that I am not being offered." Arturo's voice, low and ominous, sliced through their conversation. The couple whirled guiltily to find the captain behind them.

"Ah, Turo," Narcisse greeted him, trying not to be perturbed by his captain's fierce scowl. "We did not see you return."

"You saw nothing but each other, even when I came aboard," the privateer agreed, scowling. "I left you to command a ship, Duval, not to coddle this female."

The helmsman drew himself up and answered stiffly, "Everything is under control here, *capitaine*."

"For how long, with a woman roaming the ship, parading herself before the crew?" Arturo snarled. He turned to Danielle, his manner becoming cold and formal. "I must ask you to return to your cabin at once, *mademoiselle*, and do not come out until I say you may."

For an instant, it seemed as if she would speak, then the girl pivoted furiously and marched down the companionway. In her cabin she fumed, resentful at losing her chance to protest for fear of causing trouble for Narcisse. But she had done nothing wrong. How dared Arturo accuse her of exhibiting herself to the crew? He simply did not want her to see anyone who might help her.

Through the afternoon, the sounds of the crew at work drifted in on the breeze through the porthole, growing more boisterous as the men anticipated the night to come. Danielle considered signaling the island for help. Going to the small round window, she peered out. A boat was nearing the *Magdalena*, but the girl's cries died in her throat when she realized it contained Jacques, six heavy water butts and four straining oarsmen. She would get no help there.

Sitting down heavily on the bunk, she listened to the shouts and thumps from the deck as the barrels were hoisted aboard, and wrestled into place on deck. But soon a hush fell over the ship while the crew prepared to go ashore. Danielle observed as the men were ferried in boats to the beach. They waded ashore in the waning sunlight and disappeared merrily up the road toward town. She watched until the last boat had landed and no one could be seen among the lengthening shadows on the island.

The sun had nearly set when she decided to swim to shore after dark. But before she could carry out her plan, a knock sounded at the door and Arturo opened it.

"I would like to see you on deck, *s'il vous plaît,*" he requested sternly.

"And have me 'parade myself before your crew'?" she shot back tartly.

"The crew is ashore," the man growled, "even Narcisse, your newest conquest."

"You—you did not punish him?"

Arturo's blue eyes turned to ice at the relief in the girl's voice. "I should have thrown him in the brig. Instead I put him in charge of Pat for the night. It may hamper his *affaires de coeur,* but we will find out if he can watch the boy better than he watched my ship today. Now are you coming or not?"

Silently she followed Arturo out on the empty deck, uncertain what to expect.

Far forward near the bow, the watchman ambled, looking wistfully toward the purple-shaded shore. Without so much as a glance in his direction Arturo led Danielle aft, where a small table waited, set for two and carefully laid with crystal, silver and china Pat had retrieved earlier from the captain's trunk.

"Would you care for some wine?" he asked, pouring from a beautiful decanter. In his other hand, the crystal stopper captured the fading rays of the sun and turned them into a thousand shards of fiery radiance.

"*Merci.*" Danielle accepted the glass from him, concealing with difficulty her confusion at the sudden change in his mood. The opal ring on her finger, a reminder of the differences between them, caught the light of the setting sun when she held her glass up to admire the way the wine glowed, red and warm.

Now Arturo was silent, gratified to see Danielle's face los[t] its guarded expression. He did not look forward to what wa[s] to come. Glumly, he imagined her elation when he told her sh[e] was to be put ashore tomorrow as she wished.

The girl was still unaware of Arturo's plan as she stood be[-] side the rail, sipping her wine, savoring the last warmth of th[e] sun, breathing in the flower-scented breeze from the island[.] For the moment, all thoughts of throwing herself into the se[a] and swimming toward shore were forgotten. In the twilight, th[e] turquoise surf was gray-green and the white foam of the wave[s] took on the same rosy hue as the sunset. From a ship nearb[y] came the delicate music of a guitar. Almost happy, the gir[l] sighed, lulled by the gentle roll of the ship riding at anchor.

Arturo moved to stand beside her, reconsidering his scheme[.] Danielle was breathtakingly beautiful, silhouetted against th[e] red ball of the sun. Her face was pale from her confinement i[n] the cabin, the pallor causing her brown eyes to look wider an[d] darker than before. The wind sculpted her skirt and petti[-] coats to her willowy body and stirred her blond hair, glintin[g] with gold.

He had striven to put her from his mind. He had attempte[d] to forget how lovely she was. He had tried—unsuccessfully—[] to stay away from her, telling himself he was tired of thei[r] endless verbal sparring. Sadly, he realized he enjoyed thei[r] spirited exchanges. What he could not bear were the memo[-] ries of her wrath and the scorn he had overheard in her voic[e] this afternoon.

His eyes caressing her, he wished fleetingly that every mo[-] ment they had spent together could have been like this one. Bu[t] it had not been so. His mind was made up: Danielle would sta[y] in Nassau.

"I have something to discuss with you, *mam'selle,*" he sai[d] abruptly, his voice gruff.

"*Oui?*" She looked at him expectantly over her shoulder.

"I have decided to do as you ask. I am going to release you.[]"

"To release me?" she repeated uncertainly, her eyebrow[s] lifted in surprise.

"Tomorrow before the *Magdalena* sails, I will take yo[u] ashore and see that you are settled." Arturo felt as if the word[s] were being wrenched from him.

"Merci," she whispered, turning her face toward the sunset.

"I will ask the governor himself to watch over you," he continued, eyeing her intently, wishing he could see if she smiled triumphantly. Her stiff, erect back was to him, and beyond her, the sky glowed as if on fire.

"He will see that no one bothers you, and I will make sure you have funds enough to stay in one of the more respectable rooming houses," he continued.

"I do not want your money, *capitaine,"* she protested, still refusing to look at him.

"You may find life very hard without it, even in Nassau. Or perhaps you plan to raise funds by playing cards?"

Her unbound hair whipped behind her, a storm of gold on the wind, as the girl turned her head to glare at him.

But before she could speak, the man laid a pacifying hand on her shoulder. "I am sorry, Danielle," he apologized. "That was uncalled for. Please, let me establish you in Nassau. I owe you that much, for taking you away from New Orleans."

"You promised me a new life," she answered in a tight voice, shrinking from his touch. "I suppose that is what I am getting—whether I like it or not."

Again Arturo considered changing his mind, but Danielle wanted to be free of him. She had told him, shown him, at every turn that she hated him. She would not have him if he were offered on a silver salver, he reminded himself grimly.

"You will like Nassau." He gestured toward the settlement, where flickering lights had begun to appear in the twilight. "A beautiful, resourceful woman like you can make a good life here."

"Or I could book passage on the first passing ship and go home." She faced him suddenly, fists clenched, brown eyes flashing.

"I would not advise it," he said soberly.

"Would you still have me believe you kidnapped me for my own safety?" she asked through gritted teeth. "That all you have done has been for my benefit, *capitaine?"*

Here they were again. Right where they had started. Arturo sighed wearily and raked his fingers through his hair. "Let us

not quarrel tonight, *cher*. What is done, is done. Could we nc
part as friends?''

He led the girl to the stern where the bench had been strew
with pillows to make a comfortable seat. He took the cha
across from her and lit the lantern on the table against th
deepening evening. Then he uncovered the dishes one by on
offering each temptingly for her inspection.

Felix had prepared a feast. When Danielle tasted the fir
course, a rich soup, it was obvious what had happened to th
turtle brought from shore that afternoon. The couple als
dined on roast squab, fresh crusty bread, fried plantains an
fresh fruit, all from the island. Despite the sumptuousness o
the meal, they ate almost disinterestedly.

What was wrong with her? Danielle wondered in despai
throwing quick, veiled glances at the stony-faced man. Sh
should be happy; he was giving her her freedom. Why did sh
feel as if he was abandoning her?

Across the table, Arturo wrestled with his own emotions. H
would be well rid of Danielle Valmont, he told himself sa
agely. He had driven his crew, added more canvas and wille
the wind to blow, to speed his ship to Nassau. Why now did h
ache at the thought of her leaving?

Stars shone in the night sky by the time the diners finishe
their meal. As they sipped their wine, a harsh, thickly a
cented voice reached them from the water below.

''Ahoy, *Magdalena!* De Leon, show your face, you curs
of two parents!''

''Ah, *non*.'' Rising, Arturo glared over the gunwale at
man rowing a boat from one of the nearby ships. ''When I sa
the *Fatima*, I hoped he would be sleeping off a four-day drun
ashore.''

''Who is it?'' Danielle asked at his elbow. In the darkne
she could not see the man, but could tell that he was powe
fully built, nearly as broad as he was tall.

''It's Turk, the Ottoman pirate. What is he doing in the
waters? Danielle, get back!'' the captain ordered, shoving h
behind him. But it was too late. Mentally, Arturo cursed Na
cisse for having her in sight of every ship in the harbor this a
ternoon.

"Then it is true what I hear," the visitor bellowed up at them. "De Leon carries a woman on his ship."

Arturo swore under his breath before answering, "It is true. What are you doing in Nassau, Turk?"

"Taking on supplies, like you." He shrugged, pulling in his oars. "Are you going to ask me aboard, De Leon, or must I steal up the side of your ship with my knife in my teeth?"

"Come aboard, by all means." Arturo's invitation was surly. Although they had once been shipmates briefly, he had never been friends with Turk. But now was not the time to make an enemy.

The captain stalked forward to throw down the pilot's ladder to their guest. He did not notice Danielle trailing behind him.

"The climb is not long when the *Magdalena* sits so low in the water," Turk announced, heaving himself onto the deck. "Your ship is loaded for trading?"

Danielle gasped quietly when the bulky Ottoman landed heavily on the deck. His appearance was startling. His legs were like tree trunks, jutting up from splayed bare feet. His broad waist was encircled by a red sash into which were tucked a scimitar, a dagger, a long knife and a flintlock pistol. The swarthy skin of his bare midriff, his back, his arms and even the top of his shaved head were adorned with tattoos. A white scar crossed one of his dark, slanted eyes and traversed his cheekbone to disappear into a flowing black beard. Above his curled, waxed mustache, his nose protruded, huge and hooked. Turk smiled slyly at his host, one gold tooth gleaming in the dim light.

"Do you think I would take up trading?" Arturo answered evasively, grimacing when the other man slapped him on the shoulder, jostling his wounded arm.

"I have never known you to haul cargo, but I've never known you to carry a woman, either," Turk answered, peering around the captain at the girl. "And such a woman!"

Arturo watched with admiration as Danielle proudly met the rude inspection. He should have sent her below, he berated himself, but to do so now would offend the other man.

"We were having some wine. Would you like some, Turk?" the privateer offered grimly, hoping to divert his attention.

"Rum, De Leon. If one is to sin against Allah, it should be with rum so strong it will bring tears to your eyes."

"How long since you were a good Muslim, Turk?" Arturo asked wryly.

"There are no good or bad Muslims, only believers or unbelievers," the other man growled. "Let us not waste time on religious argument. My throat is dry."

Arturo motioned for Danielle to stay behind him. "You will find a cask of rum in the galley," he directed her softly. "Bring some, and a tankard, and be very quiet about it."

Although unaccustomed to being treated like a servant, she did not protest. Turk made her uneasy. He strode arrogantly to the stern and threw himself into the chair that had been Arturo's during dinner.

While Danielle went into the galley, the captain sat across from his unwanted guest and offered him a cigar.

"No," Turk declined curtly. "I have my own—the essence of paradise. But you do not smoke hashish, do you?"

"No."

"I tell you, no tobacco—not even perique—can give a man such escape from care." Turk watched him shrewdly, pleased to have named Arturo's cargo as his first gambit. When the privateer did not respond to his comment, the heavy man lit the pipe he had pulled from his pocket and filled the air around him with a sickly sweet-smelling haze, while Arturo smoked his cigar.

After a few silent moments, Turk spoke again, his speech already slurred from the drug. "What will you take for this woman, De Leon? She would make a fine addition to any harem. I'll give you a good price."

In the galley, Danielle's breath caught in her throat, but she did not have to strain to hear Arturo's reply.

"She is not for sale."

"She is a passenger then?"

"Only temporarily, *monsieur,*" Danielle said as she joined them, conscientiously ignoring Arturo's advice to be silent. Positioned between the two men, she set a pewter tankard in front of the visitor and filled it from the flat-bottomed decanter she carried. "Tomorrow I go ashore."

Turk was momentarily taken aback that the woman spoke for herself, but there was no accounting for Western females. This one, like all the others, needed a lesson in humility. Capturing a lock of her flowing blond hair, he drew the girl around the corner of the table toward him with a gentle but insistent tug.

"So you stay in Nassau?" His guttural voice was suggestive as he rolled the silken tress between callused fingers. "Then I will surely see you and we will enjoy each other's company, eh?"

Danielle did not answer. Her dark eyes were cold as she inclined her head and pulled her hair from the man's grasp.

With a lecherous smile, he allowed it to slide through his fingers. "I think we could become good friends," he crooned, his glittering black eyes roving over her avidly.

Suddenly, Arturo leaned forward in his seat and wrapped one possessive arm around the girl's waist, moving her to stand between his knees. "She is not staying," he announced emphatically as he pulled her onto his lap.

"But you said—" Danielle turned to protest, but her voice died when she caught the warning in his blue eyes.

"I know what I said, *ma cher,* but I was angry," Arturo said smoothly. His viselike grip at her waist belied his mild tone. "I want you to stay with me on the *Magdalena.*"

"You said this woman was not your slave, De Leon," Turk erupted, his hand seeking his knife. "Let us fight for her."

Rapidly assessing the danger of the situation, Danielle nestled back against Arturo's hard chest and looked at the hulking Ottoman, with what she hoped was a worldly smile. "No need to fight, *m'sieur,*" she protested softly. "I would be Arturo's most willing slave, but he is content to have me as his *cher amie.*"

"Then you stay with De Leon?" The pirate snorted skeptically.

"Of course. I go wherever Turo goes." She leaned her head against the privateer's shoulder and reached up to touch his cheek.

Arturo's arm tightened at her unexpected caress. Intent on playing her role, the girl lifted her eyes to look at him and discovered his lips, so close to hers, were curved in a bemused, intimate smile, which caused her heart to race.

Taking her hand in his free one, he brought it to his lips and tenderly kissed the open palm. She drew back as if burned, then hoped Turk had not noticed.

"A lovers' quarrel," Arturo explained. "As it is with all sweethearts, we say many things in anger, but I would never let her go so easily."

"So that is the way of it," Turk muttered. Righting his chair, he sank into it with a dark expression. "I did not know she was your woman. *Inshallah.*" He splashed the last of the rum into his tankard and addressed the girl. "But I tell you this, woman, when you tire of De Leon, you will be welcome aboard the *Fatima.*"

"I am sorry, but I could not leave my handsome *capitaine.* Not after he suffered such danger to accomplish our elopement."

"It was well worth every peril, *cher,*" Arturo murmured warmly, nuzzling her hair. Danielle shivered, feeling his fingers tracing a delicate, feathery pattern along her rib cage.

"Oh, Monsieur Turk. Your tankard is almost empty." She jumped to her feet and picked up the decanter. She felt Arturo's hands grasp at her waist as if he were reluctant to release her—for Turk's benefit, she supposed.

"Where are you bound, De Leon?" Turk asked.

"Back to New Orleans," Arturo lied distractedly, his eyes following the girl as she returned with the rum.

"I thought you just came from there."

"*Oui,* but we ran into a fine prize and must turn back."

"We have done well in this business, you and I," Turk remarked idly. But he watched the other man craftily as the girl sat beside him, resting in the crook of his arm. Having a woman made De Leon soft, the pirate thought with satisfaction. He did not even lie well anymore.

Turk did not press the privateer, for he already knew what the *Magdalena* carried and where she was bound. He had been delighted this afternoon to find, after years of searching, one among Arturo's crew who could be bribed for information.

"I must go ashore," the Ottoman announced, draining his tankard. "If you will not share your woman tonight, then I must find one of my own." He bounded to his feet and strode heavily toward where his boat was tied.

Arturo and Danielle watched from the main deck as Turk rowed ashore. Standing very close, they were conscious of little but each other when the man finally beached his boat on the island. The girl thought she saw him in the waning moonlight, waving toward the *Magdalena*.

"Let us give him something to remember," Arturo whispered, pulling her nearer and kissing her.

She might have protested that Turk could no longer see them, but she did not. Perhaps it was because she was grateful for Arturo's protection from the Ottoman; perhaps it was because tomorrow she would stay when he sailed; or perhaps, although it defied all understanding, it was because his kiss was what she wanted most.

The man's lips on hers were at first tender and questing, but his kiss deepened, becoming insistently ardent when she returned his caress. The desperate passion of their embrace rocked them . . . this would be their last moment together.

The ache of longing was too great for Danielle to endure. "I do not think Turk can see us," she murmured, pulling away dazedly.

"Then it will be something for me to remember," Arturo said, trying to smile with a hint of his usual bravado.

Later as the girl lay miserably in her bunk, she fought back tears. She would not cry, she told herself fiercely, not because of Arturo. She would not! At last she fell asleep, trying to think of tomorrow when she would be free again. . . .

Chapter Eleven

"Ready about!" The cries of the sailors seemed to come from far away. Yawning and stretching, Danielle drifted between sleep and wakefulness. She roused slowly, lulled by familiar sounds—the creak of taut lines, the rattle of blocks in the rigging and the snap of the sails as the wind filled them.

Her brown eyes flew open in alarm and she sat up. Placing a hand against the hull, she groaned. The brigantine vibrated with motion. The *Magdalena* was at sea.

She leaped from her bunk and hurried to the porthole. Already New Providence was out of sight and nothing could be seen but smooth, glistening blue water. She sat down heavily, stunned that her chance for freedom was gone, taken away by Arturo as unexpectedly as he had offered it. Danielle experienced the briefest moment of relief—Arturo had not left her behind. Then she recalled she had not even had a chance to set foot on solid ground. That she would be confined to this cabin for any more time seemed an intolerable fate; suddenly, the girl felt as if she would cry. Then, resignedly, she began to dress.

At least she had not been abandoned to the unwanted attentions of Turk, Danielle realized suddenly. Had Arturo decided to continue his role of protector? He had played the part well enough last night. The memory of his caresses returned unbidden, and she felt the warmth of a blush before she resolutely turned her mind to more practical matters.

The problems between them were not resolved, but perhaps since the captain had shown a willingness to free her, he could be persuaded to return her to New Orleans when this voyage was over. She knew he would refuse at first, but she would change his mind, she decided. She would remind him of his broken promise, make his life miserable if she must. Unaccountably cheered by the prospect, she smiled sweetly when Pat brought her breakfast.

"Sorry to be so late, miss," he apologized, "but 'tis a fine state the galley is in this mornin' with Felix havin' to sample a bit of his own medicine."

"Medicine?"

"Aye, his cure for hangovers. He and Narcisse and me had quite a time last night," Pat boasted, although he showed no ill effects except for red-rimmed eyes, which had rested too little. The boy joined Danielle for breakfast, nibbling her biscuits as he avidly described his well-chaperoned adventure ashore.

Poised to rap on the door, Arturo heard their laughter from the companionway. He juggled the large pink boxes he had brought from Nassau and tried to steel himself for the scene to come. Danielle would not consider his agonizing before he decided to take her with him. She would not appreciate his wisdom; she would simply be upset at the change in plans. God knew what would have happened to her if she had fallen into Turk's hands. She should be grateful...if she would only think about it.

Purposefully, he knocked and was nearly bowled over by Pat's hasty departure. Using the door as a shield, Arturo peered into the cabin and offered its occupant his most winsome smile.

"*Bonjour, cher,*" he greeted her after he was certain she would not throw anything at him. Her aim was too sure for carelessness.

"*Bonjour, capitaine.* Am I to assume you have broken your promise and are taking me to Morocco?" she asked flatly without so much as a curious glance at his burden.

He stepped into the cabin, abandoning his cover. "It is for—"

"For my own good," she finished the sentence for him.

"Be reasonable, *cher,*" he cajoled, setting the boxes on the bunk. "Would you rather I had left you for Turk?"

"No, but you promised I would be free."

"And so you shall, if it is what you want when we return from Tangier." He grinned, his old flirtatiousness returning. "But I might make you change your mind."

She leveled a humorless stare at him. "I doubt it."

"You wound me, Danielle," he declared dramatically. "Can we not declare a truce between us?"

Her acquiescence was as unexpected as it was sudden. "All right—if you promise to behave as a gentleman."

"It is a great deal to ask." The captain flashed her a rueful smile. "But I will try if you will."

"To behave as a gentleman?" She laughed. "That *is* a great deal to ask."

"Fight your baser instincts, *cher,* and all will be well," he joked. "In the meantime, would you accept the use of my bathtub this morning, as a token of my esteem?"

"Oui, merci," she accepted at once with a delightful smile.

"There is only one thing."

"What?"

"I am afraid you will be forced to use fresh water."

"Fresh water, really?" Danielle's brown eyes mirrored her pleasure at the thought of washing the salt from her body.

"Just this once. I had an extra butt brought aboard for you in Nassau. And there is a change of clothing. They were to be farewell gifts. The clothes are new," he added hastily, nodding toward the boxes on the bunk. "I swear no one else, friend or stranger, has ever worn them."

"If I am not going away, they cannot be farewell presents. You must let me pay you for them." Digging deep into her pocket, Danielle pulled out part of her winnings.

"Non," the captain insisted, closing her hand around the coins. "Can you not accept a gift from me?"

Danielle met Arturo's vexed frown and promptly returned the money to her pocket. *"Merci,* Capitaine De Leon," she thanked him prettily with a proper curtsy.

"You are welcome." The privateer bowed stiffly, as if somehow embarrassed, then he departed, leaving the girl to anticipate her bath.

With amusement, Danielle examined the contents of the boxes Arturo had brought. The eclectic assortment of clothing was opulent and unmistakably expensive. But it looked as if the captain had raided a modiste's shop, taking whatever he could grab up.

Shaking the wrinkles from a stylish day dress of cool blue-gray muslin, she inspected it critically. The workmanship was exquisite and the gown looked as if it would fit very well. Although not really a mourning dress, it had an elegant simplicity and was far more appropriate than the gowns he had offered before.

Also folded in the box were an embroidered satin petticoat, made for evening wear, a pair of silk stockings and a dainty gossamer undergarment of finest white batiste. The latter was of the latest design from Paris, a combination of camisole and pantaloons. Despite its obvious practicality, the garment was feminine and fetching. The girl touched it lovingly, blushing to think that Arturo had purchased such a personal item for her.

In the second box, Danielle found a graceful black shawl with a long silky fringe. A pair of fancy red kid slippers caught her attention and she tried them on, but they were much too large. Her black half boots would have to do.

The girl's lips twisted in a regretful smile when she saw what else Arturo had bought—a bonnet, its crown erupting with a gaudy explosion of flowers, feathers and ribbon streamers. That she felt a stir of excitement to receive the absurd creation marked her eagerness to be outside. She had no use for this hat or any other, if he was going to keep her locked in a cabin all day.

With a gusty sigh, she laid the bonnet on the bunk beside her other new things, considerately concealing the undergarments from view. Pat was already confounded at being recruited to haul bathwater to her quarters. His ruddy face would flame in mortification at the merest glimpse of lace.

Out on deck, Pat muttered a mild oath and slowed his pace as the bucket of steaming water he carried sloshed out on his feet. Behind him, the tap of Felix's peg leg did not falter as the cook collided with the cabin boy. The old sailor's curse was not so temperate as the lad's when much of the water washed over the rough planking.

Though Felix was not at his best after the night ashore, he had not complained when pressed into service to carry water.

He was curious to see the *Magdalena*'s female passenger. No matter what he had been told by the crewmen who had seen her yesterday, the cook was sure she was a hussy. He was delighted to discover instead an enchanting Creole girl. Smitten before a word passed between them, the skinny old man became inspired to sing while he worked, lifting his reedy voice in a sentimental Cajun love song.

When the job was finished, Danielle pulled a few coins from her pocket and offered shyly to pay them.

"Felix Fontaineau does not take money from a lady, no," the old man replied, drawing himself up proudly.

"Besides," Pat interjected, "'tis the cap'n's orders we're followin' and I would never let the cap'n down."

"Well, there must be something I can do for you kind gentlemen," the girl fretted. Her eyes fell on the bony knee of Felix's good leg protruding through a hole in his pants. "I am not a very good seamstress, Monsieur Fontaineau, but perhaps if you lent me your sewing kit again, I could mend your britches for you."

"When I am no longer wearing them," he told her, a twinkle in his nearsighted eyes, "I would deem it a pleasure, *mam'selle*."

Alone in the cabin, Danielle stripped rapidly and stepped into her bath. With a blissful sigh, she sank up to her neck in the hot water, causing it to lap dangerously at the edge of the tub. She soaked luxuriously until the water began to cool. Then she scrubbed the salt from her body and shampooed her hair with scented soap supplied by the captain. She must find an appropriate way to thank him for thinking of her, she mused.

Arturo warily observed a sail that had been sighted on the horizon just after dawn. The other ship, too far away for him to discern its flags or markings, seemed to be on a course parallel to the *Magdalena*'s. Perhaps it was nothing, just another trading vessel, but it disturbed him. Pirates were scarce these days, but the captain of a ship laden with valuable cargo must be cautious.

He stood on the quarterdeck beside Jacques, his feet planted wide to steady him as he looked through the spyglass at the horizon and cursed under his breath.

"There she is again," he muttered, focusing on the sail. "I do not like it. She is rigged for speed, yet she paces us."

"She may carry cargo, too," the first mate replied.

"I doubt it. She is not under full sail as we are, yet her speed matches ours. I wish she would come closer so we could know whether she was friend or foe."

"Perhaps her *capitaine* wonders the same thing about us," Jacques suggested. "When we change course, she veers to keep the distance between us—like a nervous woman, eh, Turo?"

"Well, then, *mon ami,* let us watch her closely—as we would any woman—while we continue to dance."

"Oui, capitaine." The big Baratarian chuckled throatily.

The captain and his first officer remained on the quarter-deck throughout the morning, trying to deduce who was following them. Arturo paced, the frown on his brow deepening each time the other ship matched its course to theirs. The vigil continued through the hot afternoon and his temper became shorter by the moment.

In her cabin, Danielle was unaware of the sea chase. Cool and refreshed, clad only in her new undergarment, she plunged her soiled black dress into the cold bathwater, scrubbing it ruthlessly before spreading it out to dry.

Running an appreciative hand over the cool copper rim of the bathtub, she wondered if Arturo would allow her to borrow it again. Or was its loan a salve for his conscience because he still held her captive? Truce or no truce, she was still a prisoner.

A most indulged prisoner at the moment, she reflected wryly, donning her new gown. Standing before Arturo's cracked mirror, she arranged her hair in a simple chignon. Then she took the small glass from its peg and held it at various angles, craning her neck to examine her appearance. The dress fit as if it had been made for her, and her blond hair shone from its recent washing. She returned the glass to its place, feeling pretty for the first time in months. It was too bad her efforts would be wasted in a ship's cabin.

"Glory be, miss," Pat breathed admiringly when he came to remove the bathtub, "I knew ye were pleasin' to look at, but I didn't know ye were beautiful. I mean . . ." His voice trailed off and he hung his head in embarrassment.

"I know what you mean, Pat," she said graciously. "Thank you."

"Y'er welcome. Shall I fetch the cap'n?" the boy asked eagerly. "He should see you like this."

"He is probably busy. Besides, he will see me. I am not going anywhere," the girl answered lightly.

"I don't suppose ye are. Well, if there's anything else ye need, Miss Dani, just ask and I'll get it for ye," Pat instructed, nearly stumbling over his own feet in his eagerness to help her. Blushing to the roots of his red hair, he went to get Felix to help him with the tub.

Danielle opened the door to admit a breeze, then sat down to mend Felix's torn trousers. The garment was still damp, for the old cook had insisted upon washing them before he would allow a lady to handle them. She smiled, touched by his unexpected delicacy.

It was thus Arturo found her. On his way to fetch his sextant, he paused in the doorway to observe Danielle while she sewed, unwilling to disturb the fetching picture she presented, her sleek head bent over her work.

Sensing his presence, the girl glanced up with a bright smile. "*Bonjour, capitaine,* won't you come in?"

"*Merci,*" he responded, drawn into the cabin despite himself. He had nearly half an hour until the navigational readings, and there was nothing he could do about the ship that followed them. Doffing his jacket, he draped it over the back of the chair and sat down. "Please, go on with your work. Whose . . . er . . . trousers are those?"

"They belong to Felix."

"Felix, eh?" He snorted. "You certainly made an impression on him, but then you seem to make an impression on everyone you meet."

Danielle darted a quick look at the man to see whether his words were flattery or insult, but she discovered he was smiling warmly at her.

"You look charming, *cher,*" he complimented her. Approval, and something more shone in his blue eyes as he took in her appearance. The gray-blue of the dress was a perfect foil for her blond hair and fair complexion, and it was suitable for mourning without being black. How he hated black on a woman. The gown was modest enough in cut to please her, yet the fitted bodice did not hide the curves of her bosom and the skirt flared becomingly from her trim waist.

"I am glad you think so." Suddenly nervous under his scrutiny, the girl concentrated on unsnarling a knot in her thread. "I think the dress is lovely."

"Yes . . . lovely," he murmured.

"You have excellent taste." The words rushed from her as she tried to keep the conversation alive.

"Indeed I do."

"In clothes, I mean," she stammered.

"Of course," Arturo agreed seriously, stifling a smile at her discomfiture.

"I am glad you are here, *capitaine*." Her voice steadied as she attempted to change the subject.

"So am I, *cher*, so am I."

"I want to thank you for your many kindnesses this morning."

"I could show you many more." Arturo's voice was a caress, which stirred something deep inside her.

Danielle tried to ignore the warmth of his response, the obvious gleam of admiration in his blue eyes, but she could not look away. His gaze held hers.

She found suddenly, to her distress, that she was dumbstruck. How could he have such an effect on her? Time and again he had toyed with her. Were last night's kisses part of the game? Was today's solicitude merely the effect of their truce? She was almost grateful when she pricked her finger and was forced to return her full attention to her work.

Arturo fidgeted in his chair and made a show of rolling his shirtsleeves higher on his muscular forearms. "It is too hot in here," he complained. "Wouldn't you like to go on deck?"

"During the daytime?" Danielle asked disbelievingly.

"*Oui.* Most of my men have already seen you, but stay out of their way nevertheless. If you stay on the stern, you can visit Felix."

"I promise I will keep out of the way," she pledged, her face alight with pleasure. "Your crew won't even know I'm around."

"They'll know," he assured her with certainty. "Felix extolled your beauty and kindness to anyone who would listen this afternoon, including me. Of course, I already knew what a lovely, well-bred Creole lady you are."

Danielle bit her lip and elected to ignore the jibe. "*Merci beaucoup* . . . Arturo. Of all the gifts you have given me today, being able to go out on deck is the best."

Arturo did not know which he liked best coming from her lips, the sound of his name or her word of thanks. Complacently, he stretched his long legs in front of him and tipped back his chair. Then, crossing his arms across his flat torso, he watched her. The silence between them was comfortable and companionable.

Some captains took their wives to sea with them, he thought idly, enjoying the domesticity of the scene. He had never understood it before. But this was how it would feel, right and natural, to have Danielle by his side, washing his clothes, sewing his shirts, sharing his bunk.

Wives, washing, sewing! What sort of crazy thoughts were these? He was De Leon, the freebooter. Abruptly, he sprang to his feet, a scowl on his handsome face, and was halfway to the door before the legs of his chair banged down on the floor.

Startled, Danielle looked up from her mending. "What is wrong?"

"*Nada,*" the privateer growled over his shoulder, "nothing, at all." One long arm reached back to snatch his jacket from the chair as he barreled through the open door. "I will see you later."

She sighed and shook her head. She had not said or done anything to affect him so. What was wrong with the unpredictable captain now?

After lunch, the girl held her new hat in one hand and a pair of scissors in the other, debating whether to prune any more of the flowers on it. She had already discovered, beneath the flowers, feathers and ribbon, a lovely straw leghorn bonnet. She twirled it on one finger and stepped to Arturo's mirror where she tried it on, turning her head this way and that as she regarded her handiwork with satisfaction.

Out on deck, she paused beside the hatch and blinked, unaccustomed to the bright sunlight. Adjusting her bonnet against the glare, she surveyed the ship with interest. Most of the crew were hard at work and did not notice her. She could see Arturo far forward on the foredeck, a spyglass to his eye, as he talked with Jacques. Curiously, she stared toward the horizon where his glass was trained, yet she saw nothing but ocean.

Danielle found Felix under a makeshift awning near the galley, snapping green beans and humming to himself. His song died in his throat when she appeared on the stern.

"*Mam'selle,* does the *capitaine* know you are wandering around the ship in broad daylight?" he gasped in alarm.

"*Oui,* he gave me permission if I will stay out of the way of the crew. May I sit with you for a while? Perhaps I could help."

"If you are sure it is all right," the old cook muttered fretfully, but he relinquished the bowl of beans. So pleased was he to have a new audience for his accounts of pirating days, before he had lost his leg, that he talked for two hours, stopping only when absolutely necessary for breath, keeping Danielle completely enthralled.

When the captain returned to the quarterdeck, he was moody and absorbed, chafing at the tenacity of the ship that stalked his brigantine. The heavily laden *Magdalena* seemed unable to elude the pursuer. Arturo's narrowed blue eyes focused unerringly on the distant sail as he issued curt orders over his shoulder to Narcisse at the helm.

As the captain rounded the cabin section, he slowed and surveyed the scene before him. Wearing a stylish bonnet, which looked somewhat familiar to him, Danielle sat under an awning, a metal bowl in her lap, and snapped beans. All around her, the port watch went about their duties near the mainmast, throwing frequent inquiring glances at her, but the men quickly averted their eyes when they saw the captain. No one cared to test his temper; it had been short since the girl was brought aboard.

Danielle gazed smilingly at Felix, who stood with his back to Arturo, talking animatedly. The old man gesticulated, his skinny arms flailing as he embellished the story he was telling.

Neither the girl nor Felix had spotted the captain and he was about to make his presence known when he saw the cook beckon two sailors who worked nearby: Dazet, the ship's carpenter, and Falgout, the second mate. Arturo remained where he was and watched with amusement as they hesitantly presented themselves to Danielle. He was not close enough to hear their exchange, but he grinned at the thought of it. Falgout, round-faced and amiable, was timid in the company of women; Dazet was rawboned and reticent with anyone but Falgout, his stutter making him painfully shy.

Even from a distance, Arturo could tell the introductions were brief and stilted. Danielle's face was hidden from his view, obscured by her bonnet, but he did not have to see it to know she smiled charmingly at the sailors. To his amazement, both men soon seemed completely at ease. They stood before the girl, vying for her attention as if they had known her for years.

Arturo hesitated in the shadow of the cabin section, feeling somehow excluded from the friendly gathering, even though the participants did not know he was there. His expression darkened ominously when he caught a glimpse of Danielle's beaming face as she waved in response to a call from the quarterdeck. No doubt Narcisse was hanging over the rail overlooking the stern and flirting, even though he was on duty, Arturo thought grimly.

While Dazet regaled Danielle with a story, Falgout's eyes swept the deck idly, widening when they met the captain's. He nudged the other man and signaled imperceptibly in Arturo's direction. The carpenter's plain face, wreathed with smiles, sobered when he saw Arturo standing nearby. At once, both men nodded to their leader and edged away to go about their tasks.

Curious, Danielle turned in her seat to learn whom the men had greeted. Seeing Arturo for the first time, she smiled in welcome, but he did not reciprocate. Instead, he stepped deliberately into view of the quarterdeck and glared up at Narcisse. The helmsman sketched a hasty salute of farewell toward the girl and returned his full attention to his task. Without a word to Danielle, Arturo pivoted and marched forward again.

"What do you suppose is wrong with Capitaine De Leon now?" she asked the cook.

"I could guess," Felix muttered, shrewdly considering Arturo's departure, "but I could not say for sure, no."

Before she could ask another question, he diverted her with another of his yarns.

The old man and the girl laughed and chatted until the sun was low, a crimson glow above the water. At last, Felix disappeared into the cramped galley to cook dinner. Careful not to wear out her welcome, Danielle made her way forward.

As she rounded the cabin section, she saw Arturo and Jacques on the main deck, staring into the distance. She halted and strained to see what they had spied. At last she saw it: a rare sight on the high seas, fellow voyagers on the vast ocean. The other ship was far away, too far to make contact. It looked tiny and isolated across the wide expanse, just as the *Magdalena* must look to them. An acute, alien loneliness swept the girl as her eyes followed the distant sail, rosy in the sunset. After a moment, she went below without disturbing the men at the rail.

Danielle was surprised later to find Arturo at her door, ready to escort her on their evening walk.

"We have a truce, remember?" he reminded her when she hesitated.

"*Oui,* but after this afternoon, I was not sure you wished to honor it." Danielle sighed. "I never know what you are thinking."

"Sometimes, *cher,* I do not know myself," he answered with a bleak smile, leading her out onto the deck.

The night was warm with only the slightest stir of breeze, and the moon was full and bright. Arturo seemed restless and preoccupied as they strolled, looping the main deck. He peered frequently into the night as if he thought he would see the sail. His jaw tightened tensely when a shooting star crossed his line of sight. Danielle glanced at him curiously and wondered if he believed the old Creole superstition that a shooting star foretold death.

Arturo excused himself for a brief conference around the binnacle with Jacques and Narcisse. From where she stood, Danielle heard snatches of their conversation, and when they finished talking, it seemed Arturo's men were in wholehearted agreement with his orders. Under cover of darkness, the *Magdalena* would veer while slowing to lose the other ship.

When the moon set in a few hours, Narcisse would change course and Jacques would see to reefing the sails.

His mind on his plan, Arturo returned to Danielle's side to continue their walk. However, when they neared the hatch, he halted suddenly. "There is something I must say, *cher,* something I have not said before," he confessed soberly.

"What is it?"

The girl's eyes were wide with concern and it seemed to the captain that her upturned face waited for his kiss. He ached to hold her in his arms. With difficulty, Arturo reminded himself of the agreement they had made that very morning. Being a gentleman was proving to be even harder than he had thought.

All at once, he did not trust himself to speak, even to look at her. In an attempt to collect himself, he strode to the railing and leaned against it, bracing himself with both hands.

"Arturo, please, what is it?"

Danielle's touch through the sleeve of his jacket was like a brand. With a quick intake of breath, he whirled to look at her and was taken aback to see the dread written so plainly on her face.

"Do not look at me so," he groaned. "I did not mean to frighten you. I just want to apologize for the card game the other night. I never intended for it to go so far."

"I am sorry about it, too," she whispered, relieved that his gravity was due to nothing worse. Still, she was disturbed by the reminder of her ill-conceived wager. "I should have never challenged you."

"No harm done." Now that they had addressed the constraint between them, Arturo wished to dismiss the matter lightly. In the dimness, Danielle could see the flash of his white teeth against sun-bronzed skin as he smiled at her. "We have seen more of each other than most shipmates and, I must say, I liked what I saw."

"Then why...?" she blurted, unable to stop herself. Her voice trailed off and she blushed wildly, certain he could see her face redden even in the moonlight.

"Why did I not make love to you? Do you not know the answer to that question, Danielle?" Arturo's voice was vibrant with intimacy. It thrilled her, bringing a shiver to her spine.

"I desire you, make no mistake." He stepped closer, so close their bodies nearly met. She imagined she could feel the heat emanating from him, but he did not touch her. Mesmerized by his nearness, she fought the urge to sway toward him as he continued, "But when I take you, it will be because you desire me as well. I want you to come to my arms willingly, not as payment for some foolish debt of honor.

"Now, go to your cabin." He turned from her with effort, his knuckles white as he gripped the railing. "Go," he snapped in dismissal, "before I forget my promise to behave as a gentleman."

Danielle obeyed at once, fleeing the deck as though pursued. She closed her cabin door and leaned against it, chest heaving and heart pounding as she tried to still her trembling.

It should not matter, she told herself, but it did. Arturo wanted her, after all. She knew she should be insulted that he spoke only of desire; she wanted to be loved and cherished. And still, he had spoken no words of tenderness.

Yet, inexplicably, Danielle's spirit soared. Within her, the strange exultation warred with shame; she had been as near to forgetting their agreement as he had.

Chapter Twelve

Was it wrong to feel so happy? Danielle wondered guiltily. She reveled in her freedom, savoring the fragrant aroma of coffee on the morning breeze, the sound of Felix banging pots in the galley, the warmth of the sun on her shoulders. During the past several months, she had nearly forgotten what it was to awaken with a light heart. Now it seemed easy to remember.

Nibbling a biscuit, the girl sat outside the galley and tried not to let the oppressive mood aboard the *Magdalena* dampen her spirits. She had emerged from her cabin this morning to a hushed, expectant ship. No voices were raised in song while the crew worked. All faces were turned toward the sail visible to the starboard, closer now than the day before.

On the quarterdeck, Arturo, intent and deliberate, ordered the sails trimmed. He had not even seen Danielle when she joined Felix on the stern to watch the sail bobbing hypnotically on the horizon. At last, the cook led her to the galley and gave her the same meal with which the crew had broken their fast.

"Oh, there ye are, miss, sorry to be late with yer breakfast." She turned to see the flustered cabin boy hurrying toward her.

"Do not worry, Pat," the girl replied with a soothing smile. "I found myself something to eat."

"And where have you been, M'sieur O'Reilly?" Felix called sarcastically from the galley. "Turo likes to have his second cup of *café* by now. You're going to have him angry at me, *oui*.''

"No madder than he is at me already," Pat retorted, uncharactistically negative about his hero. "I tell ye, there's no pleasin' him this mornin'."

Felix came out on deck, wiping his hands on his stained apron. "He is upset because we did not lose our shadow during the night, *oui?*" he asked sympathetically, nodding toward the other ship.

"Aye, 'tis as if that other cap'n knows what we're goin' to do 'fore we do it. Like he can read Cap'n De Leon's mind or somethin'."

"Don't be ridiculous," Felix snapped. "It was luck and nothing more."

"Cap'n De Leon thinks it's more," the boy intoned gloomily. "He thinks the other ship is the *Fatima*."

"The *Fatima!* The cook's myopic eyes squinted at their pursuer and he swore eloquently, forgetting Danielle sat nearby. The girl listened, fascinated, as a tapestry of colorful expletives unfurled before her.

"Felix! The lady..." Pat nodded uncomfortably in her direction, his face flaming.

"My apologies, *mam'selle*," Felix murmured when reminded of her presence, but he wasted no time with decorous gestures of regret. "Well, if it is Turk, we will know soon enough," he muttered. "But for now, let us go about our duties. I believe you have a deck to swab, my young friend." He dismissed the cabin boy with a perfunctory nod of his head.

Pleased that Felix would allow her to help in his galley, the girl peeled potatoes while he scoured the breakfast pots, rinsing them with seawater and emptying them overboard. While they worked, the old cook talked, his attention divided between his tasks and the distant sail. Danielle listened raptly to stories of Arturo's youth, picturing the skinny, black-haired urchin who had followed Lafitte everywhere.

"Always as nervy as a gnat, that Turo," Felix reminisced.

Suddenly a call came from a sailor on the ratline near the foremast. "She's coming closer, *capitaine!*" He gestured toward the ship, which was now approaching rapidly. Her sails billowing with wind, she seemed to skim over the surface of the water toward them.

"Finally," Arturo muttered almost eagerly to himself. He flexed his tense shoulders and called, "Can you see what colors she is flying?"

The entire company turned to watch the vessel bearing down on them, the sailors instinctively edging toward their battle positions. As the other ship neared, she again drew parallel to the *Magdalena* and slowed to pace her.

"I knew it," Arturo growled. "It *is* the *Fatima*." Turning his spyglass on the other ship, he swept it until it rested on Turk, who was arrogantly pacing his quarterdeck.

Fuming in frustration, the privateer assessed his position. What a loathsome spot for the *Magdalena!* At the moment she was a merchant vessel with a shipment to protect, prey to any fleet scavenger of the sea, while the *Fatima* rode high in the water, unencumbered by cargo, fast and easily maneuvered. Artillery mattered little at a time like this.

"Sorry, old girl," he whispered, unconsciously stroking the polished wood of the *Magdalena*'s railing. "If we get out of this one, we'll never go trading again."

Arturo ordered more canvas and the ship picked up speed, but their pursuer also hoisted more sails and easily drew even with them once again, veering closer still. It was obvious the *Magdalena* could not outrun her. The captain knew he must outfox—or outfight—Turk's crew. Quietly, he gave the command for his ship to heave to and ordered all men to their battle stations.

"Go to your cabin, *mam'selle,*" Felix bade the girl when Jacques's whistle summoned all hands on deck.

Danielle did not argue. As the cook limped to the galley to secure his gear, she hurried toward her quarters. She could see the sailors on the foredeck, scampering below to draw ammunition from the magazine and to man the cannons 'tween-decks.

She reached her cabin just as the *Magdalena* heaved to with a shudder and a mighty creak of timbers. Careening off the bulkheads in the passageway, the girl managed to open the door and stumble inside. Tossing her bonnet onto the bunk, she fought her way to the porthole and looked out at the other ship.

It, too, had slowed and now drew closer, near enough that she could distinguish the unshaved faces lining its gunwales. She could plainly see the pirate captain. Turk's mighty legs were spread solidly on deck as he looked over the *Magdalena* confidently. His hand caressed the hilt of his sword as if he were impatient for the impending battle.

She heard Arturo hail the other ship. "Ahoy, *Fatima*. What do you want, Turk?"

"I am glad I caught up with you, De Leon. I've a taste for perique and some molasses." Turk's shout came clearly across the water. "And for the woman, too."

It seemed to the girl that the pirate looked directly at her as he spoke. Hastily, she ducked away from the porthole, afraid he would see her. From the shadowy interior of the cabin, she listened to the exchange between the men.

"Too bad you made this long voyage for nothing," Arturo responded dryly. "You cannot have my cargo, and I left the girl in Nassau."

"Do not tell me you are a fool as well as a liar!" Turk bellowed without rancor. "I will take what I want, including the girl. I know you kept her with you. Send her over and let my men transfer your cargo. Then, who knows? Perhaps you will escape with your lives . . . even with your ship."

"Never!" the captain of the *Magdalena* roared amid the cheers of his crew.

"It will be a shame to send such a fine vessel to the bottom of the sea," Turk yelled, "but it is as Allah wills it. Prepare to be boarded!"

Another cheer rose, this one from the *Fatima* as the Jolly Roger was run up her mast. But the shouts of Turk's men were soon drowned by the roar of the cannon as the *Magdalena*'s crew opened fire. The boom of the guns caused the decks of the little brigantine to vibrate underfoot with each volley.

Almost immediately, the enemy ship began to return fire. The deck lurched under Danielle as the *Magdalena* took a ball in the forerigging, which splintered the bowsprit. Caught off balance, the girl staggered backward and sprawled on the bunk, crushing her new bonnet. Grimacing, she pulled it from beneath her with one hand and flung it aside while the other sought the pistol under her pillow. She tucked the tiny gun into the deep pocket of her skirt. It would afford little protection, but at least she would be armed if she needed a weapon.

Struggling back to the porthole, she watched as the *Fatima* swooped toward her prey like a hawk on its kill. But Arturo was a skillful commander and his brigantine seemed to dance on the waves, just out of reach of her assailant. The marauder fired another volley, and Danielle heard the groan of straining wood as the forward topmast swayed, then crashed to the deck below. Even in her cabin, she could hear the scream of an unfortunate sailor.

Instantly, she dashed up the companionway and burst through the hatch beneath the quarterdeck.

"Get below, Danielle," Arturo bellowed when he saw her.

The girl whirled and looked up at him, her dark eyes meeting his challengingly through the smoke of the guns.

"Get below, damn it!" he repeated his order hoarsely.

"No!" she cried. "Someone is hurt." She whirled and raced through a hail of bullets to the bow where Jacques lay amid the tangle of fallen rigging, the topmast resting on the lower part of his body. White-faced and shaken, Pat knelt beside him, calling for help to lift the mast off the first mate's injured leg.

The limb stuck out at an odd angle to his body and Jacques's face was gray and contorted with pain. Blood streamed from small cuts on his arm, but he was conscious and directing the straining sailors who labored to free him from the wreckage of the mast.

Danielle pulled the cabin boy to his feet and sent him for fresh water to cleanse the wounds. Then, rapidly, she assessed the extent of the first mate's injuries. She instructed the seamen to move the injured man carefully and lean him against the capstan.

Kneeling beside Jacques, she wadded the fallen jib into a tight bundle and placed it behind his back as a cushion. Then she busied herself ripping strips from her skirt for bandages and searching for a piece of the shattered spar to use as a splint. When Pat returned shakily with a bucket of water, she spoke to him firmly, instructing him so he could assist in setting Jacques's leg there on deck. As soon as they finished, the boy, his face pale, slipped away, leaving Danielle to tend to the man's lesser wounds.

Cannonball after cannonball thundered toward the *Magdalena*. Some fell short, barely missing the bow, sending spray up over the deck. A few balls struck high on the hull, tearing away sections of the gunwales and scoring the deck. The little ship rocked crazily with each impact, but Danielle continued to work, heedless of the battle around her. Her hands were gentle as she tended Jacques's injuries, her voice soft and encouraging. It was the last thing he remembered as he lost consciousness.

From behind her came a loud metallic clank. The ship swayed under the drag of grappling hooks from the *Fatima*. They caught the *Magdalena*'s railing, gouging deep runnels before they bit into the wood. Drawn by Turk's crew, the ships bumped together, wood grinding against wood. With a victorious shout, pirates swarmed over the main deck and the continuous clash of steel against steel was punctuated by gunfire and the screams of the wounded.

At last, Danielle stood and looked down at the battle from her vantage point. On the foredeck, men fought and died before her eyes. Arturo's crew was outnumbered, but they defended their ship valiantly and she could see few casualties among them.

Dazet and Falgout, the inseparable friends, stood back to back near the foremast, warding off all attackers. Danielle thought she saw Pat ducking through the fray, but she could not be sure. Just below her, Narcisse was cornered near the forecastle, fighting two pirates at once.

Infuriated and determined to even the competition, Danielle picked up the bucket beside her and leaned down to swing it in a wide arc. She winced when the heavy wooden bucket made contact with the skull of the man closest to her. Addled, he stumbled away, leaving his companion in arms to finish their skirmish.

With only one man to fight, Narcisse quickly dispatched his opponent. The handsome helmsman paused long enough to acknowledge Danielle's assistance with a smile and a graceful swordsman's salute.

"Do not come down, *mam'selle*," he advised. "I will stay close and you will be safer up there."

"Where is Arturo?" Danielle called in response to his advice. "Have you seen Felix or Pat?"

But he had no time to answer. Another pirate with a flashing sword and murder in his eye claimed his attention.

Poised on the bow, Danielle's anxious eyes swept the ship, but she could see no sign of the ones she sought. She gasped and looked up as a shadow fell over her. One of Turk's crewmen swung above her in the ruins of the forerigging. He swooped down, his yellowed teeth bared in a feral smile.

Muttering in a pidgin mixture of English, Spanish and Arabic, he wrenched the bucket from the girl's hand and tried to wrestle her to the deck. She resisted furiously, sickened by his clumsy efforts to drag her skirt upward and by the feel of his hot, sour breath on her neck. Suddenly losing patience, the pirate drew back his great fist and hit her, his hairy knuckles leaving vivid, red impressions on her face. Her head swimming and her ears ringing from the blow, Danielle swayed on her feet. The man grunted with satisfaction, certain she was subdued, and loosened his hold on her as one hand went to the fastening of his trousers.

Panic-stricken, she forgot the recent pain the brute had inflicted on her. She forgot the gun in her pocket. She forgot everything but escape. Galvanized into action, she emitted a bloodcurdling screech and shoved with all her might. With an angry howl, the surprised man pitched backward into the sea.

Careful to stay behind Narcisse and out of reach of his assailant, the girl climbed down to the foredeck and strained to see the combat far away on the main deck. There was so much smoke. Thick and black, it brought tears to her eyes and caused her breath to catch in her throat. Suddenly she realized where it came from. The quarterdeck was ablaze!

"Mon Dieu!" she whispered. "Arturo! Arturo!" The whisper rose in volume, becoming a wail. She did not recognize the sound that came from her own throat, did not hear Narcisse call to her, as she dodged blindly between clusters of combatants. The foredeck was nearly impassible, and tears of frustration streamed down her face as the determined girl shoved her way amidships. A skinny young pirate grasped her

arm as she sped by, receiving one well-placed kick for his efforts. He released her immediately, his lewd laugh ending in a
moan as he bent double from the pain.

When Danielle reached the ladder to the main deck, she
clambered up it, then stopped helplessly to look around. The
Fatima's crew overran the *Magdalena*'s deck, and Arturo was
nowhere to be seen.

Aware she had put herself into the thick of the fighting, she
sidled away from the ladder just as a man flew through the air
past her and landed heavily on the deck below.

"Danielle!" She thought she heard her name over the clash
of arms.

Hopefully, she lifted her stinging eyes to the burning quarterdeck, where amid billowing smoke she could see shadowy
figures locked in combat.

The girl's face paled beneath its covering of soot as she
caught sight of him. Arturo was dueling with a foppish pirate
in the inferno. His blue eyes flicked distractedly down to where
she stood, her feelings plain on her tear-streaked face.

"Danielle!" the captain shouted, his voice raw from the
smoke. "Stay where you are. I will come to you." He had been
frantic with worry, and now that he had found her he would
not let her out of his sight again. He fought with renewed energy and quickly finished his adversary, leaving the man's body
on the blazing quarterdeck.

Arturo kept his gaze firmly fixed on the girl and leaped to
the main deck, where he began to slash his way toward her. He
fought skillfully, wielding sword and knife, countering every
attack. Danielle watched apprehensively, the conflict surging
around her, pressing in on her until her back was against the
gunwale and she could retreat no farther. Every second of the
privateer's implacable advance seemed an hour to her.

Before he could reach her, Arturo was set upon by a member of Turk's crew who swung a heavy chain over his head.
The man seemed drunk with blood lust, intent on maiming
anyone who stood in his way as he cut an indiscriminate swath
through the fracas. Arturo did not see his assailant until it was
too late. He dodged at once, twisting wildly in a vain attempt
to evade the heavy chain.

"No!" Danielle screamed when the captain fell. Desperately, she tried to claw her way through the horde to reach him, but she was trapped in a cramped, narrow space, hemmed in by a solid wall of bodies as men fought all around her. Standing on tiptoe, she craned her neck to see the man lying on the deck.

Arturo lay very still for a second, addled and shaking his head. Gingerly, he sat up and touched the wound, fully expecting to discover a large hole in his skull. Instead he found that the blow had glanced off his thick hair. There was only a crease in his scalp from which surprisingly little blood flowed.

Realizing suddenly that the pirate still loomed over him, prepared to finish him, Arturo muttered on exasperated curse and threw his knife with a quick, fluid motion. It flipped end over end, its blade glinting in the dim light before it sank to the hilt in his attacker's chest.

Unsteadily, the privateer got to his feet and retrieved the embedded knife from his fallen enemy's body. He daubed at the blood trickling down his forehead with his shirtsleeve and met Danielle's anxious eyes. Smiling crookedly, he lurched toward her, shouldering his way purposefully through the crowd.

Arturo was nearing the girl when one of Turk's men jumped between them. His back to Danielle, the pirate crouched to spring on the wounded captain. Without hesitation, she seized a belaying pin from the pin rack nearby and swung it. She heard a yelp of pain from behind her, but she had no time to investigate before she brought the pin down hard on the head of the man in front of her. With a groan, Arturo's foe sprawled at her feet, unconscious.

"Two at once," the captain announced with satisfaction as he joined her. His eyes were on the deck behind her where another of Turk's crew lay, holding his head and moaning. "I am glad you are on our side, *cher*."

Danielle nodded mutely, aghast at the damage she had wreaked, even unknowingly, before turning her eyes to Arturo's smoke-blackened face. Unexpectedly, she reached up and smoothed his singed mustache. "You are burned," she murmured distractedly.

"*Non,* just scorched. Now come," he ordered, "the deck is no place for you. You must hide in the galley until this is over."

"I do not want to cower in hiding, not knowing what is happening out here."

"You prefer to fight? An admirable trait, I am sure." Arturo chuckled dryly. "But I cannot permit it. Think what an effective hostage you would be if Turk captured you. I do not want to hand over the *Magdalena* and her entire cargo just to get you back.

"Now, come on!" He thrust Danielle behind him and began to hack his way aft. She offered no resistance. Instinctively, she covered his back, brandishing the pin at anyone who looked as if he would follow.

Suddenly a crazed, triumphant laugh rent the smoky air and Turk leaped from the quarterdeck, landing on the deck in front of them. His scimitar whistling in the air, the pirate advanced ruthlessly on Arturo, forcing him back against the gunwale, pinning the girl behind him against the rail.

Danielle felt the wind leave her lungs in a rush as she was slammed against the railing. Bowed backward over it, she was held firmly in place by the weight of Arturo's body against hers. She could feel the taut muscles of his haunches and powerful legs through her skirts as he fought. Blood rushed to her head and the carved rail bit into the small of her back. The belaying pin she had used as a weapon flew from her fingers and plummeted downward as she dangled over the water. Out of the corner of her eye, she could see the dark bulk of the *Fatima* drifting ominously close at hand. If the swells washed the other ship against the *Magdalena,* Danielle would be crushed.

Gasping for air, the girl strained to grip the rigging and pull herself upright. In front of her, Arturo blinked back blood and countered Turk's attack savagely, unaware of her dilemma. With extreme effort, she straightened, clinging to the lines to keep from falling back again. Her free hand groped blindly for the pistol in her pocket, but she could not reach it. Her voluminous skirt—and the pocket holding the gun—were bunched against the gunwale.

She watched, powerless to assist the captain, as one of Turk's crewmen arrived to reinforce the big pirate, attacking

Arturo vigorously from the right. Arturo managed to hold them off, but the blow to his head and the loss of blood took their toll, slowing his reflexes. Sensing weakness in his opponent, Turk emitted a whoop and both pirates intensified their attack.

The sailor from the *Fatima* became careless when victory appeared within reach. Seeing the man's side unguarded, Arturo seized the opening, lunging forward to sink his sword in his chest. Before he could free his blade, Turk closed in for the kill.

Behind the captain, Danielle rocked backward on her heels, nearly overset by her sudden release when he leaped forward. Time seemed to stand still as she pushed herself forward and gained a firm footing on the deck. Her hand dipped into her pocket and found what she sought. As she drew the tiny weapon, she wished she had time to aim; with only one shot, she could not afford to miss. Pointing the pistol at Turk, she sent a wordless prayer skyward and pulled the trigger.

At the pistol's report, the duelists turned to her with surprise on their faces. Even the men around them paused in their fighting to stare for a moment. Turk's shoulder gushed blood from a tiny hole and he opened his mouth to speak. But before he could say anything, he crumpled and fell to the deck, where he lay motionless on his side.

At that moment, Danielle was thrown violently against Arturo's broad chest and his strong arms held her there as the *Magdalena* rocked with the recoil of a forceful explosion. An alarm went up from the pirates and they rapidly retreated, swinging back aboard their own ship in complete disorder. Lines between the two ships were hastily cut and, as they drifted apart, Arturo's crew could see their enemies rushing to man the pumps.

"What the devil?" the captain muttered, drawing Danielle with him to the railing. His narrowed eyes were fixed on a cannonball hole in the *Fatima*'s hull just at the waterline.

"We're saved, *capitaine!*" Falgout shouted from the smoldering quarterdeck. "Someone from the *Magdalena* got off a broadside."

While they watched, the *Fatima* began to founder. Their last glimpse of the marauder was as she limped away, trailing wisps of smoke behind her.

"Are you all right?" Arturo turned to Danielle in concern. He gripped her shoulders tightly, forcing her to look at him.

"*Oui.*" She gulped, tearing her horrified eyes from Turk's still body. "But I think I have just killed a man."

"Not by shooting him in the shoulder with that." He nodded at the little gun she still held in numbed fingers. Tying his scarf tightly around his head to stanch the blood, Arturo knelt beside the Ottoman to lift him. Then he frowned. "What is this?"

"Wh-what?" Danielle asked, her face blanching as he withdrew his hand from behind the man's back, covered with blood.

"He is dead. He's been stabbed." He rolled Turk's limp form over to reveal a bloody puncture wound on his back.

"But how? Who?"

"I do not know. It could have been anyone in the heat of the battle. At least you know you did not kill him, *cher.*"

Arturo rose and pulled the trembling girl against his side, comforting her softly. "It is all right, Dani. It is all over now. Come, I will walk you to your quarters."

She huddled against him for a moment, appreciating the solid warmth of his chest, drawing strength from him. Then, slowly, the couple walked toward the cabins.

"Danielle!" Narcisse, unharmed, came into view on the ladder from the foredeck. His face was pale under its covering of grime. "*Mon Dieu,* I have been mad with worry for you."

"She is all right," Arturo answered curtly for her, his arm still wrapped around her shoulders.

"So I see." The young Cajun nodded, one eyebrow lifting in mute question. But before anything more could be said, a cheer went up on the foredeck, and all three went forward to investigate.

They joined the ship's company just as Pat was lifted from the hold. The cabin boy seemed to be intact, though he held out his hands carefully in front of him. His face, smudged with soot, was jubilant.

"Am I to understand that it was you who fired at the *Fatima,* Pat?" the captain questioned.

"Aye, sir," the boy replied, his skinny chest swelling with pride. "I was 'tweendecks when our men were occupied fightin' those cutthroats, and I saw one of the cannons was unmanned. So I sez to meself, 'Tis not only an opportunity, Patrick, me lad, but yer duty.'"

"Are you badly hurt, lad?"

"Naw." He seemed embarrassed by the attention he was receiving. "Just a little burnt. The barrel was already heated and I think I may have used a wee bit too much powder. I hope the cannon is all right, sir."

"I am sure you got the worst of it," Arturo said with a chuckle. "Well done, *mon ami!*"

"Aye," Pat agreed, no practitioner of false modesty. "Don't reckon we'll be seein' the *Fatima* again soon, Cap'n. D'ye?"

"No time soon," Arturo replied. "Why don't you let Felix take a look at your hands. Where *is* Felix?"

He scowled when the old cook did not appear. Danielle felt a stir of anxiety when no one seemed to know where he was. However, when a crock of lard and a jug of rum were hastily produced from the galley to serve as medicines, she tended Pat's burns, slathering his hands with lard and wrapping them in strips from her skirt. Then she insisted on treating Arturo's cut.

"It is not bad, so do not think you must practice your embroidery on my head," he cautioned, only partly in jest.

"I would not waste the thread," the girl answered tartly, though she was relieved to see he was correct. The wound was clean and not very deep.

Arturo sat on an upturned bucket, his knees around his ears, and bore Danielle's ministrations with limited tolerance, refusing to allow her to grease his singed arms and hands with lard. He cursed expressively when she swabbed the cut on his head with rum to disinfect it. Then, impatient to see to his ship, he stood before she was finished, forcing her to tiptoe in order to tuck the ends of his bandage in place.

With a distracted word of thanks, he strode away to oversee the cleaning and repair work. Standing in front of the charred quarterdeck, where Narcisse was steering the limping brigantine, Arturo listened to a damage report from Falgout, who was filling in for Jacques. The captain was pleased to learn the *Magdalena* had suffered only three fatalities and there was no injury more serious than cuts or broken bones.

Danielle decided to return to the wounded first mate and see to his needs until he could be moved from the bow to his cabin. As she crossed the foredeck, littered with bodies, she kept her eyes fixed straight ahead. Around her, a casualty count was in progress, and the corpses were being stacked near the ruined mast. She shuddered at the grisly reminders of the afternoon's bloodshed.

Shock overcame all other emotion, however, when the girl climbed to the bow and saw Felix, his head bloody, sitting beside Jacques. Fright gave way to relief when she examined his injury and discovered it was not serious. He had only been grazed by falling rigging. Quickly she cleansed the wound and bandaged it.

"Almost had another hole to fix, *mam'selle*." The old man smiled toothlessly at her, unmindful of the pain.

"No matter, Monsieur Fontaineau," she assured him with a smile. "We would patch it as surely as we patched your pants."

Danielle looked up from her labor to discover wounded sailors clustered around her. They waited patiently, presenting their wounds for her inspection almost shyly. Most of the injuries were minor: cuts caused by splinters from flying debris, or burns, like Pat's, from the heating of the cannon. She treated all efficiently, one after another, setting up a rough clinic of sorts on the bow.

It was dusk before she finished and walked wearily toward the main deck. So exhausted was she that she did not even see Arturo supervising his crew beside the mast. He watched as Danielle passed, warmed by the sight of her.

Her new gown was in tatters; her black petticoat, visible underneath, was now bedraggled and stiff with blood. Streaks of soot and black powder smudged her sunburned face. Her hair, dull from the smoke, had tumbled around her shoulders. And she was magnificent, the man thought appreciatively.

Arturo spoke a few brief words of instruction to Falgout and Dazet regarding the repairs. Then he followed Danielle, wanting to speak to her, to comfort her, but uncertain what to say.

As the girl mounted the ladder to the main deck, the atrocities she had seen during the day finally reached her numbed brain and she swayed.

Stepping forward, the captain swept her lightly into his arms where she nestled, already half unconscious.

Chapter Thirteen

Danielle awakened, surprised to find herself in her cabin. She had been on deck for hours after the battle, but she remembered nothing after that. Someone must have carried her to her cabin, undressed her and put her to bed. Mortified, she realized she was clad in only her gossamer undergarment. Her tattered, bloodstained clothing was nowhere to be seen. Her old black gown and chemise and the elaborate petticoat Arturo had given her were laid out with care.

The cabin was hot and the girl's head throbbed, the ache made worse by the lingering smell of smoke. Lifting a hand to her forehead, she found her face was black with soot. She sat up and looked around sluggishly. She must wash . . . but first things first.

She opened the porthole and stood in front of it, breathing in the fresh air in hungry gulps. Outside, rain fell in huge drops from a dark cloud directly overhead. No wind drove the clouds or slanted the rain hitting the deck. The *Magdalena* was nearly motionless, rocking gently on the green waters.

The brigantine was extraordinarily quiet. Only a few muffled sounds came from far forward. Surely repairs to the ship were not complete, she thought sleepily; she could not have slept that long.

Emptying the tepid contents of the ewer into the basin, Danielle washed her face, the soot leaving the water gray and cloudy. She sighed, disappointed that she must dress without the benefit of a bath. Her body itched at the thought of pulling on her stiff mourning gown over the grime. But there were more important considerations than baths aboard the *Magdalena* today.

Cautiously, the girl approached the mirror, dreading what she would see. Her fears were confirmed. She would hardly pass for a Creole lady now, she thought bleakly. Her tangled hair was dull from the smoke; her face was puffy from sleep; her jaw was bruised where the pirate had hit her yesterday; her nose was a decidedly unladylike shade of red from the sun.

"What difference does it make?" she asked her reflection. The wounded men she had tended were more important than her complexion.

She dressed quickly and sat down to a breakfast of fruit and cheese, discovering suddenly that she was ravenous. Her meal was interrupted almost before it began by a light rap at the door.

Pat, his freckled face alight with pleasure, peered into the cabin. "Top of the mornin', Miss Dani," he greeted her cheerfully. "Saw yer porthole was open and figured ye were stirrin', so I brought somethin' to go with yer breakfast." He entered, wearing a dripping oilskin jacket and gingerly carrying a pot of coffee in his bandaged hands.

"*Merci*, Pat. How thoughtful of you."

"Y'er welcome. How're ye feelin'?" he asked. "Ye sure had us worried, ye know, faintin' like that."

"I am fine," she assured him. "How are you?"

"Gonna be good as new soon," he pronounced with satisfaction, holding up one hand, now wrapped in white gauze. "But please don't tell anybody yet. I'm enjoyin' bein' a wounded hero . . . not that I've gotten out of much work."

"All right, I will not tell—right away." Danielle smiled. "Where did you get the clean bandages?"

"From Felix. He doctored my hands this mornin', though he hadn't much time, what with mendin' sails and sewin' shrouds."

The girl shivered involuntarily at the reminder of yesterday's carnage. Quickly, she changed the subject. "Tell me, Pat. How did I get back to my cabin?"

"The cap'n. He put ye to bed and let no one disturb ye."

"Capitaine De Leon put me to bed?" Inwardly, she cringed.

"Aye, and mighty anxious about ye, he was. He threatened anyone who woke ye. Though he assured us ye were restin' easy, some of the lads might have braved a floggin' if ye did not stir soon. It's good ye woke when ye did."

The boy fidgeted for a moment, then shyly drew a bundle from inside his jacket. "I . . . well, Felix and I have somethin' for ye, since ye ruined yer new dress puttin' us back together." Beneath his damp hair, Pat's face flamed as he presented the girl with a parcel wrapped in brown paper.

"What is this?" Tentatively, she opened the package and pulled out a petticoat of bright red flannel.

"'Twas for me mother," he stammered, "but I won't be seein' her anytime soon. I thought 'twould serve as a skirt. I hope y'er not embarrassed, but 'twas the only female garb I could find, though I searched the *Magdalena* high and low."

"It will make a fine skirt," Danielle agreed obligingly.

"Felix sent this to hold it up since 'tis a bit large." He produced an embroidered black sash. "And we figured, for a shirt, ye might be able to use one of the cap'n's."

"Thank you both, Pat," she replied, moved by their generosity.

"No, ma'am, thank you." The cabin boy gathered the dishes clumsily in his wounded hands and hastened toward the door. "I know ye'll be wantin' to wash the smoke from yer hair and all. Though I can't bring the tub for there's too much work to be done, I will fetch ye more water.

"But I have to be goin' now." He preened with youthful self-importance. "'Tis up to me to tell the captain y'er awake. He's been waitin'. He set the lads to doin' the quieter work for he didn't want to disturb ye with too much hammerin', but as I said, there's a great deal of work to be done, 'specially on the quarterdeck."

The boy had hardly left before the pounding commenced. Only moments later, another rap sounded on Danielle's door and Arturo came in. His head was no longer bandaged and he looked hale and hearty . . . and handsome, despite the dark circles under his eyes, which bespoke a lack of sleep.

"*Bonjour,* Danielle," he greeted her warmly. Crossing to the basin, he helped himself to her towel and dried the rain from his face. "I am glad to see you look none the worse for wear."

"Merci," the girl thanked him coolly, all too aware of her appearance. He could have waited until she had washed. But she did not let him know of her discomfiture. *"Café?"* she asked graciously. Out of habit, Pat had brought two cups with her breakfast tray. One of these she filled and handed to the captain.

"Merci. I must say, you were *magnifique* yesterday, *cher,"* Arturo said, dropping into the chair across from her. "I cannot tell you how grateful I am to you for the care you gave my crew."

"I was happy to help," she said simply. "How is Monsieur Foucher this morning?"

"Jacques is as well as can be expected. Considering."

"Considering?" Her eyes widened in alarm for her patient.

"It is nothing serious," he assured her. "It's just that, well, we gave him rum for the pain and he . . . er . . . got drunk."

"But how is his leg? I would like to look at it."

"Perhaps a bit later. Felix looked in on him this morning. Now what is this?" he asked idly, picking up the red petticoat from where it lay, still folded. He roared with laughter as he held the outsize garment up in front of him. "Where did you get this?"

Danielle rushed to defend her youthful benefactor. "Pat gave it to me, and it was very sweet of him. He wanted me to have something to wear besides this." Distastefully, she pinched a fold of her black skirt and held it out for his inspection.

"I am sorry about your new dress, *ma petite,"* the captain apologized sincerely. "You know, I think I have something that would be better than a petticoat." He pulled a key from his pocket and went to kneel beside his trunk.

"Non, s'il vous plaît—"

"Shhh, you do not even know yet what I have for you, *cher."*

As he rummaged in the trunk, she glimpsed the flamboyant gowns he had offered earlier. Finally he lifted out several bolts of fabric, two of them quite rich and opulent.

"Will you accept these as a token of my appreciation? With Felix's sewing kit, I am sure you could fashion them into gowns worthy of your beauty."

"They are beautiful. *Merci,*" Danielle murmured gratefully, fingering the rich textiles.

"It is the least I can do," the man answered gravely. He stacked the bolts on the table, then moved to stand beside her chair. "After all, I owe you my life."

"Oh, *non.*"

"Oh, *oui.* Turk would have finished me, if you had not shot him. I found your concern for me quite touching. In fact, one of my fondest memories will always be the sight of your face with tears streaming down it." Reaching toward her, his fingers twined in her hair and he traced her cheekbone with his thumb. "And after you said you would never cry for me," he chided lightly, a glint of amusement replacing the gravity in his blue eyes.

"I was not crying!"

"But you were," he contradicted firmly.

"Well, it was not for you. It was…it was because of the smoke," she pronounced, equally resolute.

"Ah, Danielle," he said with a sigh, pulling her from her chair. "You always deny your feelings. Why can you not admit that you are simply mad for me?"

"Arturo De Leon…" she began scorchingly.

"Admit it, *ma petite,*" he coaxed, cupping her chin to tilt her face toward his. "You love me."

"No," she denied weakly, shifting her eyes to look over his shoulder.

"Not even a little?" He bent to kiss the corner of her mouth softly.

"*Non.*" The whispered word was a painful denial as the realization rocked her. She was in love with Arturo De Leon. He was maddeningly arrogant and certain of his charm; he was a roué who flirted shamelessly with every female he encountered; he would never be true to one woman. He was attracted to her, she was certain; that was lust. But love? Not Arturo. She could not, *would* not, love him.

Danielle refused to meet his gaze, afraid the raw emotion in her eyes would give her away. Inwardly she raged. How could she care for the insufferable, impossible captain? She had never admitted it, even to herself, but she had known it since the night they met at the Winter Masque. She had known on deck yesterday when she had feared for his life. She recalled the fierce, overpowering pain when she thought he might be dead.

She did not want to love him. She wanted to hate him. She did hate him, she told herself stubbornly, mentally reciting a litany of his faults. He took her from the only life she had known. He kept her prisoner on a ship bound for distant ports. He controlled her life, even her comings and goings aboard ship. He toyed with her, first flirting, then rejecting her, embarrassing her at every opportunity. She could never even hint at her feelings for him or her humiliation would be complete.

"Won't you confess your passion for me?" Arturo teased insistently, his warm breath stirring the hair beside her ear. "Shall I offer more encouragement?" His smiling mouth descended on hers, claiming it confidently. It was an easy, playful kiss that might have deepened if the girl had not stiffened in his embrace and withdrawn.

She drew a deep, quaking breath, feeling as if she would smother, engulfed in his nearness. Her head pounded and tears burned at the back of her throat, but she addressed him coldly, "Release me."

"As you wish." The timbre of Arturo's voice was unsteady for an instant, as well. Dropping his hands to his side, the privateer sought to cover his loss of composure by quipping lightly, "You will not object if I continue to encourage you, *cheri?* Surely you will surrender to my charms someday."

"I do mind," she declared emphatically, glaring up at him. "I will not surrender. And I do not find your jokes funny, *capitaine.*"

"How do you know I am joking?" His sapphire eyes caught and held hers compellingly.

The girl was saved from having to respond by a knock at the door. Dazet stood in the passageway with a bashful smile and two buckets of rainwater. Uncomfortably, she wondered how much of the conversation between Arturo and herself he had overheard.

"Why didn't Pat bring the water?" the captain asked at once, casting a hard look at the ship's carpenter.

"Th-the boy could not c-carry it in his injured h-hands," Dazet stammered. "Since the w-water supply is my r-responsibility, I decided to bring it myself, *c-capitaine*."

"I see." Arturo could not argue with the man's reasonable explanation, but he did not like it. "Put it over there," he growled.

"Th-this is the f-first of the runoff," the sailor told Danielle shyly, his stutter aggravated by nervousness. "W-W-We couldn't drink it anyway. You sh-should have it."

"*Merci*, Monsieur Dazet, you are very kind." Danielle smiled brightly, rendering the carpenter completely speechless.

"Do you not have duties, Dazet, like repairing this ship?" Arturo interjected tersely.

"*Oui, c-capitaine*," he conceded at once, backing out the door. "*B-bonjour, mam'selle*."

Danielle wheeled on the captain when he did not follow his crewman. "Do you not have duties, *capitaine*, like commanding this ship?" she asked acidly.

With a dark scowl, Arturo marched out of the cabin, slamming the door behind him.

By the time Danielle finished bathing and washing her hair, the rain had stopped and the sun was slanting through the clouds in golden shafts. The girl stepped out on deck and sniffed the clean wind, which carried on it the smell of the new wood used to replace damaged sections of gunwales. The deck shimmered in the heat and her black dress felt stiflingly hot.

The *Magdalena* moved slowly but steadily, propelled by a slight breeze, which billowed the undamaged sails near the stern. The skeletal look of the foredeck was altered while Danielle watched. Under Arturo's supervision, the crew hoisted the mended foresail.

As the girl made her way toward the galley, she was hailed by the smiling Narcisse from the quarterdeck and greeted by several of Arturo's crewmen. They saluted her jauntily with bandaged hands she had treated the day before.

On the stern, she found Felix and Falgout stitching the flying jib, the last of the mangled sails. Each wearing a sailor's palm, a leather protector over the hand, they chattered like a pair of old ladies as they worked huge needles and coarse thread through the bulky canvas. When he saw her, Felix grinned and motioned for the girl to take a seat beside him.

Soon Falgout found the courage to ask Danielle to tend Achille Pleasance's wounds. The young man, his nephew, had a sliver of wood embedded in his leg from the battle. His uncle did not know whether the young fool was playing hero or whether he simply he had not realized how bad his injury was. But the leg had swollen badly overnight and Falgout feared it would fester.

"I will be happy to see to it, *monsieur,*" she agreed at once.

"Why didn't he ask me?" Felix demanded petulantly.

"Er . . . because you once pulled a tooth for him."

"Fair enough." The cook nodded. "I will get my medicines for you, *mam'selle,* and some clean linen for bandages."

"Felix is a fine cook, him," Falgout assured her when the old man disappeared into the galley, "but no damn good as a doctor."

The reluctant Achille, not much older than Pat, was brought to Danielle. His wound was halfway up his leg, just above the knee in the fleshy part of his thigh, and she realized it had been modesty that kept him from seeking treatment; he was horrified at having his leg examined by a female.

The wound was inflamed and Achille's pants had to ripped along the seam to his thigh so it could be doctored. A few men working nearby emitted catcalls at the sight of his bare limb, but Danielle quelled them with a glance. Then she spoke kindly to her patient, hoping to set him at ease.

His face pale, the boy wrung his cloth cap nervously in his hands before she even started. She cleansed the angry-looking wound and probed gently, locating the splinter and extracting it without much difficulty, though she was distracted by Achille's muttering. Eyes tightly closed, he recited the Twenty-Third Psalm as though he thought he would meet his end at her hand.

When she had applied ointment and bandaged the leg, Achille stopped in mid psalm and opened his eyes to ask, "I can go now, *oui?*"

"*Oui,* but try to stay off it as much as you can."

"Merci." He stood up and placed his weight on his leg to test it. "It feels much better. That was not so bad, was it, *mam'selle?"*

"No," she said, laughing, and watched him return to his comrades. Then she turned her attention to Felix.

He allowed her to change the dressing on his wound without a sound, but when she made her next request, the old man emitted a loud squawk of protest. "It is not a good idea for you to go see Jacques, no, *mam'selle*. When I saw him this morning, he was in no mood for company."

"I know he is drunk," she answered, unperturbed.

"Then let Turo go with you. He's the only one who can handle Jacques when he's had too much to drink."

"Oui, mam'selle," Falgout readily concurred. "If you will wait here, I fetch the *capitaine."*

Danielle dreaded seeing Arturo so soon after their meeting in her cabin. Her trepidation was not eased when he came quickly, his face ominously dark.

"What is this about you going to Jacques's cabin?"

"Monsieur Foucher's wound must be tended."

"Aren't you carrying this angel of mercy act too far?" he inquired crossly. "I have heard nothing all day from my crew but Mam'selle Danielle this and Mam'selle Danielle that."

"As you well know, *capitaine,"* she cut in, undaunted, "in this heat, gangrene is a danger. He could lose his leg."

"All right," he growled, annoyed to admit she was right. "But stay behind me until I find out what kind of mood he is in."

They paused outside the door next to Arturo's cabin. Jacques could be heard inside, singing one line of a song repeatedly in a low monotone.

"Turo, 'm glad you're here," Jacques greeted his captain. "I can't remember th' nex' line." The first mate was fully clothed, propped on his bunk with a jug of rum cradled at his side. In a booming basso, he sang a line from a popular risqué song and regarded Arturo expectantly.

"Not now, *mon ami."* The captain stepped aside so Jacques could see Danielle in the passageway behind him.

Jacques tried to focus on the slender black-clad figure, but his glazed eyes crossed with the effort. "Where'd you getta nun, Turo?'' he whispered loudly. ''You shoulda tol' me an' I wouldn' sing such a song in front of her, no.

''Sorry, S-sister,'' he apologized expansively to Danielle. ''F'rgive me, *s'il vous plaît*.'' He hiccupped loudly, then grinned sheepishly. *''Pardon.''*

''Do not concern yourself, Monsieur Foucher,'' Danielle answered, fighting a smile. She moved into the cabin, which reeked of sweat and alcohol, and bent over Jacques's injured leg. There was some swelling, but nothing about which to be alarmed, she decided.

She touched the first mate's forehead. ''He has a fever. He must be gotten out of these clothes and bathed with cool water. And he must *drink* water as well. Get rid of that.'' She nodded toward the rum jug.

''It is for the pain,'' the captain argued defensively.

''Then water it down.''

''Jacques is not overly fond of grog.'' Arturo's expression was dubious.

''I'll drink grog, if tha's wha' th' sister wants,'' Jacques muttered, tugging on Arturo's sleeve. ''But please, Turo, don' let 'er see me 'thout my clothes.''

''I won't,'' the other man promised. He turned to Danielle. *''Très bien,* I will undress him while you send Achille with water. He can bathe Jacques. You see to the rest of your patients, who undoubtedly need your tender nursing.''

Danielle ignored his sarcasm and went out on deck to doctor and rebandage numerous wounds. Later, she made a tisane of quinine for Jacques's fever and sent Pat to his cabin with it. The boy returned to report the first mate had drunk every drop, complaining loudly before he rolled over and began to snore.

Pleased with her afternoon's work, the girl borrowed Felix's sewing kit and went below to construct a new gown. Since she had little aptitude for sewing, she selected a plain blue cotton to experiment upon and began to cut. While she sewed, she thought longingly of the gown she had worn to the Parker ball. She had felt beautiful, and when she and Arturo had danced, his eyes had confirmed it. Jabbing herself with the needle, Danielle uttered a short cry of pain and put away her memories.

The ship was under full sail the next morning when the girl ventured out of her cabin. At first, she felt foolish wearing Arturo's shirt, the red flannel petticoat and Felix's sash, but rewarded by a joyful smile from Pat, she decided she did not care what anyone else thought. Her confidence was bolstered when none of the men seemed to notice she wore an undergarment for a skirt.

Danielle saw Jacques sitting on the foredeck, his back against the mast, a crude crutch beside him. The first mate looked haggard, and though he nodded at her, his attitude did not invite company.

Turning toward the stern, she was beckoned by Narcisse, who stood at the helm. "*Bonjour, ma belle,* I wish to speak with you, but I cannot leave my post. You will join me for a moment, *oui?*"

"Are you sure it will be all right?" Danielle asked cautiously, remembering Arturo's order to stay out of the way.

"I think so, just this once."

When the girl had climbed up to join him on the quarterdeck, the handsome Cajun remarked, "I was wondering, *cher,* what happened to that charming bonnet Turo gave you?"

"It was ruined during the battle."

"So I thought. Now, me, I would hate to see you ruin your lovely complexion. This sun will turn you brown." He smiled at her, his teeth white against his tanned skin. "Good for a dashing sailor, yes, but for a beautiful woman, not so good. So if you will allow me . . ." He produced a dainty lace parasol from a hiding place nearby.

"Oh, Narcisse, it is lovely," she breathed as she accepted the frivolous sunshade. "*Merci.*"

"It is nothing." He shrugged. "I bought it for you in Nassau."

"You are a dear friend and a terrible liar," Danielle teased. "The tag on the handle says Balliet's of New Orleans."

"A dear friend," the young man echoed gloomily. Then he grinned, unabashed. "Ah, well, if I am caught in a lie, the truth then. I bought it for a—an acquaintance of mine, but I think she will have forgotten me by the time we return to Tortuga."

"I doubt it," the girl disagreed gently.

"No matter. She will have to pine away. You have the parasol . . . and my heart," he flirted extravagantly.

Gaily, Danielle opened the parasol and twirled it artfully, throwing Narcisse a brilliant smile. Her smile faded, however, when she caught sight of Arturo, watching them with a scowl on his face.

"I believe I must excuse myself, Monsieur Duval," she murmured, her eyes on the volatile captain.

"Oui," Narcisse agreed quickly, "I think it would be best."

She went to seek Felix on the stern, but he had no task to occupy her. After days of feeding the crew hardtack, the old man had returned to his cooking duties. He had sacrificed one of his chickens, and now the savory aroma of gumbo filled the air. The girl sat with him, idle and bored, until Dazet approached with a light spar rigged as a fishing pole.

"I thought y-you might enjoy f-fishing to p-pass the time," he suggested shyly. "You c-could have fresh f-fish for d-dinner . . . if F-Felix w-will cook it for you."

"Ah, *très bon!* Fresh fish." The cook smacked his lips loudly. "I will make you a bargain, Mam'selle Danielle. The first fish you catch is for you. The second is for the *capitaine.* But the third, it is for me, yes?"

The captain stood at the helm, frowning as the smell of fish frying in the galley reached him. He should have felt happier. The wind was with the *Magdalena;* repairs were complete, and the ship was almost as good as new. Things were back to normal—as normal as they could be since Danielle Valmont had turned life upside down on his vessel, he brooded.

Arturo's frown deepened when he recalled the sight that was so common aboard the *Magdalena* the past few days: Danielle in her outlandish costume, shaded by that ridiculous parasol. Each day she fished on the stern, watched over indulgently by his rough men.

There was no doubt, the girl had captured the hearts of his crew. Since she had nursed the wounded, she had discovered many small anonymous gifts in her cabin: hair ribbons, a lacquered brooch, a bar of rose-scented soap. Achille had given her a small cloth bag of horehound candies, kept too long in his sea chest. The lozenges had been stuck together in a gooey ball and coated with lint from the cotton sack, but she had made as much of them as if they had been the finest confections, Arturo thought testily.

Only Jacques seemed impervious to her charm. Good old Jacques, the captain thought appreciatively. The first mate kept to himself, nodding when the girl's eyes fell on him, but he never spoke or beckoned her to his side. At least, *he* was not behaving like a lovesick schoolboy.

Danielle had a smile and a kind word for everyone; yet Arturo felt the distance between them each night when they walked together. His pride smarted. Accustomed to success with the ladies, he was nonplussed when Danielle skillfully evaded his advances. She was not unkind; she simply refused to be drawn into those flirtations or clashes that ended inevitably with her in his arms. During the past few weeks, she had been transformed before his eyes from a spoiled, uncertain girl to a confident, serene woman.

He cursed softly under his breath to think of it, for she stirred his blood more than ever, but she would not let him close. At times, he was not sure he wanted to be. Taking her from New Orleans had been a bad idea.

Still, his breath caught in his throat now when Danielle emerged from below. Cool and composed in the heat, she wore a simple blue dress and twirled her parasol over her shoulder. She lifted her eyes to the quarterdeck, smiling in casual greeting when she saw the captain there. Frowning, he nodded and watched her progress to the stern.

When she rounded the cabin section, the girl was greeted by a most peculiar sight. Felix leaned far over the port rail, his wooden leg tracing circles in the air behind him. Dropping her parasol, she rushed to grasp his belt and pull him to safety. The cook cursed and scowled over his shoulder, but his frown turned into a toothless smile and when he saw it was Danielle who held him.

"Look, *mam'selle,* just look at them!" He gestured down toward the water.

Stepping to the rail, she saw a school of adventurous dolphins playing tag beside the ship. She knelt on the bench on the stern and leaned out over the side almost as far as Felix had, laughing exuberantly as the old man called to them. The graceful creatures seemed to dance and caper, first falling back in the wake of the ship, then leaping forward effortlessly. The sun glistened on their sleek skin as they rose on their tails and bleated up at them, seeming to invite the humans to join them for a swim.

Suddenly, Danielle's enjoyment was marred by the awareness she was being watched. Shifting uncomfortably, she glanced over her shoulder. She could not see Arturo on the quarterdeck. Her eyes swept the deck near the mainmast. Harry Hinson nodded slightly when she discovered his scrutiny, but he made no effort to avert his gaze. His greedy eyes roamed boldly over her body. Self-consciously, Danielle sidled forward along the gunwale, maneuvering to put the mast between them and block his view of her.

Lately the Cockney's leering face seemed to be everywhere she looked when Danielle went out on deck. Sometimes he loitered near the stern and practiced throwing his knife at the mast. But when he went to retrieve it, his eyes slid suggestively toward the girl. He never spoke, but his increasingly audacious gaze was constantly upon her.

One evening at dusk when most of the crew were at leisure on the foredeck, Danielle sat with Felix, sorting dried beans in the waning light. At last, Felix rose and lugged the basin of beans into the galley where they would soak overnight.

In the stillness, Danielle could hear the beans bouncing against metal as the cook poured them into a huge pot. She stretched lazily and got to her feet.

"*Bonsoir,* Felix," she said softly. "I am going to my cabin."

"*Bonsoir, mam'selle,*" the old man answered distractedly, intent on his task. "Until tomorrow then."

As the girl ambled along the narrow, deserted deck that ran just outside her cabin, Harry appeared around the corner. His lecherous eyes fixed firmly on her, the little Cockney blocked her path, making no move to yield as she drew near.

"Lovely evenin', hain't hit, miss?" He spoke in hushed tones so he would not alert Narcisse on the quarterdeck above them. His hot gaze roved over the girl's trim figure.

"Lovely." Danielle nodded perfunctorily and attempted to pass next to the bulkhead.

"Stay haround and talk wiv a lonely sailor, duck. Since we're shipmates, don't ye think we should get to know each other better?" The suggestion sounded obscene from his leering lips.

"I cannot stay."

"Cannot stay or will not?" The man's thin face flushed, and he gripped her wrist tightly as she tried to pass again.

"Let me go, *monsieur*." Danielle's tone was icy.

"Not bloody likely," he whispered, his hot breath on her neck. "I've fancied ye since that penny-ante gambler brought ye aboard. Ye're not goin' to begrudge a bloke one small kiss, are ye?"

Harry was a small man but he was surprisingly strong, and his painful hold did not slacken when the girl tried to wrench her arm from his grasp. He pinioned the arm he held behind her, pressing it against the bulkhead as he ground his pelvis against her.

"I said, let me go," Danielle ordered through clenched teeth, "or Capitaine De Leon will hear about this."

"Will 'e? Ye've been leading 'im by the nose, 'aven't ye? Well, ye can't lead 'Arry 'Inson because 'e won't be led."

They grappled silently in the dusk for a moment, Danielle giving a muffled cry when Harry endeavored to plant a wet kiss on her mouth.

As she looked around desperately for a weapon, she saw Jacques over her assailant's shoulder. His face black with rancor, the first mate approached as rapidly as his injured leg would permit.

"That's more like hit," Harry muttered, mistaking reprieve for surrender when the girl sagged with relief. He eased his grip somewhat, but did not release her. Engrossed in his quest, he did not hear the tap of the crutch on deck as the burly Baratarian advanced on him. "Now has I was sayin'—"

Harry's statement was never finished. With an inarticulate bellow, Jacques swung his crutch, catching him in the small of the back.

Yelping with pain, the Englishman drew his knife and whirled to face his assailant. When he discovered who it was, he dropped his defensive pose, but the anger did not leave his eyes.

"Jack, me boy, I thought we were friends," he greeted the first mate cajolingly.

"Get forward, Harry," Jacques commanded menacingly.

"What's wrong, mate? Me and the girl was just talkin' a spell. Hain't that so, miss?" Harry looked innocently to Danielle for confirmation.

When none was forthcoming, he drew himself up cockily and sheathed his knife. "I'll go, hawright, 'cause I can't find hit in me 'eart to fight a wounded man. Ye're a lucky bucko, Jack...this time." With that warning, he swaggered away, leaving the angry pair to watch his departure.

"*Merci,* Monsieur Foucher," the girl said, sighing with relief and rubbing her wrist tenderly.

"It is nothing, *mam'selle,* after what you did for me," the big man told her gravely. "I thank you."

"You are more than welcome, sir." Danielle smiled. Behind her, she could hear another tap on the deck. It was Felix's wooden leg as he hurried forward to see what the trouble was.

"You saved my leg, if not my life," Jacques told her, raising his voice enough so the cook could hear. "If you had not been here, I do not know what would have happened to me, no. Because he can gut fish, Felix fancies himself a surgeon." He nodded fondly toward the old man, who eavesdropped nearby.

"See if I waste any more of my doctoring on you, Jacques Foucher," the cook fussed and stumped back toward the galley.

"I wish, too, to apologize for what has been done to you," Jacques continued quietly when they were alone. "We should never have taken you from New Orleans. I have talked to Turo about it, but he does not always listen...especially when he wants something. He wants you and he insists he will take you to Tortuga. You may yet win, *mam'selle,* but you must be patient."

"Please," she entreated hesitantly, "you will not say anything to him about what just happened with Harry, will you?" She feared if Arturo knew, he would confine her to her cabin again.

"*Non,*" Jacques agreed. Nor would he say anything to Narcisse, he added silently. Either of the men might kill Harry for what he had done, and the *Magdalena* needed every hand. "I will keep a close watch on him," he promised, "and I suggest you do the same."

"*Merci.*" She sighed. As the first mate turned to leave, she blurted, "*Monsieur,* before you go..."

He halted and looked back at her. "You can call me Jacques, *mam'selle.*"

"Very well, Jacques. Harry just said something about a gambler bringing me aboard. Didn't—I mean, was it not Arturo who kidnapped me in New Orleans?"

"*Non, mam'selle.*"

"Who then?"

"A Kaintock, *un américain coquin* with a bad look about him."

"*Un américain?*" the girl repeated with a blank look. Then realization dawned in her dark eyes. "I was at Monsieur Soulé's town house, alone in the courtyard, when I heard a noise. A man stepped out of the shadows, but before I could call out, he put a sweet-smelling cloth over my face. I struggled, but could not escape. I remember now, I heard a voice...a Kaintock voice. It was Jack Lynch! But why?"

"I do not know."

"What happened to Monsieur Lynch?"

"Him, he learned to swim when Turo threw him in the river," the first mate said with a wolfish smile.

"You mean Arturo tried to kill a man because of me?"

"I do not believe the man was in any real danger. Turo only did what he thought was necessary. He took you from New Orleans to save your life. This I believe. But the problem is, now he does not want to let you go. Me, I think he loves you."

Arturo strolled around the cabin section just in time to hear Jacques's last declaration.

"Well, here you are with your heads together, exchanging confidences," he greeted them, his voice deceptively mild. They whirled to look at him guiltily. "Even though you are wounded, I would think you had better things to do, Jacques, than to meddle in my affairs."

"Sorry, *capitaine,*" the big sailor muttered insincerely. His eyes showed his resentment of Arturo's accusation, no matter how true. He hobbled away on his crutch without a backward look.

"I thought I asked you to stay out of the way of my crew," the captain reminded Danielle coldly.

"I have tried," she snapped. "But you can hardly expect me to jump overboard when one passes me on a narrow deck."

"Allow me to walk you back to your cabin before you are accosted by any more of my men," he insisted nastily.

She darted a quick glance at him, but was oddly relieved to see his temper was no worse than usual. He must not have witnessed the scene with Harry. She allowed him to take her arm and lead her toward the companionway, but she stopped abruptly when they reached the hatch. "Arturo, please, I must know . . ."

"What?" his voice rapped out harshly.

"Why did you take me from New Orleans?"

"Didn't Jacques tell you?"

"He said it was to save my life because Jack Lynch kidnapped me." Her eyes sought his and held them. "But I don't understand. Why would he wish to do me harm?"

"He planned to sell you to recoup some of the money Yves owed him for gambling debts."

"So you bought me from him?"

"I *took* you from him," the privateer amended. "And I have regretted it every day since."

"Then why did you keep me with you?"

"I heard Jacques tell you why." Arturo's voice was mocking. "Because I love you, remember?"

Stricken, Danielle stared up into his taunting blue eyes, her heart aching at his contempt. She drew herself up to answer icily, "Oh, yes, how could I have forgotten?"

She hoped the man did not notice the tightness in her voice or the tears that lurked dangerously close to the surface. Her chin rising proudly, Danielle swept haughtily down the companionway and disappeared into her cabin.

Chapter Fourteen

The ship was quiet as Arturo lounged near the stern and lit a cheroot. Drawing on it, he rubbed the back of his neck wearily. He was tired, but well pleased by their progress. If the wind held, they would soon reach Morocco.

When he saw Danielle on the deserted deck farther forward, the privateer's eyes narrowed. She did not see him and he did not alert her to his presence. She was motionless, lost in thought, her face turned toward the last vestiges of sunset. The girl's finely chiseled profile was dark against the red-streaked sky. Arturo watched as the wind whipped her skirt and lifted the fringe of the shawl she wore against the chill of the evening.

As if she felt his eyes upon her, she glanced in his direction. Because he did not want to seem to be spying on her, he acknowledged her notice with a nod; he met her gaze evenly. Coolly, she returned his nod, holding her ground, knowing he would avoid her as she had tried to avoid him.

I love you, remember? His cold taunt still rang in her ears. Even now his presence reminded her of the hurt she tried to forget.

Abruptly, the girl wheeled and disappeared from Arturo's view. With a savage curse, he jammed his cigar between clenched teeth and turned his muscular back to the spot where she had stood.

Safe from the captain's probing eyes, Danielle threw herself on her bunk and massaged the temples of her aching head with trembling hands. Should she try to set things right between thém? she asked herself for the hundredth time since that night on deck.

No! Her pride would not allow it. Henceforth, she would learn not to love Arturo De Leon.

But how, when his very presence made her heart race and every fiber of her being yearned toward him? She could not give in to the longing. To keep her resolution strong, she had begun to avoid him.

Her life had settled into a new routine . . . quiet, monotonous, without Arturo. It amazed her the distance two people could maintain even aboard a cramped ship. Their inevitable meetings were civil, if somewhat strained. Since they no longer walked together in the evenings, the girl walked with first one, then another of the ship's officers, careful to alternate so Arturo could not concentrate his anger on any one man. She was especially circumspect in her behavior toward Narcisse, who had become a good friend to her. It would take little to intensify the strain between the captain and his helmsman, a tension that Danielle seemed helpless to control.

One gray November morning, she could barely drag herself out of bed, so disheartened was she. After considering whether to pull the covers over her head, she forced herself to rise and dress in a gown she had made, a cheerful yellow creation she hoped would lighten her mood. Pat would soon arrive with her breakfast, and she was determined not to take her discouragement out on him.

When he appeared, the cabin boy loftily presented Danielle with a battered-looking orange, the last of the fruit from Nassau, and one of the scarce, treasured eggs.

"One egg was all Felix could spare," Pat explained, "because he used the rest for this." With a pleased flourish, he uncovered a small plate of sweet rolls with raisins.

"How nice," Danielle exclaimed, pleasure overcoming her ennui.

"He wanted ye to have something special this mornin'," the boy informed her, "since 'tis yer birthday."

"How did you know?" she asked, taken aback.

"The cap'n told us, miss."

"The *capitaine* told you?" She was puzzled for a moment before remembering a day that seemed a lifetime ago...the day he had escorted her so gallantly in Barataria.

Pat interrupted her sad reverie. "Many happy returns, Miss Danielle. This is from me." Proudly, he handed her a small package, wrapped in wrinkled paper. "I made it for ye meself."

Unwrapping it, she discovered a simple necklace, painstakingly fashioned of intricately knotted cord. "It is beautiful, Pat!"

"'Tis nothin'," he said with a bashful shrug.

"*Merci beaucoup.* You know, we have a custom in my family. Anyone who gives a birthday gift receives a kiss for luck." Leaning forward, she brushed his cheek lightly with her lips. The boy's eyes widened and his face turned as red as his checked shirt before he retreated rapidly, backing out the door.

The gifts from Felix and Pat were the first surprises in a day filled with unexpected events for Danielle. When she emerged from her cabin, the girl went to express her gratitude for Felix's extravagant breakfast by placing a kiss on his wrinkled cheek. Flustered and chattering even faster than usual, the cook gave her another cup of coffee and a seat beside the galley.

The mood was light among those collected around the bench on the stern. Of Arturo's officers, only Jacques did not join in, seemingly busy on the foredeck. Dazet and Falgout presented themselves to Danielle, each offering a gift. Delightedly, she accepted a small wooden box, which Dazet had carved to hold her few pieces of jewelry. Then she admired the elegant purse Falgout had fashioned for her from the skin of a shark the sailors had pulled onto the deck a couple of weeks before. The head of the man-eater was now nailed on the bow as a warning to others of his kind.

When she thanked them, both men surprised her. Having heard of the Valmont family tradition, they leaned forward to present their rough-stubbled cheeks, merriment sparkling in their dark eyes. She could hardly refuse. Laughing, she bussed each of them on the cheek and they went away, flushed and pleased.

On the quarterdeck, Arturo gripped the rail with white-knuckled fingers and muttered murderously under his breath.

What the hell was going on? His temper, already dangerously strained, was near breaking when Jacques joined the group on the stern.

"May I speak with you a moment, Mam'selle Danielle?" the big Baratarian asked politely.

"Of course." Excusing herself, the girl followed him to the gunwale. "It is good to see you without your crutch, Jacques," she said with a smile.

"*Oui,* my leg is completely healed," he rumbled. Then he fell silent, seeming to grope for words as Danielle waited expectantly. "Even though you smile and act as if you are happy, I can see you are troubled, *mam'selle,*" he blurted at last. "I have something which I hope will lift your spirits. Happy birthday, *ma petite.*" Without fanfare, the first mate held out a small tobacco sack.

Opening it, Danielle found a scrimshaw medallion. On its polished ivory surface, her fingers traced a delicate carving of a ship braving a stormy sea. The vessel, not unlike the *Magdalena,* was valiant and beautiful, sailing on as the waves broke over her bow and a violent wind billowed her sails. Even the etched rigging seemed to strain with effort.

"This is the most beautiful carving I have ever seen," she murmured with honest delight.

The rough seaman ducked his head in embarrassment. "It is right that you should have it. You are like the little ship and you will weather the storm, *oui?*"

"*Oui.*" She nodded, tears springing to her eyes. "*Merci, mon ami.*" Immediately, she fastened the pendant to the cord necklace Pat had made for her. "It is beautiful, yes, Jacques?"

"*Très jolie,* Danielle," the sailor said in approval, his eyes shining as she stood on tiptoe to hug him. He watched fondly as the girl hurried back to show the others, then he limped to the foredeck.

Even surrounded by friends, Danielle felt her spirits flag late in the afternoon. She attempted to sustain the festive mood, but her smile began to feel as if it were painted on as she accepted the congratulations of the crew. She was uneasy when Harry Hinson appeared to offer his felicitations, but he departed quickly. Her humor was not improved, however, when she realized Arturo was watching her from above. Their eyes locked for an instant before the girl fled to her cabin, her breath short and her heart pounding with tightly restrained emotion.

Pat joined Danielle for dinner in her cabin, but when it became apparent she was not in the mood to talk or play cards, the lad went in search of more entertaining company.

She waited for full darkness, then went restlessly to the main deck. Pleased to find it deserted, she stepped to the railing to look at the sea, faintly silvered by the quarter moon. At the sound of footsteps, she did not turn, but steeled herself for an encounter with Arturo. She was relieved to hear Narcisse's cheerful voice behind her.

"Ah, Danielle, I have been looking for you."

"*Bonsoir,* Narcisse." She turned to welcome the handsome young Cajun with a smile. "I thought you were at the helm this evening."

"Later." He gestured negligently, joining her at the rail. "For now Achille has it. Me, I am glad to find you here because I have something for you." He pulled an exquisite lace-edged handkerchief from his pocket, originally bought, no doubt, for one of his many conquests, and presented it with a flourish. "My compliments to the loveliest lady aboard the *Magdalena.*"

"I'll wager you say that to every lady you find on a moon-lit deck," she teased.

"Have you no faith in men, *mam'selle?*" he winced playfully.

"I have every faith in you, you roué," she retorted with a companionable smile. The carefree banter was familiar territory for both of them. The man could not help but flirt, Danielle thought comfortably, and she could not help but enjoy it. She admired the fine square of linen and lace and added seriously, "This is beautiful, Narcisse. *Merci.*"

"*Bon anniversaire,* Danielle," he answered softly, leaning slightly toward her.

Lifting her eyes to his dark ones, she faltered, alarmed by the unexpected ardor in them. She knew instinctively that she must not kiss him, even on the cheek, so she extended her hand graciously. "*Merci beaucoup,* my friend."

"Still only a friend?" He sighed dramatically and straightened at once. "But a good friend, *oui?*" In an instant, the devoted admirer was gone and the familiar, flirtatious Narcisse reappeared. Pressing a kiss on the back of Danielle's hand, he continued to hold it, maintaining, "You look so sad, *ma petite*. Do you not wish to talk to me about the reason?"

"Surely you cannot believe I would be sad on my birthday," she countered lightly.

"I know you do not wish me—or anyone else—to think so, but you have carried this sorrow with you for many days. I do not know what passed between you and the *capitaine*," he went on hesitantly, hoping to chase the haunted expression from her eyes, "but now you are unhappy. Why not let me talk to him for you?"

Danielle reclaimed her hand. *"Non, merci."*

"Come now, I have known Turo all of my life. He is hotheaded and proud, but he is not a fool. It is not like him to leave things so confused between you."

"He did try to apologize, but I would not let him."

"That would have been a blow to him." Narcisse shook with silent laughter. "He has uncommon success with the ladies, him."

"So I have heard," she responded stiffly.

"Now I see," the helmsman breathed wonderingly. Grasping the girl's shoulders, he turned her to face him so he could look directly into her eyes. "You are in love with him," he said, almost accusingly.

"No," she protested in alarm, trying to withdraw. But when he did not loosen his grip, she met his gaze despairingly and whispered, "Oh, Narcisse, does it show so much?"

"Only if one knows women ... and I know women," he boasted with a sad smile. Releasing her, he leaned against the gunwale and stared out at the sea. "You cannot go on this way, no, *cher*. Let me talk to Turo."

"No!" she objected again. "Please say nothing to him."

"As you wish, Dani. You know whatever service I may perform for you, I will."

"Merci, you are a good friend." Standing on tiptoe, she kissed his cheek, then returned to her cabin.

The handsome young man watched her disappear down the companionway, grateful that the darkness had masked the painful longing in his eyes. He shook his head and sighed deeply. Now things were becoming clear to him. He had enjoyed flirting with Danielle during the past few weeks, and he had not minded the dark looks Arturo had given him each time he saw them walking together. In fact, Narcisse had savored twitting the big captain. But he had not realized that Danielle loved Arturo and Arturo loved her. And neither would admit it.

What could he do? Narcisse wondered. He had agreed not to speak to Turo. Although he could not have Danielle, he could make sure she was not hurt, even if he had to pound on the captain to keep that vow.

The young Cajun did not see Arturo poised above him on the quarterdeck. The captain had not been able to hear the conversation between the couple, but he fumed at the intimacy of the scene he had witnessed and his jaw tightened at the memory of Danielle kissing Narcisse. Glaring down at his old friend, Arturo mused darkly. Narcisse was probably not to blame. After all, Danielle had kissed first one member, then another of his crew throughout the day. Well, enough was enough. He was going to find out what was going on, even if he had to pound on the helmsman to find out.

Springing down the ladder, he confronted Narcisse on the maindeck. "A word with you," he commanded brusquely.

"*Bonsoir,* Turo," the handsome young man greeted the captain mildly, ignoring the murderous gleam in his blue eyes.

"I want to know what is going on between you and Danielle."

"A mild flirtation on my part," he said, shrugging carelessly, "and nothing on hers, much to my regret."

"Narcisse Duval, I ought to—" Arturo's big hands tightened involuntarily into fists.

"Do you think you can bully me the way you bully Danielle?" the other man asked hotly without retreating a step.

"What do you mean by that?" the captain asked dangerously.

"I mean you have browbeaten her from the moment you took her from New Orleans. You kidnapped her, locked her in her cabin, shouted at her, ignored her. And do not think I haven't noticed how you scowl at her wherever she goes, whatever she does!''

''And why shouldn't I? It is up to me to keep peace aboard this ship. All day she kissed my officers and flirted with my entire crew. And now *you* have decided to become her protector. What is she to you?'' He advanced menacingly on the slender helmsman.

Narcisse wavered for an instant. Never one to back down from a fight, he yearned to rid himself of his frustrations, and Arturo would be a good opponent. But Arturo was also his captain and one of his oldest friends, so he controlled his anger with effort and said quietly, ''Calm down, Turo. You know I would never come between you and your woman.''

''She is not my woman,'' the privateer responded stiffly. ''She is nothing but trouble. I just want to know what she is trying to do to me.''

Fury flickered behind Narcisse's dark eyes. ''I told Danielle you are not a fool, but I was wrong.'' Then he stalked forward, his shoulders rigid with anger, and left the captain to stare after him in dumb surprise.

Having gotten no satisfaction from Narcisse, Arturo decided he would have this out with Danielle. He marched down the companionway and halted in front of her cabin. ''Danielle Valmont, I want to talk to you,'' he bellowed, pounding until the door rattled on its hinges.

''What is it?'' The girl opened the door and peered out at him with an air of quiet dignity. She had removed her hairpins and was brushing her hair in preparation for bed. It billowed around shoulders in a golden cloud, illuminated by the lamp behind her.

''I want to know what the hell is going on,'' he roared, determinedly ignoring the fetching picture she presented.

''I do not know what you mean, *capitaine,* but I am sure it can wait until morning,'' she said to dismiss him, and began to close the door.

''No, it cannot wait until morning,'' Arturo insisted, pushing his way into the cabin. ''I saw you out on deck just now with Narcisse.''

"You were spying on me?" Danielle's dark eyes flashed in indignation.

"If you conduct your indiscretions on deck, you cannot expect privacy," he barked, pacing the length of the cabin.

"How dare you?" she accused, following on his heels.

The man wheeled suddenly, looming over her. "I want you to tell me right now just what you are trying to do to me."

"To do to you?" she snapped, at the end of her patience. In her fury, she did not retreat from him. "I cannot believe such conceit, even from you! What could I have done, when I have taken such care to avoid you? My very presence on this ship brings you displeasure, yet you fault me for staying out of your way? Mark me well, Arturo De Leon, I have done nothing to you."

"You have done nothing to me," he growled, gripping her wrist tightly and yanking her toward him, "except to drive me mad every moment since the first time I saw you."

"Only in the beginning," she admitted honestly, her fingers working in vain to pry his fingers from her arm. "I know I was difficult, but so were you. You cannot deny that for the past month I have left you alone."

"Yes, you have left me alone," he crooned, "alone with only my burning desire for company. Is it a game you play, *ma petite?*"

"*Non,*" she whispered. She ceased her struggles, her mesmerized gaze fixed on Arturo's tormented face.

"You looked like the light of the sun today in your yellow dress, but each time your eyes met mine, they were cold," the man grated. "I could melt the ice in you, Danielle, but I will not force you, no matter how much I want you. I promised that your very first day aboard the *Magdalena*. But I warn you, I'm about to reconsider that misguided bit of chivalry. You try me, woman!"

"I have not—" she spit through stiff, white lips.

"Not tried me?" he cut in to ask dangerously. One muscular arm encircled her waist tightly, drawing her against him so her hands were trapped against his hard chest. "I saw you kiss Narcisse."

"It was only a kiss on the cheek," she whispered, breathless from his embrace.

But Arturo refused to hear. "Tell me...did he make you feel like this?" he demanded before his mouth possessed hers in a bruising kiss. Tearing his lips from hers with difficulty, he said hoarsely, "Today I have watched you throw yourself at my crew. Yet you treat me with disdain. I want to know why."

"You don't understand." She nodded feebly toward the birthday gifts that lay on the table.

"No, *you* don't understand," he corrected grimly, his expression bleak as he stared down at her. "You may think to leave me alone, but it is impossible. You are always with me, *mon coeur,* in my blood, in every breath I breathe. I think of you in the light of day. Your face haunts my dreams at night.

"You are inescapable, drawing me as surely as a flame draws a moth. Even if you were to be the ruin of me, I would seek no escape. You stopped being my prisoner when I became yours. I am captive to my own desires. I want you, Danielle, as I have never wanted another woman."

"Desires, Arturo? Always desires." She sighed, looking away for fear he would see the longing in her eyes.

"Why not desires?" he asked harshly, tilting her face so she was forced to meet his passionate gaze. "Desires consume me, the desire to hold you, to have you as my own, to keep you with me always ... to love you and to be loved by you in return."

"Love?" the girl repeated, pushing away to step back within the circle of his arms and gaze up at him doubtfully.

"Yes, love." The man's deep voice shook with emotion and his hand on her face was tender. "I never meant it to happen, but God help me, it did. I love you more than sanity or reason allows. I have always loved you. I knew it a month ago, but I did not want to admit it, even to myself."

"It took you so long to realize?" she asked with the beginnings of a radiant smile. "I knew I cared for you on the day of the battle, and I did not want to admit it, either."

"You love me?" Arturo's blue eyes were hopeful as they caught and held hers. Gone was the smirking, superior rake, Danielle realized, and in his place was a man she could love for the rest of her life.

"With all my heart." Her arms encircled his neck and she regarded him teasingly. "I am mad for you, *mon capitaine.*

Remember? Have you not told me that I find you irresistible?"

"*Oui, cher,* but I did not think you were listening." An exultant smile on his face, the man enfolded her in his arms, his fingers gliding upward along her ribs, bringing a quiver of delicious anticipation to her.

Their lips met in a kiss, sweet and unhurried, untainted by reluctance or resentment. Danielle's eyes closed and her lips grew soft and warm and inviting, parting under his with the merest hint of pressure. Enraptured, he explored, his tongue darting and caressing, teasing hers into response.

The girl moaned softly, a sigh of pleasure from deep within her throat. She moved in the tender circle of his arms as he enfolded her in a strong, loving embrace. Her breath quickened as Arturo's kiss deepened, becoming more demanding, and she felt a liquid heat spreading through her body. It tingled first in her breasts, which heaved against his hard chest, then swept downward, making its molten way to the very core of her body.

She returned his kiss with unexpected passion. The intuitive heat of her response, the feel of her willing body pressed against his, kindled a ravaging fire in his loins that inflamed him, causing the flare of desire, too long denied, to ignite within him.

He repeated her name again and again, murmuring against her cheek when his mouth left hers to move downward. His mustache grazing the slender ivory column of her throat caused the girl to shiver, enthralled by the intimacy of his touch. Mindlessly, she tilted her head back to expose her neck to the fiery trail of his kisses, until at last his lips reached their destination at the gentle rounding of her breasts. The bare flesh exposed above her décolletage was warm and fragrant and wonderfully firm under his gentle, kneading hand.

She ran her open palms languorously over the rippling muscles of Arturo's back, her hands closing convulsively on his rugged shoulders, gripping them tightly when his head dipped lower to kiss and nip gently at the breast swelling beneath his hand. She shuddered to feel the heat of his mouth through the bodice of her dress, the fabric rough and wet against the hard peak underneath. She lifted her hands to clasp his head, her fingers weaving through his thick, curling hair as she strained ever closer to him.

Arturo thrilled to the feel of her, to her touch, savoring each euphoric sensation she aroused in him. Slowly, his mouth moved up again to linger pleasurably below her ear, where her pulse pounded wildly beneath firm white skin.

"Turo, please," she entreated huskily as his arms tightened around her. Whatever she would have said was lost when his lips traced her jaw and came to rest again, hungrily, on her mouth.

Arturo was like a man starved. He feasted on the taste, the textures, the feel of Danielle. With staggering intensity, the realization came. He could partake of her for the rest of his life and never be sated. After a long, sweet moment, he withdrew, shaken, and looked down at her.

Her long lashes lifted to reveal brown eyes clouded by desire. "Please... love me," she whispered hesitantly as if still afraid of his response. Her fingers brushed delicately at the corner of his mouth and traced a line of his cheek, caressing, smoothing his brow, which was knit with an uncertain frown.

"Are you sure?" The question held a note of caution.

"I am sure," Danielle answered, although she knew full well what she offered. She knew at this moment, and forever, that she wanted nothing more than to love Arturo and to be loved by him. He had been right, after all; she would go to him willingly. There was no pride, no honor, no debt to repay. There was simply a gift. The gift of herself.

His face alight with love, Arturo accepted her offering. Carefully, he unbuttoned the bodice of her dress, pausing as he slipped it down to string hot kisses across her shoulder. She assisted him in sliding her arms from the sleeves of her dress, but immediately those arms twined around his neck. Danielle molded herself against Arturo's lean length, her lovely face eagerly lifted for his kiss.

When he had obliged her, delighting all her senses, the man freed himself enough to lift her dress over her head, then he dropped it onto the chair nearby and turned his attention to the tape of her petticoat. It fell with a silken whisper to the floor and was followed by her pantaloons. She stood naked before him.

Danielle approached shyly to perform a similar service for him, easing the jacket from his broad shoulders. Her usually adept fingers fumbled nervously with the buttons on his shirt, slowly stripping them from their holes, her unpracticed manner stimulating Arturo all the more.

"Danielle," he groaned, his desire torturous in its urgency.

"Yes, my love?" she murmured dreamily, her arms sliding under his shirt to link around his bare waist. Her hands lightly stroked the smooth, warm skin of his back, feathering along his spine. Drawing a shuddering breath, he embraced her, burying his face in the sweet-scented cloud of her hair. He reveled in the resilient softness of her breasts as they flattened against his furred chest. Cupping her buttocks with both hands, he pressed her against him, making his painful need known.

His mouth melded to hers in a fiery kiss, Arturo swept Danielle into his arms and carried her to the bunk. His blue eyes were filled with promise and they caressed her waiting body as he laid her down gently. His gaze never left her as he shed his clothing in a few swift moves. The innocent girl's eyes widened when he stood beside the bed for an instant, his body gilded by lamplight, the evidence of his desire jutting and magnificent. Then he joined her on the bunk, stretching his long, lean body beside her. She trembled to feel the solid, searing pressure of his unmistakable maleness against her hip. The muscles of her abdomen contracted at his touch before his hand drifted downward to stroke the inside of her thigh with gentle intimacy. She did not protest; Arturo touched her as if he believed she were precious.

"It is not too late to change your mind," he advised, his breath harsh and ragged. She could not know how the warning cost him; he was not sure he could allow her to leave the bed.

"I am not afraid." Her dark eyes were fixed trustingly on his face, and she was awed by the love she saw there.

Danielle was not frightened for she was certain Arturo would not hurt her. She knew about mating. She had seen the coupling of animals on the plantation. Conversations between some of the older women when they thought she was not listening had taught her that lying together was more pleasurable for the man than for the woman. She did not care. She wanted to give herself to him, but she was hardly prepared for the overwhelming emotions the man aroused in her.

Skillfully, he stroked; he nuzzled; his mouth wandered over her, licking, nibbling, kissing, until she thought he must surely intend to drive her mad. Indeed, her sanity deserted her, but it was such a rapturous madness she experienced, she hoped never to regain her senses. Abandoned to passion, the girl responded instinctively to Arturo's caresses.

"Gently, *mon amour*," he whispered against her mouth as he entered her. "The pain will be over soon and then comes the pleasure. I promise you."

There was a moment of burning pain as he had said, but it was quickly forgotten as Arturo surged inside her, filling Danielle with an ecstasy that blossomed, its singular warmth unfurling within her. She arched her lithe body beneath him, matching her rhythm naturally to his, rising to meet his thrusts as he moved inside her. Clinging together, they rose higher and higher, born on a wave of mounting passion until the release they sought swept over them. Their soft cries of fulfillment mingled in the night.

They lay together afterward, the sheen of perspiration that coated their bodies glistening in the lamplight. Arturo lay awake for a long time, listening to the even breathing that told him the girl slept. He pressed a grateful kiss on the blond head nestled at his shoulder and pondered the gift she had given him.

He had never before made love to a virgin, making it a point not to take what a girl should save for her husband. But Danielle was his woman now. The realization stunned Arturo as much as it exhilarated him. When he had taken the innocence she offered him so freely, he had taken her to be his own. They belonged together and nothing in the world would ever part them again.

He turned on his side and wrapped one arm around Danielle's waist, fitting her against him. Then Arturo slept, enjoying his first blissful, undisturbed slumber since leaving New Orleans.

The girl could not say what awakened her later. Perhaps she woke because it was nearly dawn. But more likely, it was the presence of a warm, hard male body in the bed beside her... unaccustomed, but indisputable and so wondrously right. Arturo! Her eyes flew open abruptly as memories of last night flooded back, causing her pulse to race and bringing a hot blush to her face.

She might have risen then, but she found she could not. She lay as Arturo had held her through the night, curled in the curve of his body. The man's broad shoulder was her pillow and one of his brawny arms was thrown carelessly over her midriff. She could not even turn her head to look at him for a long golden strand of her hair was captured under his powerful body. Because she could not move without awakening him, she stayed very still. She was not sure she was ready to face him after last night.

Danielle caught her breath and her body stiffened when yet another unfamiliar sensation made itself felt. Soft and warm, it stirred faintly against her hip as if it had a life of its own. Behind her, Arturo sighed deeply and his arm tightened about her.

His breath stirred the loose tendrils at her temples and she shivered when he murmured huskily in her ear, "So you are awake. *Bonjour, mon coeur.*"

"*Bonjour,*" she answered tentatively, wishing she could see him. She moved her head slightly, attempting to free her hair from beneath him.

Obligingly, he shifted, bringing himself up on one elbow so he leaned over her. All at once, Danielle was not sure she wanted to look at him, after all. She could not bear it if his handsome face was smug or disapproving. There was no escaping what she had done last night; she had been certain when she gave herself to him. She only wished she felt the same assurance this morning.

Well, she thought, swallowing deeply, she would have to face him sometime. Filled with misgivings, she eased onto her back, managing at the same time to slide away from him as far as the narrow bunk would permit. She lifted hesitant eyes to meet his in the predawn light.

Her movement did not allow her to see the sleepy passion lurking in Arturo's eyes. His amorous expression rearranged itself into a fearsome scowl, however, at her reluctance to be near him.

"What is wrong?" she asked, dreading the answer.

"I was about to ask you the same question. You regret last night?"

"No." She shook her head in certainty. How could he be so devastatingly attractive with tousled hair and unshaven jaw? she wondered.

"I would not want you to be sorry, Danielle, because you made me very happy."

"I—I was a complete wanton, wasn't I?" she asked shyly. She had to know how he felt, even as a wave of shame washed over her.

"Completely," he agreed into a lazy smile, tracing her lips lightly with his finger. "You left nothing to be desired, *cher,* except perhaps for another taste of your sweetness."

His playful expression left him abruptly when he saw her stricken look. "Danielle," he chided gently, "do you think I do not still love you this morning? Or perhaps you think I lied when I said I loved you at all?"

"No," she whispered, turning to bury her face against his chest. She did not want him to see her relief at his words, to know that she had doubted him.

"Listen to me, *cher,*" Arturo commanded, cupping her chin in his big hand, turning her face to his. "I love you even more this morning than I did last night. And last night I was already quite addled for the love of you. By this time tomorrow I should be a perfect idiot," he added with a mischievous grin.

"An idiot? I don't know." She laughed softly, almost weak with relief, and slipped her arm around his waist. "But perfect? Yes, absolutely perfect."

"*Dieu,* but you look beautiful in the morning," he murmured, smoothing her hair.

You cannot condemn a man because he enjoys awakening beside a beautiful woman, he had said long ago, speaking of daughters of joy. Was she any better? Danielle wondered. Resolutely, she put the question behind her. That memory had nothing to do with what she felt now—love, only love. Joyfully, she snuggled against him, reveling in the scent, the taste, the feel of him.

Leisurely, tenderly, they explored, discovering unimagined pleasures to be had in their merging.

Land ho!

The shout awoke the lovers several hours later. Arturo bounded from the bed and strained to peer out the porthole.

"I cannot see a thing. The view is better from the quarter-deck," he muttered distractedly.

"No, I take that back," he amended with a roguish grin when he turned to see Danielle propped on the bunk, the sheet slipping dangerously low over her bare breasts. "The view is better here. It is just too bad I cannot stay to enjoy it." He bent to plant a quick kiss on her lips before going to the basin to wash.

Arturo strode about the cabin, totally unconcerned and gloriously nude. The girl watched, fascinated by the magnificence of his body, while he hurriedly dressed.

As he picked up his jacket, a muffled metallic clank came from it. "Ah, before I forget," he said, delving into the pocket. "*Bon anniversaire, cher.* A belated birthday present for you." Smiling broadly, he handed her a pair of elaborate silver combs.

"You mean you had a gift for me yesterday, in spite of..." Her voice trailed off and she looked up at him in dismay.

"In spite of our differences?" he finished for her. "*Oui,* I carried them around all day, but I did not know whether I was going to be able to give them to you or not. You were so difficult."

"Difficult? Is that what you call it today?" she baited him merrily. "*Merci,* Turo, they are beautiful." Immediately, her hands went to her hair and the captain watched as she attempted, without a mirror, to secure her thick golden tresses with the combs. Her concentration was so complete, she failed to notice the sheet's steady downward progress, which finally left her firm, white breasts bare and lifted high by her upstretched arms.

"Cover yourself, Danielle," Arturo ordered with a groan, "or I will not be able to leave this cabin."

"Sorry," she mumbled, hastening to tug the errant sheet up over her nakedness.

"I am sorry I must go now." Arturo kissed her in farewell though he was going no farther than the deck. "I will see you later, *cher*. We have much to talk about, *oui?*"

"*Oui,*" she echoed softly, watching the door swing closed behind him.

Danielle did not linger in bed after Arturo had gone. She rose immediately and retrieved her clothing from where it had fallen last night when he removed it. Her lips curved in a smile when she thought of that.

But while she dressed, Danielle's mind was working. Arturo loved her. She was secure in that knowledge, but she still did not know what to do. What could she do? There was no turning back. No decent Creole girl would have allowed him to take her to bed, yet she had surrendered her innocence to him gladly. But she did not feel indecent or immoral. Far from it. What had happened between them was natural and right, an act of love between a man and a woman.

A man and woman who were married, her genteel upbringing reminded her. When she yielded her virginity, had she surrendered all claims to marriage? Arturo had said last night that he wanted to keep her with him always, and she had thrilled to the words.

But would he marry her? Or would he expect her to be his mistress? If he asked it of her, could she do it? Danielle was shocked to admit, even to herself, that she loved Arturo enough that she would stay with him whatever the price. If she must, she would learn to live only for the present, without the promise of a future together.

It was a high price. And how she hoped she would not have to pay it.

Chapter Fifteen

The sun was high in the cloudless sky when the *Magdalena* sailed into the Strait of Gibraltar. On a bay facing out toward the Atlantic Ocean, Tangier, the white sunbaked city, stretched enticingly to the cliff looming behind it.

Al Gharb, the west wind, ruffled Arturo's hair as he stood on the main deck, one arm encircling Danielle's trim waist. She leaned back contentedly against his chest and watched with interest as the ship approached the busy harbor. Absorbed in the sights and in each other, neither was aware of the significant glances that passed between Narcisse and Jacques on the quarterdeck behind them.

In the turquoise water before them, small boats darted back and forth. Large sailing ships flying ensigns from innumerable nations were tied at docks lined with warehouses and the bagnios that held slaves for transport in and out of northern Africa.

"You must go below now," Arturo said when they drew close enough to glimpse turbaned laborers, toiling along the waterfront. "I am sorry, but it could be dangerous if you were seen."

"I know." The girl sighed, reluctant to take her eyes off the curious beast called the camel, but she did not argue.

"I know you would like to see Tangier, but you may have a chance later, at least, to meet a Moroccan." He smiled at her. "Diego Montera will surely come to call before we sail for home."

In her cabin, the girl followed Arturo's orders, careful to stay out of sight as she peered through the curtain. Before the bowline was even in place, merchants and beggars converged upon the wharf and raised their voices toward the ship in a cacophony of unfamiliar tongues.

In the midst of this teeming throng, a visitor waited under a tree near the dock while the mooring lines were made fast. Seated in a battered armchair while a black slave fanned him, the big bearded man watched the proceedings with a bored yawn. When the gangplank was in place, he rose ponderously and spoke to his retainers before making his way toward the ship.

Diego Montera, known to his neighbors as Muhammad ibn Francisco al Montera was a man of considerable bulk. The gangplank swayed and creaked under his weight as he boarded the *Magdalena*. Under his white turban, the Spanish merchant's round, swarthy face lit with a smile when he spied Arturo De Leon awaiting him on deck.

"Welcome, Diego," Arturo called genially.

"*As salaam 'alaykum, effendi.* Peace be unto you." The mountainous man's voice erupted from somewhere deep in his chest. Halting in front of his old friend, he placed his forehead against Arturo's and greeted him in Muslim fashion, extending his right arm so they could slap palms. "Now you say to me, '*Wa 'alaykum as salaam,*'" he instructed happily "'And unto you be peace.'"

"*Wa 'alaykum as salaam,*" the privateer repeated, and wa immediately rewarded with a smothering bear hug against Diego's expansive silk-clad chest.

"I know I lack dignity," the merchant boomed, kissing his friend on both cheeks, "but, oh, *mi amigo,* I am glad to see you again. Welcome to al Maghrib al Aqsa, 'the land farthest west.'"

"*Gracias,* Diego . . . or should I call you Muhammad?" Arturo was unfazed by the other man's affectionate demonstration.

"Call me whatever you bloody well please while we are aboard your ship," Diego requested with a negligent wave of his hand. "I have time enough ashore to be Muhammad.

"Wallahi," he declared, surveying his surroundings with an appreciative eye. "It is good to have a deck under my feet again, even if the *Magdalena* is moored. My ships spend more time sailing the seas of the Orient than they spend here. Still, I manage to keep up with the comings and goings of the harbor."

"I knew you would meet us," Arturo said with a nod. "Your intelligence was always the best. Come, let us go where we can talk."

"Good! And on the way, I will tell you what I would like."

"Name it. My ship is your ship," his host said chuckling as they strolled toward the cabins.

"Gracias. First," Diego began, ticking off the list on his fingers, "I would like a glass of fine French wine. I know you must have some—you always do. Then perhaps a bite of cold meat. Is that old rascal Felix still with you?"

"Of course." The captain smiled.

"Then your last chicken must have met its fate when land was in sight. Felix could always prepare a fine poached bird."

"And you could always eat one," the captain teased.

"Sí, always. Finally, I would like a fine Cuban cigar. Are these things possible?"

"Are you sure there isn't anything else?" Arturo bellowed with laughter.

"It will do for a start," Diego replied, unperturbed.

"I thought your religion did not allow you to drink alcohol or—"

Diego silenced the other man with a mock-severe frown. "I am a good Muslim when on solid ground, but at sea—and the harbor is close enough to that—Allah does not look upon my transgressions. Truly, I will be forgiven when next I attend mosque."

"Truly." Arturo stifled a grin.

"Besides, there are some things a man misses. Ham, bacon—"

Arturo interrupted the playful recital. "Diego, before we go to my cabin, there is something you should know. A woman is using my quarters and she is not veiled. I don't know if that makes a difference to you now."

"Makes no difference to me, but I never thought you one to bring a doxy aboard," the merchant replied almost primly.

"She is not a doxy," the captain corrected, a dangerous edge to his voice. "Danielle Valmont is a lady, and as I told you, she is using my cabin."

Diego's eyebrows rose, almost disappearing under his turban. This woman meant something to his old friend, it was plain to see.

"Come along now," Arturo insisted. "She is expecting us. I told her if you came aboard, I would bring you to meet her."

"Turo, this Danielle . . . she is pretty?"

"Beautiful."

"*Bueno,* I always enjoy a woman who is fair of face. And it's a good thing, for feminine companionship is one thing I do not lack, you know." The Spaniard chuckled. "A Muslim can have as many as four wives if he will treat them all justly."

"Yet you have only one."

"Yes, only one, praise Allah. Though as a Muslim I should not speak of her in public, any more than I should tell you about my flock of daughters. But since we are alone . . ."

"How many daughters *do* you have now?"

"Five and still no sons. *Inshallah.* As Allah wills it. But with so many girls, think of the clothes and the jewelry. If one has something, the rest must have it, too," he moaned dramatically. "If I had any more daughters, I would die a pauper." Quaking with laughter, he angled narrowly into the passageway behind his host.

In the cabin, the merchant met one of the most ravishing women he had ever seen in his extensive experience. She was young, but every inch a lady, carrying herself with a proud grace, which transcended age. Diego studied her with open admiration. Clad in a simple, elegant gown of rose-colored silk, she was indeed a joy to look upon. Her ivory skin was tinged with gold by the sun, and her cheeks and full lips were pink from the fresh air of the sea voyage. Her lustrous golden hair was upswept in a simple chignon and held with a pair of elaborate silver combs.

But there was more to her beauty than that. She seemed to glow with an inner light and her eyes, deep and brown, were tender when she looked at the captain. She was obviously a woman in love.

Danielle greeted the men with a dazzling smile and urged them to be seated. Pouring rich red wine from a crystal decanter into two glasses, she served them graciously.

Diego picked up his glass, sniffing the wine in anticipation before he drank. His eyes lit with gratification when he sipped it and he smacked his lips appreciatively. But before he could comment, the cook appeared, bearing a platter of cold chicken.

"Felix, you old devil, you have come to save my life," Diego greeted him heartily.

"As if half a chicken could save your life, Montera," the old man said with a snort. Still, he was delighted to note before he left that Diego pounced upon his dish instantly.

The Spaniard made short work of the chicken. "Not yet, amigo." He shook his head when Arturo offered him a cigar. "I wish now only to savor the wine."

"You are sated already? You must be slipping."

"Inshallah," Diego retorted, "for we are only growing older."

Danielle refilled Diego's wineglass, then sat quietly on the bunk while the two men talked. Soon the conversation turned to business.

"I see you carry cargo, Turo. A good idea. What have you brought with you?" the merchant asked.

"A little sugar and some tobacco."

"Perique? *Muy bien!* I will take it off your hands. Tell me, how do you like shipping?"

"Honest trading is no pastime for a privateer, or his ship," Arturo answered ruefully.

"You could get used to it over time and I could use a partner," the other man cajoled. "The work is easy enough these days, for pirates are few."

"They number one less now," Arturo responded. "The *Magdalena* was set upon by Turk three days out of Nassau. He was killed during the battle, but his men escaped."

"Turk, eh? I did not know he still plied his trade. Well, he was no friend of mine. Did you kill him, Turo?" Diego asked, mildly curious.

Arturo heard Danielle's intake of breath behind him. "No, he fell in the thick of the battle—I do not know who dealt him the blow. It does not matter, but the whole experience was enough to put me off trading."

"Ah, well." The merchant sighed in resignation. "In truth, amigo, business is difficult here in northern Africa. My profits dwindle every day as I am forced to pay baksheesh in every port. The bribery here could bankrupt a man. Even so, it is better than piracy in this day and age. Even the Barbary pirates are being run out of the Mediterranean. I ask you, what is this world coming to?"

Before the men's melancholy could deepen, there was a swift rap at the door and Pat bounded into the room.

"Jacques warns ye to stow the wine, sir," he rattled, hastily shoving all evidences of alcoholic refreshment into the locker. "Some Turkish gentlemen are comin' and they seem in fine dudgeon."

"That would be Khalid al Hammid, I imagine, commander of the sultan's police force here in Tangier. He certainly wasted no time in getting here," Diego ruminated. "Khalid is a most powerful man, an Arab. He is temporarily serving as the customs inspector, since the last one met with an accident. He lost his head when he ran into Khalid's sword—on the sultan's orders, of course.

"I will handle this," he assured the captain. "Just be calm. And hide that humidor."

Pat scurried to comply only seconds before the Moroccan official threw open the door. Khalid al Hammid, representative of the Ottoman sultan in this far-flung western port, strode haughtily into the captain's quarters. Diego hoisted his bulk from the chair with remarkable agility and bowed, motioning slightly for Arturo and Pat to do the same. He positioned himself so his massive body hid Danielle from view.

"May your day be happy, Khalid al Hammid," he greeted the man in Arabic.

"May your day be happy and blessed," the official answered indifferently, by rote.

"We are as honored by your visit today as if the sultan himself, may Allah heap blessings upon him, stood before us," Diego welcomed him humbly.

Khalid responded with no more than a curt nod. Taller and more muscular than his men, the commander cut an imposing figure, pausing just inside the door as if contact with the infidel captain would contaminate him. His stance was arrogant, his legs spread slightly, and his hand was upon his sword. Below his carefully wrapped turban, his pale, colorless eyes looked somehow alien to his narrow brown face. They were cold and cruel as they flicked toward Arturo. "Who is the captain of this vessel?" he demanded of Diego.

"Arturo al De Leon, a great warrior and a commander in his own country."

"And what country might that be?"

"America, far across the ocean."

"I have never heard of it. He is a Kaffir?" he asked with a disdainful curl to his thin lips.

"An infidel, yes." Diego sighed gustily, "But I keep trying. Someday he will understand the wisdom of the Prophet, *Inshallah*."

The commander cocked a skeptical eyebrow. "Not all Kaffirs are civilized enough to speak French. Does this one?"

At Diego's nod, he turned to Arturo and addressed him in flawless French. "Welcome to Tangier, Capitaine De Leon. I am Khalid al Hammid, chief of police and acting customs inspector. It will be necessary for me to see your cargo before you unload it. It is only a formality, you understand, but we cannot issue a pratique until we see it." His intonation did nothing to hide his boredom at the entire procedure.

All at once, the ship rocked slightly in its moorings, and Khalid's eyes fell on Danielle, sitting quietly on the bunk behind Diego. His eyes widened incredulously, not only at the presence of an unveiled woman, but at her seeming unconcern and immodesty. Her brown eyes when they met his shocked gaze held nothing but lively interest. She did not even attempt to cover her face.

Enthralled, he could not pull his gaze from the girl in the rose gown. *Mashallah!* What a beautiful woman, a houri made for a harem, where she would be a favorite. But she was brazen, he could see at a glance; she would need taming. A vision of her pleading with him flitted enjoyably through his mind.

But Khalid's fantasies were interrupted when he became aware that Arturo was speaking to him.

"Who is this woman?" the commander demanded impatiently, ignoring Arturo. "A slave?"

"Pay her no mind," Diego answered swiftly. The big merchant glanced intensely at the couple, the warning clear in his eyes. "She is a free woman of America, here only because she serves Capitaine De Leon."

"I care not if the captain brings his entire harem, but she is not suitably attired. In this barbaric land, America, they do not veil their women as the Prophet commands?"

"No, they are Christians, Nasranis."

"I know what Christians are," the commander snapped irritably. "But in Morocco, even Christians veil their women."

"And so she *would* be veiled, if she were going ashore," Diego promised the incensed Muslim. "I would see to it myself."

"See to it instead that she is not even permitted on deck. Keep her out of sight," the official ordered brusquely.

"Now, *capitaine,* let us inspect your cargo." Khalid led his men from the cabin, but he could not resist a final glance over his shoulder at Danielle, repelled and fascinated at the same time.

When the inspection was completed and Khalid al Hammid had departed with his men, Arturo and Diego returned to the captain's quarters to discover that Danielle was not there. Certain she had been kidnapped by an unseen band of brigands, Arturo called her name and raced toward the passageway, nearly colliding with the object of his concern when she opened the door and stepped inside.

"Where have you been?" the privateer roared. "I told you not to go on deck."

"I didn't," Danielle answered calmly. "I went to your cabin. I decided it would be safer if you had to bring Khalid al Hammid back to mine."

"Safer?" Arturo repeated dully. "I would not let anything happen to you on the *Magdalena.*"

"The girl is right to be cautious," Diego interjected soberly. "Did you see how he looked at her? She is a beauty, true enough, but it was more. Her face is unveiled and her hair the color of honey. Danielle is a white woman in northern Africa and that is a dangerous thing to be. She should be safe enough, however, if she stays here.

"Now, as for you, Turo, I will expect you this evening to finish our business. The *funduq* where I lodge provides a fine Aribi dinner and I have Djebeli tobacco. I will send a servant for you later. And I would suggest you do not wear that scarf ashore. The color green is held in great reverence by the Muslims.

"Unfortunately, *mademoiselle*, I cannot entertain you. I think you understand," he concluded, visibly relieved when the girl nodded. "*Bonjour* then, Danielle Valmont. Allah watch over you on your journey."

Danielle listened as voices of the men on deck faded and were replaced by the wailing of a muezzin calling the Muslims to prayer.

Late in the afternoon, Arturo granted shore leave to his crew. Only Felix stayed behind, claiming he was too old for the fleshpots of Morocco. Eager to explore those dens of iniquity, the other men wasted no time in pouring off the ship. They left the *Magdalena* with hardly a glance for their less fortunate mates who stood anchor watch.

At sundown, Arturo appeared at Danielle's door to bid her good-night. "I am sorry to leave you, *cher,* when I know how you hate to be confined," he apologized, "but it is too dangerous...."

"I know." She sighed. "I only wish I could learn more about this world before it was time to leave."

"Come here a moment." He led her to the porthole to look out at the nearly deserted waterfront. "The Muslims are at their sunset prayers, but I can show you a little of what Diego taught me today. It seems almost everyone in the Ottoman empire can be identified by his clothing. See those men over there in brown? They are Christians ... Copts. The fellow in the black-and-white djellaba with the cross tattooed on the end of his nose is a Berber from the mountains. Yellow means they're Zoroastrian. And the man in the black robes and skullcap is a Jew."

"How simple that makes everything," Danielle commented dryly.

"Indeed." Arturo laughed. "That concludes the lesson for this evening. Please remember what Diego said and stay below."

"I will," she answered glumly.

"How will you pass the time?"

"I don't know. Perhaps I will sew. I have one more piece of the fabric you gave me." She nodded toward a glistening length of champagne-colored brocade spread on the table.

"A beautiful color for you. What will you make of it?" Arturo asked, fingering the rich textile.

"Since my sewing skills have improved on this voyage, I plan to test them by making the most exquisite ball gown you have ever seen. Though where I will wear it on the *Magdalena,* I do not know."

"You could wear it when we return to New Orleans . . . as a wedding gown, perhaps?" He eyed her expectantly.

"To New Orleans? A wedding gown?" The meaning of his words reached her, but she was still uncertain she had understood him.

"*Oui.* What is wrong? I thought after last night you would want to marry me."

"Is that what you want, Arturo? I thought you were not the marrying kind."

"So did I," he admitted with a grin, "but I've changed my mind. Very recently.

"I understand your uncertainty, Danielle," he continued more seriously. "You should have time to consider whether you want to be my wife. I am not a rich man. The *Magdalena* and Désir du Coeur, my small plantation, are all I own. I know you are accustomed to much better. But I love you, and I want to marry you.

"No, do not answer now." Hastily, he placed a silencing hand against her lips when she would speak. "All I ask is that you think on it and give me your answer in the morning."

"Arturo De Leon!" she erupted, slapping his hand away in exasperation. "I vow, sometimes you try my patience. Why must I wait until tomorrow to tell you what I already know? Of course, I want to marry you!" she cried jubilantly, throwing her arms around his neck.

Arturo blinked down at her blankly for an instant, then he whooped exuberantly, swinging her off her feet and kissing her soundly. "You will marry me? I will make you happy, Danielle, I swear to you."

"Cap'n." Pat's voice could be heard through the door. "Mr. Montera's servant is here, sir, to lead ye to his inn."

"I will be right there," the privateer called, smiling tenderly at the girl in his arms. "I must go. It will probably be quite late when I return, so do not wait up. *Bonsoir,* I will wake you with a kiss very much like this one," he murmured teasingly and covered her mouth lovingly with his own.

"*Bonsoir,*" Danielle responded breathlessly when he released her. "Turo!" She stopped him suddenly, catching his arm.

"Yes, *cher?*"

"Be careful. Diego says Tangier can be dangerous."

"Not even an army of Arabs could keep us apart now." Pleased by her concern, Arturo departed with a broad smile on his face.

The faithful had been summoned to their evening prayers when Harry Hinson set out alone on his errand. He wended his way through the narrow streets of Tangier, stopping in the souk to ask in his faulty French for directions to a disreputable coffeehouse that had once been described to him by an old shipmate. There Harry would find Omar al Nasr, a slave broker he knew only by reputation.

In the waning light, the Cockney located the café down one of the alleys of the Casbah, the Arab quarter. Ducking inside, he entered a twilight world that smelled of smoke, fragrant coffees and unwashed bodies. Men in the white dress of city Arabs and in the colorful djellabas of desert tribes reclined on cushions on the dirt floor and talked among themselves.

Uncertain what to do next, Harry seated himself nervously at a low, unoccupied table beside the door. When the server appeared, the sailor asked for Omar. Silently, the server pointed to an unsavory-looking character, clad in the red robes of a slave trader, who lounged nearby.

Harry approached the stringy, greasy-looking man, addressing him in his poor French, "Pardon me, are you Omar al Nasr?"

"Oui," the Arab affirmed lazily, scrutinizing the foreigner from behind hooded eyelids. "You seek to do business with me, effendi?"

"Yes, sir."

"Then sit." Omar gestured toward the soiled cushion across the table. "Two cups of *keshreh,*" he ordered when Harry complied.

Omar sat smoking his pipe without a word until the coffee was set before them. Harry eyed the tiny cup dubiously before taking a sip. *Keshreh* proved to be a tasty aromatic brew made of the shell of coffee beans and spiced with cinnamon and clove. Smacking his lips loudly, the sailor gulped the entire serving and held out the cup for more.

With a disapproving frown for the *Inglayzi*'s manners, Omar beckoned the server again. Then, sipping his own coffee politely, he spoke at last. "You say you wish to do business, effendi. Do you wish to buy or to sell?"

"D'ye speak English, Omar?" Harry asked, eager to improve his position for the haggling to come.

"In my business it is necessary to speak many languages," Omar answered in English. "But French is our second language in Morocco."

"Well, then," Harry went on confidently in English, "I'm sellin'. An' a sweeter piece of merchandise, ye haint never seen . . . a white woman."

The only sign of interest Omar exhibited was to raise his bushy eyebrows skeptically. "This woman is European?"

"Hamerican." The sailor shrugged his scrawny shoulders indifferently. "But there haint much difference, ye know."

"She has light hair?"

"Ye dark people like that, d'ye? Well, 'er 'air is golden," he confirmed. "An' 'er skin is white. Like Devon cream, hit is."

Omar tried to look unimpressed, but his interest was obvious when he looked around to make sure no one was listening. White women were a rare commodity in northern Africa and with fair hair, the woman would be extremely valuable.

"How old is this woman?" he asked, still attempting to seem indifferent.

"Nineteen or twenty years old and pretty has a picture," Harry said, warming to his sales pitch.

"She is a virgin?"

The sailor did his best to look offended. "Of course."

"Where is she? I would like to see her."

"She's on my ship, but I could bring 'er to ye if I could get some of them veils and such that women are s'posed to wear 'ere."

"I will supply you with a yashmak," Omar offered. "Let us go to my home."

The men left the coffeehouse and walked through the mazelike streets. At last they halted in front of a building that looked like every other building along the shabby thoroughfare. Only one narrow door broke the expanse of wall facing the street. Opening it, Omar gestured for the sailor to precede him.

They entered a tiny courtyard where a puny mimosa grew in one corner and a small fountain gurgled in the center of the weed-choked patio. From the shadowy interior of the run-down two-story house, a dusky young eunuch materialized. The slave broker did not invite the English sailor into his home, but waited with him in the courtyard while he sent the slave to bring a woman's garments to them. The eunuch returned after a few moments with the voluminous costume neatly folded in a large basket.

"Yasir will accompany you to your ship, then lead you back here," the slave trader told the sailor.

"Kind of ye, Omar." Harry slapped the Moroccan familiarly on the back. Things were going even better than he had hoped. He was going to be a rich man. When he killed Turk to keep him from taking the girl, he had known it would pay off.

"Come on then, Yasir," he ordered importantly. "Let's not keep your master waitin'."

Omar watched distastefully as the pair departed, then went to the fountain to plunge his arms into the water and wash. He knew he was not the best of Muslims; sometimes he prayed only twice a day, but he could not bear the taint of the infidel upon him. When Omar was clean again, he went into the house to wait.

Harry bade the slave to wait for him in the shadows of one of the wharfside buildings. Then the little Englishman sauntered up the gangplank to the *Magdalena*.

The guard watched his swaggering progress, but did not speak. Harry was an odd one—sometimes friendly and talkative, at others surly and uncommunicative.

Tonight he was friendly. "Evenin', Paul," he greeted the watch as he trudged up the plank.

"*Bonsoir,* Harry. Did you have a good time in the city?"

"Good enough."

"What have you there?" Paul's eyes fastened on the basket the other man carried.

"A gift for me muvver, bless 'er," the Cockney responded sentimentally. "I try to buy 'er something at every port."

Paul nodded approvingly as Harry passed. "A man should remember his mother. Me, I buy little presents for my children, all six of them. They—"

The end of his sentence never came. Once past him, Harry pulled a heavy stick from the basket and hit Paul on the back of the head. Without a sound, the sailor's knees buckled and he pitched forward on the deck.

Harry looked around rapidly for Jean, the other sentinel, but he did not see him. Creeping stealthily to the other side of the ship, he surveyed the decks, forward and after. Jean was on the foredeck, leaning against the port gunwale, staring out to sea as he fought drowsiness. It was simple enough for Harry to come from behind and surprise him.

With both guards out of the way, Harry made his way to the captain's quarters, careful not to make too much noise. He did not want to alarm the girl. He ducked through the hatch and tiptoed to her door, cautiously opening it a crack.

Through it, he could see Danielle standing in the circle of light cast by the lantern. Her blond hair gleamed like molten gold as she leaned over the table, cutting a length of shiny fabric.

Carefully, the man set down his basket and pulled a tiny vial from his pocket. Uncorking it, he doused a dingy handkerchief with elixir of poppy and stepped into the cabin without a sound.

Because her back was to the door, Danielle sensed, rather than heard, someone approach. She glanced over her shoulder and her eyes widened with alarm when she saw Harry advancing on her, the drug-soaked cloth in his hand.

The sailor did not hesitate. He pounced upon his prey and tried to clamp the handkerchief over her face. Galvanized by the sickening-sweet scent she remembered, Danielle lunged toward the bed, determined to reach her pistol. Harry seized the struggling girl from behind, grunting with effort until he managed to get his hands around her throat and squeeze just hard enough to cut off her breathing. Gradually, her resistance lessened, but she slashed weakly at her assailant with the scissors she held in her hand.

Their blades caught him on the back of his hand and brought forth a gush of blood. With a muffled cry, the man yanked his hand away, throwing beads of blood around the room. He clutched at his wound, releasing the girl so she slumped to the floor.

Blood dripped from his hand, leaving red splotches on the carpet, as Harry stepped over Danielle's inert body to reach for a towel. He stanched the flow of blood and cursed the girl under his breath as he rolled her over none too gently to be sure she was still alive.

She was unconscious, though whether from the opium or from the lack of oxygen, he could not be sure. Dark bruises already showed on her neck, and he hoped they would not lessen her value. He retrieved the basket from the passageway and clumsily drew the unfamiliar yashmak over her clothes, uncertain whether he had put it on correctly. It did not matter, he decided, as long as she was covered. Then he tossed her limp form over his shoulder and carried her out.

As Harry made his way across the deck toward the gangplank with his burden, Felix limped forward from the stern. Even in the dark, the myopic old man could tell something was amiss. "Wait, you," he sputtered. "What have you got there?"

Harry stopped obligingly to let Felix come a bit nearer, while with his free hand he sought and found his knife. Taking quick aim, the Cockney threw the knife with deadly accuracy, catching the old cook in the chest. With a groan and a look of incomprehension, Felix collapsed to the deck.

Harry carried his valuable cargo past the unconscious guard, down the gangplank to the eunuch who waited in the shadows. Together, they braced the girl and half carried, half walked her through the dark streets to the house of Omar al Nasr.

Chapter Sixteen

Grinning broadly, Arturo listened to Pat's riotous description of Tangier by night as they walked toward the wharf. He had met the boy and Jacques on a street near the waterfront, and now they sauntered companionably toward the *Magdalena*.

The captain's blue eyes swept his ship, lighting on the porthole of Danielle's cabin. His smile broadened when he saw that her lamp was still burning; she was waiting up for him. The smile was replaced by a frown, however, when no guard hailed them at the gangplank.

Suddenly uneasy, Arturo bellowed for the watch and set off toward the ship at a run. Jacques and Pat were at his heels as he bounded up the ramp, nearly tripping over Paul's unconscious body.

"Pat, stay with him," the privateer ordered after ascertaining the man was alive. "Jacques, see if you can find Jean.

"Danielle!" he shouted anxiously, tearing toward the hatch.

When Arturo burst into her cabin, his worst fears were confirmed. The girl was gone, but she had not gone willingly. There had been a struggle. A pair of bloodstained scissors were on the floor, and flecks of blood dotted the rug and the fabric crumpled on the table. He lifted the disarranged pillow on the bunk to find her pistol still in its hiding place. An unfamiliar empty basket rolled in the corner under the pegged rack that still held her clothes. He peered into it distractedly.

His investigation was interrupted by a howl of anguish from deck. "Come quick, Cap'n, someone's killed Felix," Pat sobbed, kneeling beside the cook's body in the shadow of the quarterdeck. Arturo had not seen him when he charged toward the cabins.

"Why would anyone want to hurt him?" the lad said, weeping.

Arturo knelt beside the old man, his face grim at the sight of the knife protruding from his skinny chest. Placing his fingers on Felix's neck, he was relieved to feel a faint pulse.

"He is alive." Carefully, the captain pulled the knife from the old man's chest and stanched his bleeding. Then he called for Jacques over his shoulder.

"Here, Turo." The first mate hovered over them, concern for Felix evident on his rough face.

"Find a doctor."

"*Oui,* right away."

Arturo lifted Felix tenderly and carried him through the galley to his cabin. As he laid him on his bunk, the cook's eyes fluttered open. "Mam'selle Danielle?" he croaked with effort.

"Gone," Arturo answered bleakly.

"Harry...took her, Turo. You must find her."

"We will get her back, *mon ami.* Rest now. A doctor will be here soon."

"A foreigner?" Felix whispered disapprovingly. "I don't think..." His voice trailed off as he lost consciousness.

Arturo bade Pat to stay with Felix until the Muslim hakim arrived. Then the captain strode up on deck again.

In twos and threes, the *Magdalena*'s crew had all returned by then from their evening's entertainment—except for Harry Hinson. They stood in a worried knot near the gangplank, muttering among themselves. At the sight of Arturo's anguished expression, Narcisse detached himself from the group and drew his captain aside.

"It is true what Jacques says, Turo? Danielle is gone?"

"Felix says Harry Hinson took her," Arturo answered hoarsely.

"You are going to look for her, *oui?*" the helmsman demanded urgently.

"Of course, though what we will find at this time of night, I do not know."

"I am going with you," Narcisse announced in a tone that would brook no argument.

"I will go as well," rumbled Jacques from behind him.

"And I," Falgout chimed.

"M-me too," Dazet echoed the sentiment.

The captain stared at them dully, knowing he must fight the paralyzing fear he felt for Danielle's safety. It was up to him to organize a search for her and her abductor. Shaking his head as if to clear it, he turned to his first mate. "Jacques, you are in command of the *Magdalena*. If Felix awakens, tell him not to worry, we are searching for Danielle. Falgout, Dazet, you may hunt for Hinson, but stay together. If you find him, bring him here," he ordered. "Narcisse, you come with me."

Grimly, the men set out to question the denizens of the waterfront, who might have a clue to Danielle's whereabouts.

Morning was about to break when Arturo and Narcisse returned to the ship. Jacques awaited them at the gangplank, shaking his head sadly at the unspoken question in the searchers' eyes.

"No news of her, but the hakim says Felix will live."

The captain waited, pacing the deck impatiently, until Falgout and Dazet returned. At the sight of the shaken captain, they shook their heads sorrowfully, then retired to the forecastle for a well-deserved rest.

At last, only Arturo remained on deck, listening to the cry of a muezzin in the dawn while he decided what to do. Danielle must be rescued before it was too late. If he found Harry first, he would beat him until the Cockney revealed what he had done to her. One way or the other, the captain resolved to get her back. If he had to take Tangier apart, brick by sun-baked brick.

Danielle huddled in the corner of a dark, airless chamber. She had awakened with a raging headache and a great thirst. Her throat hurt so, it was hard to swallow and her stomach did not want to hold the water set out for her once she got it down.

In the dim light, which filtered through a high window, the girl could see nearly thirty women crammed into the narrow room. Some were curled on the floor sleeping; most, however, were awake, clustered together, weeping and wailing loudly in Arabic.

Only one, Layla, a Persian who spoke a little broken French, approached the blond-haired girl. From her, Danielle learned she had been purchased by Omar al Nasr, a slave trader.

"I cannot be bought or sold," she stormed. "I am a free woman."

"Perhaps free you were, *mademoiselle,* but you are free no more," someone said behind her in a husky but feminine-sounding voice. "Try to accept your kismet. It is for the best."

Danielle wheeled and blinked in amazement at the moon-faced man with dark liquid eyes. Was he the person who had just spoken?

He confirmed her suspicions. "I am Yasir, head eunuch of Omar al Nasr. You have nothing to fear here."

"Nothing but slavery!"

"But *mademoiselle,*" he said indulgently, "you are a great beauty and will occupy a place of honor in a rich man's harem. You are no common slave. In fact," he confided soothingly, "my master plans to sell you to a marriage broker. You will be fortunate indeed, never to see the public souk."

"I would like to speak to your master," she requested icily.

Yasir looked hurt. "If you insist. But he will not listen."

Already framing her plea, the girl hardly heard him. She would offer ransom. She would beg if she must. But she would get back to Arturo somehow.

When Omar appeared, Danielle went immediately to speak to the dirty, gap-toothed man. "*Bonjour.* You are Omar al Nasr?" she inquired politely.

"I am." He frowned at her. Her eyes were bold; not even a veil would hide her audacity. He had not known this when he purchased the unconscious girl. There were several things he had not known, he thought gloomily, but *inshallah,* he must make the best of the situation.

"Please, *monsieur,*" she began confidently, "there must be a mistake. I am not a slave."

"Thus your old master said you would speak, deceitful woman," Omar countered scornfully. "It will do you no good. You are my property now and will obey me without argument."

"I am no one's property," she responded angrily, her chin rising rebelliously. She felt the incredulous eyes of the Arab women upon her; they did not understand her words, but they could not have mistaken her outrage.

"Worthless female! Cursed of your two parents! Do not use such a tone with me," Omar exploded, fingering for effect the dagger he wore thrust into his sash. "Or I will personally teach you the exquisite tortures of bastinado. I assure you, after ten strokes of the rod upon the soles of your feet, you will cooperate."

Layla edged near to whisper, "You do not wish to be punished in such a way, *mademoiselle*. I hear bastinado is painful indeed."

"You hear correctly," Omar assured them with a smirk. "Now, infidel, you will stay here, showing proper respect to all you meet until I send my eunuch for you."

Arturo trudged wearily through the streets of Tangier, one hand massaging the tense muscles of his neck. Just after dawn, he had sent word to Diego Montera, but his messenger had returned alone. The Spaniard had been in such haste to return home, he had left before daybreak. Now the American was on his way alone to find the commander of the sultan's police.

Locating the correct building, he pounded heavily on the locked door. A night porter, disgruntled at being awakened from a nap, opened a small wooden panel in the door and informed the infidel that no one would be there to see him until halfway between morning and noon prayers. Then he slammed the door within a door and left the Kaffir in the street.

Arturo wandered through the deserted maze of narrow streets past households whose occupants were just waking up and past mosques where beggars slept lining the walls. At last, he entered the *millah,* the Jewish quarter, where he came upon a merchant getting ready to begin the day's business.

Gideon ben Amasa, money changer and seller of olive oil, wine and fruit, sat on a rug-covered bench in the souk, sipping thick, syrupy coffee. While he warmed his old bones in the early-morning sun, he waited patiently for his first customer. He scrutinized the foreigner with keen interest, and, catching Arturo's eye, the black-clad man motioned for him to join him for coffee.

When he discovered the American spoke French, Spanish and English, the old Jew was delighted at the opportunity to converse in all three languages. He spoke them fluently, slipping back and forth with ease. Soon the two men, so different in age and culture, were on a first-name basis. And, in the course of their conversation, Gideon learned what had brought Arturo ashore.

"I am afraid, Capitaine De Leon, you will receive no help from al Hammid," he warned.

"Surely he cannot ignore kidnapping and attempted murder."

"He can and he will. What happens aboard your ship, he will consider your responsibility. The representative of the sultan has more important concerns, such as collecting baksheesh."

"Are you saying I should offer him a bribe?"

"It wouldn't hurt." The old man shrugged. "But I cannot be sure even that would help. He has little liking for infidels. I will tell you, young friend," Gideon suggested gently, "do what you can. Though it is unlikely, I will inquire within the *millah* whether anyone has knowledge of the girl. If you come back at sunset, I will tell you what I have learned."

"*Merci, Gideon, merci beaucoup.*"

The sun was high in the faded blue Mediterranean sky when the captain returned to police headquarters. The door to the street had been open for only a few moments when Khalid's fresh-faced young adjutant reluctantly showed the *Inglayzi* into the reception room, then went to tell his commander that Arturo was waiting.

At the far end of the narrow room, a few old men sat on divans, talking loudly. Their conversation halted when Arturo entered the room. But when he sat quietly on a pillow and did not disturb them, they returned to their gossip, though they threw frequent wary glances his way.

He waited until everyone else had been taken to see Khalid al Hammid. Arturo began to get restless so he strolled into the courtyard to clear his head. He did not stray far from the room, but he had had enough of fidgeting in the hot reception area, wondering if Khalid would see him at all.

He leaned against an orange tree, listening for movement inside the house, and stared out at the street through the gate, watching the passersby without really seeing them.

"So there you are, Capitaine De Leon." Khalid al Hammid spoke almost accusingly from the doorway.

Arturo turned to face the disdainful Arab. "*Bonjour,* Commander. Thank you for seeing me today."

"Since you were willing to wait until I finished more pressing business . . ." Khalid did not finish, but shrugged discourteously. "What did you require of me?"

"I need your help. The girl I brought with me has been kidnapped."

"How unfortunate to lose a valued servant," the official responded coldly. "I warned you of the dangers to an unveiled woman in Morocco."

"She did not go ashore!" Arturo protested hotly. Then he forced himself to continue in a more moderate tone. "She was taken from my ship last night."

"Your guards are very careless. I trust you have punished them."

"Danielle's abduction was not due to their carelessness, but to the treachery of one of my men."

"Allah preserve us from disloyal servants," Khalid intoned piously, rolling his eyes skyward. "I do not understand. How do you think I can help you?"

"By organizing a search."

The commander threw back his head and laughed aloud. "You think that you, or I, will find the woman in Tangier? That is quite unlikely, *monsieur*. It would take an army to search the Casbah alone. Besides, she has probably been spirited from the city by now and is on her way to a harem in Cairo or Damascus, even Arabia. You will never find her."

Arturo had to stifle the jolt of pain he felt at Khalid's hopeless words. "Perhaps, but my failure is almost certain if you will not help me."

"Very well," Khalid said, sighing grudgingly. "I will have some of my men question the owners of the larger auction houses in the city. But beyond that . . ."

"*Merci* for your kind assistance," Arturo acknowledged sarcastically. "I will find her myself." Turning on his heel, the privateer marched out.

"Yes, Kaffir," the Arab muttered under his breath, watching him depart, "I can almost believe you would."

"He will help us, Turo?" Jacques was waiting when Arturo stepped from the shady courtyard into the sunbaked street.

"His men will search the slave market. That is all."

"What do we do now?"

"We are going to the Casbah," the captain answered decisively. "We'll ask questions in the bazaar, then work our way into every part of the city, if we must. If Danielle is in Tangier, we will find her."

From the house of Farhan ibn Sa'id high on the hill, Danielle could see the *Magdalena* still moored at the wharf. Even though it was past time for the brigantine to sail, she knew Arturo would continue to search for her. But how would he find her in a country where women wore garments that made them indistinguishable? How could he locate her in the harems of the Muslim world? The girl looked around in discouragement at the luxurious apartment that was her prison.

She was well treated by Farhan. The marriage broker made sure she had abundant food, plenteous baths, opulent clothing, even slaves to serve her. She wanted for nothing...but her freedom.

She did not weep and wail at her plight, behaving instead with a quiet dignity, which seemed to have earned the respect of Abdul, Farhan's head eunuch. After only a few days, the old man even seemed to be fond of her. Despite his role as her jailer, she was grateful to him for his kindness of the first night at Farhan's house when the broker had sent for her.

"Do not fear, *mademoiselle,*" Abdul had told her as he led her through the breezeway to where the marriage broker waited. The old eunuch was impressed with the quiet golden-haired girl when he glanced back at her. Her pale face was white and composed, showing none of the fear she must feel. Her golden hair was plaited in a thick braid that hung down her back, and the lavender caftan he had chosen for her was perfect for her coloring. She had such a regal bearing that she was probably a princess in her own country, Abdul decided. After all, only royalty could face adversity with such grace. This *Inglayzi* was indeed a pearl of great price.

When they paused outside Farhan's door, Abdul removed Danielle's shoes, leaving them outside the door. He did not know the act gave her time to scrutinize Farhan without appearing to look at him at all.

Danielle's purchaser was a tired-looking middle-aged man. A marriage broker for many years, he had bought and sold thousands of women. He had little interest in his merchandise outside of what price a female might bring.

When she stood before him, her head high and unbowed although Abdul had instructed her otherwise, Farhan began the interview.

"You know who I am?" he asked gruffly in French.

"Farhan ibn Sa'id," she answered distinctly.

"Sidi Farhan ibn Sa'id," he corrected, "your master for now. What are you called?"

"Danielle Marie-Christiane Valmont." The girl was ready to present her case when he interrupted.

"You are from America?"

"*Oui.*"

"What was your father's name?" he demanded suddenly.

"Laurent Valmont," she stammered, surprised by the question.

"Very well then, Danielle bint Laurent, daughter of Laurent. I understand that you are in good health. *Alhamdulilah,* praise be to God for that! But I have also learned you are not a virgin."

"How—how did you know that?"

"If you must know, Omar examined you while you were unconscious," he replied testily. "Now what I must know is whether you have borne children."

"*Non,*" she whispered, horrified by the invasion of her body and the broker's intimate knowledge.

"*Inshallah.*" Farhan was disappointed. A proved childbearer could bring a good price, particularly when that trait was combined with comeliness. "No matter. You are young and will give your husband many sons."

"Please... I am already promised in marriage. You must release me."

Farhan frowned in annoyance. "You must learn, Danielle bint Laurent, whatever shall be, shall be as Allah wills. Now you may undress," he ordered with a negligent wave of his hand.

Danielle stared at him dully. Although Abdul had told her what to expect, she shook her head disbelievingly.

"It is useless to protest." The marriage broker scowled at her. "I wish you no harm, but I must see what I have purchased. If you do not remove your clothing, I will have Abdul do it for you."

"Obey, *mademoiselle,*" she heard the eunuch whisper from the doorway behind her.

Reluctantly, Danielle unbuttoned the caftan, her fingers fumbling over the tiny pearl buttons. Slipping the garment past her shoulders, she let it slide over her hips to fall in a heap around her bare feet. With effort, she forced herself not to cover herself when she felt Farhan's gaze upon her, but faced him proudly. An ivory necklace as pale as her skin rested at the base of her graceful neck, hiding a ring of bruises. Just above its carved pendant, the girl's pulse fluttered wildly, the only sign of her distress.

"You are lovely," he noted approvingly. "Now turn around." He ran a practiced eye over her full, round breasts rising proudly from her trim torso as she complied with his order. The sleek curves of her long legs glistened in the lamplight as she slowly revolved, and the long, golden braid brushed white, flawless skin at the small of her back where her hips flared provocatively.

"Your body is well formed, indeed," he declared with satisfaction, "and you are fair of face. I will find you a good husband, Danielle bint Laurent. One with wealth and power, so that your sons will be lions of the desert. You may dress," he said, abruptly concluding the interview. "Then Abdul will escort you to your room."

Danielle obeyed and departed, appalled that she was considered merchandise and nothing more.

* * *

"*Hayya 'ala s-sala,* come to prayers." The imam's call floated over the city, but Falgout hardly noticed it. The second mate paced the decks of the *Magdalena* and watched the dock anxiously, half expecting Diego Montera to materialize at any moment and demand to know why the ship had not sailed. The brigantine was loaded with spices and waited only for the captain's word to set sail for home.

But now Arturo was sleeping in his cabin, succumbing to exhaustion after several days of endless searching. Jacques, too, was asleep; the first mate had looked dead on his feet when he and the captain returned to the ship last night. Each day the men had combed the bazaars where Arabs haggled in strident voices, adding to the general din of the marketplace, until temporary silence fell at each call of the muezzin. It seemed that when the girl was abducted from the *Magdalena,* she had been swallowed up by the close, hostile alleyways of Tangier. How long they could keep up the search, Falgout did not know.

As if in response to his musing, a haggard-looking Arturo emerged from the hatch and was greeted by Pat.

"How is Felix this morning?" the captain asked at once.

"Restin' easy, but chafin' to be up and around," the boy replied with a grin. "Can I bring ye some breakfast, sir?"

"No time," Arturo grunted. "I have wasted too much time already. Why didn't someone wake me?"

"Because, me, I told them not to," Narcisse answered, climbing up from the foredeck.

"Since when do you give orders?" the captain growled.

"I don't, but Falgout agreed with me that you should sleep. Just as he agrees you must eat. Is that not so, Falgout?" he called loudly.

"*Oui,*" the second mate responded from nearby, his round face serious. "Pat, go and fetch the *capitaine* some breakfast."

"You will do Danielle no good if you make yourself sick," the helmsman argued logically.

"I must find her," the privateer muttered distractedly, going to stand at the railing, where he looked out over the waterfront as if he thought he would find an answer there.

"Turo," Narcisse said hesitantly, "I have waited each day, as you ordered, at Khalid's, but still there is no word. I hate to say it, my old friend, but I fear Danielle is lost to us."

"You would give up without a fight?" Arturo wheeled on him belligerently.

"Show me an enemy to fight and I will fight him," Narcisse retorted hotly. "But you search from morning to night without even a rest in the heat of the day. Al Hammid says the Arabs think you are crazy. That is why they do not help you."

"They do not harm me, either," Arturo answered dryly.

"This is true," Narcisse admitted soberly. "It is considered bad luck to harm a madman." He did not say it, but privately he wondered if Arturo was mad—mad with grief at his loss of Danielle.

"I must find her, *mon ami,*" the captain muttered. "It is my fault she was kidnapped. If I had never taken her from New Orleans, if I had not left her that night, if I had protected her..." His voice broke in anguish.

"If, if, if." Narcisse sighed. "If only you did not love her, you could sail away on the next tide, eh, *mon capitaine?*"

"You love her, too," Arturo said quietly.

"Oui," the handsome young man answered unhappily, "but she belongs to you and I will help you get her back."

"Très bien. I will return to police headquarters and you will continue your search. We are both mad."

Fortified by Pat's inexpert cooking, the privateer left Jacques sleeping and went to visit Gideon, as he had every morning for the past few days. Each sundown, he went to the old Jew's home to see what he had learned. Gideon had befriended Arturo as had every member of the ben Amasa household, including the numerous cousins, nieces and nephews, and they were anxious to help the desperate man.

Zared, the old merchant's handsome, reckless nephew had recently wed the lovely, black-eyed Mahalah. When the young couple had been unable to get the approval of Mahalah's Christian family for their marriage, they had eloped from Jidda where Zared had handled the family business interests in Arabia. Especially sympathetic to Arturo's plight, the newlyweds were determined to help him rescue his lost love.

Zared had called upon his experience among the Arabs and, disguising himself as a desert tribesman, went to the waterfront to question the Arab sailors there. He had hoped to succeed where Arturo's men had failed, but he, too, had come back empty-handed.

Even Gideon's grandson, Isaac, wanted to assist the captain. Dark-eyed, skinny and smiling, he had posted himself among the street urchins outside the bagnios. Though he was only twelve, the boy could not hope to catch sight of an unveiled female. So he eavesdropped on the conversations of the dealers, but he learned nothing.

Several hours later, Arturo was about to give up the search until after the evening prayer hour when he spotted Danielle's silver combs in a jewelry stall in a souk.

"Where did you get these?" he roared, snatching them up and wheeling on the fearful merchant.

The Armenian trader retreated so quickly, his fez was nearly knocked off by the top of the tent. Struggling to right it on his head, he answered defensively in adequate French, "I bought them, effendi. I did not steal them. As Allah is my witness, I am a respectable businessman."

"I did not think otherwise. But please tell me," the tired American requested calmly, "from whom did you buy them?"

"From another effendi."

"Do you know his name?"

"We traded. We were not friends." The man was aggrieved at being associated with a nonbeliever.

"Had you ever seen this man before?"

"No, effendi. He was *Inglayzi,* but he came with someone who was familiar to me."

"Who?" Arturo kept his voice low with effort. "Can you tell me who that was?"

"Yasir, servant of Omar al Nasr, brought him here. And it was he with whom I bargained," the trader replied guardedly. All of Tangier buzzed with news of the half-crazed infidel captain who wore a blasphemous green scarf at his neck and sought information about the abduction of a white woman by one of his own servants. Who knew what he would do, the Armenian thought, if he knew how he and Yasir had conspired to outsmart the insufferable little Kaffir?

They had put on a good show for the *Inglayzi,* shouting in Arabic and waving their arms. He had never known he was paid an insultingly low price for such fine merchandise. When the silver combs were resold, Yasir and the trader would split a tidy profit.

This delicious anticipation was forgotten when the big American pressed, "Where does this Omar live?"

Silently, the Armenian extended a palm, his message clear. Arturo frowned and dug into his pocket again. Diego was right. Baksheesh could be the financial ruin of any man who did business in the Ottoman empire. Scowling, he laid a silver coin in the man's outstretched hand.

"The house of Omar al Nasr is near the South Gate. Just ask one of the beggars at the gate when you arrive."

"*Merci,*" Arturo muttered. Remembering the combs he was still gripping, he asked, "How much for these?"

The merchant named an outrageous price, which the man paid without flinching; the sale was a boon, though he missed the fun of haggling. Foolish Americans! He shook his head in bemusement.

As the captain neared his destination, he tried to shed the beggars he had picked up when he stopped to ask directions at the South Gate. He shot foul looks at them as they bobbed in front of him. "Hakim, baksheesh," they shouted, their hands extended, crying out for alms at the top of their lungs. Scowling darkly, he stepped up his pace and finally outdistanced them.

Finding the home of Omar al Nasr, the privateer went to the gate and began to pound. A wide-eyed servant opened it slightly and peered out.

"I must see your master," Arturo informed him in French. "It is very important."

"That is not possible."

"Are you Yasir?"

"Why do you seek Yasir?" the eunuch sputtered, frightened by the big, unshaven Kaffir.

"Because I think he knows something about the woman who wore these." Arturo held the combs out for his inspection.

Yasir looked up at Arturo shrewdly. "If this Yasir—Allah preserve him as a true believer—had such information, would you make it worth his while?"

Without a word, Arturo dug in his pocket and presented a handful of coins.

"I am Yasir," the slave admitted after making a quick mental inventory of the contents of the other man's hand.

"I thought as much. Where is the woman who wore these?"

"Indeed, effendi, you have the key which will unlock that gate." Deliberately, Yasir extended his palm.

An exasperated sigh exploded from Arturo as he laid a silver coin in Yasir's hand.

"She was here," the eunuch answered promptly, "but she was sold several days ago."

"Who bought her?"

Shamelessly, Yasir nodded toward his still-outstretched hand. When Arturo laid another coin in it, the eunuch glanced down at his palm disapprovingly and pursed his lips, refusing to speak.

"All right," Arturo snapped and placed another silver coin beside the first.

"Why, she was sold to Farhan ibn Sa'id, hakim," Yasir gushed, "the marriage broker."

"Marriage broker!" Arturo groaned. "Where will I find him?"

"Effendi, that is a gate that only a golden key will open." Yasir rattled the coins in his palm. Arturo put another one in it. After ascertaining it was indeed gold, Yasir smiled brightly. "*Alhamdulldah,* most generous of men, I will take you there myself."

"Do you charge as much for guiding as you do for speaking?" Arturo growled with dwindling patience.

"No, *monsieur,* only one small piece of silver for that. But come, we must hurry." With a quick glance over his shoulder, Yasir slipped out of the gate and headed down the street.

The slave led Arturo a long way before they passed through a gate and climbed a steep hill. At last, Yasir stopped in front of a big buff-colored house.

"This is the home of Farhan ibn Sa'id, effendi, but I do not see his guards. I do not think you will find the girl within."

"We will never know unless we ask." Arturo began to beat adamantly on the wide, double doors.

"You cannot simply knock on the door and ask for a harem slave!" Yasir protested in horror.

"She is not a harem slave," the other man maintained, knocking even harder, causing the sturdy doors to rattle against each other.

"Please, *monsieur*," the eunuch muttered uneasily. "This is one of the wealthiest streets in the city. You will bring the constabulary upon us, if not Farhan's guards.

"Let them come." Arturo continued to pound.

"I must bid you adieu, *monsieur*," Yasir blurted hastily, "for I must hurry home to my master."

The privateer did not answer. The young eunuch rushed away, looking back over his shoulder while Arturo continued to bang on the door.

At last, a shuffling step could be heard from the other side of the wall. One of the doors opened a crack and an old eunuch squinted suspiciously at the persistent American. "What do you want?" he demanded in Arabic.

"I am looking for a Monsieur Farhan ibn Sa'id. Do you speak French?" Arturo asked frantically.

"*Oui.*" Abdul nodded, but he did not open the door to let the stranger in. His master and most of the guards had just departed with several Arab women to a *funduq*, where the women would be kept safe until their sale tomorrow.

"I am looking for Farhan," the white man insisted.

"He is my master," Abdul answered pompously. "What do you wish of him?"

"I am Capitaine Arturo De Leon and I am seeking a girl—"

"You have come to the right place." The old man smiled insinuatingly.

"No, no, not just any girl. This one is American, with golden hair and brown eyes."

So this common infidel was searching for his princess. Abdul inspected Arturo critically, before replying tersely, "There are no women here, Kaffir."

"No, wait!" Arturo shoved on the door desperately when the old man prepared to close it.

"Allah save me from the devil," the eunuch cried, panic-stricken. "Go away, cursed one! Leave before I call the guards!"

"Please," Arturo entreated. "I only want to find the girl."

"I told you there is no girl here."

"Then let me speak to your master."

"My master is not here, either."

"Please, you must help me. I must find her!" Even the stern Abdul felt a stab of remorse at Arturo's torment.

"Listen to me, young effendi," he said almost kindly. "If my master bought this girl—and I do not say that he did—it would do you no good to speak to him. Such a woman has probably already been auctioned. Many men search for wives in the souks. Heed my advice and give up your search. You will never find her within harem walls," the eunuch concluded and slammed the door shut.

"I will not give up," Arturo swore, though his shoulders sagged despondently as he trudged toward the *millah* and Gideon's house.

Go back to your world, Kaffir, the eunuch thought, after the big American left. The woman you seek belongs to my world now. Here she will be better served. They will call her *umm emir*, mother of princes.

Abdul sighed and returned to the women's apartments to see to the needs of his princess.

"*Capitaine*, wait until you hear my news!" His dark eyes flashing, Isaac greeted Arturo exuberantly when he was ushered onto the roof. Gideon's family sat around a table, enjoying the cool of the late afternoon, and with them were Jacques, Narcisse, Dazet and Falgout.

"What are you doing here? Is there news?" Arturo asked his officers hopefully.

"Ask the boy." Jacques nodded at Isaac, who danced around Arturo with barely contained excitement.

"Calm down," Gideon ordered his grandson with an indulgent smile, "and tell Arturo what you have learned."

The boy stopped and drew himself up proudly. "A private auction is being held tomorrow at a *funduq* near the harbor. Farhan ibn Sa'id will offer ten women for marriage. Among them will be three white women: one with dark hair, one with red and one of unsurpassed beauty with hair of gold...a houri such as those who await good Muslims in paradise. She will be sold last."

"Danielle," Arturo breathed, sinking down beside Gideon.

"We think so," the old Jew conceded cautiously.

"She was at Farhan's all the time!" the privateer roared, pounding the table in his anger.

"You were there?"

"*Oui*, and the eunuch told me she was not. I should have forced my way in."

"The guards would have killed you. Farhan employs a small army."

"Then let us all go," Narcisse interjected hotly. "They cannot stand against all five of us."

"Six," Zared amended. "I offer my sword as well."

Gideon quelled them with a fierce frown. "Be reasonable, young men. You cannot storm the house guarded by so many. You cannot steal the girl without a fight. If you fought...if you got her out of the house, what would you do then? It is too far from the harbor for you to reach your ship in safety. It would be madness even to try."

"But I must try," Arturo insisted doggedly. "Danielle is everything to me. I will not leave her behind."

"I loved a woman so, once." Gideon nodded knowingly. "Very well. I think there may be another way. If we cannot get into Farhan's house, we must steal her from under his nose—in public. I know a man, Ibn al Mahsin, an Arab who owes me a favor. Perhaps he could obtain an invitation to the auction for another of my Arab customers."

The men hunched around the table, their heads close while they planned. Mahalah came and went, bringing food and drink. Though she was silent, Arturo noticed concern in her eyes, which rarely strayed from her husband as their daring scheme took shape.

"This could be dangerous to you and your family, Gideon," the privateer protested.

"No." The man shook his gray head with confidence. "Once I secure the invitation, my part is finished."

"And Zared?"

Everyone assured Arturo that the young Jew was best equipped to pose as the son of a sheikh and a potential buyer of a wife.

"Mahalah and I planned to leave for Spain next week. Now we will leave a little earlier." The young man shrugged. "Besides, I am not known here. I can melt into the crowd before your Danielle's absence is noticed. There is no danger to me. It is you and your crew who must devise a scheme to get back to your ship and sail away before anyone can stop you. I do not envy you that task."

"We worry for each other's well-being while time runs out," Gideon cut in impatiently. "Do we put our plans of words into action?" He looked directly at Arturo as he asked the question.

The captain did not answer. His worried study was interrupted by Mahalah's soft voice. "Do not hesitate because of me, *capitaine*. Zared says he will be in no danger and I believe him. But that would make no difference to my husband. He would still help you, for he lives as much for danger as for love. We would not want you to miss the joy we share as husband and wife. To have it, you must take back the woman of your heart."

"It is decided then," Gideon said with a sigh when Arturo nodded. "I will go now and request payment for a debt of long standing." Rising, the old merchant went to call on Ibn al Mahsin, the client whose unwitting assistance would set their plan into motion.

Chapter Seventeen

Just after noonday prayers, the handsome young "desert lord" and his retinue rode out of the stable yard of Ibn al Mahsin, the man who was honored to ensure their entry to the slave auction that very afternoon.

The "personal slave" of the lord perched on the back of a donkey behind his master and choked on the dust. Under his *kaffiyeh,* the flowing headdress of the nomadic Arabs, his blue eyes mirrored his impatience. Arturo disapproved of the plan that required Zared to pose as Turkia bin Ali, son of a desert sheikh, and young Isaac and himself as slaves; he would have preferred to storm the auction, his crew behind him, and spirit Danielle away. But Gideon insisted the present plan was their only chance for success.

Arturo's mood was not helped by a lack of sleep and the sweltering robes he wore. But he could not help but smile when Isaac caught his eye, grinning as he walked beside Zared's stirrup, loudly crying, "Make way, make way!"

The privateer watched Zared as he rode in front, his robes flowing behind him. He sat proudly erect on the swift desert pony his uncle had managed to secure. There was no doubt the young man could carry out his impersonation. His experience among the Arabs would serve him in good stead. He looked every inch the young lordling as he conversed with the stout man who bounced awkwardly on the horse at his side.

Zared's companion was effusive, showing no sign of suspicion. It was as Gideon said, the captain mused: the portly Tangerine was thrilled to be host to the son—even a fifth or sixth son—of an influential sheikh. No matter that Gideon's client had not been able to place the face of that exalted personage in his mind; he truly believed that he, Ibn al Mahsin, had a role to play in the marriage of the son of a desert chieftain.

Arturo flexed his broad shoulders and forced himself to relax. He glanced back at bin Ali's three fierce "men at arms" riding behind him. With their black hair, dark eyes and bronze skin, Falgout, Dazet and Narcisse also looked their parts.

By the time the party approached the *funduq,* a crowd had gathered in the narrow street. News traveled fast in this part of the world and many had hurried to witness the arrival of such important visitors. A score of Farhan's white-uniformed guards stood among the spectators.

The marriage broker emerged at once from the inn, trailed by the innkeeper. Both men were obviously excited by the presence of a sheikh's son at the auction. Farhan's appraising eyes raked over the young noble greedily.

The lordling's bearing proved his claim to a noble house, he decided at once. Except for one large ruby ring, a jewel-encrusted dagger and a rare white manservant, the young man showed no sign of his wealth, though desert tribesmen rarely did. A glance assured him that the goatskin purse concealed under the noble's outer robe looked fat enough . . . fat enough to buy any woman auctioned today, even the aloof Danielle bint Laurent.

A look of irritation flitted over the marriage broker's face at the thought of the girl. Locked in a room upstairs, she conducted herself as if she held court, allowing only Abdul to enter. She had bewitched the old eunuch so he nearly yielded to her urging that she be allowed to wear a caftan instead of the gauzy costume of the other women.

Farhan was pleased to remember how she had drunk the drugged wine he gave her. She dared dispute Abdul's orders, but not his. Drugging slaves had to be handled carefully—not too much, not too little. The right amount was necessary, especially for this *Inglayzi.* If she protested when the time of the sale came, her willfulness would drive the price lower and lower. Allah protect me! Farhan thought.

When Arturo saw Farhan's momentary grimace of impatience, his heart stood still, fearful they were found out. But the marriage broker greeted them cordially, "*As salaam 'alaykum,* Ibn al Mahsin."

"*Wa 'alaykum as salaam,* Farhan ibn Sa'id," the stout Tangerine answered importantly. "May I present Turkia bin Ali?"

"I bid you welcome, most noble one." Farhan made an obeisance.

Zared returned the greeting politely. "May Allah bless your day and ten thousand more for allowing my presence at your auction, ibn Sa'id."

"You are gracious, my lord. The honor is mine. Will you dismount? My servants will take your horses to the stable."

"My retainers will see to them," Zared commanded imperiously. "It is my wish that they await me here."

Zared dismounted first, then Ibn al Mahsin. Then the noble nodded brusquely at his manservant, giving him permission to do the same. Arturo complied at once, keeping his head low in an attempt not to call any attention to himself.

Shooing the nervous innkeeper out of the way, Farhan led his honored guests inside. As page, Isaac led the way proudly for his master, Ibn al Mahsin followed them and Arturo brought up the rear. Behind him, he heard the horses nicker as his ship's officers silently dismounted to wait, eyeing Farhan's guards distrustfully.

The room they entered was long and low-ceilinged with a raised platform at the front. Zared stopped and postured arrogantly, his hands on his hips and his disdainful eyes sweeping the room, taking in the cramped, low tables and the Arabs seated at them. Conversation died as Farhan led them to a table he had reserved for them by the dais.

Zared dropped into the best seat as if he expected no less. His eyes bugging at the preferential treatment, Ibn al Mahsin took the other. Isaac stood behind Zared, energetically wielding a fan, looking as if he were enjoying his role.

Arturo stood at Zared's side, his eyes roving the room, taking in every detail. To the right of the platform was a narrow archway through which a stairway could be seen, apparently the back entrance to the second floor. That the women were upstairs was evidenced by the sturdy eunuch who guarded the arch.

About fifty Arab men were gathered for the auction. Some wore the costumes of city Arabs; some had come from the desert. There were even some marriage brokers who would pay Farhan's price for a rare, white woman to sell in remote regions of Arabia. The men glanced curiously at Zared, but he was haughty and unapproachable. Their curiosity was reserved for the son of a desert lord; fortunately no one spared a glance for the manservant by his side.

As if Farhan had been waiting for Zared's arrival, the auction started at once. Arturo had trouble maintaining his disguise as he watched woman after woman being led through the archway to the platform. Obviously drugged, they swayed on their feet and gazed around in confusion as bids flew through the air.

Zared was silent, for he had made it clear that he sought a white wife. If he was having the same thoughts as Arturo about the humiliating auction, he did not show it. He stirred restlessly, occasionally honoring Ibn al Mahsin with his observations on the women being offered.

There was a stir of anticipation when the last Arab woman was sold. That left only the white women. Zared sat forward in his seat and impatiently motioned Isaac away from him as if his fanning annoyed him. The boy feigned a disappointed pout at his dismissal, but stepped back obediently against the wall near the door.

All eyes were on the dais when the first woman, a petite, curvaceous brunette, was brought out for inspection. Her green eyes had been lined with kohl and the lids drooped under the effects of the drug. Dressed in an emerald-green harem costume, she gazed stupidly at the sea of masculine faces as if she could not quite comprehend what was happening to her.

No one but Arturo noticed when Isaac slipped out the door. The boy sped through narrow streets, slowed by the crowds as he neared the souk on his way to the waterfront. To glimpse him, one would think he was a mere servant hastening on an errand for his master, but Isaac knew better and his grin widened proudly; Arturo's plan depended on him. At Isaac's signal from the wharf, the *Magdalena*'s cannons would boom, creating a diversion so the Americans could escape and he and Zared could melt into the crowd.

His skinny legs pumped, and little puffs of dust rose as his sandaled feet pelted along the ground. When he burst into the small square around which the market was built, Isaac sniffed the air, drawing deep breaths as he ran, smelling the scent of the ocean. The docks were straight ahead, but could not yet be seen for the crowd.

Somewhere in front of him the traffic slowed to a sluggish crawl. The boy ducked and dodged, twisting his small wiry body, forcing his way through the slow-moving press until he could not move at all.

It seemed one of the camels being led to the camel dealer in the nearby souk had rebelled and knelt crosswise in the middle of the narrow street. Nothing the driver did—whistling, shouting, jabbing with his *mashab*—could stir the animal. Spitting and roaring, it rolled its eyes and snapped at the man each time he got close.

Elbowing his way back through the crowd, Isaac doggedly retraced his steps to the square where he could take another street to the harbor. He quickened his pace, breaking into a run as the crowd thinned. He had lost some time, but he hoped he was not too late.

"*Mashallah*," Zared muttered when the redhead was led onto the dais. "Her hair is like a fire that causes my blood to boil. I must have this woman," he announced loudly to Ibn al Mahsin.

The Tangerine looked uncomfortable as Zared began to bid wildly for the white woman, making his desire known to all. For a moment, Farhan, looking down from his post on the dais, feared no one would bid against the son of a powerful sheikh. But greed was strong and soon one of the richly dressed marriage brokers bid for the blue-clad beauty. Immediately, Zared upped his bid. Then another man joined in. His bid was a dare that young Turkia bin Ali accepted at once.

Zared arrogantly countered every offer the other men made. Ibn al Mahsin sank lower in his seat with each exchange. Neither he nor anyone else noticed when the young noble's servant left his master's side to lounge against the wall at the side of the room.

The blue-eyed slave leaned against the wall, his attention seemingly on the hectic bidding. But his gaze drifted regularly toward the archway. The eunuch still guarded it, but part of his concentration was claimed by the scene unfolding before him.

Under the cover of his robe, Arturo's fingers found the small but lethal dagger concealed there. As a slave he could not carry a sword. He would depend mostly on the confusion when he spirited Danielle away. What was delaying the cannons? The sound of their firing was guaranteed to draw the eunuch's attention from the door, if only for an instant. And an instant was all Arturo needed.

A flurry of disbelief swept the room when Zared bid not only an entire purse of gold, but a rare, valuable, Tuareg-trained camel. Even the woman seemed to realize something unusual was happening. The marriage broker retired from the bidding and the young lord's taunting eyes lit on the only other remaining bidder in a personal challenge.

Enthralled, the eunuch stepped forward for a better view as Zared laid his purse on the table with a heavy clank.

This was the opportunity Arturo had waited for. He could wait no longer for the guns. Cautiously, he drew his knife and, slipping behind the guard, stole silently up the stairs. He found himself in a long, shadowy hallway lined with doors. Dim light filtered in from an arch at the other end of the hall where a staircase mounted to the second floor from the street. In the murkiness, he saw that all the doors stood slightly ajar—all save one. And Arturo had no doubt that he would find Danielle behind that door.

He could hear Zared's voice downstairs, growing more strident as he continued to bid. Where were the cannons? Arturo raced to the door and tried the latch. Locked...as he had known it would be. He paused, trying to decide how to gain entry to the chamber. He could hardly break down the door, at least not until the cannons sounded from the harbor.

Why hadn't Jacques commenced firing? None of the crewmen had wanted to stay aboard the *Magdalena,* but they had their orders and would do their parts. Had Isaac failed? Why had he entrusted the important task of signaling the ship to a boy? Arturo agonized.

The sound of someone ascending the front staircase came to the privateer's alert ears. He stepped back into the shadows as Abdul shuffled into view up the stairs. The old eunuch must have been watching the bidding from the front door of the inn and only now returned to his charge.

As Abdul approached Danielle's door, it seemed to him that the big man materialized from the shadows. "You!" Abdul whispered when he recognized the infidel under the Arab costume. The old eunuch's eyes widened but before he could call out to the guards at the bottom of the stairs, Arturo was at his side, his blade pressed to his throat.

"Open the door," he rasped in his ear.

"I will not. I will die first," Abdul replied with dignity, staring straight ahead.

"That can be arranged," the American growled dangerously. The tip of his dagger pricked the eunuch's skin, drawing a bright bead of blood.

"You will never escape, Kaffir," Abdul insisted, but he fumbled blindly at his thick waist until he found the key to Danielle's room. "There are guards at every door. You will die if you take Danielle bint Laurent."

"I cannot live if I do not."

Abdul's brows lifted in surprise and his eyes shifted toward the captain. "Tell me one thing before you kill me, effendi. My princess...will she have an honored place in your harem? Will she be your first wife?"

"She will be my only wife," Arturo replied softly and brought the hilt of his dagger down on the old man's bald head. He caught Abdul as he slumped and laid him gently on the floor. "Rest now, old man," he muttered.

It must be time! Danielle's breath caught in her throat when she heard muffled voices from the hallway. This might be her only opportunity to escape. Her hand closed on the heavy clay lamp she had chosen as a weapon and she crept to stand behind the door.

They thought her drugged and helpless. How she relished the idea of their surprise. She had poured the drugged wine Farhan had given her out the window when no one was

watching. Then she had lain down on her divan as if suddenly
sleepy. Through slitted eyes she had watched him leave the
room, a smug expression on his thin face. He would not look
smug for long. Raising the lamp over her head, she hoped it
would be the marriage broker who opened the door, for she
did not really want to hurt Abdul.

The man who entered was tall and muscular, wearing the
clothes of a desert Arab, probably one of Farhan's mercenar-
ies. Though she could not see his face, from the back he looked
powerful under his voluminous robes. She must land a solid,
well-placed blow if she was to incapacitate such a formidable
foe.

She brought the lamp down hard toward his head, but the
man whirled in a flurry of robes and one strong, browned hand
lashed out to capture hers in an iron grip. The lamp fell with a
muted thud on the thick carpet and rolled away, spilling oil.

With a frustrated cry, the girl lashed out at him, determined to reach the door, which he had closed quietly behind
him. She fought wildly, never noticing in her fury that his hold
was oddly gentle. He pinned her against the door with his hard
body, holding her arms above her head almost tenderly.

Unmindful of the consequences, she tried to double her leg
and land a blow to his most sensitive area.

"Careful, woman! You will ruin what hopes we may have
for a family—if we can get out of here alive."

Her flailing ceased when Arturo's deep, teasing voice pen-
etrated her panic.

"Danielle, *mon coeur,* don't you recognize me?" He continued to hold her with one hand until he had raked the
kaffiyeh from his head with the other.

"T-turo?" the stunned girl stammered. "You came for me."

"Of course I came for you. I love you," he answered simply. Releasing her hands, he took her in his arms.

With a low, joyful cry, Danielle wrapped her arms around
him, lifting her face to his. The man crushed her against his
chest and his mouth found hers, communicating his love
without words.

"Are you all right?" he asked. Stepping back, he gripped
her shoulders and looked her over. When he saw her costume, his blue eyes darkened with desire, unanticipated and

unwanted at the moment. A small vest of gold satin barely covered Danielle's naked breasts and her long, trim legs could be plainly seen through trousers made of a diaphanous golden cloth.

"It is too bad we do not have much time, *cher,*" he said huskily. Still gripping her shoulders, he poised, listening. Where the devil were the cannons?

From downstairs he could faintly hear Zared's voice, desperation edging it. Soon the bidding must cease, and the guards would come for Danielle.

It was dangerous to linger. But without the roar of the cannons from the harbor, escape was nearly impossible. They could not leave by either staircase, for they were too well guarded.

Arturo crossed to the window and looked out at a small, walled garden. It was completely deserted, the auction holding the attention of everyone in the *funduq*. Then he spied a door to the street. Their only hope.

He went to the divan and began to cut strips from the bedclothes with his dagger. His nimble fingers tied sturdy sailor's knots until he had created a rope that would reach from the window to the ground below. His brow furrowed with concentration, Arturo tugged at each end of the fabric, straining it, hastily checking the strength of the binding. When he was satisfied, he turned back to the girl and swiftly removed his robe and sash.

"You must have a disguise," he explained before she could ask. "There would be a riot if you were seen dressed like that."

The robe swallowed Danielle's slender figure, but Arturo draped it over her and belted it, blousing the extra length of material over the sash. Then he cut what remained of the bedclothes into thick strips, which he wrapped around her head to form a crude turban to cover her blond hair. The clumsy headgear wobbled precariously every time she moved her head, but when Arturo finished, she looked like a small, pale-skinned urchin dressed in the clothes of an older brother.

The privateer retrieved his *kaffiyeh* and arranged it on his head. "Now maybe we won't attract too much attention too soon."

Lowering the rope out the window, he turned to Danielle. "Do you think you can do this?"

"Oui." She nodded gamely, her turban bobbing.

He lifted her to the window ledge and ordered quietly, "When you reach the ground, stay close to the wall until I join you."

"Oui, mon capitaine," she said, smiling nervously at him. Then she planted a quick kiss on his lips and slid over the ledge and out of sight, wriggling as she let herself carefully down the rope.

Arturo held his breath, certain she would be spotted at any moment, listening for an alarm. But he heard nothing, not even the long-awaited sound of the cannon. When the girl stood safely on the ground, pressed against the wall, he lowered himself down beside her.

Taking her hand in his, he led Danielle to the door in the garden wall. They paused for an instant, steeling themselves for the perilous journey back to the ship. With only one disguise between them, it would not be easy.

At that moment, the *Magdalena*'s cannons boomed from the harbor, where the brigantine had cast off from the wharf and now rode at anchor. Isaac had signaled the ship! Determined to use the confusion to their advantage, Arturo opened the door and headed purposefully toward the horses his officers held in readiness. Across the dusty space, he could see the relief in his men's eyes. Narcisse looked as if he would burst with joy.

Before they could reach their party, people begin to pour out of the *funduq,* drawn by the cannon's fire. Arturo ran toward the horses, dragging Danielle behind him. To avoid tripping over the long robe, she freed her hand and hiked it up to her knees. Then she raced after him.

All at once, Farhan vaulted down the stairs and onto the street. He had gone to rescue his valuable slave, only to find Abdul unconscious and the girl missing. When he caught a quick glimpse of golden-clad leg under Danielle's robe, he pointed and shouted, *"Wallahi,* my slave is being stolen!"

Instantly, Dazet and Falgout flanked the fleeing pair, their swords drawn. Narcisse drew his own sword and relinquished the reins of the horses into the hands of a man who loitered nearby. In a flash, Arturo recognized him as one of Gideon's cousins in the guise of a city Arab. The man smiled and hurried to take the horses to the back of the inn where Zared waited.

"Turo!" Narcisse shouted over the din, tossing his captain a saber he seized from a bystander.

"Merci," Arturo called, hefting the sword to get its feel. He frowned at the shoddiness of the weapon, but it would have to do.

"My pleasure," Narcisse shouted before eagerly crossing swords with one of Farhan's guards.

Gathered in a tight cluster, the Americans changed direction, retreating from the mob, following the same route Isaac had taken. They had to try to get through the crowded souk on foot.

One of Farhan's eunuchs appeared from the garden where he had been searching for the girl. When he recognized the urchin tearing past him, a pleased smile split his dark face and he opened his arms to grab at her retreating figure. His smile disappeared when he grasped nothing more than her unwieldy turban. She ran, reaching for Arturo's outstretched hand, her blond hair streaming out behind her.

Danielle collided with the captain's sturdy back when he halted abruptly. Two guards had rounded the corner of the inn and were blocking their path. Bidding the girl to stay back, Arturo met them with sword and dagger. The clash of the swords was deafening as the blades flashed in the sunlight. She watched fearfully, hardly aware that she was the center of a protective circle. Behind her, battles were being waged by Narcisse, Dazet and Falgout against Farhan's guards and the horde of irate Arabs. No one at all seemed to notice Ibn al Mahsin, standing in the doorway of the *funduq,* searching forlornly for Turkia bin Ali. Nor did they see the two white slave women who'd been Danielle's fellow captives, as they dashed away in the opposite direction, vivid flashes of green and blue in the dust of the battle.

Arturo disarmed both guards, wounding one so he cried out hoarsely and no longer followed. The second guard retrieved his sword and chased the fleeing couple into the souk.

Arturo and Danielle raced through the maze of streets, weaving among the crowd. Though they did not stop to look over their shoulders, they heard the shouts and the clash of swords behind them as the *Magdalena*'s officers followed, fighting to hold off the onslaught. The blue-eyed foreigner and the unveiled white woman streaked past most of the passers-by before they realized what was happening. But when they did, the Arabs joined the chase.

Hands grabbed at the infidels, at their clothes and Danielle's bright hair, ripping Arturo's *kaffiyeh* from his head. The couple burst into the square at the center of the souk with the determined guard on their heels. The eunuch engaged Arturo in battle again, attacking so ruthlessly the big captain was not even aware when his officers erupted into the square with Farhan and his guards right behind.

Frightened by the armed combat and the intermittent boom of the cannons from the harbor, veiled women screamed, adding to the commotion. Startled camels shied at the tumult, hissing and prancing as they knocked down the stalls, and crushed baskets underfoot. With an intimidating roar, Dazet lifted a bamboo cage filled with live chickens over his head and flung it at their pursuers. The cage broke when it hit the ground and squawking chickens emerged amid flapping wings and flying feathers. The square exploded into pandemonium.

Seeing that Danielle's protectors were occupied, Farhan advanced on his prize. Racing to a pottery stall, the girl picked up a bowl and threw it at him. Her aim did not fail her. She hit his shoulder and slowed him for a moment.

Infuriated at seeing his wares flying through the air, the potter deserted his wheel and charged toward the girl with an angry shout. Without a second thought, she hurled a pot in his direction as well. Well supplied with ammunition, she held her position, bombarding her attackers, while watching Arturo anxiously out of the corner of her eye.

He battled his tenacious opponent until, at last, he sank his dagger into the man's chest. The injured eunuch staggered away, his hands locked around the hilt of Arturo's knife. Gripping his sword, the privateer surveyed the chaotic souk for Danielle. His eyes found her and noted the menacing circle of attackers that tightened around her. Quickly, he hurried to snatch her from danger.

Fending off attacks on every side, the captain roughly shoved Farhan aside and grasped Danielle's hand. Together, they sprinted toward the gate to the street that led to the harbor. The thoroughfare ahead of them was nearly impassable, but Arturo was ready to plunge into the crowd when a mountainous eunuch, carrying a huge scimitar, appeared from nowhere to plant himself solidly in front of them.

Arturo slowly retreated, cursing under his breath in five languages. Suddenly he dodged into a dye seller's booth, dragging Danielle with him into the multicolored tunnels created by drying fabric. With a furious bellow, the eunuch pursued them, slashing with his scimitar in the narrow space, cutting lines of richly tinted material so they fell to be trampled underfoot.

Staying low, Arturo and Danielle ran as quietly as possible. From two aisles over, they could hear the wheezing and thrashing of their pursuer as he slashed and stabbed viciously at the fabric.

They reached the small clearing at the end of the aisle where the vendor boiled his dyes. They were hurrying toward the opening when they were spotted by the irate owner of the stall.

Concealed behind a stack of folded fabric until the danger was over, he now forgot his caution, waving his arms and shouting for help. When he lunged toward the girl, a sword flashed, reflecting the rich-hued surroundings, and the ropes that held the stall's awning in place were cut. As the Arab was swallowed by yards of billowing, brightly colored fabric, Arturo and Danielle turned to find Narcisse in the square behind them.

"You look well, Mam'selle Danielle." He grinned appreciatively. "We have wasted enough time here, *oui, mes amis?*"

"*Oui,*" Arturo answered soberly, "let us get back to the *Magdalena.*"

But before the trio could make their escape, they heard a triumphant laugh behind them. The big eunuch, breathing heavily, advanced on Arturo and Danielle.

His eyes locked on the menacing guard's, Arturo extended one foot and tipped a simmering pot of dye. The eunuch gave a shrill scream as the hot liquid spilled over his feet and splashed up in lavender waves onto his white uniform.

The fugitives did not stay to admire their handiwork. Dashing back into the square, they scanned the ruin of the souk. Most of Farhan's guards had been disabled. The marriage broker himself groaned near the fountain, nursing a lump on his head. The fighting had dwindled and townspeople now milled amid the havoc, stepping over bodies, mostly unconscious, which lay where they had fallen.

The captain whistled three sharp blasts over the lessening din. Immediately, Falgout and Dazet joined the others.

"They are going to get away," an angry merchant shouted.

"Seize them!" another bellowed.

"This way, effendis! This way!" a pair of youthful voices called to the foreigners.

Arturo turned to see Isaac and his younger cousin, Nathan, gesturing to them. At once, the party of Americans wheeled and followed the two boys.

The dwindling but persistent mob chased them through the narrow streets, hardly wide enough for two men. Anger gave the Arabs extra speed and they gained steadily until the Americans passed a cross street. The crowd was caught short when a tiny, two-wheeled cart pulled by a shabby-looking donkey lumbered into the intersection. Driven by a bent, ancient farmer, the cart was loaded with a cask of wine, a huge jar of olive oil and baskets of oranges. The shaky load was steadied by a heavily veiled woman who rode on the side of the wagon, one braceleted arm thrown across the jar of oil.

At the shouts of the mob and the boom of the cannons, the donkey balked, causing the cart to lurch forward at an angle so it was firmly wedged in the narrow street. The woman shrieked in panic and released her hold on the olive oil to catch herself. Suddenly, the load shifted in the open cart and hundreds of oranges rolled to the ground under the feet of the pedestrians. The cask and the jar also fell and broke, their rich contents mingling in the dust.

The old man whistled and shouted at the donkey as he apologized profusely to the bystanders and upbraided the wailing woman. The cart rolled forward a few inches, then back, but would not come unstuck. The driver seemed powerless to free it.

Powerless, at least, until the Americans disappeared from view down the street. By the time the farmer had straightened the wagon, most of the mob had given up and returned to the souk to clean up the damage.

"Are you all right, young one?" the old farmer asked the woman, who now sat silently in the back of the cart.

"Yes, Uncle Gideon." Mahalah's chuckle could be heard from within the concealing yashmak. "Do you think they got away?"

"That is in the hands of Yahweh. Let us go home now. We have done what we can to help him."

Chapter Eighteen

"Shoot over their heads," Jacques commanded from the quarterdeck. "We do not wish to kill, only to frighten."

"Aye, aye." The small detail of men at the gunwales pointed pistols and muskets at the Turks who approached in three small rowboats.

Immediately, the crack of small-weapon fire punctuated the monotonous boom of the cannon. A cheer went up from the *Magdalena*'s crew when they realized how quickly confusion brought about the Turks' retreat. In the water below them, the little boats rocked violently and men were pitched overboard as they attempted to escape the sudden fusillade.

Khalid al Hammid stood on the covered porch of a water-front *bagnio* and watched small puffs of dust rising as bits of rock peppered down on the arid clearing in front of him. In the middle of the bay, the brigantine rode at anchor, well away from the other ships, and fired heavy charges of gunpowder and broken ballast rock into the air, causing a hail of stinging stone to rain down from above.

From the building behind him, the chief of police could hear the frightened moans of the slaves held there. Idiots, he thought impatiently. They were in no danger.

In fact, the barrage brought little real damage. But the threat was enough that the waterfront, usually teeming with laborers and beggars, was deserted. The burly sailors from nearby *boums* and merchant ships sought safety below decks. Even the old water seller had abandoned his open tent stall although it was pitched under the protective branches of a huge acacia tree.

Why did the Americans do this? Khalid wondered in exasperation. They were firing on the city with no intent to kill or destroy. What did they hope to accomplish? His eyes narrowed when he peered through the shower of rock to see the havoc being created among the men he had sent to seize the ship. More than half of them splashed in the murky water of the harbor, and one of the boats was completely unmanned; the other half of the troop rowed wildly for shore, unmindful of the rock raining down on them.

Khalid was irritated by their incompetence, incensed at being assigned to such a troublesome post as Tangier, but mostly he was furious that he had underestimated the *Inglayzi* captain. From the beginning he had sensed De Leon was dangerous, but the man must have been mad if he thought he could intimidate the chief of police. If this was a challenge, let the Kaffir make it himself, the Arab seethed.

He would not accept this humiliation. When the reinforcements he had summoned arrived, he would send a detail to the cannon emplacement in the heights to blow the American ship out of the water.

But the police chief wavered, unsure that course of action would be wise. It was a difficult situation: infidels firing their cannons in the harbor of an Ottoman city. To leave the attack unanswered looked bad, for he was the representative of the sultan in this far-flung province. But if the ship was destroyed, the sultan would not like having to deal with an angry American president. If only he could get his hands on the *Inglayzi* captain, he would make him pay.

Suddenly, a flurry of activity a short distance down the waterfront caught Khalid's attention. A group of people spilled out of the street into the marketplace and onto the deserted wharf. After a moment, Khalid recognized the man in the lead, crouching as he ran, using his big body to shield the pale-haired beauty at his side. Bareheaded before God and clad in only a *thobe,* Arturo De Leon was racing in his direction!

Alhamdulilah! His prayers were answered. Khalid assumed the American would be a splendid opponent. Now was the time to find out. He would settle this thing personally with the infidel.

When the American sailors recognized their captain and shipmates, the cannon fire abruptly ceased. The uncanny silence was broken only by the sound of the fugitives' feet drumming on the wooden wharf. Their path angled slightly and Khalid realized they were running toward a small boat tied at the end of the pier not far from where he stood.

With no hesitation, the commander of Tangier's police placed himself directly in the path of the fleeing Americans. When Arturo spied him, he straightened and slowed his step. His blue eyes were fixed warily on Khalid as the Arab brought up his sword in a mocking salute.

The privateer halted and acknowledged the unmistakable challenge with a nod and a wolfish smile. Gently, he pushed Danielle behind him, into Narcisse's arms. "If I lose, look after her," he instructed his old friend. "Do not let him take her."

"You know I would die first," Narcisse assured him quietly. "But have no fear, you will not lose. You have much to live for."

"Oui." Arturo smiled down into the girl's stricken face for an instant, his love showing in his eyes. Then he walked forward to meet Khalid.

"No, no," Danielle whispered to herself, "we were so close to escape."

"Come, *cher,*" Narcisse urged, tugging her after him. "We must go on to the boat. Turo will join us when he has won."

The girl did not argue, but her step faltered as the Cajun led her down the dock to the boat. She strained to look over her shoulder, unable to take her eyes off the men as they took the *en garde* position in the clearing in front of the wharfside buildings.

Their deadly curved blades glistened in the sun, engaging with a faint metallic rasp. Slowly, assessingly, Arturo and Khalid circled, their swords crossing almost lazily as they tested each other's steel.

"What a welcome meeting this is, *capitaine,*" the commander offered casually. "I knew, somehow, it would come to this."

"I have been looking forward to it as well," Arturo said, grinning unabashedly.

Khalid gathered himself to lunge. But Arturo was ready for his vigorous offensive. He parried the other man's blows easily, maintaining the distance between them, his blue eyes watching for the briefest of openings.

When he saw it, he seized it, the tip of his sword slicing the front of Khalid's loose shirt. As he withdrew, the Arab's cold gray eyes raked over Arturo appraisingly.

His opponent was an even better swordsman than he had hoped, Khalid mused. A light hand and a supple wrist bespoke practiced skill with a saber. Arturo was taller and more muscular than he, but the Arab felt no fear, only a surge of anticipation, as he reevaluated his foe. The *Inglayzi* would be a fine opponent indeed!

Khalid resumed the conversation as if it had never been interrupted. "I see you have your woman back."

"I told you I would find her," Arturo replied scornfully. "Did you not believe me?"

"I had my doubts. Although I realized you wanted her, I did not know you were possessed."

"Ah, you underestimated me." The American advanced, seeking to improve his position, while Khalid wasted valuable breath.

"There is no accounting what a madman will do." The commander shrugged.

Arturo merely grunted in response, pressing him farther back toward the buildings that lined the wharf.

Khalid's eyes narrowed, and for a time discussion ceased as the men dueled in earnest, steel clashing against steel.

Danielle watched anxiously as Khalid tried to maneuver Arturo to the water's edge. She stifled her cries of warning, afraid she would distract him. The privateer teetered for a instant on the edge of the pier, but he withstood the onslaught, refusing to be driven over the side. The heated battle raged over the hard-packed clearing as the men advanced and retreated savagely.

"You grow weary." Khalid panted from exertion, but his cruel lips curled with a smile when he brought first blood.

"It has been a long morning," was Arturo's dry, reply. He spared no more than a glance at the slight wound on his left arm. A trickle of blood was quickly absorbed into the fabric of his *thobe,* crimson spreading slowly on white.

Arturo did not want the Arab to know how the chase through the souk had tired him, but he knew he must end this battle quickly. Over Khalid's shoulder, he could see the water seller's tent pitched under the tree. He renewed his attack to press the Arab toward it, step by step, bent on lessening the other man's mobility.

But Khalid seemed determined to talk. His gaze flickered toward the end of the pier where Danielle watched the sword-play, supported by Narcisse.

"Your woman is lovely, *capitaine,*" he taunted, feinting a cut to the other man's flank. "Perhaps I will take her into my own harem when you are out of the way."

"You would have to kill me and all of my men first." Arturo ignored the invitation to thrust, which would have left his guard down.

"I do not care about the others, but it will be a shame to kill you, *Inglayzi,*" Khalid said, puffing. "You would make such a fine galley slave."

"You would have to kill me to have Danielle," the privateer repeated doggedly, redoubling his efforts, catching the other man off guard. "And still you would not be rid of me. I would come back to haunt you."

So taken aback was he by the infidel's words, Khalid quickly found himself driven against the stall of the water seller. His sword caught in the goat-hair roof as he slashed, its curved edge slicing through it as easily as gauze. As Arturo launched himself toward him, the Arab ducked through the tent, upsetting a jar of precious water and losing his turban in the maneuver. When he managed to emerge on the other side, the American was just behind.

Around the acacia tree they fenced, both men dripping with sweat in the afternoon sun, their sabers clashing with a hideous clamor. Arturo fought like the madman Khalid suspected he was, until he had backed the official against the trunk of the massive tree.

This time when the American lunged, Khalid's eyes widened and he whirled out of the way at the last moment. His feet sliding in the mud from the spilled water jar, the commander tripped among the tent ropes. The blade of Arturo's borrowed sword whistled near his ear, then struck the tree and broke off, almost at the hilt.

"Zut!" the privateer bellowed in frustration, glaring disbelievingly at the useless weapon in his hand.

Recovering his balance, Khalid walked slowly toward his foe, his sword at the ready. "I really do not wish to kill you, Kaffir," he said softly. "You are a worthy foe. I am sorry our battle is over so quickly."

"It is not over yet," the American grated, diving for a stick that supported a corner of the tent. He rolled and landed on his feet, holding it before him like a quarterstaff. Then he advanced on the Arab with a roar of anger.

A shadow of apprehension flitted through Khalid's pale eyes. The *Inglayzi* would attack him with a tent pole? He was indeed mad! He met the jolting attack, swinging his sword fiercely. But Arturo thwarted every blow, grasping the stick with a hand on each end. Then, cursing vehemently in every language he knew, the captain gripped the sturdy stick at one end and swung it like a bludgeon.

His blustering tactic was successful. Khalid retreated, unnerved by the flailing stick, the shouts, the unintelligible babble. For the first time in his memory, he felt real fear.

Arturo's staff hit the end of Khalid's fingers where they curled around the hilt of his sword, bringing sudden numbing pain. But the police commander kept a tenacious hold on his sword, parrying a storm of jarring blows until he was backed against the wall of the *bagnio*.

Khalid tried to clench his sword with throbbing fingers, but the pain was too great. By the beard of the Prophet, they were surely broken. When he loosened his grasp for a mere second to adjust his grip, Arturo brought the end of his staff up to slam against the hilt of the sword. The saber flew from Khalid's hand and skittered on the ground, landing against the side of the building, just out of reach.

The Arab's eyes slid toward it desperately, but he could not move. The madman's staff was pressed against his neck, pinning him against the mud wall. The least pressure from the big man and Khalid knew his neck would snap. "Go on, finish it," he said hoarsely.

"I could easily kill you," his opponent panted, his breathing harsh and ragged, "but I do not think I will."

"You would leave an enemy alive to fight another day?"

The American expelled a deep breath and loosened his hold somewhat. "There won't be another day for us, al Hammid. Besides, as you say, there is no accounting what a madman will do." Stepping back, he saluted the baffled Arab with the stick he used as a weapon. Then he threw it down in the dust, turned his back deliberately and strode toward the waiting boat without even a glance over his shoulder.

Supported by the wall, Khalid heard the cheer from the Americans as the big captain walked away from the battleground. Arturo carried himself confidently, but his broad shoulders slumped wearily and his left arm hung limp at his side, trailing occasional drops of blood. The *Inglayzi* had been weakening, Khalid thought triumphantly, somehow comforted by the thought. He did not like to dwell on it, but he had been defeated at arms for the first time in many years.

Khalid watched as Danielle stepped forward, then stopped to stand motionless, poised at the end of the pier while the victorious man walked toward her.

What a picture she was, the commander mused as he ambled toward the water's edge. Still wrapped in Arturo's robe, she was unveiled, her unbound hair gilded by the sun. The smile she turned toward De Leon was radiant and welcoming and open for anyone to see. A woman made for loving... and she belonged to the American captain. Unexpectedly, Khalid felt a stir of envy.

Suddenly the girl ran to Arturo with a jubilant cry and was swept into a fervent one-armed embrace, which conveyed, even at a distance, relief and joy. Then, hand in hand, they went to the waiting boat and were rowed to the ship.

As the little boat neared the brigantine, the commander of the sultan's police moved stiffly to the end of the pier and sat down on a barrel. He heard the rattle of sheathed sabers before his men appeared around the corner from the souk, led by his adjutant, Mustafa, the only man in the entire company of swordsman to own a gun.

Seeing that the Americans had escaped, the young Ottoman raced to the end of the pier and dropped to one knee beside Khalid, taking careful aim at the inviting target Arturo's powerful back presented. But he did not fire, for suddenly he felt the cold blade of his superior's sword at his throat.

"Do not, Mustafa," the police commander growled. "I warn you, if you kill the *Inglayzi*, ill luck will follow you to the grave, perhaps even beyond. He is mad...possessed by a jinni with golden hair."

"Then what—what shall I do, venerable one?" the adjutant stammered. "They are getting away."

"Let them go. In fact, watch to make sure they leave the harbor without incident. Tangier cannot be rid of such undesirables too quickly."

With that, Khalid al Hammid departed, leaving the young man to wonder if the exalted commander of police, the sultan's own representative in Morocco, was himself possessed.

The cry of the muezzin drifted across the water from the city as Danielle was pulled aboard the *Magdalena* by friendly hands. On deck, she found herself surrounded by weathered, bewhiskered faces, all lit with welcoming smiles. Suddenly overwhelmed, she returned the smiles tremulously and blinked back tears of joy.

"It is about time Turo brings you home, yes," Felix announced disapprovingly, still looking a bit pale, but intact.

"Aye," Pat agreed, darting a nervous look at his hero. "Welcome back, Miss Dani. 'Tis good to see ye again."

"*Oui,*" came the heartfelt agreement from the crew.

"The *mam'selle* knows we are glad for her safe return," the first mate cut in, his voice gruff with emotion. "Pretty words can wait until later."

"Jacques is right," Arturo affirmed. Only the captain's head and shoulders were visible as he ascended the pilot ladder from the boat below. He stepped aboard, his wounded arm bound with a strip of Falgout's *kaffiyeh*, the ends fluttering in the brisk breeze. "Clap to, *mes amis,*" he shouted as he was joined by his officers. "Weigh anchor! We sail now!"

At once, the crew prepared to set sail. Capturing Danielle's hand, Arturo led her toward the ladder to the quarterdeck, but she balked near the hatch.

"Should we not go below? To see to the cut on your arm," she added quickly, noting the lecherous gleam in Arturo's eyes.

"Ah, and I thought you meant to reward me for my valor." He sighed dramatically.

"Perhaps I will, *mon cher,*" she breathed with a dazzling, provocative smile, "after I tend your wound."

"We will see to both my wound and my reward when we have cleared Tangier harbor," he promised warmly. There was work to be done first. He drew her after him to the quarterdeck.

The couple overlooked the activity on the foredeck while Narcisse contentedly took his place at the wheel. Then at a signal from Jacques, the crew began to hoist the sails. Still clad in the oversize robe, Danielle leaned back gratefully against the captain's strong chest. Arturo held her, his sinewy arms encircling her trim waist, his face close beside hers as he breathed in the fragrance of her hair.

"Look, *capitaine,*" Jacques called as they sailed out of the harbor. He pointed toward the horizon where the faint outline of another sailing ship could be seen approaching. "It is the *Clara Corey*. We will win this race, *oui?*"

"We will win," Arturo confirmed, looking up at the sails billowing with the wind from the Levant that bore them toward home.

The *Magdalena*'s last sight of Morocco was a sandy spit of land stretching far out into the blue waters of the Atlantic. A horseman astride a magnificent white stallion galloped along the strand, his robes streaming out behind him. When he reached land's end, he stopped and cupped his hands over his mouth to shout at the departing ship.

"Kaffir! Can you hear me?" came Khalid's distant call over the water.

"I hear you, al Hammid!" Arturo led Danielle to the railing as he answered the Arab.

"You are a worthy opponent, but I warn you never to return to Tangier. You bring with you too many problems."

"Do not worry, I won't trouble you further," Arturo shouted back with a laugh, throwing his arm loosely over Danielle's shoulder.

"And in the future—" Khalid's voice was nearly lost over the roar of the waves as the *Magdalena* broke into the open sea "—see that you take better care of your woman!"

"I assure you, she will never leave my side," Arturo murmured. Smiling tenderly, he took her in his arms. "I would never want to lose her again."

"Never," Danielle agreed in the instant before their lips met.

* * * * *

HARLEQUIN
American Romance®

THE ROMANCE THAT STARTED IT ALL!

For Diane Bauer and Nick Granatelli, the walk down the aisle
was a rocky road....

Don't miss the romantic prequel to WITH THIS RING—

I THEE WED
BY ANNE McALLISTER

Harlequin American Romance #387

Let Anne McAllister take you to Cambridge, Massachusetts, to
the night when an innocent blind date brought a reluctant Diane
Bauer and Nick Granatelli together. For Diane, a smoldering
attraction like theirs had only one fate, one future—marriage.
The hard part, she learned, was convincing her intended....

Watch for Anne McAllister's I THEE WED, available *now* from
Harlequin American Romance.

ITW

Everyone loves a spring wedding, and this April,
Harlequin cordially invites you to read the most
romantic wedding book of the year.

With This Ring

ONE WEDDING—FOUR LOVE STORIES
FROM OUR MOST DISTINGUISHED
HARLEQUIN AUTHORS:

BETHANY CAMPBELL
BARBARA DELINSKY
BOBBY HUTCHINSON
ANN McALLISTER

*The church is booked, the reception arranged and the
invitations mailed. All Diane Bauer and Nick Granatelli
have to do is walk down the aisle. Little do they realize that
the most cherished day of their lives will spark so many
romantic notions....*

Available wherever Harlequin books are sold.   HWED-1AR

HARLEQUIN'S WISHBOOK
SWEEPSTAKES RULES & REGULATIONS
NO PURCHASE NECESSARY TO ENTER OR RECEIVE A PRIZE

1. To enter the Sweepstakes and join the Reader Service, affix the Four Free Books and Free Gifts sticker along with both of your Sweepstakes stickers to the Sweepstakes Entry Form. If you do not wish to take advantage of our Reader Service, but wish to enter the Sweepstakes only, do not affix the Four Free Books and Free Gifts sticker; affix only the Sweepstakes stickers to the Sweepstakes Entry Form. Incomplete and/or inaccurate entries are ineligible for that section or sections of prizes. Torstar Corp. and its affiliates are not responsible for mutilated or unreadable entries or inadvertent printing errors. Mechanically reproduced entries are null and void.

2. Whether you take advantage of this offer or not, on or about April 30, 1992 at the offices of Marden-Kane Inc., Lake Success, NY, your Sweepstakes number will be compared against a list of winning numbers generated at random by the computer. However, prizes will only be awarded to individuals who have entered the Sweepstakes. In the event that all prizes are not claimed, a random drawing will be held from all qualified entries received from March 30, 1990 to March 31, 1992, to award all unclaimed prizes. All cash prizes (Grand to Sixth), will be mailed to the winners and are payable by check in U.S. funds. Seventh prize to be shipped to winners via third-class mail. These prizes are in addition to any free, surprise or mystery gifts that might be offered. Versions of this sweepstakes with different prizes of approximate equal value may appear in other mailings or at retail outlets by Torstar Corp. and its affiliates.

3. The following prizes are awarded in this sweepstakes: ★ Grand Prize (1) $1,000,000; First Prize (1) $25,000; Second Prize (1) $10,000; Third Prize (5) $5,000; Fourth Prize (10) $1,000; Fifth Prize (100) $250; Sixth Prize (2,500) $10; ★ ★ Seventh Prize (6,000) $12.95 ARV.

   ★ This Sweepstakes contains a Grand Prize offering of a $1,000,000 annuity. Winner will receive $33,333.33 a year for 30 years without interest totalling $1,000,000.

   ★ ★ Seventh Prize: A fully illustrated hardcover book published by Torstar Corp. Approximate Retail Value of the book is $12.95.

   Entrants may cancel the Reader Service at anytime without cost or obligation to buy (see details in center insert card).

4. Extra Bonus! This presentation offers two extra bonus prizes valued at a total of $33,000 to be awarded in a random drawing from all qualified entries received by March 31, 1992. No purchase necessary to enter or receive a prize. To qualify, see instructions on the insert card. Winner will have the choice of merchandise offered or a $33,000 check payable in U.S. funds. All other published rules and regulations apply.

5. This Sweepstakes is being conducted under the supervision of Marden-Kane, Inc., an independent judging organization. By entering this Sweepstakes, each entrant accepts and agrees to be bound by these rules and the decisions of the judges, which shall be final and binding. Odds of winning in the random drawing are dependent upon the total number of entries received. Taxes, if any, are the sole responsibility of the winners. Prizes are nontransferable. All entries must be received at the address printed on the reply card and must be postmarked no later than 12:00 MIDNIGHT on March 31, 1992. The drawing for all unclaimed Sweepstakes prizes and for the Bonus Sweepstakes Prize will take place May 30, 1992, at 12:00 NOON at the offices of Marden-Kane, Inc., Lake Success, NY.

6. This offer is open to residents of the U.S., the United Kingdom, France and Canada, 18 years or older, except employees and their immediate family members of Torstar Corp., its affiliates, subsidiaries, and all other agencies and persons connected with the use, marketing or conduct of this Sweepstakes. All Federal, State, Provincial and local laws apply. Void wherever prohibited or restricted by law. Any litigation within the Province of Quebec respecting the conduct and awarding of a prize in this publicity contest must be submitted to the Régie des Loteries et Courses du Québec.

7. Winners will be notified by mail and may be required to execute an affidavit of eligibility and release, which must be returned within 14 days after notification or an alternative winner will be selected. Canadian winners will be required to correctly answer an arithmetical skill-testing question administered by mail, which must be returned within a limited time. Winners consent to the use of their names, photographs and/or likenesses for advertising and publicity in conjunction with this and similar promotions without additional compensation.

8. For a list of our major winners, send a stamped, self-addressed envelope to: WINNERS LIST, c/o MARDEN-KANE, INC., P.O. BOX 701, SAYREVILLE, NJ 08871. Winners Lists will be fulfilled after the May 30, 1992 drawing date.

ALTERNATE MEANS OF ENTRY: Print your name and address on a 3" × 5" piece of plain paper and send to:

In the U.S.	In Canada
Harlequin's WISHBOOK Sweepstakes	Harlequin's WISHBOOK Sweepstakes
3010 Walden Ave.	P.O. Box 609
P.O. Box 1867, Buffalo, NY 14269-1867	Fort Erie, Ontario L2A 5X3

© 1991 Harlequin Enterprises Limited   Printed in the U.S.A.

LTY-H491RRD

Back by Popular Demand

Janet Dailey
Americana

A romantic tour of America through fifty favorite Harlequin Presents®, each set in a different state researched by Janet and her husband, Bill. A journey of a lifetime in one cherished collection.

In April, don't miss the first six states followed by two new states each month!

April titles # 1 - **ALABAMA**
        Dangerous Masquerade
      2 - **ALASKA**
        Northern Magic
      3 - **ARIZONA**
        Sonora Sundown
      4 - **ARKANSAS**
        Valley of the Vapours
      5 - **CALIFORNIA**
        Fire and Ice
      6 - **COLORADO**
        After the Storm

May titles # 7 - **CONNECTICUT**
        Difficult Decision
      8 - **DELAWARE**
        The Matchmakers

Available wherever
Harlequin books are sold.

JD-AR